River
PEOPLE

T0307166

MARGARET LUKAS

BQB
Virginia

Published in the United States by BQB Publishing
(an imprint of Boutique of Quality Books Publishing Company)
www.bqbpublishing.com

978-1-945448-22-5 (p)
978-1-945448-23-2 (e)

Library of Congress Control Number: 20189622660

Book design by Robin Krauss, www.bookformatters.com
Cover design by Marla Thompson, www.edgeofwater.com
Editor, Olivia Swenson

Praise for *River People* and Margaret Lukas

"In this big, ambitious novel, Lukas renders the changing world of the Midwest in the late 19th century, a world as brutal as it is beautiful. The players on its stage are admiringly human and deeply flawed. In clean, beautiful prose, and an unflinching eye, Lukas illuminates the ways in which the relentless work of survival both builds and destroys kinship and community. Threaded through, as constant as the Missouri River at the physical center of this story, is a desire for belonging that flourishes in the unexpected."

- Rebecca Rotert,
author of *All the Animals We Ever Were*

"Wonderfully redemptive, *River People* brings alive a surprising group of underdogs, their life in the backwaters, and a scoundrel or two who care more for propriety than taking care of their own. A spirited tale of early Omaha you will want to share with your friends."

- Theodore Wheeler,
author of *Kings of Broken Things*

"*River People* is a wonderful novel full of heart and humanity. A delightful read."

- Jeffrey Koterba,
Nationally Syndicated Cartoonist, author of *Inklings*

River People explores the harsh reality of women's lives at a time when their days were shaped by toil, poverty, and abusive patriarchy.

But against the backdrop of that dark world, *River People* reveals another steeped in myth, the beauty of the Missouri River, and a woods where trees breathe, and their leaves "listen high where the spirits speak."

A mesmerizing tale of love and redemption.

Jeff Kurrus,
Editor of Nebraskaland Magazine;
author of *Can You Dance Like John*

Thanks to my husband, Jim, and our four gorgeous children: Jen, Emily, Julie, and Dan. You stood by me, never doubting, even when it might have seemed I ignored you. I loved you every day.

Thanks to the tireless help of Kim Stokely (*In the Shadow of a Queen*) and Gail Weiland, (finishing her novel) who both spent endless hours reading and critiquing with me. You gave me insight, friendship, and encouragement when I struggled.

Thanks to everyone at BQB Publishing, especially Olivia Swenson, my editor for her care and wisdom, and Terri Leidich, a woman as dedicated to literature as she is to the writers she encourages and nurtures. I needed both of you, and you were there for me.

And to readers along the way who've given me valuable feedback: Sue Bristol, Gina Barlean, Rhonda Hall, Trish Lynn, and Heather Traymor.

One

1898

Grandma Teegan was dying. They shouldn't have come.

Eleven-year-old Bridget trudged up the dark stairwell. Her legs and arms ached. Water sloshed over the rim of her heavy pail. The heat in the tenement house swelled floor by floor, and sweat rolled down her neck and shoulders and dampened the back of her wool dress. She'd taken off her broken shoes and even her bloomers beneath her long skirt, but she was still hot as "frying mutton." Through July and now into August, Grandma Teegan had muttered about the heat, but for the last week, she'd been too sick for talking or humor.

Bridget set the pail down on the next riser and wiped sweat off her face. She'd made it up three flights. Only one more to go. She changed hands, gripped the handle again, and climbed. Grandma Teegan waited for her.

Opening the door to their small room was hottest of all.

Grandma Teegan, hunched on the cot, gasped to catch her breath. Bridget let the pail thud to the floor, socked herself in the stomach, and hurried to drop to her knees in front of the elderly woman.

Moisture beaded on Grandma Teegan's sunken cheeks though she wore only her threadbare nightshirt. Beside her lay the newsprint Bridget had stolen from a street vendor a week earlier. She picked it up and began to fan the sweaty face. Stealing the paper when she might have been caught was stupid. They couldn't eat it. She'd tried and hadn't been able to swallow.

She waved the paper, trying to both cool her grandmother and sweep away the shadows filling the million lines on Grandma Teegan's face. Wisps of white hair fluttered. Was she a hundred years old? Even Mum and Pappy had called her Grandma, and in the stories she told, the women who carried their people's history and legends in the books of their hearts, often reached a hundred years. And more.

"I'm taking care of you," Bridget promised. And she would. Somehow. She couldn't let Grandma Teegan die. She couldn't have murder number two. "You're going to get better."

The wrinkles in Grandma Teegan's sagging cheeks didn't lift, her watery eyes didn't clear, and she didn't nod with assurance. She also didn't place her palms on Bridget's cheeks and say, "We yet find your mum." She coughed and then sucked and gasped for air with a sound like soup in her lungs.

Bridget rose from her knees and sat beside her on the mattress—no more than paper sewn between rags. *Nera, Nera*, she prayed. *I won't be scared.*

Fish lived in Bridget's stomach. Ten, she decided. T-E-N. They swam back and forth when Grandma Teegan coughed. And other times. Lately, they never stopped swimming, even at night. Bridget's arms and legs slept, but the fish swam. Back and forth.

"I brought water." She hurried to dip their tin cup and hold it to Grandma Teegan's lips. The streets below were cooler and had an occasional breeze. Ought she try and coax Grandma Teegan down the stairs and outside for a few hours? But what if Grandma Teegan couldn't make it back? She couldn't spend the night sleeping on the street like the homeless children who piled into brick stoops and slept huddled together like puppies. Grandma Teegan's bones would break. Her disappearing skin made her arms and legs into sticks; her shoulders, knees, and elbows, doorknobs.

Bridget tried to think back over the months to when the coughing started. Coughing neither spring's warmth nor summer's awful heat had helped.

Grandma Teegan hadn't coughed when they first arrived in New York a year ago. Hadn't coughed in the fall when for weeks they walked up and down the Irish quarter searching for Mum and Pappy. The coughing began in winter when they continued hunting—even at night during snowstorms. Shivering up and down city blocks, Grandma Teegan yelled "Darcy!" over the biting wind. Bridget yelled, "Pappy!"

More than once, a man scooping snow into the lines of horse-drawn wagons had leaned on his shovel and looked up. But he was never Pappy. At first, she and Grandma Teegan were glad not to find him so desperate he worked with the unemployed Irish who came out during storms—men often without hats or gloves but with hungry children huddling in cold rooms.

Winter ended, the coughing worsened, and they quit walking the streets and asking strangers if they knew a Kathleen, a Darcy.

Bridget even quit insisting her parents were West—though she knew they were. Before leaving Ireland, Pappy had talked about getting to Dublin then Liverpool, the cost of steerage, surviving in New York without a sponsor, and earning enough money to outfit a rig for homesteading in the West. Mum and Pappy were there now. Nothing else explained their absence in New York. But when she insisted, Grandma Teegan's eyes stared off until Bridget could no longer bear the sadness. Being eleven, she understood now what she hadn't at ten. Grandma Teegan didn't know where "West" was. They didn't have money for next winter's coal, even for today's food. There was no money for a train ride into the unknown.

"Tomorrow, the ticket," Grandma Teegan managed. "Ye sell. Ye eat."

Bridget drew in a sharp breath, and all the fish in her stomach jumped at once. She socked them.

Grandma Teegan's bony hand dropped on Bridget's wrist. "Na, na afraid."

Bridget wanted nothing more than to have Grandma Teegan's return ticket to Ireland sold—had it cost ten or fifteen pounds? But what then?

"When I'm a doctor," she said, "I'll make you well." *I won't let you die. Not like Uncle Rowan.*

But she wasn't a doctor and Grandma Teegan was growing down. She missed her croft, Ireland's green hills, her sheep, and her dog, Ogan. She missed all the graves too.

"You're still going home." Bridget nearly choked on the words. "You need to keep your passage."

"Find ticket."

"Tell me about selkies. Tell me how Mum swims in the sea and can visit us wherever there's water."

"Ticket."

Bridget stood and took a step back. "I can't. We'll find Mum and Pappy."

In the year since arriving, Grandma Teegan hadn't once reminded Bridget she'd only crossed to make sure Bridget found her parents. Hadn't once reminded Bridget she planned to leave as soon as that was done. "I'll lie me down with ye Grandfather Seamus," she'd said in Ireland. "My resting place be here." As she always did at the mention of the great-grandfather Bridget had never met, she'd looked at his old tools leaning in the croft corner: a rake, a spade, and a hoe. Grave-tending tools now.

"You can't sell your ticket," Bridget tried again. *You'll die here.* But how could she live without her? *And you can't ever leave me.* Grandma Teegan had always been her most mum. Though the entire family had lived together, Grandma Teegan even then shared Bridget's bed. It was Grandma Teegan who told the old stories, who held her when Mum and Pappy had red fights. Grandma Teegan who loved her in spite of Uncle Rowan's death—murder number one.

She backed slowly toward the door with Uncle Rowan's words banging in her head. *It be us now who must take care of her.* But Rowan grew a shadow around his body and though Bridget had seen it, she'd not been able to keep him from falling through the gloom of it. Now, Grandma Teegan was hers to take care of. Without the ticket, Grandma Teegan had no hope of ever returning home. Dark shadow would grow like a grave around her, too.

"We don't need to sell it," Bridget said. "I can get us food."

"Ye take ticket. Dunot steal."

Bridget ran out and to the stairs. Chased by Grandma Teegan's coughing, she raced down the twisting flights, not slowing until she reached the first floor. She was relieved to see Mr. Wilcox, the man who slept in the foyer, wasn't there with his blankets. He had a room on the top floor across from theirs, but he was so scared of fires he slept nights in the entryway, begging pardon every time someone needed to step over him. Yet, when a candle fell onto an old straw mattress and people cried "Fire!", Mr. Wilcox ran against the flow of people fleeing and up the stairs to bang on doors and help people to safety. He'd been Nera.

Outside, the afternoon sun hung low behind buildings, and much of the street lay draped in shadow. People sat on stoops to escape the heat inside; cranky babies bounced on mothers' laps; men smoked in their ragged clothing; children shot marbles and chased one another. Bridget's heavy feet shuffled. She had to stay close. She wished she hadn't run, but for a moment she'd been certain darkness, the death space, swirled around Grandma Teegan's head.

I didn't see shadow. She was eleven. Grown up. She had to be as brave as Nera, who in the old story stole a finger bone from an angry skeleton. She rounded the building, stepped into the empty alley, and leaned against the wall. *I didn't see shadow.* She slid down the brick into a squat, tucking up her skirt to keep it off the filth. The narrow space between two buildings was quiet but smelled bad. Fifteen families emptied their chamber pots into the hole in the middle. Or not wanting to get too close, flung their smelly waste in the direction of the hole.

She dropped her head back against the brick and closed her eyes. She wasn't taking care of Grandma Teegan, and Grandma Teegan couldn't die in America, couldn't be buried this side of the water. That was Bridget's biggest fear. Grandma Teegan had sold all her sheep and bought a return ticket to make sure it didn't happen. She needed to go back for the coughing to stop and for her skin to turn pink again, not blue and see-through as paper. And years and years in the future, if she ever did die, she needed to be buried with Grandpa Seamus. But how to live without her? And without all her stories? Folktales, Brothers Grimm, and Irish legends. Especially stories of selkies, who lived in water and on land. Grandma Teegan told stories about them the way she told all her stories. The way she'd spun wool, combing and carding and pumping the treadle of their deeper meanings. She told them holy.

Buzzing made Bridget look up. Mud dauber wasps were building a nest on the bricks several feet above her head. She watched them, blue-black in the dimming light, their long legs dangling as they swarmed. Pushing her feet out, she sank the last inches, forgetting the dirt. Grandma Teegan was dying because of her. Nera would do even the scariest thing to save her grandma. Nera would step up to a skeleton and yank off a finger bone.

Bridget sniffled. How could she do it? Being left again, being without Grandma Teegan, would be scarier than sneaking up to an old, stupid skeleton. Scarier than its bones dancing in the air. Scarier than its eyes turning red and coming alive.

She hugged her knees. Grandma Teegan would never leave her,

no matter what. She couldn't be forced into leaving her behind the way Pappy and Mum had. N-E-V-E-R. There was only one way to save Grandma Teegan: leave her. Then she'd have no reason to stay in America. She'd take her ticket and board a ship.

The nice Irish cop who'd caught Bridget stealing had told them about a train taking children West. At the suggestion, Grandma Teegan gripped her red shawl tighter around her shoulders and shook her head. "Olc! Na, strangers!" And would say no more.

In the alley, the shadows deepened. A wasp landed on the wall inches from Bridget's shoulder and began walking up. A cart with a loud squeaking wheel rolled along the walk. Bridget sat up straighter. The cart belonged to the apple vendor who claimed a spot at the end of the street.

She walked out. Indecision and fear kept her well back of the vendor. If she did it, she had to be caught by the Irish copper. The one who'd talked about the train and only pulled her up the four flights to Grandma Teegan—twice, though the second time he'd been much angrier.

There, with him tut-tutting, Grandma Teegan had clutched Bridget as if she herself were the one who'd stolen and needed forgiveness. "Dunot steal," she begged. "Promise."

Bridget hadn't promised. A nod was not a promise.

But the last time she'd tried to steal, a mean and scary cop dragged her blocks and blocks to a police station. He shoved a slate into her hands with her name chalked in large letters. In even larger letters below her name was the word "thief." As she mumbled "Nera, Nera" to try and stop her sobbing, a man used a big camera to take her picture. Then four men pushed her into a chair, circled her, breathed on her. They called her a "street rat," said girls were the worst because they "gnawed away at society." They threatened to make her an inmate of a house of refuge. Then they shoved her out onto a now-dark street, and she walked hours until she found her way home.

Watching the apple cart, she shivered and took slow steps forward. She could never go to the police station again. Not even Nera was that brave. But she couldn't let Grandma Teegan die in America, either.

The vendor in his cap watched her. Gray haired, he'd not been quick enough to catch her before, but he remembered her. This theft, she wanted him to know, wasn't about two apples.

She waited, hardly aware of the street noise surrounding her. Finally, a blue uniform with its flash of shiny buttons appeared half a block ahead. She waited still longer. The cop ambled and talked with people while she socked her stomach. When it was time, she took a deep breath. "Nera, Nera." Would he take her to jail this time? Or would he only huff and puff like before, trying to scare her into believing he would?

She ran at the cart. Though the vendor tried to block her, she ducked under his arm and snatched an apple. "Thief!" he yelled. "Thief!"

Pretending not to see the policeman, she ran in his direction, not veering off until he was nearly upon her. She screamed, but he grabbed her, shook her by the arm, and peeled the apple from her hand. She struggled. "I'll give it back. I promise, I'll never steal again."

He pulled her down the street to shaking heads, whispers from stoops of "caught again" and "poor lass." In front of her building, when he'd shown the occupants on the street he meant business, Bridget quit resisting.

"I have to go West," she said. "I have to go on your train."

He studied her, frowning. "She won't have it."

He had red hair too, and his accent sounded like home—though home and its sounds seemed from another lifetime. Was that why he had patience with her?

"You have to make her let me go. She's dying." She'd not cried in front of the man before and slapped at tears she hated now. "When I'm gone, you have to help her to the boat. She has a ticket. One ticket."

"Oh lass," Grandma Teegan moaned and coughed at seeing the policeman and his grip on Bridget. "Oh lass," the words full of defeat and heartbreak.

Bridget pulled free. Grandma Teegan's face looked as stricken as it had the day her grandson Rowan died. "It's not your fault," she said.

"How many times?" the copper asked. "Next time it won't be me arresting her." He sighed and took off his cap, tucking it under his arm. "Me mum," he said, "I can't let her go free again. The whole street be crying me foul. She don't smoke, drink beer, sniff the powder. She ain't in a gang of street rats. But all that be coming for her. She best take the train—"

"Na." Grandma Teegan moaned the word and was struck with coughing.

Bridget knelt and dropped her head in Grandma Teegan's lap. Had she gone too far? Would the policeman lock her up if Grandma Teegan didn't agree? Even then, Grandma Teegan would at least be free of her.

"Look at ye," the man said. "Ye pass this winter and what of her? It'll be jail soon enough."

Pass this winter? Bridget licked her lips, then wider, searching for the taste of Mum's tears. Was the copper seeing the death shadow? "I want to go. I want to go," she said again. "The train goes West. I'll find Mum and Pappy. I know I will."

Grandma Teegan made a gasping, wet noise. Tears filled her eyes, bubbled over, and disappeared in her wrinkles.

Bridget licked again, promising herself she did taste Mum's tears. They'd lain together in the grass, watching clouds. Shoulder to shoulder, their hair spilled into one color, and they couldn't tell the long curls apart. Mum rolled to her side, stared into Bridget's face, and a tear dropped onto Bridget's lips. The salty taste of that tear and their matching hair were the two best memories she had of Mum. The rest was all Grandma Teegan.

"I have to get on the train," Bridget said. Her heart was ripping. She'd find Mum and tell her how she'd been brave enough to let Grandma Teegan go home. She'd also tell Mum about her brother Rowan, although she wouldn't admit the death was her fault. "Please. He's going to put me in jail."

The cop nodded.

"Mum wants me to go West," Bridget begged. "Grandma Teegan, you can't put me in jail."

The next day, they stood together in a large room before a wide desk, Grandma Teegan more stooped than upright. Her white head was bare, her long braid sawed off with a knife and wrapped in her red shawl—the bundle tied around Bridget's waist. A man sitting behind the desk shoved papers across to be signed. Bridget held her hands over her mouth to keep her trembling lips quiet. She watched as Grandma Teegan, with her hands shaking so hard Bridget didn't think she could do it, the great-grandmother she'd lived with and loved all her life, picked up the pen and signed her away.

Two

Four months earlier

Seventeen-year-old Effie sat on the porch steps of her family's Minnesota farmhouse. Out over the pasture not a bur oak, slippery elm, or any other tree had been left standing to mar the surface. Or for an Injun to hide in. Sticking a hand out from a trunk, then pushing a foot through bark—as Granny described it—emerging fully formed with a nearly-naked, painted body. Complete with raised tomahawk.

Even the massive oak, once standing only yards from the porch and holding a swing and giving picnic shade, had been taken down. All that remained was a thick round stump, waist high for Ma's washtub. The tub sat there now, glaring in the sun. The same tub in which seven years earlier Baby Sally had drowned.

Effie's stomach churned. Seven years and yet it might have been seven minutes since the terrible afternoon she'd fallen asleep while tending the toddler.

The screen door behind her banged, followed by two quick raps, one on top of the next. She turned to see her little brothers, the four-year-old twins, opening and slamming the door just for the noise.

"Stop," she scolded. "Let Granny sleep so I can have a moment of peace."

When they banged the door again, she half stood as if she had the will to get up and give chase. They squealed and ran inside. The door rapped closed.

She slumped back down, her gaze fixing again on the washtub. For the last year, she'd been able to shift Baby Sally's death to a smaller room in her mind. She'd been in love and dreamed of a future with nineteen-year-old Jury.

She swallowed against the knot in her throat, wanting to run off the porch and away. But where to go and cry without being seen by Granny, her parents, or one of her brothers? She wasn't going *alone* into a pasture—even one stripped of its trees—and sharing a tiny bedroom with Granny meant she had no private space even inside the house. Only the small, dark place beneath Baby Sally's black burial cloth.

The screen door squeaked open again. She started, ready to take the twins in hand. Instead, seven-year-old Johnny came out, his sweet face pinched with sadness. He sat down beside her. "I couldn't find you." He didn't ask for the hundredth time how to tie his shoes or why night was dark. Or even why Granny screamed. "I couldn't find you," he said again.

Her sadness was affecting him. She tried to smile. He'd been hers to care for since infancy when Ma shoved the newborn into her arms.

"I been right here," Effie said. He didn't deserve to carry her grief. "Show me your marbles."

He sniffled and curled, putting his head in her lap. "Skeet," he said, his bottom lip trembling.

She brushed hair off his forehead. Yellow-white hair like her own and in need of her scissors. "I'll make Skeet give them back. Okay?"

He moved, wiping his teary cheek on the skirt of her only good dress. It was Sunday, and though for the second week the family wasn't showing their faces in church, Granny coaxed Effie into the green silk. Then Granny insisted the old preacher, who came down the lane days earlier in a rickety buggy pulled by a rickety horse, read from his Bible. He arrived two days after Effie heard the news about Jury. One day after Pa sent her to Jury to "do what you must. Wife him, need be."

Johnny pinched fabric on Effie's skirt and used it to wipe his nose. Granny would scold when she saw the stain, angry that Effie hadn't bothered to change back into a farm dress after the Bible reading. The green had been Granny's, and she'd paid twenty-five cents to have the seams let out and the hem let down for Effie.

A cow lowed in the distance, and Effie's gaze lifted again to the stark and barren pasture. She ached for the shelter of the black cloth she kept under her pillow. She'd draw it over her head and shut out the world so she could weep in private. Suppose she was pregnant? What then? How long could she hide her condition? And where could she go to escape when she no longer could? Pregnant and no husband? There was no greater shame, not just for her, but for the whole family. She couldn't hurt her parents, especially Ma. Not again.

Only ten days earlier, the whole world had seemed fixed to pop wide open for her. She thought she'd soon be leaving on Jury's arm. Thought the two of them would live six miles up the road, not far from Johnny and the others, but far enough away to allow her to sleep at night and escape Homeplace's ghosts.

Then Pa returned from New Ulm with their weekly supplies, his face wound tight. He dropped a sack of coffee beans on the table and turned to Effie. "Jury ain't marrying you."

The words gusted in her head, quick and strong. Standing at the sink washing dishes, she'd needed to grab the sides and hang on.

"He's marrying someone else."

She'd loved Jury long before he even noticed her. All through the winter, he'd come Sundays to court. Courting not just her, but her parents, her brothers, even Granny. Well-mannered as a man fixing any day to ask for her hand.

She dropped her eyes to the pans still needing scrubbed. Jury was marrying someone else? The hurt struck deep, knifed her where all along she'd known she wasn't good enough for him. Couldn't ever be enough. She'd let Baby Sally die.

Johnny, his head still in her lap, turned over. "Now this side," he said, pressing his other cheek to the silk.

She rested her hand on Johnny's shoulder. She'd been his mother, changing his diapers, feeding him until he was old enough to hold his own cup, and keeping him from the washtub. She was still his mama, drying his tears, scolding him when he got too close to a horse, teaching him his letters. She knew how to be a mama all right, but how could she put a roof over a child's head and food in a child's belly? She had no hope of ever getting a job. She couldn't read more than the word "soda" or "salt" on a can. And no respectable family would have an unwed mother in their house, even as a maid.

She stifled a moan. She couldn't bring such awful grief to Ma. So that Ma couldn't walk down the street in town without people gawking even more. Ma, who'd already lost a baby daughter to drowning, given birth to a boy people thought simple, and lived with a crazy mother-in-law. A woman surely unfavored in God's eyes.

The door to the house opened, and the old preacher stepped out. Since Reverend Jackdaw's arrival, she'd been so consumed with losing Jury and possibly being pregnant, she'd scarce paid the man any attention. He was nearest Granny in age, and Granny was the only reason Pa tolerated the man sleeping in the barn.

The afternoon Rev. Jackdaw arrived, Effie had also been sitting on the porch, Granny sniffling and rocking behind her. Pa marched from the barn at the sound of a squeaking buggy and a horse clopping down the lane. He listened to three words of the man's complaint and pointed down the road toward New Ulm. "Blacksmith on ahead. Take your troubles there."

The preacher spied Granny wrapped in her quilt. He jumped down, rushed up the steps, and lifted Granny's hand. "Rev. Jackdaw," he said. "The Lord's blessing on you."

Granny sputtered.

"I see by the light in your eyes, Sister. You are one of God's elect."

The tip of Granny's tongue poked around the teeth on the right side of her mouth and out the gaping hole on the left. She found her voice, insisted he stay for coffee. A piece of pie. A prayer for her nerves. When Pa objected, she pointed at him. "That one wath off fithing with hith pole."

Pa turned and headed back to the barn.

Granny wasn't on the porch now, nor Pa, only Rev. Jackdaw stepping up too close. His body blocked the sunlight, casting her and Johnny in shadow. She thought he wanted to pass, but he only stared down at them, his large, worn shoes inches from Johnny's small fingers. She pulled his hand to safety.

"There's wisdom for you in the good book." He fisted his Bible, holding it in the air like a rock or hammer. "Passages to deliver you from your suffering."

He recognized her suffering? She could feel Johnny beginning to tremble. "It's all right," she soothed, but he scrambled up and ran back into the house.

Rev. Jackdaw peered down his long nose. "Just desserts that one."

"No," Effie said. The man had no right. People thought the seven-year-old simple, but only Granny and Skeet—older than Effie by two years and heavier than her by thirty pounds—used words like imbecile and stupid. Said them in Johnny's presence. Granny didn't mean any harm; she couldn't help the holes in her mind. How it clutched coins of reason one minute and lost them the next.

"Johnny gets scared," Effie said. The preacher had one eye old and one scarred, twitchy, and mean. "You scare him, that's all."

"Follow me," Rev. Jackdaw ordered. "I'll deliver your soul."

His manner, sharp as his voice, proved to Granny that God Himself had come down the lane and slept the last week in their barn. Effie didn't agree, despite the man's age and the long white beard. Still, suppose the half-twisted face and the shaking Bible could help her?

He struck out across the yard, his long shadow reaching back for her. "Follow me."

"If-*fee*!" The cry came from deep in the house. Granny was awake. Then more insistent, "If-*fee*!"

She ached to run screaming down the long lane to the county road. Only Pa knew the full story of Jury. But even he didn't know how scared she was, or how she contemplated jumping off the Redstone Bridge. Wasn't that the best way out of her misery and the only way to save the family from more shame?

"Effie!" Ma's voice this time. "I need you in here."

Effie hurried after Rev. Jackdaw.

They used the cow path, walking along the crest of the pasture hill, she several steps behind. At the pond, its banks swollen by snowmelt, they stopped. Large startled frogs—last year's survivors—jumped from the crusty edges, splashed, and disappeared under the water. She sat a few feet from Rev. Jackdaw, his teeth yellow and horsey under his beard and his strange eye. She struggled not to turn away in disgust. Instead, she concentrated on keeping as much of her skirt as possible bunched in her lap, off the ground and away from ants.

Rev. Jackdaw opened his Bible and began to read, each verse louder than the last. Suddenly, strange sounds sprung from his mouth—not words at all, but some goofy language of his devising. She'd heard of people speaking in "tongues" at revivals, but this jumble of sounds reminded her of the Pig Latin she and Skeet spoke. A way of cursing each other without Ma understanding the bickering.

Rev. Jackdaw continued spouting, shiny bits of spittle flashing in the sunlight, his voice rising and falling as he lifted his Bible heavenward.

Several minutes passed. Effie began doubting that what she saw was a show. The sounds went on too long, without hesitation, and he'd forgotten she was there. When he remembered her finally, his bad eye, looking blind only a minute earlier, burrowed into her.

"Lord, save her from her sins of the flesh."

She froze. The sky was a hard blue, and yet she felt certain the heavens were thick with eyes. How could he know her sin without God having seen and told him?

Over the next hour, the preacher's attentiveness held her like a pair of hands. The choice was hers, he said. Salvation could open her chest and put in the glow of a stained-glass window. Or she could refuse the invitation and send her soul to the fire of ever-lasting damnation.

She couldn't undo her past, couldn't bring Sally back or take back the hour in Jury's loft. Not by herself. If she didn't even try to be saved by this man, who was willing to do it, what other hope did she have?

He drummed his fingers, nails chipped and dirty, on his Bible. His shirt smelled of days without being washed. "Are you ready to accept baptism?"

She nodded and rose to her feet. Her family, especially Pa, needed to witness and know she'd been saved. "I'll run and get the others, change my dress."

"Don't you know," the good and the bad eye settled on her, "it's better to pray and receive in private?"

Her face burned; she'd acted childish. She looked down, pinched the green silk of her skirt. "I couldn't . . . Granny." She kept from adding, *It's the only decent piece of clothing I have.*

"Why take ye thought for raiment?"

He plopped a heavy hand on her head. She thought he meant to bless her, but he pushed until her knees lowered to the grass. He prayed, long and loud—his hand still heavy—that on the day of her baptism into eternal life she might be saved from her heathen shyness and false pride in her mortal body.

He drew her up by the elbow and began removing his shoes.

Her fingers found the buttons on her bodice. Rev. Jackdaw was a holy old man, and she was in need of being saved. She slid the dress off her shoulders and stepped out. Standing in only her underslip, she let him take her hand and tug her into the pond.

The icy water stung her ankles and calves. She winced. Then winced again with each step and the cold crawling higher on her legs.

With his arm around her waist, he pulled her forward. "Do not fear the Kingdom of God."

She couldn't stop now. Her dress was off, the water above her knees. She'd already begun moving away from this miserable world and into another full of promise. When the water reached her waist, he stopped. He prayed with more force, his words again lurching and strange. She thought of a gaggle of geese and then again of the Pig Latin she used to fight with Skeet.

When Rev. Jackdaw leaned her back, cold water raced up her spine. She jerked and clutched his arms to keep from going too deep. He draped his body over hers and held her so close she felt his chest pounding. The awful backward bending and the cold replaced by her fear of drowning, she clung to him. *Baby Sally died in less than half a washtub.*

He cupped water and dripped it over her forehead. Her legs trembled with the cold, the continued bending back, and fear. She turned her head away, trying to keep his unwashed beard out of her face. The horsey teeth chomping words she still didn't understand.

His arm pulled out from beneath her. She sank. Water rushed over her. Her arms slapped and splashed. Pond water filled her mouth. She twisted and managed to turn over. Her feet found the slippery bottom. Spitting and gasping, she splashed for shore.

On the bank, her thin slip dripped and clung to her skin. He came close, as though he'd pray over her again. Hunched and hugging herself, she quaked with cold. "You made me fall."

His wool pants dripped water over his bare feet. His nails the color of cow hoofs. He picked up her green silk, and she reached out, but he kept the dress at arm's length. She scolded herself for still being so self-conscious of her body. She quit grabbing, closed her eyes and tried to feel the sun on her skin and the hand of the Divine on her shoulders.

She felt only cold. Where was the stained-glass window in her heart? Where was the clapper of dove wings? She opened her eyes.

Rev. Jackdaw stared at her breasts. She was near naked with her cold nipples erect, their shape and color stark through the thin cotton. She spun, putting her back to him and slapping her arms across her chest.

She wasn't blessed. No tongues of fire crackled over her head. She felt sick the way she'd felt leaving the hayloft with Jury, the sick way she'd felt realizing how much Pa wanted her gone.

She faced Rev. Jackdaw. "Give it!"

His one eye lusted. But the other eye, the eye twisted by a scar, held such obituary she could not name the darkness. That eye hated her for her nakedness.

Grabbing back the dress, she stepped into the silk. As her cold fingers worked, button by button, the fabric turned wet and dark. She turned for home. She deserved the Redstone Bridge. One step off and it would be over.

Skeet lay in the weeds not ten yards away. "Skeet!"

He stood, gave a lopsided smirk—more a snarl—and started back at a lope.

"Skeet! Don't tell Pa. Please, it's not what you think!"

Coming into the yard, she saw Pa and Skeet standing side by side just outside the barn. To Skeet's grin, Pa's face was foreboding, his large, calloused hands fisted. His glare pierced her and then slid to her right. Only then did she hear Rev. Jackdaw just a few feet behind her.

Three

Wearing a faded but dry farm dress, Effie sat at the crowded supper table, holding two-year-old Curly in her lap. Meat from an old hen, boiled from the bone, doused in white gravy and layered over pasty-bread, stared up from her plate. She couldn't eat. Earlier, she'd told Ma she was ill and didn't want to sup, but Ma scowled. "You'll help me, same as always."

The others ate, knives and forks clicking on plates. Ten around a table better suited for four or six. Skeet balanced on a narrow milking stool, his shoulder brushing Effie's. He always brought his stool next to her, the better to pinch her leg under the table—the only sibling he could torment without their screaming.

Effie let Curly pick food from the plate they shared, gravy dribbling off his chin and into her lap. She felt no anger toward the old preacher for what had happened earlier, only emptiness. In taking advantage of her, he'd tried to steal from her, but she'd already been emptied out.

From her end of the table, Granny shrieked suddenly. "Murdering thavages."

Johnny dropped his fork in alarm and looked with wide eyes across the table at Effie.

"Savages," Skeet sneered. "It starts with an s."

Effie kicked him, glad to see him wobble on the peg of his stool. "Don't correct her."

Granny, a thin arm poking out from the folds of the patchwork quilt she'd named Never Forget, stabbed the air with a spoon. "Wanting to kill white Chrithians. Wanting our land. That what thavages want."

Rev. Jackdaw scooped more chicken in his mouth. "Fancy shooting and God-sent plagues wiped out the heathens."

Granny's spoon jabbed in Pa's direction, a trail of gravy sliding down her quilt. "He let the thavages kill my children right here in *my* kitchen. Thavages ain't dead. Lincoln left all them nooths empty."

At the other end of the table, Pa's jaw blanched with the pressure of his gritted teeth.

Skeet jerked his leg out of Effie's reach. "Nooses."

"There's worse 'an redskins," Rev. Jackdaw said. "Whores." He wiped the beard around his mouth with his sleeve cuff and looked directly at Pa. "I'll take your daughter's hand in marriage."

Effie needed a moment to make sense of what she'd heard. Then felt something she hadn't in over a week: the urge to laugh.

Pa wasn't laughing, and Ma's eyes widened as if she'd been slapped. Neither parent spoke.

The quiet grew, clutching at Effie's throat. Why was no one roaring objections? Why wasn't Pa using the barrel of his shotgun to nudge Rev. Jackdaw across the floor and out the door?

Granny clapped her bony hands together. "God-a-mercy!" she shrieked. "If-fee, you're to be a preacher'th wife."

Pa's eyes still didn't lift. He still didn't rise from his chair, bang on the table, and shout, *No! Not my daughter.*

Rev. Jackdaw went on eating. Across the table, Johnny's face looked fixed to weep. Skeet leaned closer to Effie. "Istressmay Ackdawjay." *Mistress Jackdaw.*

"God-a-mercy!" Granny cried a second time. As though she'd just received the white dove that failed to descend on Effie at the pond. "A preacher'th wife."

"Pa?" Effie managed. What did he suppose she'd done with the preacher? He'd sent her to Jury. He'd stood in the dark that night holding the reins of a saddled horse. "Go," he'd ordered. "Go see that boy. Go see that boy. Wife him, need be. He'll do what's right by you." He'll do what's right by you."

When she arrived back home two hours later, Pa sat in the dark on the porch. He nodded and took the reins to stable the horse.

But the ploy hadn't worked; they'd both misjudged Jury. She'd made a fool of herself, and suppose she was pregnant? If she was, she needed to wed quickly in order to fool a new husband into thinking he'd sired the baby. There were no other suitors in the picture, and if they waited too long, there might never be.

Pa took another bite; his eyes on his plate.

He'd sent her to Jury, but he hadn't sent her off with Rev. Jackdaw. She'd listened again to what someone else wanted for her, this time the preacher.

Rev. Jackdaw spoke around the pale, pasty glob in his mouth. "We'll be off to Nebraska. Omaha."

Pa looked up, his eyes full of misery, or was it shame? "Omaha?" The question asked as if he wanted Rev. Jackdaw's word on it.

"I'm to build a church there."

Effie's head spun. The preacher was older than Pa by nearly two decades, but her parents' silence proved they were considering it for her. They wanted her gone. The knowing—or was it knowing again?—struck her like a fist. But leave Minnesota? Johnny, Curley, and the other boys? Leave Pa and Granny and Ma?

"Why do fish like water?" Johnny shouted.

"Cause they're fish," Skeet barked.

"Because," Effie said as calmly as she could, "it's quiet, very quiet, under there."

"Like under the black?"

Effie listened to the silence winging around the room, telling her she was leaving. Jury didn't want her, and she'd let Baby Sally die. One way or another, she'd killed her little sister. With the grief she'd already caused the family, she would not heap on a scandal. She deserved Rev. Jackdaw's battered face, yellowing beard, and weak shoulders. He was the furthest thing from Jury's youth, broad shoulders, and handsome face. But Rev. Jackdaw would take her away. He offered an escape, and maybe that would be one breath better than a watery grave in the river.

Her legs began to tremble. In her lap, Curly felt the vibration and hummed a long O sound. His voice warbled out over the table.

Pa made grunting noises in Rev. Jackdaw's direction. Effie had heard him wrangle with more spirit over a puppy he'd trade for a few garden vegetables. And if the deal failed, he'd shrug and a week later have Skeet drown the puppy.

Granny sputtered. Her jaws and tongue worked to keep the tough chicken under her remaining teeth. "If-fee will be the pill-her of the community."

Ma, her white hair hanging, squinted at Rev. Jackdaw as though looking at him hurt her eyes. Her gaze shifted to Pa. "He's likely to drop dead and leave her with mouths to feed."

"Thut up!" Granny said. "You're a fool."

An hour later, with Rev. Jackdaw's trouser legs still damp, Effie stood beside him at the table not yet cleared of dishes. She'd refused to change, despite Granny's fretting that she ought to be in green silk. Ma watched, one tired hip braced against the stove for support. Her eyes swam, but she offered no protest. Pa, eyes steely, waited at the back door, needing to hear the words spoken before he left the house, stepping out into the quick-gathering dark.

Johnny stood at Effie's side. They grasped hands as Effie placed her other trembling hand on Rev. Jackdaw's Bible. "I do."

"In the name of the Lord, I pronounce us man and wife."

He carried in his valise and journal from the barn and pulled the slim mattress from Johnny's bed up the ladder to the dark attic. He motioned for Effie to climb.

She'd never been in the attic, and she stood motionless in the musty-smelling hold amidst cobwebs and the skittering of mice. Rev. Jackdaw left the trap door open and pointed to the mattress just visible in the meager lantern light rising from below. She lay down. He lifted her dress to her waist. His pants came off, and he dropped onto her to seal the deal he'd struck with Pa. In the kitchen, he'd pronounced them married, but the real binding, this consummation, needed done before anyone changed their mind.

She tried to quiet her weeping as he rutted, her face turned from his sour breath and from his sweeping, unwashed beard.

"Quiet," he growled.

When he finished, she turned on her side, a fist between her teeth.

He growled again, louder. "I said quiet. That's enough."

The deed was done. She was his wife. Jury, her family, everything else was gone.

Later still, despite her best efforts to stop crying, he shoved at her. "Go sleep with the crazy bat."

Only then did she realize that two stories below, Granny wailed for her. She hurried, her bare feet finding their way across the rough attic floor, her toes finding the ladder rungs down. Her body made no sound, and she had no shadow. She felt empty as the kitchen ghosts.

The upstairs lantern was out, but moonlight coming in the windows allowed her to see the open door to the room where her little brothers slept. She couldn't see whether Johnny had crawled in with Curly or the twins. The door to the smaller room—little more than an over-large closet where Skeet slept—was closed, and Pa had dropped the bar across it. Skeet claimed the bar kept annoying siblings from disturbing his sleep. Effie believed otherwise: Pa dropped the bar each night to keep Skeet from running away. Something Skeet often threatened to do.

The open door to her parents' room gave only a perfect, cold silence. No rhythmic breathing from Ma saying she slept. No snoring from

Pa. Effie wanted to stand in the doorway, make them look at her, but sorrow threatened to buckle her knees.

"If-*fee*!" Granny's cries were louder. Effie took the unlit stairs to the first floor, her tears making her way even harder to see.

"Where you been?" Granny cried.

Fumbling in the darkness, Effie found the black cloth she kept folded beneath her pillow. "In Rev. Jackdaw's bed."

The baby suddenly wailed overhead and Granny gasped, "Thavages killing my baby!"

Dropping onto the bed, Effie pulled up her knees and hugged them to try and stop her shaking. "No," she managed. "That's not your baby." She drew the black cloth over her head.

In the attic, Rev. Jackdaw turned on his side, tried to stretch out the ache in his lower back. Effie had sobbed. Gagged when he'd done his duty and planted seed in her. If he ever felt himself growing soft in regards to her, he'd remember she gagged. He clenched and unclenched his fists, fought the demon convulsing his eye, sending the whole side of his face into a fury.

He'd lingered a week at the farm just watching Effie, waiting, knowing God was presenting him with an opportunity. After three barren wives, God was giving him Effie. She had six brothers and would bear him as many sons. Building a church could take a decade or more, and only sons could be sworn to finish the work, should it come to that.

He'd take the necessary measures to bring Effie into submission. The Bible was clear. He was husband of his property: horse, wife, and soon sons. He was a stronger man than his father, would not let his wife run off, would never let her go to a house like Miss Myra's.

He fumbled in his valise for matches, struck a single stick and held the flame over the spot where Effie had lain. Back and forth. Another match, squinting, covering the area inch by inch. Flame burned his thumb and forefinger and went out.

Just as he suspected. No blood. That explained her father's willingness to have her gone and out of his household. It also meant she was unclean and needed watching.

Four

Effie stood on the porch and Pa close by, both of them watching Rev. Jackdaw climb into his buggy and slap the reins over his old horse, Nell. Every time the preacher walked the nag in from the pasture and began hitching her to the buggy—saying he was going into town to check for a letter—Pa sent Effie to the attic to be sure the man was leaving his belongings.

In the spring, she'd said, "I do." Now it was late August and yet they remained at the farm. Week after week Rev. Jackdaw reported he still hadn't received news from Omaha. And week after week Effie watched Pa's frustration grow. He came in the house only for meals and sleep, biting his tongue, avoiding any rift that might cause his son-in-law to try and sneak away without the daughter. His only compensation for tolerating the situation was that Granny screamed less. Rev. Jackdaw knew to keep her occupied and distracted, reading to her from his Bible. Or from Granny's Jonathan Edwards tract: "God holds you over a pit of hell. He holds you as one holds a spider or some loathsome insect over the fire."

With the buggy heading down the lane, the dust rising and blowing along the pasture fence, Pa turned back to his work in the field. Effie saw Ma and Skeet bending over baskets, the twins carrying ears of corn. As always, she'd been left with the baby and Curly. Granny and Johnny too, who were no help in the field.

She shared Pa's fears. The preacher could not leave her behind in shame. She hadn't been pregnant, but everyone in New Ulm knew she was married—even Jury. She wouldn't be left behind now, not with his wedding so close.

When she was sure Rev. Jackdaw wasn't turning around for any reason, she ran through the house, climbed the attic ladder, and stepped into the heat. With shaking hands, she opened his valise. When she'd accidentally seen the dress hidden there, he'd explained it had been a favorite of his dear sister, and that he kept it in memory of her. Effie touched the edge of the red, wanting to take out the satin and feel it glide over her body. Perhaps she and his sister were the same size. But she didn't dare. She wouldn't get the dress refolded and tucked in exactly right. Just poking fingers down through his two extra shirts and touching the softness made her nervous.

"If-*fee*! Injuns!"

She turned and hurried back down. Johnny and Granny sat at the kitchen table. Granny wore her Never Forget quilt around her shoulders, patches made from the clothes of her murdered children. Red slashes of ripped cloth randomly placed on top. Symbols of spilled blood. Her cane banged up and down on the floor. "If-*fee*, If-*fee*!"

"I'm right here, Granny. Shush, you'll wake the babies." And to Johnny, "Everything is all right."

Johnny held his slate but no longer practiced his name. He covered his ears against Granny's screaming, but his eyes fixed on the rapping cane as though it were about to attack him.

"I'm right here," Effie said again. She grabbed Granny's hand, stopping the noise. It was always the same, Granny needing her every second, day and night. For seven years she'd slept in Granny's bed, seven years of brushing up against aged and chiseled bones, Granny's nightmares and stories, dozing in them and waking startled, pulled from her own nightmares by Granny's screams.

And times like this with Granny mentally resurrecting her children. And the day they died. Her mind so crippled there was no way to save her from having to watch them be murdered over and over.

"Get my gun," Granny cried, her eyes wild.

"There aren't any Injuns," Effie said again.

Johnny's face, red with fear, and Granny's stark terror were a cold wind weaseling into the room. When Ma and Pa were there, the screaming was less frightening, but with them off in the fields with the other boys, fear came up through the floorboards, crept out from the corners of the shadowy kitchen where children had died. The cold blew over Effie, stroked her with icy fingers.

"Breathe," she coaxed Johnny. "Work on your letters." And to Granny, "No one's coming. Look." She lifted a corner of the quilt and knocked hard on the stock of the gun in Granny's lap. "Your gun is right here."

Granny's eyes narrowed on her, as if Effie were lying, trying to fool a poor old woman in her distress. Even on the first day after Baby Sally's death, Granny hadn't noticed the toddler's absence. She'd had no understanding of how her screaming for her dead babies filled Effie's mind, rocked Ma to the core, and sent Pa fleeing to chores he'd already done.

The chalk Johnny used snapped in two under his pressing and he howled.

"No Injuns are coming," Effie told him. With a shaking finger she traced a J on his dusty slate. "Like this, you're doing it backwards again." She couldn't read well, but she knew how to spell and write the names of her family. "Johnny starts with a J. The letter comes down and out. This direction."

Granny's cane swung again, pointed to a spot on the floor. Effie couldn't keep herself from checking to be sure no blood suddenly pooled there. No children's ghost faces looked up at her.

Granny's fits could scare the bee-jesus out of a fence post, and Effie searched the kitchen for distraction. Bread dough beneath a floury cloth rose over the top of a pan and waited to be kneaded down. Rinsing her hands at the kitchen pump, she told herself she wouldn't give in to fear this time. She'd carry on as naturally as possible, let Granny's fit of derangement pass. She punched the dough. Slapped it.

Granny cried, the toothless gap in her mouth wide. Her body cowering.

Effie stopped, grabbed the dishcloth and dropped her face into it. Never a moment of peace. Even at night while Rev. Jackdaw huffed and puffed on her in the attic, Granny called from below. The whole house listening to the length of the mating through Granny's wails. When finally Rev. Jackdaw rolled off her and wanted quiet and the small mattress to himself, she rose to go to Granny. Who could blame her for wanting away from Homeplace? Even if it were the devil himself taking her.

Johnny sobbed. Granny's face was blanched and the terror in her eyes sent a new rash of chills snaking up Effie's back. She saw no dead children, but they'd all been killed right there, the blood, the crying. Painted savages stood in the very spot where her feet now trembled. Her heart raced. Even if no one else could see them, Granny saw actual ghosts. The spirits of her dead children lay scattered across the floor. Dying again.

"Let's get out of here," Effie said. Was Baby Sally's ghost also there? "Bring your slate, Johnny." She wrapped an arm around Granny's waist, hefting her up. "We'll sit on the porch. You can look out and see how all the trees are gone."

Moving Granny along with the dragging quilt and a clutching Johnny was slow and felt nearly impossible. Behind them, Effie was certain that faces on the floor watched them leave.

Five

The train pulling into the Minnesota station blew a loud, high whistle of warning. The sound and the slowing made Bridget stretch to look out the window. She was West now. *West.* The word sounded like wind and the warmth inside promises. Men in the West didn't have to work in mines. They didn't have to be carried home on stretchers. West was wonder. West was where she'd find her parents.

Craning her neck, she searched the line of women standing along the tracks. In their bonnets, she couldn't see much of their hair and wasn't sure of the colors. She squeezed the red wool tied around her waist and licked her lips.

She'd been licking since leaving Grandma Teegan, three days ago, and the skin around her lips was raw and stung when her tongue rubbed over the chafing. No matter. She licked again, searching for the taste of salt and the distant memory of Mum's tears when they'd hugged good-bye in Ireland.

The train came to a complete stop. The matron in charge of the thirty-four children—some so small they still needed nappies and had just begun toddling—rose from her seat. Her eyes scanned the group but landed hard on Bridget, a warning as shrill as the train whistle. *Because,* Bridget thought, *my hair is red, and she says that means I have "no soul", and I'm a "half orphan", "the worst kind." And "a thief."*

Matron marched to Bridget's seat with spectacles slipping down her long nose. "That disgusting habit of yours. I see your tongue again, I'll cut it off."

Other orphans watched; an older boy snickered.

Bridget squeezed harder at the band of wool and the thick coil of Grandma Teegan's braid inside. She'd fight sadness and how much she missed Grandma Teegan. If you didn't fight, one day you went to work, and three days later, a strange man stepped up to your bed and ran a dirty string from the top of your dead head to your dead toes. Measuring you for a burying box. Just like what happened to Rowan.

Matron clapped her hands over the group. "Silence. We are in New Ulm, Minnesota. You will behave exactly as I say." She raised her palms and both sides of the aisle rose together. Bridget stepped in line, holding the hand of the two-year-old girl she'd been assigned.

Surrounded by a crowd of people eager to adopt, they followed Matron in pairs down a busy street filled with shops, horses, and buggies. The toddler under Bridget's care, Penny, grew tired and wanted to be carried. Bridget managed the weight on her hip, walking crookedly to keep up. With each step, she fought a growing uneasiness. Why hadn't Pappy and Mum pulled her out of the line—Mum crying tears of joy?

The adults hurrying alongside the procession talked too loud and began picking out the child they meant to have for themselves. A bright hat leaned close to Bridget. *Mum?* But Mum never owned such a large hat with colored feathers and a dead bird. The woman didn't have hair that matched Mum's, and she was only interested in Penny. "You're a cute baby girl."

Bridget held tight to her charge and walked faster as Matron ushered them into a school and then a classroom. The strange faces, not Mum's or Pappy's, crowded in, lining the four walls. They shouted over one another and pointed at the child they wanted. In the noise and confusion, Matron struggled to keep order. "Form a line, please. This will not do." An old pen scratched down names as she filled out paperwork and tried to settle disputes.

The sinking feeling in Bridget's stomach grew. Where were Pappy and Mum? She wanted to sock her stomach, but Grandma Teegan's braid was there, and anyway, she had to hold Penny.

The woman in the hat with the colored feathers and a dead bird spied a small, blond boy. She grabbed his hand though he screamed and squirmed to get away.

"It's okay," Bridget whispered to Penny. "Someone else will want you."

On the desktop in front of her, a large, lopsided heart had been carved into the wood with a penknife. She tried to distract Penny by having her trace the heart with a finger.

The littlest boys were fought over first. The room began to empty, with happy couples grasping small hands and couples unwilling to accept anything but a little boy leaving empty handed.

Then the little girls mattered: *second choices*. Penny was pulled away crying. Bridget concentrated on the carved heart, not letting her eyes meet and promise anything to Penny, who'd begun to scream and reach back for her. She clutched Grandma Teegan's red scarf. *Nera. Nera.*

The older boys, able to work in fields, went next. Bridget sat with four other girls, all of them staring at their hands or straight ahead. Their eyes were open, but their faces were closed. A few minutes more and Bridget sat alone. Matron narrowed her eyes on the last remaining woman and repeated what Bridget had heard her say to another couple: "A thief that one." And then, "Those worthy of placement are gone." When the woman still hesitated, "She'll be locked up. I'll see to that."

The woman started for the door but glanced back, her eyes scolding Bridget. "I'll not have a thief in my house."

While Matron fussed over the ledger she'd filled out, Bridget pressed her finger deep into the heart, felt the skin push into the tiny hollowed-out shape. She wasn't really a thief. Just, sometimes she couldn't stop herself. Grandma Teegan had understood.

Bridget kept her fingertip pressed in the carving. "How long until the train leaves?" How much time did Mum and Pappy have to rescue her? They *were* hurrying. Any minute they'd run into the room crying, "Bridget! Bridget! We found you!"

Matron didn't answer. She studied her ledger, her breath beginning to puff.

Minutes passed. Bridget twisted the fabric of the blue cotton dress she'd been given. "Why did they take my clothes? It wasn't true, they weren't full of bugs."

Matron still didn't answer.

Bridget couldn't go back to New York. And not to prison. Grandma Teegan wasn't even there. By now, she was on a steamer and would never know what happened.

Matron gasped, the color draining from her face. "Who took him?" She wiped her brow with a handkerchief yanked from her dress bosom. "Who took him? A runaway? Losing a child. My job. They won't stand for this."

Bridget hadn't learned names on the trip, but she remembered faces. "Who did you lose?"

"Not a word to anyone!"

"You're going to lose your job?"

For a long moment, cold eyes pinned Bridget, then Matron looked back to her book.

Out the window, horses pulled rumbling drays. Inside, a large horsefly tapped against the glass. Bridget wished she had a pocketknife. She'd carve a B. Then if Mum and Pappy arrived too late, they'd know she'd been there.

Rev. Jackdaw stood outside the New Ulm post office and clutched the letter he'd waited all summer to receive. He looked heavenward; it was time to be about his high commission. He crossed the street to the mercantile for the supplies he'd need for the trip to Omaha: beans, flour, sugar, coffee, a roll of bed ticking. Before leaving the establishment, he checked the letter again and added a long length of new hemp rope to his purchases.

He put what he could in the boot of his buggy and left the rest up front on the floor. At last, everything was coming to pass. In Omaha, he'd have a community of followers, prosperous men and women who'd hold their Rev. Jackdaw in high esteem. There, he'd build his church. More. An edifice. Like the great cathedral he'd seen in Miss Myra's stereoscope. Putting the small apparatus to his eyes, sliding the picture up and back until it came into focus, he'd stared into what settled over him like heaven. Endless arches and domes vaulting great sweeps of space spoke of man's power and indomitable will. Thinking about it made him breathe deep. He'd teach himself to read complex building plans and instruct men to build the tallest, grandest church in Omaha. He'd be remembered as an architect of God.

He climbed into the buggy and lifted the reins. His commission was clear this time and, as it had been for Moses, it could be written on two golden tablets. The first was building that church. The second was raising sons to carry on his work after he'd gone to his eternal reward. At sixty-three, he wasn't too old to sire them. Abraham had been even older, and from his loins had come the twelve tribes of Israel. When Isaac was born, Sarah had already advanced far past a woman's worthwhile years. Effie was only seventeen, ripe for bearing.

Just as he was ready to slap the reins over Nell's back, the Lord stopped him. Two whores came screaming out of the saloon. They screeched and stomped on the other's parasol, breaking the stays and ruining the paper. Cheap paper. Their sin-dazzled skirts flung, their lurid ankles and calves flashed in red stockings, and their groping hands threatened to rip open the other's indecent bodice—bright, low-cut. Necks and heaving bosoms bare.

Dresses nothing like his own. The dress he kept hidden in the bottom of his valise was a scourge, assuring him he would never burn in hell. He'd struck a deal with God: when weakness threatened to overcome him and punishment was in order, the dress served as flagellation. Just as it had in childhood: punishment for his two grievous sins.

Watching the whores, he understood what the grinning male spectators didn't. Thanks to the staged brawl, the "ladies" would be the talk in every saloon. By nightfall, men who'd lost interest in them would be standing in line again, eager for a two-dollar ticket to hell.

He sat, considering the magnitude of the Lord's work waiting for him in Omaha, a city with the reputation of being the largest Gomorrah between Kansas City and Los Angeles. Over two hundred and fifty legal brothels. The newspapers claimed only ten times that many prostitutes, but he'd heard the real numbers were so high the city wouldn't let them be reported.

The whores' spectacle, unfolding in front of his eyes, the perfect timing of it, was divine orchestration. Had to be. He reached for his journal. Sitting in the buggy, his small inkbottle balanced on his knee, he began to write: *I'm leaving this record lest God forget.*

When he closed his journal, over an hour had passed. Writing the whole account of that long ago event was always necessary. The story was the roots of him. And like the tree stump in Effie's yard, the roots plunged too deep and too wide to be removed.

He laid the book back on the seat, his name tooled on the front filling him with satisfaction. *Rev. Jackdaw.* He'd spent a long time considering the alias. It commanded authority and befit his mission.

As if nodding His head in wild approval, the Lord sent him the third gift of the day. The letter, the whores, and now a flyer nailed on the post, fluttering suddenly not four feet away: Free Orphans.

He hadn't planned on bringing back an orphan, but females had poor constitutions, and Effie needed watching while he worked in

Omaha. There were too many stories of wives out west jumping into swollen rivers or dressing in their Sunday best and sucking pistol barrels. Or running off when their husbands turned their backs.

A dark shadow filled the doorway of the schoolroom and made Bridget start. For a fleeting moment, hope surged again at the sight of a man. Just as quickly, her shoulders fell. This wasn't Pappy. This man was too tall and thin and . . . something else she didn't like.

"You're not Pappy."

She'd meant to whisper, but her disappointment sounded loud in the empty room. She peeked at Matron, who still dabbed at her sweaty temples. The woman flashed her a cold look of warning: *Not a word from you.*

The man stood framed. With his height and the black hat he didn't remove, he nearly brushed the top of the doorway. "I'm looking for a free girl."

A chill like stepping into cold seawater started at Bridget's ankles and raced up the length of her body. The fish in her stomach said, "Yes. Yes." But mostly they said, "No. No."

Matron stabbed a crooked finger to her place in the ledger—the knuckle round as a marble—her eyes flashing. "You're late," she said to the man. "The adoptable orphans are gone."

He spoke through lips buried in white beard. "What about that one? She free?"

Bridget tried to make her lips smile, but they wouldn't do it. He wore black clothes. His black coat hung to his knees, then black trousers and black boots. Not coal black, not the way she remembered Uncle Rowan's clothes after a day in the mine. Nor was this man's hair covered in dust. Long and white, it hung beneath the black hat he still hadn't removed. Where his hair stopped beneath his ears, his beard had already begun, covering his cheeks and ending long and skinny at the second button on his coat. In the center of the bush was the crack she'd seen: the twisted twig of his mouth.

She knew the man! The realization made her breath suck in. That's why she'd felt such cold the moment before. She'd dreamed him. Remembering made her clutch again at the red wool. She'd dreamed him her last night with Grandma Teegan. She'd cried out and Grandma Teegan, beside her on the cot, pulled her even closer.

"Only a dream," Grandma Teegan said. Pretending she hadn't also been dreaming the same dream, and that her own throat hadn't also cried out. Pretending the awake world and the dream world were separate. Which Bridget knew wasn't true. Too many dreams followed her out of the night, banged on the door of her daytime world, and stepped in.

"Not all children deserve homes." Matron's brows were two angry moths struggling to reach one another. "Some need to pay for what they've done."

The man didn't hear or didn't care. His hard boots with thick heels came knocking into the room. *Knocking, knocking* across the wooden floor. He leveled his eyes on Bridget. "This one left for me?" *Me* echoed in the nearly empty room. "I need a free girl."

Matron's bosom lifted with frustration. "Those *fit* for homes are gone. It's the jailhouse for this one. Now, I have pressing matters."

Bridget traced the heart, losing count of the number of times her finger had gone around the shape. Losing a boy scared the woman, but losing her silver writing pen made her mean. She'd turned out Bridget's pockets, emptied the paper suitcase holding Bridget's two pair of bloomers, and even untied the wool around Bridget's waist. The pen wasn't there, only the long length of Grandma Teegan's hair. "Evil." She crossed herself.

The man tipped his chin in Bridget's direction. "That one? She free?"

Across the top of the slate board, the alphabet stretched out on green cards. A, upper and lowercase, and then B, for Bridget, upper and lowercase. She skipped ahead to K, upper and lowercase for Kathleen. Mum.

"I have a use for her," the man said.

"It's a thief you're wanting?" Matron let the question hang in the air.

"The name is Rev. Jackdaw. I've been about the Lord's work." He grabbed his chin hair and slid his hand down the length of his beard. "The Lord's work needs no apology."

Bridget fought an urge to run out the door. If a boy could get away, she could. But even so scared she might be sick, she'd stay. Nera hadn't run. Nera—who was always Bridget's exact age—faced the skeleton no matter how it rattled. Even knowing the bones would clamber down from the tree and chase her and never quit.

"The Children's Aid Society," Matron faced Rev. Jackdaw squarely, though Bridget saw how the woman's round finger never lifted from the ledger, "promises to place out only healthy, honest children. This one is a criminal." She threw Bridget a hard look. "She should have been locked up, the key thrown away. Some fool thought she deserved another chance." She sniffed her dry nose. "It was my father's silver pen."

"It's your business to place them out." Finger by finger, Rev. Jackdaw pulled a black glove off one hand. Then the other hand. "She's got no family likely to come after her?"

"She lost one of the orphans . . . a boy," Bridget said. "She lost a *boy*."

Matron's face blanched. She glared at Bridget. "That one's a half orphan. She had a grandmother," the words hot and bitten off the tip of her tongue "but the woman sent her away. Signed Surrender Papers. It isn't a wonder she did. Half orphans are the worst—"

"What's that mean, half orphan? I'm looking for a free girl."

"Families don't want them. They push the burden onto good Christians. Lazy folks, not willing to work, they are."

"No." Bridget licked her lips, then wider. "Grandma Teegan didn't just give me away."

Rev. Jackdaw scoffed. He stepped up too close and pinched Bridget's lower jaw so hard her mouth opened. He bent down and looked in at her teeth, his beard falling forward and touching her chest. "You ain't the first to be put out. No use mourning that."

Bridget wanted to yank his beard until he howled on one foot like an angry leprechaun. With his crow clothes, crow hands, and crow way of strutting, he looked like a creature from one of Grandma Teegan's stories. A creature that could step out of fog or white sea-spray, touch people on the shoulder, and lead them away for a thousand years.

His eyes raked her freckles, her red hair, even the thinness of her arms. With his hat pulled low and so much hair covering his face, she hadn't noticed his bad scar until now. It puckered from beneath his hat at his temple and came across and curled in. The twist ended at his eye like a thick, round caterpillar.

"Family." The worm twitched. "They stick the knife. Know where the blade goes deepest." His eyes stayed on her though he spoke in Matron's direction. "She won't steal in my house. I'll see to that. She can be schooled to be of use? I won't suffer a squawk."

He smelled of sweat and horses. "I went to school," Bridget said. "I can read."

He straightened, a hand on his lower back. "A free girl that reads. You ain't scared of animals?"

She'd loved Grandma Teegan's spring lambs and especially their dog Ogan, who at night always slept by her side of the bed.

"Trees?" Rev. Jackdaw's eyes were narrow. "You scared of trees?"

She looked at him hard, afraid she hadn't heard correctly. "Nobody is scared of trees." *I'm not afraid of selkies either.*

"She ain't a papist?" Rev. Jackdaw jutted his chin up, stretching the loose skin of his neck and peering at the ledger. "You ain't holding out on me? You ain't got something better?"

"She lost a boy." Bridget nearly shouted this time and watched Matron's face turn a sickly color. There were only two choices: prison or this man. "I want to go with Rev. Jackdaw." She slid out from behind the desk and forced herself to stand straight as a stick. A skeleton was clambering out of a tree. "Then I can't tell on you."

Matron began to sink slowly, landing in the chair behind her. "You!" Then hardly more than a whisper in Rev. Jackdaw's direction. "You aren't seventy yet?" Her voice gathered strength. "Only those between seventeen and seventy are eligible to take a child." She cleared her throat, dabbed at her sweaty brow with her handkerchief, and glared at Bridget. "Thousands more just like her. Clogging the streets, stealing. Going to prison just to get their greedy hands on food."

Rev. Jackdaw took quick steps to the desk and reached for the pen beside the ledger. "Free and clear now? She's mine."

"You'll see she goes to school?"

He gripped his gloves in his left hand and slapped them against a trouser leg. "Hardship clause." He scowled. "Hardship clause says a girl can be kept home and at her work."

Bridget stood beside him as he signed on the line Matron indicated. On the left of the sheet was a list of children's names. On the right, signatures or X's if the person couldn't write. The pen scratched: *Rev. Jackdaw*. The nib fell off and flecks of indigo ink ruined the signature.

Rev. Jackdaw's eyes widened. The worm cornering his right eye twitched. "Damn pen's worthless."

Matron stared at the spot. "My work . . ." Slowly, she picked up the pen, pushed the nib back in place, and dipped it in ink. Holding it over the empty line where Bridget knew a signature for a lost boy should go, Matron flicked the tip with her thumb. A splotch landed and spread, filling that space and the one above. Her sharp eyes landed on Bridget. "I'm rid of you."

Nera, Nera. She'd be brave. But would a skeleton follow her now? She told her heart to stop banging so loud: she'd only be with Rev. Jackdaw until Mum and Pappy found her. Besides, until then, maybe he had a wife who wanted to be her mum. Maybe they'd all live together happy. When she went to bed at night, she'd close her eyes knowing in the morning she'd wake in the same place. The day after that, too. Until she was found.

Walking out of the room together, she reached for his hand and felt his flinch at her touch.

When the school doors closed behind them, he pulled away.

Six

Rev. Jackdaw cleared the plank walkway ahead of Bridget and stepped onto the hard-packed dirt street. His longer strides widened the distance between them, but he'd signed a paper on her, and so she hurried to keep up. They crossed to a buggy with a graying horse hitched to the front. Was this the animal he thought she might be afraid of? She wanted to run her hand down the horse's neck and look into the large eyes. She'd tell the horse she was adopted and see what the eyes said.

"Git in," Rev. Jackdaw ordered. He climbed in after her, making the buggy dip with his weight, then shudder as he sat down. He lifted the reins, shook them, and the horse started forward.

"Thank you," Bridget said. She wasn't at all sure she should be thankful, but she wanted to make him a friend and make her knees stop shaking.

"Charity don't mean kinship," he said. "With that hair, I'll call you Rooster."

"My name is Bridget."

"Was. Rooster now."

Rev. Jackdaw *was*, she spelled silently, M-E-A-N.

The back of his hand smacked her mouth. Pain shot through her top lip. "Quit licking. You a dog?"

She sucked at the hurt and tasted blood. She wanted to spell mean out loud, but that would make him hit again. She pressed her lips together and listened to the squeaking buggy, the rumble of the wheels, and the jingling of the horse's traces. They passed a shopkeeper sweeping out a doorway, boys shooting marbles, and two old men rocking. For several blocks, she tried not to think about Rev. Jackdaw or where they were going.

The sight of a huge brick building just ahead caught her attention. The sign said, Martin Luther College. Its wide staircase stretched across the front and went a dozen or more steps high. Many buildings in New York were as large; it was the activity on the stairs that made her stare. She was in the West where Mum lived, and a group of young ladies mingled in long skirts and waists with leg-o-mutton sleeves. Was one of them Mum? They shuffled, some going up a step, some down, laughing, arranging and rearranging themselves in two rows by height. Unable to decide who was taller, they passed their hands back and forth over each other's heads. At the foot of the stairs, an older woman waited for them with her tripod and camera.

"Squawks," Rev. Jackdaw said. "Suffrages."

The group settled as the buggy reached them. The older woman bent to her camera and ducked under a small curtain. As she did, the back row of girls pinched the widest part of the sleeve of the girl in front and lifted the fabric like stretching up a wing. They laughed when the woman popped her head out again and frowned.

Their glee grabbed Bridget. Could one of them be Mum? Maybe Mum wasn't lost, only going to school. Studying each as the buggy continued to roll, not letting her eyes slide too quickly over even one, her hope faded as one after another of the faces belonged to strangers. No hair the color of hers. By the time she studied the last face, she was leaning out of the buggy and looking back.

The force of Rev. Jackdaw's hit knocked her back. "What'd I tell you?"

She sat stunned. Pinching her eyes closed, she imagined the last young woman in line picking up the hem of her skirt, running down off the steps and starting after the buggy. The girl ran like Cinderella at the stroke of midnight. Her white petticoat swished back and forth around her ankles. She ran down one block and then up another, never stopping, never getting winded. She ran and ran because she wanted to be Bridget's mum.

"No stealing outta you. No trouble at all."

Bridget opened her eyes. The girl was gone. No one chased the buggy with her petticoats flying. Only thinking about Rev. Jackdaw's scar kept tears away. Rowan, the best uncle in the world, died with a cut on the side of his face. That wound had been longer than Rev. Jackdaw's, though it didn't have time to grow into a scar. When they pounded nails into Rowan's coffin lid, the gash was still open, the trough of it pale as the rest of his face.

Seven

In the rhythmic rocking of the buggy wheels and the horse's hooves clopping up soft puffs of dust, Bridget watched the road—its curves and washed out areas, the houses they passed, and the landmarks of big trees.

Rev. Jackdaw wasn't talking to her, but he kept glancing at the sky where the sun was sinking and dark clouds rumbled. He shook the reins harder. "Git up!"

When the horse, without a word or tug on the reins, turned down a long, rutted lane, Bridget smiled and breathed a sigh of relief. Shelter was up ahead. A barn, a pigsty, and a house. Was this her home until Mum and Pappy found her? As they went down the dusty lane, the comfort of seeing shelter faded. The land either side of the buggy made her stomach hot and shaky. She grabbed hold of the red wool, imagining not just the braid inside, but Grandma Teegan too, small as a fairy.

Every tree had been cut down. They lay scattered, trunks and branches bleached white. She counted several, then stopped, not wanting to count more or to study the small grove where stumps jutted up out of weeds grown thick between them. The trees hadn't been chopped for firewood, but axed and sawed down and left to rot. No new growth was allowed either; not even a seed dropped by a bird allowed to root. The land looked haunted.

Bridget closed her eyes and let go of Grandma Teegan's braid. She didn't want Grandma Teegan, who loved trees and especially sacred groves, to see. *I won't be afraid.* She had the story of Nera, she was

West, and she had Matron's silver writing pen threaded into the hem of her dress. The pen promised she could out-smart grownups, which meant she could survive the things they took from her. Stealing from their world brought back pieces of her own.

But how could she live here? Without trees, the birds left and took their songs. Squirrels left too, and deer and turkey and shade and singing leaves and a hundred things she couldn't name. The whole world of fairy left. Without trees, even the land tried to run away. She covered her mouth and licked once before she brought her hands down. "I don't want to live where the trees are chopped down."

Several people moved in the yard ahead, and as the buggy rolled into their midst they stopped what they were doing to stare. Brows scrunched and mouths frowned. Counting their numbers helped distract her: . . . *six . . . seven . . . eight.*

Rev. Jackdaw whoaed the horse, lifted a gloved hand, and pointed to a girl standing at a clothesline. Her long, yellow hair was pinned back and held in place by a row of shiny copper combs running from one ear up and over the crown of her head to the other. She looked ready to cry. "That's Efffie."

Seeing the girl helped ease the tension in Bridget's stomach.

"When I'm away," Rev. Jackdaw said, "my wife's in charge. You mind her."

Bridget was confused. Mind that girl? She was pretty and young enough to be Bridget's sister. "It's unlucky to sleep in a house where an old man sleeps with a young woman."

She flinched as Rev. Jackdaw's hand lifted, his face saying she needed to be hit again. Before she could say, "It's in a story," he scanned the group watching them. His arm dropped. Bridget turned back to study not just the one named Effie, but the whole family. Three naked little boys, their winkels in plain sight, played with squirming puppies. A woman, looking too young for the long hair white that blew thin as wind around her head, sat on the porch step and shucked corn. A man stopped digging in his garden and stared with anger in his eyes. His face looked as cold and hard as his shovel blade. A mean-looking boy-man worked in the garden too. He held a pumpkin and stood in front of a wheelbarrow filled with other pumpkins. A baby sat on a blanket, one end of a rope tied around his waist and the other tied to the porch rail. A boy who looked no older than Bridget sat on the blanket too. He watched Effie.

Movement higher on the porch caught Bridget's attention. She'd not seen the very old woman hunkered in a rocker, sitting in shadows as dark as the rumbling clouds. One of her thin, aged hands clutched the rim of a tin bowl in her lap. Slowly the hand began to move, leaving the bowl, sliding across her flat thigh and onto a gun propped against one bony knee. Her lined face leaned forward, her eyes—dark and small and hooded—fixed on Bridget. That woman's hair was white too. Rowan once said Grandma Teegan had cried herself into her old age. Had these women cried themselves into white hair?

"God-a-mercy!" The screech from the woman in the rocker wheeled through the air. "The devil'th hair." A claw-like hand gripped a cane, the other still fisted the gun. She struggled to stand, the bowl of snap beans clattering onto the porch floor, the empty rocker bucking behind her. "Bad luck, that one." Her open mouth revealed missing teeth. "Thoot it."

Rev. Jackdaw kept his tongue. He knew their lifeless routine. They'd come in from the fields, eaten supper, and now they worked again in the last bit of dusky light. Never once picking up a Bible.

"Nith." The word spat from the porch.

Nits? Lice? He hadn't thought to wonder. He'd have Effie part Rooster's hair and see if she spied movement. As soon as they were away. He tied the reins around the brake. He hated them all. Especially the Mad Matriarch in her rocker. Like Effie's parents—locked up in their shallow minds and untouched by the Holy Ghost—the Mad Matriarch knew nothing of the world beyond her barren scrap of land. And the hell of her madness. He did his best to keep her quiet with Bible reading because her wailing made the hair on the back of his neck bristle. Worse at night. Screaming about children dead over a quarter century. The Mad Matriarch had seen the righteousness in the union of him and Effie, but any crumb of sense she'd had then was gone now.

"The train came through town." He spoke loud enough for his voice to carry to the porch and garden both. "Free orphans for the taking. This one's Irish, so she'll be good at scrubbing floors and hauling wood."

The buggy had served as his pulpit on more than one occasion. "This here's Rooster. Until Effie has sons, this one'll keep her company and do the chores. Now that's the end of it."

He stepped out and down. Rooster would do more than keep Effie company; she'd be another set of eyes. She'd know if Effie started wandering, or men started sniffing around in his absence. Effie was a pretty thing, though she didn't know it. Nor was her family the type to notice, or give a kind word if they did. All that spoke well of her. Still, she was awful young and had already lain with at least one. He couldn't spare the time to find another wife.

He ran his hand over Nell's rump and then lower to the fetlock, lifting the spavined back leg to check the hoof. Studying the injury in the fading light, he reassured himself that even if he'd spent money to keep Nell properly shoed, the puncture might have happened. Twice he'd opened the wound with his knife and forced out pus. Then he dipped a rag in hot water and held the compress, drawing out whatever additional infection he could. The long trip to Nebraska might just be the end of the horse, but there was no other option.

The matter of when to leave settled in his mind. Regardless of the weather, or the late hour, he'd pack up Effie. Her folks wouldn't tolerate another mouth to feed even for a day or two, and leaving Rooster in the barn for the night might tempt her to run off. Soon as the squall passed, he'd put at least a few miles between Effie and her crazy family. "We leave tonight," he called out.

Turning for the barn, he refused to look back. A hasty exit was best. Like he'd done at fourteen, the night he left for good. With the stars so close they swam around his head and sat on his shoulders—God whispering in his ear—he'd saddled a horse. The horse he chose might have been common as pig muck, but that night it was a grand stallion. Together they shooed off every pig and cow and swayback on the property.

He'd gotten far enough away before his old man came thundering out of the house in his union suit. Mister fired at him, but missed. Without a horse left in the corral, there was no way to give chase.

The tension in all of them rolled with as much threat as in the clouds. Effie wanted nothing to do with the redheaded girl in the buggy. Rev. Jackdaw hadn't discussed taking a child with them. If he thought she needed help so badly, why not take Johnny? Skeet eyed the orphan, Granny clutched her gun, and though Ma held an ear of corn needing shucked, her hands had gone still. Pa thrust his shovel so deep into the ground he'd nearly buried it to the hilt. They were all upset and no telling what any of them might say next. On top of that, she was leaving yet that night!

The first drops of rain plopped, and she grabbed clothes from the line. The Lord was punishing her with the orphan. She'd bled four times since she'd married, and now she was leaving home with no baby in her womb and an orphan as a substitute.

She looked out over the pasture where cows hung heavy heads and trees lay rotting. The world around her was dying. The land, Granny, even her parents were headed that way. At least Rev. Jackdaw had dreams. He would build her a big house in Omaha. No one around New Ulm, not even young men like Skeet and Jury—thinking of Jury made her stomach fold up in to a tight little square—wanted more than a strip of land to plow and a hog to butcher in the fall.

"Effie," Ma yelled, her face pinched and twisting, "quit your daydreaming. Get that washing in!"

Effie didn't understand Ma, and now she never would. She hurried down the line, pulling pins and filling her arms with small britches and shirts. Life with Rev. Jackdaw would be different, not always "Effie do this. Effie do that." There'd be invitations to fine homes, community picnics with races and cakewalks and chips of ice in lemonade. She'd experience new things, meet people with hope in their eyes.

The rain came harder. Startled by the heavy drops, the twins ran for the porch, their bare backsides still showing signs of the chubby-legged toddlers they'd been. The baby blinked from his blanket, and two-year-old Curly ran for her. She dropped her armload of clothes into the basket and knelt. His baby-boy body rushed into her arms, and she inhaled his dusty scent. Tears dampened her eyes. How could she leave these boys? It was her fault Ma was cold to every child born since Baby Sally's death. Ma preferred washing, slopping pigs, or even fixing fence to rocking a child. Scared to love something fragile as a baby again. Effie understood, yet who would the little boys have when she was gone?

The redheaded creature in the buggy watched her with large eyes. A girl—worthless as herself. How did Rev. Jackdaw expect her to accept that and forget these little boys? The child looked sweet enough, not yet the way newspapers depicted the Irish. At what age would her face change and take on the ugly features of a bulldog? Rev. Jackdaw ought to climb back in his contraption, slap the reins on his old mule of a horse, and take himself and the one he called Rooster away.

She kissed Curly's cheeks and hurried for the baby. There was no going back. Rev. Jackdaw had married them himself, and night after night he'd done to her. She'd not been pregnant with Jury's seed, but she was ruined now. She belonged to the preacher.

Lightning flashed, thunder rumbled, and Johnny screamed, "Effie!" Carrying the baby on one hip and the basket of laundry on the other, she let Curly hold a fistful of her skirt to help tug him along. On the porch, Granny hooked the handle of her cane over her chair, laid the shotgun across the rail and let Ma steer her inside. "Lith." She grabbed at Ma's hair. "Lith."

Effie followed with Johnny on her skirts now too, remembering how Ma's hair had once been a golden yellow. Would her new life in Nebraska turn her own hair white before its time?

Eight

Rain hammered the roof. Evening faded to darkness. Effie couldn't bear seeing the orphan huddled in the buggy, alone and wet. Earlier, Rev. Jackdaw told the child to get down, but he hadn't insisted—as though it hardly mattered to him. The girl hadn't obeyed.

"Come in," Effie shouted. She stood in her wool cape and cotton bonnet at the edge of the covered porch as water rattled overhead and rolled off in a screen. "You'll catch your death." Her yelling didn't make the orphan stir, but the next lightning strike, so close Effie jumped back with a shriek, sent the girl running through the rain and onto the porch. Standing beside her, Effie bit her lip. Weren't the Irish all trouble? Thieves, even murderers?

The house was warm and dry, but Skeet was there with his meanness and Granny who'd screamed at the child.

"Stay out here." Effie hesitated. "Ma don't want water dripping on her floor."

The girl turned toward a dry porch corner where the pups curled with their mama.

"Anyway," Effie said, "we're leaving as soon as all the packing is done."

Lightning flashed again and for a long second, night blinked to day. Rev. Jackdaw stood just inside the barn door looking like the storm itself. He watched her.

She turned back to the orphan. It would be the two of them traveling alone with Rev. Jackdaw. "What's your name?"

"Bridget."

Nearly an hour passed before the rain slowed to a mist. Effie watched from the window as Rev. Jackdaw pulled the wobbly cart he'd concealed behind the barn to the back of the buggy. Days earlier, he'd *found* the two-wheeled thing along the road and recognized "the gift the Lord sent him." She hadn't asked why he needed to hide something sent from God. He set a burlap sack of oats in the corner of the cart—*found*, no doubt, in Pa's granary. She hugged herself thinking of the small mouse-proof granary. Cement walls, windowless, so that no matter the hour of the day it held a pitch blackness as deep as hell and just as full of evil.

Rev. Jackdaw punched at the top of the burlap bag, making it squatter and less visible. He laid his new rope, thick and heavy, on top. With wire he'd also claim he *found* in the barn—as though Pa saved wire especially for him—he began lashing the cart to the buggy.

"Come on," he shouted through the glass.

She hurried out with the first of what she planned to take: mostly scraps of housewares stored in the barn for thirty years.

He finished twisting and bending the wire. Water dripped off the brim of his hat, and he frowned at what she carried: two dented pans and a tin coffee kettle. "You're bringing nonsense. Consider the weight."

She hurried back inside, glancing over her shoulder at the tired horse. Nell was accustomed to pulling the buggy with Rev. Jackdaw, but now she'd have the additional weight of the cart, Effie's things, and the heaviness of two more people. Suppose the old horse died on the way to Nebraska? Would they end up walking, carrying what they could on their backs? Abandoning the rest?

Granny sat at the table muttering, her cane jittering on the floor, her mind winding up now that darkness had descended. She pushed at items on the table. "Take!"

Effie considered the copy of Dr. Chase's *Third Last and Complete*

Receipt Book. The tome was nearly a thousand pages and covered everything from making pies, to diseases of the bowel, to curing horse tumors with arsenic. She couldn't read—though Rev. Jackdaw could—but the weight?

Granny's cane lifted like a skinny, wooden arm. The tip poked the book. "Nith!"

"The recipe's in here for getting rid of lice?" Effie slowly picked up the book. She hesitated longer when Granny nudged her gun. "Are you sure?"

"Nebrathka full of Injun." Granny's remaining teeth clicked. "Thoot 'em!" Then almost instantly, "Who will thleep with me? Not thupid one!"

Effie put the book on top of a crate of old dishes packed in straw and carried them through the door. She faltered before stepping off the porch. Bridget remained huddled in the same dark corner, the odd red scarf Effie noticed earlier still around her waist. Puppies slept in her lap, and another in the warmth of her neck. Effie fought an urge to set down the crate and join her. They were both heading into the unknown, both scared of what lay ahead in the world and with a man driven by his passion. A man who saw *only* his passion.

She took a deep breath and stepped off. New worlds took courage, and at the moment, she'd have to rely on Rev. Jackdaw's.

He waited at the cart. "They got nothing better for you?"

She set the box next to the sack of oats and stared at it. After the Sioux massacred Granny's husband and children—all but Pa—Granny was taken to a hospital with half her teeth knocked out and a deep gash in her back. When she'd recovered enough to leave, she wanted nothing to do with Homeplace, or the fourteen-year-old son who'd been off fishing that Sunday morning and "not there to die like a man." She traveled straight to her brother's house in Chicago, not even informing Pa she was going. Neighbors helped the boy Pa was then. They picked up the salvageable plates and cups strewn across the floor. But Pa had seen the blood of his family splashed across the white clay. He built crates and packed the dishes away in the barn, praying that one day his mother would return to him. On that day, she'd want her things.

Effie brushed past Rev. Jackdaw's scowl and headed back for the house. How had Pa stayed on the farm after the massacre and survived living alone in the house haunted by his dead family? Was it all for his mother? Waiting for the day she'd come home to him? Even knowing she'd ran not just from the horror, but from him as well? Still, he'd milked, slopped, and plowed because his dead father would expect him to "heed the chores."

Rev. Jackdaw grabbed the next crate from her hands and dropped the box into the cart. "No more. Git in."

"My clothes." She ran back before he could grab her arm and stop her. Ma was walking into the bedroom where for the last seven years Effie had slept slept with Granny. Ma had one arm around the old woman's waist, nearly dragging her, and with the other arm she held the baby on her hip. Once in the bedroom, Ma kicked the door closed behind her with such force the lantern on the kitchen table flickered. Granny's increasingly loud and guttural wails had the baby crying, Curly sticking a dirty thumb in his mouth, and Johnny squatting in a corner staring at the marbles in his hand.

Effie's tears bubbled over as she knelt down to Curly and the twins, pulling each one close, squeezing and kissing. Henry at five years old stood with his arms folded across his chest, not wanting kissed, but standing near enough to be caught and hugged despite his seeming protests. Johnny shuffled over, his body heavy with uncertainty, and she held him, aching at his desperate clutching.

"Don't go," he cried. "Don't go."

She peeled his arms off as gently as possible and kissed his forehead. Skeet, from his head-taller stance glowered at her. "Leave him be," she said. "Don't torment him." She paused, softened her tone. "Please, leave him be."

"Indmay ouryay ownway usinessbay." *Mind your own business.*

He had no intention of letting up. She grabbed Johnny again, wanting suddenly to even put her arms one last time around Skeet. As children, before everything went bad, he'd pulled bee stingers from her arm and they'd shared apples, passing them back and forth, each biting into the sour green where the other left teeth marks and an opening. The day she fell climbing the hen house roof, after being told numerous times to stay off, Skeet washed the blood from her knee and kept quiet about her injury. When she found him sobbing behind the barn at eleven—the first time he'd been ordered to and had finished drowning three unwanted puppies—she put her arm around him. They sat in the dust talking while his soaked sleeves dried. The awful puppy-drowning job would be his every year now, and realizing the new burden he faced made her want to sob with him. But how would that help? She had to make him brave. "Stop crying. You're not a baby anymore."

He'd pushed her over and stalked off. Was that the start of their resentments toward one another?

Rev. Jackdaw rapped hard on the window. She couldn't see his face clearly, but there was no mistaking his growing anger. Kissing the top of Johnny's head again, she wondered if she dared go into the bedroom and hug Ma. Fresh tears slid down her cheeks. She and Ma had not wrapped their arms around each other in seven years. Day by day, there'd been too much to say and no words. At night, Effie had lain in bed and thought, *Tomorrow Ma will hold me again.* But tomorrow had not come. Now, Ma knew she was leaving and chose not to say good-bye. Opening the door to her would set Granny off to new heights, which meant the baby too, and Ma would have to deal with both. Granny's screaming would be the worst, though she had spoken loudest in favor of the marriage when Rev. Jackdaw asked Pa.

Asked Pa. Man business. Bartering the daughter. Something that would never cross Pa's mind when it came to the boys. Pa was nowhere around either. He'd slipped out in the night, wrestling with his emotions, avoiding telling her good-bye.

The front door flew open and Rev. Jackdaw filled its frame, his face a sermon. His having to walk up the porch steps to fetch her had claimed the last of his patience.

She dropped her arms from Johnny and lifted a corner of her cape to scrub her eyes. She'd have him remember her with a brave face. The other boys—though it broke her heart to leave them—would grow and survive, but Johnny? She turned again to Skeet. "Please."

His gaze cut her.

She grabbed the pillowcase stuffed with her personal things: two bloomers, her three farm dresses, the green silk with its pond-damaged fabric, and the black funeral cloth. With her vision a teary blur, she clamped a hand onto the gun and the small box still on the table and ran out past Rev. Jackdaw.

In the buggy, she kept Granny's shotgun across her lap. Beneath it, the small cedar box that held her six silver teaspoons wrapped in flannel. The night she first unwrapped them for Rev. Jackdaw and candlelight fell on the silver, she'd expected him to be pleased. He scolded her for being proud.

He wouldn't want the spoons up front, but she didn't own so much as a broach or ring—only the six teaspoons. She couldn't risk them to the orphan's hands or the wobbly, bouncing cart.

She jumped and nearly screamed when Pa appeared at her side. In the bit of light streaming through the window his face was gray stone.

"Not a blanket?" Rev. Jackdaw stood on the other side of the buggy, and like Pa, seemed to appear from the night itself. "You owe us a blanket."

Pa turned for the house and moments later, Granny's screams

rose higher. Before Effie could steady her breathing, Pa was back. He shoved Granny's still-warm quilt into her lap.

"You think you best take her? You ain't the one she hates."

Shock parted Effie's lips.

His chin lifted, and he took a step back. Hatless in the mist, his hair lay flat over his scalp. "You're married to that man now. I done my best by you." His eyelashes wet with rain. "A wife leaves her husband, comes home, it shames the family. You understand me? This ain't your home no more."

Her heart shook. "Bye Pa."

He stepped back and vanished. The orphan appeared as if she'd simply witched him away and replaced him. She held a sleeping puppy. "Can I bring him? He'll keep bad things away."

"Put it down!" Effie wanted to blame the child for Pa's disappearance. She clutched her spoons. She'd wanted a puppy, too, but Rev. Jackdaw refused her. She looked back through the drizzle at the house. "That pup isn't ready to leave. It needs its family."

Soon enough, any puppies that hadn't been traded to neighbors for eggs or a jar of canned beans would be drowned in the washtub. "Get rid of them," Pa would tell Skeet, and Skeet would do the deed just as he did every year. Without her being there to prevent it, he'd make Johnny watch as the puppies were one-by-one held under water. They'd struggle and splash, but Skeet's big hands would keep them under until they slowed and quit and the last air bubbles rose to the surface. Then he'd take the soaked and still-warm bodies, toss them over the sty fence, and make a horrified Johnny watch the pigs come.

"You plan on holding 'em spoons the whole way?" Rev. Jackdaw climbed up, his weight rocking the light buggy. He noticed the orphan and the puppy. "Put that down. I told you to git in." When Bridget obeyed, he slapped the reins and scowled down at the box Effie clutched. "What you're holding there is false gold."

The buggy started forward, but before they'd gone the length of the porch, the door opened and Skeet stepped outside. Not grinning now, his hands in his pockets, his face twisted with anger and jealousy. As if only now realizing what Johnny realized an hour ago: she was leaving.

As if suddenly whacked with a stick, he rushed down the stairs, grabbed up a handful of mud, and flung it. The muck struck Bridget's shoulder. Had she goaded him? Done something Effie hadn't seen? Or did her seeming escape anger him too?

Effie gasped as Bridget jumped up and stood wide-legged in the wobbly, rolling cart. Was she going to jump out and challenge Skeet? She leaned over the side, and as the cart passed the tree stump, she snatched the big washtub. The scrub board inside banged and nearly fell out, but she grabbed that too, bringing both in the cart.

Skeet's mouth opened and his eyes narrowed, but Effie wasn't surprised to see him do no more than stand there gawking. He wouldn't dirty his shoes and give chase for Ma's washtub.

"Git up," Rev. Jackdaw shook Nell's reins. He'd heard the tub bang too, seen Bridget pull it in.

Behind Skeet, the door burst open again. Johnny ran out, jumped off the porch, but tripped and fell over the leg Skeet stuck into his path. Johnny scrambled to his feet, his front covered in mud, and started running again for the buggy. "Effie!"

At his cry, Rev. Jackdaw slapped the reins harder. "Git up there."

"Effie!" Johnny's outstretched arms reached toward her as he ran. "Effie!"

She leaned around the side of the buggy. "No! You have to go back. Please Johnny, go back."

Slipping in the mud, he kept running, catching the back of the cart. "Effie!"

Rev. Jackdaw cussed, "The damned fool."

"Stop the buggy," Effie said. "Please, I love him."

"You can quit that right now. I got you a free girl."

She stared at him. "Quit loving Johnny?"

"Change her name. Cut off that hair, make her a boy, that's what you want."

Effie turned back around. With the help of the cart, Johnny was pulling himself up alongside. "Effie." His hand reached out. "Effie, here!"

The front of his clothes were dark with mud and tears streaked his face. Winded and gasping for air, he still held on, dangerously close to the buggy wheels. She reached out to the hand he extended, and two muddy marbles passed from his wet fist into hers.

She clutched the marbles and he fell back. What sort of life would he have without her protection?

He'd been born only days after Granny's arrival and then Baby Sally's death. In Ma's womb, he'd heard all the screaming. When he was born, the dirt on Baby Sally's grave still loose and dry, Ma put him in the cradle and walked away. Effie let a day pass, then another, and finally on the third, with Johnny gone quiet, she carried him to Ma.

"Please," she begged. "I love him."

The front of Ma's dress was soaked with breast milk. She didn't look at the baby, only into Effie's eyes. Slowly, she unbuttoned her dress bodice and took the infant. Johnny suckled as Ma remained standing at the stove stirring tomatoes she'd bottle. A few minutes later, she passed him back and began washing jars.

Why, Effie wondered then and still wondered, *when I killed Baby Sally, did Ma feed him for me? Pass him back to me?*

She turned to see Johnny still visible in the dark watching her, smiling through his tears. Skeet could never again steal the marbles.

Nine

The trip to Nebraska took nearly three weeks. They slept fitfully in the buggy on rainy nights. Other nights, under. When they found wood and the wind was low and didn't blow sparks across the dry fall grass, they slept around small campfires. They spent nights in haylofts and twice in rough homes that welcomed a preacher and his unlikely family.

As the days dragged on, Bridget bounced in the cart on a crate stuffed with Effie's dresses. More often, she walked alongside. She ached for Grandma Teegan and one of her stories. The story of Salt Woman said only by refusing to look back could you walk forward. Even the ancient gods advised against looking back. But how could she give up thinking about Grandma Teegan?

With each day's westward travel toward the Big Sioux River, Effie's uncertainty grew. The eyes of eagles, hawks, and whooping cranes spied her from the air. She imagined foxes, coyotes, and wolves watching her from dark lairs and wind-swept hilltops. Even many of the human eyes that peered from solitary doors at the sight of an old horse dragging a wobbly cart held suspicion and threat. And with each mile, they traveled deeper into Indian Territory. One old man was little protection against nature's wild things, and he was no protection against heathen Injuns.

When they passed towering trees—thankfully few and far between—and her nerves made her grab the shotgun and her black cloth, Rev. Jackdaw lied to her. Told her again how the Injun was completely wiped out. As though he didn't know that after the Sioux uprising Mr. Lincoln let over two hundred murdering savages go free. Squaws and papooses weren't even arrested. Lincoln not only spared the noose, he sent the whole murdering bunch to Nebraska. On top of that, the Injun chief, Big Foot, and his band—another mob of murderers—had killed over thirty United States Calvary men right on the Nebraska border. The papooses who escaped that December morning were grown now. Angry too.

Reaching the Big Sioux River, Rev. Jackdaw turned Nell south, followed the course down to where it joined the Missouri, and then continued on roads and tracks alongside the wide, brown water. When they reached Council Bluffs days later, they camped again. In the morning, Rev. Jackdaw covered Nell's eyes and tugged the skittish beast across the fifty-foot-high Union Pacific Railroad Bridge into Omaha.

For the first time since leaving Homeplace, Effie relaxed. Shopkeepers, men in wagons and on horses, men in top hats, and men in laborer's caps. With so many men, all with guns in their homes and tucked under their coats, no Injun dared attack.

"We made it," she breathed and turned to shout at Bridget through the back window.

"You aren't staying here." Rev. Jackdaw's voice rose over the rattle of the buggy.

"What do you mean?"

"You're staying at a trapping lodge just outside town."

"But Omaha? You said—"

"You got yourself free boarding and a free girl to do your chores." He told her about the profitable deal he'd made, how nothing was required of her but keeping an eye about the place. "Report any greedy poor stealing Mr. Deet's firewood."

Effie's stomach twisted into coils. He'd lied to her. Made arrangements with a man named Deet. She wanted to scream in protest, but she knew it wouldn't change his mind. She'd only anger him, and that anger would come back and hit her with more force.

They went on, the sun striking her side of the buggy, then hot over the top, and finally low on Rev. Jackdaw's side. Near dusk, with Nell lathered in sweat and hitching her hind foot, they rolled down the main street of a small town: a train depot, mercantile, post office, livery, and a two-story building with a large sign—Bleaksville Hotel.

At the end of the street, just before a narrow wooden bridge leading out of town, a school. Bridget had mentioned going to school early in their trip when they passed a similar clapboard building, it earned her a slap across the face. Effie dared not turn around to see if the girl was looking to that side of the road.

Rev. Jackdaw was. "Rooster's yours to watch. I best not hear she's stepped in there, wasting time, acting like an uppity squawk."

They crossed the bridge and for over a mile kept on a dusty road. Trees began appearing, then growing thick. They stretched on and on as the buggy rolled slowly by, with nothing but Rev. Jackdaw between her and all that might lurk in them.

On a ridge with flat, open land on one side and a drop on the other, he pulled hard on Nell's reins, brought her to a stop.

Darkness was gathering fast, and she wanted to shout, "Go, go." They couldn't camp there. Her gaze followed Rev. Jackdaw's. At the bottom of the slope, through even more trees, the Missouri River looked little more than a mud flat. For days they'd trailed alongside the water, sometimes with a clear view, at other times the road swung out and the river disappeared. Seeing it again, she had the sinking feeling the river followed them rather than the other way around. Or that despite the long, awful days, they'd covered no ground at all.

She batted whining mosquitoes, her stomach rolling and her eyes adjusting in the waning light. Not a stone's throw from the water, on an apron of sandy ground, two small shacks sat looking for all the world as sinister as the woods surrounding them. Floating three or four feet off the ground. The sight made her cross her arms over her stomach, hold tight to herself, and look to Rev. Jackdaw. His bad eye twitched, delivered the awful news he hadn't yet spoken. This was the lodge where he expected her to live.

"No," she managed. "Not here." She'd never imagined a house perched on sticks, and its unnaturalness seemed as evil as the lurking trees with their dark, swaying shadows and branches. This couldn't be where she had to stay. Not down there. Not for days, maybe even a week.

Rev. Jackdaw drew back his shoulders, scrubbed his chin, and slid a hand down his long beard. His unsettled eye jumped. "It won't take long. I'll have a house built in Omaha."

Effie had no words, her throat so tight breathing was labor. She studied the stilted boxes he'd called a trapping lodge. She'd expected two stories, as many as a dozen rooms. She'd expected a busy place with plenty of men carrying plenty of guns. She'd expected a fort. Never such an abandoned place. And never so many trees. Traveling from Omaha, she'd prayed the trees he spoke of would be off at some civilized distance from the lodge. Off like a field of wheat, not bleak and ugly and looming over every breath she drew. A huge walnut towered over the lodge. It looked half on the apron of land and half in the unquiet river. How many Injuns lived in that tree alone?

Rev. Jackdaw scowled as he handed her the reins. "Keep it slow." He climbed out, made a shoving motion to Bridget, telling her to get out of the cart. He grabbed the bridle at the throatlatch and tugged. "Step on."

Effie's eyes widened as they started down, rolling over ruts and holes, some as deep as a foot. The cuts, from seasons of neglect and water washing down, made her think of monstrous claw marks. She clutched the reins as the buggy rocked and lurched. Each time she bounced inches above the seat, she slammed her foot harder on the brake and struggled to keep herself from flying off. She wished she'd been allowed to walk with Bridget, but she had no more say in how she descended than Nell.

"Slow!" Rev. Jackdaw yelled at her.

She tried to concentrate, to stay focused just on braking and keeping the reins taut. She couldn't look at the lodge, couldn't think right now about living in the uncivilized West with trees, an orphan, and a man who paid no more mind to her wants than he did to his horse's.

"Slow!"

She stomped her full weight on the brake, the wood and leather pads gripping and squeaking. They had no choice but to go down. No one would risk leaving a horse and buggy unattended in this wild. But if a wheel sank into a furrow, though they moved against the cuts, or the bouncing snapped the old buggy's axel, even if Nell stepped into a hole, splintering a cannon bone, Effie didn't care. What lay at the bottom felt like dropping off the edge of civilization.

"Slow! Can't you hear?"

Bridget stood fixed, watching Nell. The poor horse was gentle and kind no matter how many times Rev. Jackdaw struck her with the tips of the leather reins, or how bad her leg hurt. Now her eyes were wide and rimmed in white as she hitched her way down, and Rev. Jackdaw kept hollering at Effie, right in Nell's ear.

Bridget turned away—she couldn't watch any longer. She started for the river. Her whole body had bruises from the weeks of bouncing, and her feet blisters from the hours she walked each day, but with every step closer to the water, her fingers opened wider and her hands lifted as if to grab up the wonder. The new world surrounding her reminded her of Ireland. Not rocks and stones and crashing waves, but trees and more trees like a sacred grove, and a river for selkies.

Picking up speed, laughing and breathless, Bridget ran past the cabin on stilts, stopping only when her toes reached the water. Mum could be in the river. All water was connected.

She twirled with her arms wide. "If I was a bird," she told Mum, "I'd fly up and see how far the trees grow. But you can't measure woods." She knew from walking with Grandma Teegan, and from the stories, that trees liked to stretch out or bunch up.

Ten

"Whoa," Rev. Jackdaw yelled as they finished the descent and the buggy wheels caught where clay soil met silt and sand. He kept hold of the bridle and stood staring at the shack. His cussed eye twitched. For starters, the trip from Omaha had taken several hours, not the two or three he'd expected. He pulled the letter from Deet out of his breast pocket and flung it open. *Just a piece upriver from Bleaksville.*

True enough, but where did he get the idea Bleaksville was only a couple of miles outside of Omaha? Not somewhere close to twenty. With that much distance and Nell's age, each ride to Effie would be spending the miles in a horse that couldn't spare them. Plus time away from his work in Omaha.

He glanced again at the letter. *The place ain't fit for a white woman.* Reading those words back in Minnesota, the penmanship so poor it needed study, he'd shrugged off the comment. Certain the unschooled Deet didn't know the Lord provided according to one's merit. But this abomination? A chimney falling down, a roof no better, walls with crumbling mortar between rotting logs and chinks open to rain, cold, and varmints? At least a good supply of wood had been cut, and he owed Deet for keeping his word on that.

Effie still sat frozen in the buggy, rigid and sickly looking. Even knowing she carried the sin of lying with a man out of wedlock, he'd expected she'd earned herself a nicer place. *Vengeance is mine, saith the Lord.*

He refolded the letter, shoved it back in his pocket, and felt the warm touch of vindication. The state of her soul, not his, warranted the shanty. He whispered a prayer that God still thought her worthy of bearing sons. She'd bled into her rags again on the trip down. His bad eye gave a sharp twitch, and he tried to force his mind into obedience. Forbidding himself doubt.

He worked at the harness, pulling the traces from the rings on the hames. Shacks up and down the roads they'd traveled showed women living in poorer conditions than this lodge. Even dugouts with snakes likely to stick their heads down over the supper table. Effie had no cause to complain.

Unfastening the poles from the buggy and resting them on the ground, he gave thanks. The trip was over, the buggy had survived in a single piece, and with a night's rest, Nell could muster gimp enough for the trip back to Omaha. All of which meant the Lord's favor. Even the ruined state of the lodge was advantageous to his cause. The disrepair explained why Deet agreed to free rent in exchange for watching over an ox, drying pelts, and his trees. Deet was no fool. Having someone living in the lodge also meant simple repairs would be done, rats and raccoons kept out.

"Lucky for you," he said in Effie's direction. The Lord's ways were indeed mysterious. "If the place weren't in such dire need, I couldn't have struck my deal."

His free girl skipped alongside the river as if she'd never seen water. "Rooster!" he called. "Git over here." She started back, her red hair bouncing off her shoulders, a big grin on her face. To his credit, he'd gotten the right orphan. He held Nell's reins. "Water her. Then find her something to eat. Don't wander too far and get lost in the dark." He nodded at a cleft in the trees. "Go along in there, not back up that damn ridge." Being so close to his dreams made him nervous, and the gleam in Rooster's eyes added to that unease. She hadn't tried any funny business yet, but that was because of his firm hand. He'd keep on her. "People in these parts hang horse thieves. Children or no. Especially orphans."

She reached for the reins, but he kept hold of them. Was she scared enough to behave? "You ever saw a hanging? Ever watched a man gurgle and twist? It's a slow and miserable trip to hell." He paused. "I'm keeping an eye on you."

Her gaze swept back and forth between his eyes as if she tried to figure out which eye that would be. His good eye, or the bad? "Git!" he bellowed.

With Rooster leading Nell, he looked back to Effie. She still hadn't moved and looked close to bawling. "Don't make me step up there and pull you out."

Obeying Rev. Jackdaw took a force of will Effie could scarcely muster. Both sides of the tiny clearing were a dark wall of trees. Broken branches hung caught in limbs and swung suspended in the air, wholly unnatural and looking like bleached bones. On the ground amongst the trunks, weeds grew knee-high over felled wood, and vines reddened by the fall temperatures twisted sinister as red snakes up massive trunks. Everything from bears to Injuns hid in such unholy places.

An eerie, raucous sound rose as if from the bowels of the earth. From the large tree half in the river, its shadow looming over the lodge where she was expected to sleep, blackness spilled out and upward, swelled to three times the size of the tree. As if signaled, an endless flood of shadowy birds rose from other nearby trees: starlings, cowbirds, blackbirds, crows. The inky net darkened an already pewter sky. The clicking, hissing, and clattering was deafening. Five hundred? A thousand? Just as suddenly, the flock reared and the evil-looking torrent swung back like a thick funeral cloth, resettled and shrouded the tree.

She trembled. Surely now they would leave, but Rev. Jackdaw in his black clothing climbed the lodge stairs and disappeared through the black maw of its doorway.

She waited for the nightmare to end. By the time his face reappeared, floating above a black-clothed body she could not make out in the darkness, she struggled to keep from fainting.

"Come down from there," he yelled over the roar of the crows. "It's clear. No raccoons, skunks. No varmints of any size."

"It's on sticks," Effie managed.

"Necessary this close to the river. Flood waters will wash under."

Holding Granny's gun, the spoons in their box, and her black cloth, Effie climbed down. She'd welcome skunks and raccoons over the birds sounding like torrents of rushing water, a roar of rasping, and wings tearing at the air. She forced herself up the rickety steps and across the landing only four paces wide, but stopped at the door.

Inside, Rev. Jackdaw walked along the far wall holding a lit candle stub. "You got yourself a regular lady's commode." He stopped, used the toe of his boot, nudged a wooden box with a hole cut in the top. A rusty metal bucket sat beneath. "You want, you can do your business right here."

Wooziness made Effie reach out for the doorjamb.

He leveled his eyes on her. "You're trying me." He walked on, flicked a large spider off a pump handle, and wiped the web clear with his hand. "Looky here, you got water inside." Several pumps failed to draw up even a trickle. "I'll prime it. You'll scrub off that table and start coffee. Rooster gets back with my horse, she can help you carry in."

Effie didn't watch him walk out the back door, only the scuff of his footprints in the dust. The single room reeked of mouse droppings and mold. Cracks spattered the walls, some large enough for Injuns outside to squat and leer through. Four small, grimy windows, two on the front wall and two on the back. The glass crusty with wooly strings of gray webs, untold filth and leaf bits—as though the trees themselves had coughed onto the panes. Cobwebs also hung tattered from the rafters like long fingers of hundred-year-old lace. Or worse, like strong new sewing threads. Dust lay thick over a table and two mismatched chairs. Ropes sagged on a bedstead lacking a mattress. No curtains, no rugs, though one corner held a couple more rusty buckets and an aging broom so thick with cobwebs she'd never touch it. In another corner, what looked to be a pile of old and dirty furs. So lumpy they could be covering a skeleton.

When Rev. Jackdaw stepped back in through the rear door and began to slowly pour water down the pipe of the pump, she hadn't yet moved. "Deet wrote the well rope's frayed," he said, "but I ain't going to bother changing it. You got water here. Dang waste of money buying that rope." He poured water until the pipe overflowed and then he pumped again. Brown water trickled from the spout, but with each pump the amount increased. With each pump too, the clarity of the water increased. Satisfied, he crossed to her, pulled away Granny's gun, and hung it with an angry flourish on nails beside the back door. He returned, reached for her spoons.

"No." She twisted away. "I see what's needing done." She moved slowly. How could she ever make the place livable? And where to start trying? Everything needed done at once, and she lacked the energy for any of it.

She took another measure of the room. Was it fifteen feet across? Only the cook stove eased some of her upset. Next to it, a battered box held kindling. She took up a pail. The table Rev. Jackdaw wanted washed consisted of three stained and battered planks. Most of the damage looked like slits in the wood, as though rather than laying down their knives during meals, a dozen men over several years simply stabbed them into the wood. She knew and the knowing struck her hard: no woman had ever lived in the place.

She found the unbleached sugar sack they'd emptied on the trip. Traveling, she'd wondered what she might make with it and folded and tucked the soft fabric in with her dresses. Holding it now, she decided not to tear the cotton in half and limit its possibilities. She dunked the whole cloth into her cold well water and started on the table's thick grunge. With the first muddy swipe, the sugar sack turned a dark brown, ruined, as lost as if it had disappeared in her hand.

The fire Rev. Jackdaw built helped light the room, and the smell of burning wood helped mask the lodge's musty odors. As the room gradually warmed and coffee boiled, Effie promised herself things would be all right. Until she could solve the rodent problem though, she'd keep Dr. Chase's book and her dresses in the sink. The orphan likely never had a bed and preferred sleeping on the floor, but for the first night she'd best sleep on the table. *And maybe*, Effie decided, *I'll join her*. Rats could drop from the rafters onto the table too, or crawl up the knobby table legs just as they could bedstead legs, but the table stood higher, and the furry, ugly things would at least have to claw with more effort.

Bridget was still outside, moving around in the night with the hideous dark birds and sinister trees. Why wasn't she afraid? What sort of pagan kinship with feral nature kept her from being terrified?

Stars hung overhead and Bridget imagined they buzzed like bees around the full moon. She tied Nell to the large tree in back. The tree stood only twenty steps from the cabin—she counted them. The river had cut in and washed away soil, leaving many of its roots exposed and creating a thick and watery basket of tawny ropes. She'd call him Wilcox for the old man she'd loved in their New York tenement.

She stroked Nell's long, soft neck, and kissed her cheek. "We're here. You can rest now."

The back of the lodge didn't have steps but a ramp that led up to the narrow landing and the door. Full of excitement, she ran up and inside. Effie had thrown the empty ticking over the ropes and knelt on the floor in front of the bed, her pretty face lowered and half hidden in her steepled hands. Bridget sighed. Her praying, which Rev. Jackdaw liked, and her hiding beneath the black cloth, which he didn't, were Effie's only ways of being alone.

While Effie prayed, Rev. Jackdaw sat at the table, his pen scratching across a page of his journal. Neither of them were concerned with her. She turned and went back out, stopping to stroke Nell's long nose again, and then hurrying on to the river's edge. Along the shore, small watery indentations—each harboring a moon—wandered off in both directions. A woman's footprints? A selkie's? Had Mum already been there?

She thought of the day Rowan explained all about selkies. She'd stood in the yard with him and Grandma Teegan, watching Pappy and Mum leave. Pappy sat up tall in the small wagon he'd hired to carry them and looked forward. Mum looked back at Bridget, her eyes full of tears as they rolled away. Grandma Teegan took up the hoe Great-grandpa Seamus had used throughout his life—stains from his hands still on the handle. She walked toward the village cemetery. When Ogan went loping after her, his ears flapping, Rowan let the dog go, but he grabbed Bridget and held her back.

"Leave her," he said. "She's wanting to be alone."

"Why?" Bridget cried. "Why do they all need to be alone of me?"

Rowan held her hand as Grandma Teegan walked away. She moved slow, her back bent, and she used the hoe like a walking stick. Every few steps the metal blade landed with a click on some small rock half buried in the turf.

Rowan headed for the rocky path leading down to the sea. "Come on."

They moved around waist-high boulders and stepped over rocks pot-sized. At the sea, waves crashed and threw sprays of water. To Bridget, the whole world was crying, and for good reason. Sitting on a flat rock, paying no attention to the spray turning their clothes damp, they watched the waves turn gold and violet beneath the setting sun.

"I want Mum," Bridget said.

He squinted at her. "What ye doing there?"

She shrugged.

"Ye been licking an hour."

"Mum's tears taste like salt."

"Ye like the taste of tears?"

"No. I love Mum."

He pulled her close. "Ye keep crying like that, it'll turn ye into an old woman. Don't look at me so. Grandma Teegan cried herself that age. Crying over all the people she's lost, believing ye mum be lost, too."

Sea birds dove out of the air and then leveled just above the water's surface, flying straight as sticks for several yards before lifting again. "Ye know about selkies?" Rowan asked.

Bridget nodded. Everyone knew selkies came ashore and took off their sealskins and were beautiful people who never got old. Men could be selkies, but Bridget only liked the stories of girl selkies. They married fishermen and had fishermen's babies and were happy. But the sea was their real home, and they could put on their sealskin whenever they wanted and return to the water for an hour or a day or forever.

"Ye haven't been told," Rowan said. With calloused hands, he wiped tears off her cheeks. "Yer mum," he made a show of looking around, being sure they were alone, and then he leaned down to her ear, "she hasn't really left you. She be a selkie."

Bridget sniffed and wiped her nose on her sleeve. "She went to America to get a farm with Pappy. Someday, we're going, too."

"That be true." He made a diving motion with one hand, a swoop up and then down. "But one fine day, sitting right here on this rock, I saw her out there in her sealskin."

"What color was she? Brown? Or black?"

"Silver. Shiny."

"I don't want her to be a fish."

"Only now and again, just for visiting a little girl who won't stop licking her face." He kept his arm around Bridget, his gaze out over the sea. "All the water in the world is connected: rivers, streams, underground paths, even root-ways through trees. Clouds too. If ye be by water anywhere, yer mum can sneak away from yer pappy, put on her silver skin, and visit ye."

Bridget turned her face to the sea. "Mum?"

"She can't hear that pip o' noise. If ye haven't got a tune for calling, shout."

"Mum!"

"There!" Rowan pointed. He jumped up so quick the surprise nearly knocked Bridget from the rock. He raced into the water, not bothering to remove his only shoes, only stopping when the sea reached his knees.

She scrambled after him, splashing to her ankles and scanning the water for Mum. Though she couldn't see anything, now she knew Mum hadn't really left her.

Sitting along the Missouri, Bridget couldn't see any shapes swimming in the river, and no selkie lifted out and walked up to the shore to her. "Mum!" She waited. An hour passed and exhaustion made her finally rise and head back for the lodge. She stopped again to pet Nell's neck. "Watch for Mum," she said. "Sing or yell really loud. If she comes, tell her to visit the croft and see if Grandma Teegan got home."

Rev. Jackdaw still wrote at the table. "Two thousand five hundred prostitutes," he was saying as Bridget entered. Effie had risen to sit pale and frightened on the bed ropes. "No way to get a real count of the sinners," Rev. Jackdaw said. "That's just an estimate."

Bridget had heard him say before that prostitutes were evil, yet the number in Omaha clearly thrilled him. She couldn't imagine two thousand five hundred. If they all stretched out holding hands, how long would the line be? Was the number so many it included all the unmarried and all the poor women in the West? If something had happened to Pappy, would Mum have to be a prostitute? *Nera, Nera,* Bridget chanted for courage. "Are some of the women Irish?"

Rev. Jackdaw looked up, his face pinched. "They swarm to America. Dirty, infected whores."

Bridget was confused. Mum wasn't a bad woman, no matter what name Rev. Jackdaw called her. And she and Grandma Teegan hadn't been dirty. They washed every day. She and Effie were dirty now, but they'd been traveling in dust for days. Rev. Jackdaw was dirty too.

"How do they get so dirty and infected?"

His twitching eye focused on her. "Come here."

She went to stand close; he had an answer she needed to know.

He grabbed her arm, shook her. "Ain't you had a biscuit to eat?" A long finger pointed around at the lodge. "Ain't you got a roof over your head? What makes you think whores are any of your business?"

Despite his grip, she wished she could ask him to look for Mum in Omaha. *She has hair the color of mine.* But she couldn't sic him on Mum. One day, she'd find a way to get to Omaha and look herself. She'd walk up and down the streets yelling, "Mum, Mum."

Two hours later, Bridget woke to the sound of knocking. She lay on the table top, and the noise came from across the dark room. Rev. Jackdaw and Effie were in the bed. Moonlight threaded through the branches of Wilcox, and though she couldn't see all they'd spread out for a mattress—was it every stitch of their clothing?—she could see Rev. Jackdaw on top of Effie. The Never Forget quilt covered his backside, but moonglow spread across his white shoulders and over his beard hanging down and swaying. Effie's face was turned sharply away so that his beard drug across her cheek and ear. She stared into the room.

Rev. Jackdaw panted and grunted and the ropes under the empty bed ticking winced and squeaked. The four bedposts shuffled on the floor making *whomp, whomp* sounds. During their long trip down from

Minnesota, Bridget had seen him take Effie off a few yards from the campfire and grunt on her while she lay still as the dead. Just like now.

The bed on its narrow legs bounced and Rev. Jackdaw's breathing increased. When he rolled off, Effie's face in shadow didn't move. Only a tear, its shine caught, rolled across the bridge of her nose.

Bridget closed her eyes. She wished she could tell Effie a story. Living with her, she'd have to remember Grandma Teegan's happiest ones because Effie had also brought along stories. Unhappy stories.

When Mum and Pappy find me, Bridget promised herself, *we'll bring Effie away too.*

Eleven

In the crisp morning air, Rev. Jackdaw brought Nell around to the front of the lodge. The trees were full of waking birds, the undersides of clouds pink, and he was at last ready to begin his commission.

The lodge door opened and Effie stepped out wrapped in her granny's quilt, her thin, white slip beneath ending at her ankles. She rushed down the steps. "Please, you can't leave us here."

Her young flesh was a temptation to stay. Being his wife had awakened her beauty, but he didn't have the luxury of young men, able to lie around bedding young wives. It was time to be about his Father's business in Omaha. *The desires of the flesh are against the Spirit and the desires of the Spirit are against the flesh.* He'd planted plenty of his seed already—he wasn't young, but able enough. Hopefully, last night's hadn't fallen yet again on barren ground.

"Don't leave us here," Effie cried a second time. Her golden hair flowed over her white shoulders. "Not after one night!"

He stretched his stiff back. He'd endured the long trip down with her shaking every time she needed to step ten paces away to relieve herself, her gasping every time a buggy wheel bogged, and her constant nightmares. How could she accuse him of leaving her after one night? It wasn't even him she wanted. She was scared of Indians. Maybe his being away for a spell would knock some sense in her, remind her she was lucky to have a husband.

He lined Nell up in front of the buggy. "Back, back," he coaxed and pushed, getting the horse between the two shafts and ignoring the frightened way Effie's eyes raked the trees. When she stepped forward and grabbed his arm, he stuck out an elbow and forced her to take a step back. "Give me room."

He'd put the shafts in the loops of the traces and hooked the tugs before the door opened again and Rooster stood watching them. "Hey, you," he called. "Get my valise and journal." No need for him to walk back inside; he had a free girl. "Be careful now with that book."

When she returned, he motioned for her to put his bag in the buggy boot, but he took the journal and laid it on the seat. *Rev. Jackdaw.* The name tooled into the leather helped soothe his growing irritation with Effie. It also made him think of Mister. If his father were alive—not burning in hell—what would he think now of the son he'd put in a dress and referred to as "the girl"? What would Mister think if he read the repeated accounts in the journal?

Effie sniffled, and he considered the fear twisting her face. It wasn't likely a female could understand a man's deep communion with God. Heaven's gates opened for men; wives as needed. Nor could a woman understand a man's need for breathing space, but Effie's lack of understanding would not be the thing to stop him. He checked the rub of the bit in Nell's tired mouth and ran a hand along the reins, feeling the severity of the cracks. He wouldn't check Nell's sore foot. No matter what sort of swelling she had, he couldn't afford to lose a full day or two letting her rest. Limp or no, Nell could make it back to Omaha. Then he'd see a blacksmith, have her foot tended, even rest her up a few weeks before he put her back in harness. He'd make Omaha.

Omaha. The name was a promised land. One day he'd stand over his congregation, look out from the pulpit of his stone church, three sons flanking each side.

"Will you be back tomorrow? Or the day after?"

Was she such a fool? "I'll set up credit for you at the mercantile. Now stand back, I tell you. Leave me to my commission and building a house."

"How long?"

Before she caught sight of his firing eye, he turned and climbed into the buggy. "I won't tolerate a wife telling me what to do. You understand that?"

"What if Injuns come?"

He looked down at her. "Ain't I told you soldiers took care of 'em." She opened her mouth, but he raised his hand to stop her. "None of your claptrap about Lincoln sending redskins to Nebraska."

Rooster stood, gawking as though their business was hers. "Find that ox. Goes by Jake. Has a Flying D brand. You know what a D looks like? Do that quick." He gripped his hat brim, tugged it down tighter, and seized the reins. Hopefully wolves hadn't already moved into the trees and taken the animal. Would Deet hold him responsible? Or suppose the ox had gone wild over the months of not being handled and Rooster was no match. Once again, doubt threatened to make him a non-believer. "Mr. Deet will be here trapping soon as pelts are ripe. He'll expect the ox here. You best find it. Carry a big stick and take the rope. I tied you a good noose knot."

Rooster wasn't nodding or showing any sign she intended to stay put in his absence. He scowled, not wanting to climb down with his tired back and give her a taste of how disobeying felt. "Tending that ox is a small price for a roof over your head. You mind it, and I hear you been sniffing around that school, neglecting the reason I'm keeping you, I'll make sure you don't forget again."

Twelve

Effie crawled back into the sagging bed and tried to steady her breathing. The drifting away squeaks of the buggy whined in her ears. Rev. Jackdaw knew how much being alone in the wild scared her, but he didn't care. His rejection was no different than Jury's. She didn't love him, though he'd rescued her and married her. She owed him for that, but he also had a duty to keep her safe. How could he do that from miles away? Pa had been only half a mile away when Injuns massacred his family.

She grabbed the black cloth. Only large enough to swathe a baby's coffin, it covered just her head and shoulders. Beneath it, she bit her lip. Not even her body could keep a man, though she always submitted to Rev. Jackdaw. Having him work on top of her was worse than hoeing beans in August heat, but she always submitted. Why wasn't she pregnant by now? If she were, Rev. Jackdaw wouldn't leave her. He'd take her straightaway to Omaha.

She fisted her hands. She wouldn't give up. Soon, there'd be a proper home and children. With those two things, she'd make a happy life. One day, maybe she and Rev. Jackdaw would find that over the years they'd grown fond of each other.

"Should I go find the ox now?"

Effie slapped the black cloth down. Bridget was at the table, Dr. Chase's book in front of her. "No, you're not leaving me too. Read that book."

"He said find the ox."

Effie sat up. She'd not slept the previous night, only listened to the wind tumble down the river and through the trees with a cruel, breathy nearness. Owls had hooted, and in the distance howling and yipping from what must have been a dozen coyotes. Any of the sounds might have been Injuns signaling one another. She'd listened hard for the whispered weight of moccasins at the door.

She forced herself to stand. What if she fell asleep and Bridget ran off after the ox and left her alone? She pulled yesterday's dress from the bedpost and stepped into it. She was scaring herself with her thoughts about Injuns. Just as Granny had scared herself. She couldn't let her mind run loose as a spooked horse. Without the distractions of little brothers and Homeplace chores, she had to find ways of harnessing her mind.

"I know what Rev. Jackdaw said," she pulled combs from her hair, ran her fingers back through it, and reinserted the combs. "I just can't be left alone right now."

"Mum and Pappy will find us," Bridget said. Her eyes still on the world outside.

"They won't." Effie headed for the stove. A bit of cold coffee remained from the night before. "They aren't even your parents now. Rev. Jackdaw is." She saw Pa's face beside the buggy, heard him say, *This ain't your home no more.* "We're stuck here, Bridget. Stuck."

"Why did you marry him?"

"Life isn't one of your fairytales. I had no choice."

"You could have gotten away. A boy would get away. Nera would get away."

Effie leaned on the cold stove. She felt no energy even for lighting kindling in the firebox, and she wasn't going to ask who Nera was. "I never thought it would be like this."

"What happened at your house?"

The coffee in the pot sloshed. Effie set it down and wiped her suddenly cold hands down her sides. "How do you know something happened?"

"When I was on your porch with the puppies, I could feel a bad story."

The child was frightful, clutching now at dead hair wrapped in a red scarf around her waist. Claiming to know something she couldn't possibly know. Effie pointed slowly to the stolen washtub Rev. Jackdaw had hung on the wall. "You should have left it there."

"What happened?"

A walnut thumped on the roof and rolled down with a rattle. It struck the porch, making Effie jump a second time, and bounced off. "We don't talk about it."

"In Grandma Teegan's stories, if a girl gets in trouble, she gets herself away as fast as she can."

Effie lifted an iron burner plate, clanged it down. "You don't know what you're saying. Rev. Jackdaw heard you talk like that, he'd give you a well-deserved licking." She put in kindling from the box on the floor. "I would be no better off leaving. Not a penny to my name. No way of getting one. I got to keep believing the Lord will send me babies when I've earned them. Then everything will turn out all right."

Talk about conceiving wasn't something a girl Bridget's age should hear. "I had an aunt," Effie said. "She made a doily out of her husband's hair and beard." She'd keep them both busy. "You know how to make a doily out of that hair you're holding on to?"

"It's Grandma Teegan's hair."

"Hair is hair. It doesn't have to be a doily."

"It's mine."

"It's not." She'd tried to be nice. Rev. Jackdaw had warned her about being soft on Bridget and the trouble that could cause. "Rev. Jackdaw's signing a paper on you means everything you own is his. The Bible says a wife is under her husband and children are under the wife." *And orphans don't count at all.* Though of course, neither did wives, really.

Bridget squinted at Effie as though she were the strange one.

"Anyway," Effie said, "who wants a doily you're going to talk to? Get rid of it."

"No."

"I can't live with you clutching dead hair, whispering to dead people. I left that all at Homeplace. Get rid of it."

"Grandma Teegan gave it to me so we can stay together."

"That woman gave you away. That hair was to cover up her shame. She wanted rid of you."

"You don't know the story."

"I'm warning you," Effie said, "If you don't get rid of it, I'll throw it in the river."

She'd put Johnny's marbles in a front window, and as the sun rose higher, light struck them. He'd given them to her to keep them safe from Skeet. She was being Skeet now. Or was it Granny, who'd certainly fret over dead hair? Her sanity rattled.

Thirteen

Scrubbing at the window's grime—layers of grease, flyspecks, and abandonment—Effie struggled to keep her mind on the work and not on the sinister-looking world outside. This was the second day since being pulled off the buggy and into the shanty perched on stilts. She had no idea how many days—surely not a week—before Rev. Jackdaw returned. Seeing the amount of wood he'd hired cut for winter fires had made her nearly sag to her knees. It ran along one entire side of the lodge. So high, Bridget needed to stand on a chair to take from the top. What was Rev. Jackdaw planning?

She'd try not to worry. Rev. Jackdaw would come back for her. When he did, he'd expect proof that she'd worked hard in his absence. Both she and Bridget had, sweeping out dirt, mouse droppings, dead frogs. They'd even dragged the fur from the corner and found it was one huge buffalo hide. She'd wanted to lug the ugly thing all the way to the river, but Bridget wanted it for a bed. Without a mattress of any sort for her, Effie relented. They wrestled it over the back porch railing, and Bridget spent hours beating it with a stick, pounding it free of dust.

Effie turned back to her pail and rag. She couldn't imagine sleeping on something so awful, but Bridget, working now at plastering—little more than slapping mud over holes in the wall—had drug the hide back in and happily stretched out on it.

"Look," Bridget squealed and pointed to a mouse hugging the base of a wall. The mouse ran a few inches and stopped, its whiskers trembling.

Effie hurried for the broom. Only a mouse. She could handle a mouse. On tiptoes, keeping her dress hem off the floor and standing as far back as possible, she stretched, slamming the rodent with the old bristles. Her own shrieking helped, though it sent Bridget into a fit of laughter. The mouse ran and Effie whacked again. The furry body rolled like a stone under her sweeping, its pink toes in the air, its tail flicking in a circle like a tiny whip, then on its feet again. And gone. Through a hole no bigger than Effie's thumb.

Bridget was still giggling and Effie nearly smiled. Only a mouse, and she'd handled it just fine. She returned to her pail and squeezed out the ruined sugar sacking. Brown water smelling of scum ran over her red-chapped hands. Still, today she was handling things—so long as God kept Injuns away.

She scrubbed again at the pocked glass. *Injuns.* Her gaze skittered right and then left across the yard. The trees, so tall she lived in dark shadows, felt like bars. Granny, whose mind had frayed to one thin strand, wouldn't survive a single night in the lodge. How many nights, Effie wondered, before the ropes of her own mind began fraying?

"That was funny," Bridget said.

The lightness of the previous moment was already gone for Effie. She looked from the trees to the building Rev. Jackdaw called the skinning shed. Also perched on sticks. He hadn't mentioned snakes, but where there was water, there were snakes. Their muscled bodies climbed. She'd seen one in the chicken coop at Homeplace, draped in a long S over a high roost. In one slick upward glide, a snake could scale any of the poles holding up the lodge. Arch its back and reach up through the rotting floor. Or slither in under a door.

Effie scrubbed. The river scared her more than the snakes it harbored. Every time she checked for Injuns in narrow canoes, the unquiet water had changed from brown and solid to some shade of peril. At sunset it was blood red.

"I'm hungry," Bridget said.

"I know." Effie scrubbed. Bridget needed to eat. She'd complained of hunger several times that morning, a chant she'd started the day before. But she hadn't gotten rid of the braid yet, only left it on the disgusting hide. And the walk into town and the mercantile was two miles. Along a road lined with trees. "I told you, make a thick paste. That's running down the wall."

"I'll get more dirt. Maybe I'll see the ox."

"Don't run off." There were walnuts to eat, but how filling were they? "Just add weeds, dung if you see any."

At the back door, Bridget hesitated. "Remember what he said."

"I know he said for you to find the ox. But you're likely to get lost. Quit pestering me."

It shamed Effie the way she ordered and barked at Bridget. *It's fear brings out meanness,* Ma once said of Granny. "Only fear," Effie whispered to herself. She moved to the front window and set the pail down. The sound was a soft clunk on the rotting boards. She dipped her rag in the water, wrung out the excess, drew it up to the glass, and stopped. "Someone's coming."

"There's a boy," Bridget said. She'd dropped her pail too, and raced to Effie's side.

At the top of the ridge, he stood between the long handles of a worn, wooden cart and watched a woman in a wide, mustard-colored dress slowly traverse the slope.

"Our first visitor," Effie said.

Bridget ran for the door. "Is it Mum?"

"Stop!" Effie shouted. "You aren't dressed fit. Your hands . . ." She gave chase, but the bar hit the floor and Bridget ran out.

They stood together on the narrow landing and stared at the approaching woman.

"It's not Mum." Bridget's words a near sob.

The closer the woman came, the more uneasy and stung with disappointment Effie felt. The strange, young-old woman looked to be in her last week or even in her last day of a long pregnancy. With a face pale as old sheets, the only color was her fatigue, curved under her eyes like slack, blue thumbs. Loose strands of hair dangled at her cheeks and the rest was piled atop her head and held with twigs. *Like a nest.* The woman's bare feet scuffed dust. The puckered and bunched waist of her worn dress rode curved over the top of her huge stomach, tucked under her breasts. The hemline a foot higher in the front than the back. She carried a loaf of unwrapped bread and a red rooster. Reaching the bottom of the slope and crossing the sand, she shifted the bread and the chicken with its dull red comb and yellow eyes from one hand to the other. Smiling, she offered the bread to Effie. "I brung this here for you."

Spurred by the fear of the wretched-looking creature possibly climbing onto the porch, Effie left Bridget's side and forced herself to move down the steps. She felt upended. Not knowing what else to do, she accepted the hard, dry loaf with an unsteady hand.

The woman smiled again. "I go by Mae Thayer." A lilt in her voice. "You can call me Mae." The name given with satisfaction, as if the woman thought it as much a gift as the week-old bread. And at Effie's stunned silence, "I'm your neighbor. My man, Mr. Thayer, he said a woman was down here, but I didn't believe it. I was right. Yous just a couple of kids." A bee buzzed around the chicken's head and she swatted at it. "How old you be?"

How old are you? Effie wondered. Was Mae twenty years older than herself? Or only ten, maybe five? Her face, with study, looked young enough beneath the pallor. Was it the number of years she'd lived or their harshness that had ruined her? Were all Nebraska women so beaten? Effie hadn't married out of love—few women had that luxury—but she'd married with the hope of being secure, with a home and children. Not the sort of existence this creature bespoke in her ragged dress with its sorry-looking bit of old lace around the neck.

Lace Mae had tried to fix with too-thick thread and clumsy hands, needing to hold on to the idea of owning lace.

"This place ain't fit for winter," Mae said.

Effie dared not turn and look at the lodge or down at her own dress. The brown hadn't been washed in several days, but there was no soap, and with the lodge needing so much sweeping and scrubbing, bothering to rinse the dress out in a pail would be wasted effort. She reached up, brushed her cheeks as if for dust, but pressed them hard, hoping to rub in a bit of color. With little sleep since leaving Homeplace, did her own face look as tired and old as Mae's?

"Hello in there," Mae said. "Can't you say nothin'?"

Effie's free hand swung behind her back and fisted. She clenched it until her broken nails bit hard into her palm. Her disappointment at seeing Mae Thayer in a mustard dress was unchristian, but the woman was so stark poor she had to be unfavored in the eyes of God. Why'd God bless her?

"I'm married to Reverend Jackdaw," Effie managed. Both "Reverend" and "Jackdaw" increased her importance. "He preaches in Omaha."

"You got a name? What they call you?"

"Her name is Effie," Bridget cut in. She leaned on the porch rail. "I'm Bridget."

"I can speak for myself," Effie said. Something in Mae's eyes looked addled. Since stepping out of the lodge and getting a good look at her, Effie had felt as though she were sliding slowly down the damp and cold sides of a well.

Once, in twilight sleep, her hand brushed her face and the old and loose skin she touched startled her awake. She realized she'd touched Granny's face, but the moment when she'd thought her own face miserably old lingered, spreading chill like a broad stain over the floor of her mind. Now, here it was again, the sinking sense of premonition she got looking at Mae—the first woman she encountered in Nebraska. This time, she wasn't sleeping.

Bridget came down the stairs and stood beside her. "Have you seen my mum? She's West."

Mae's eyes narrowed first on Bridget then on Effie. "You ain't sisters. Least not by the same daddy." She quit petting the chicken's head and used that hand to cradle her stomach. "You ain't lost?" she asked Bridget. "You's cared for?"

"She isn't lost," Effie said. She swung the loaf behind her back alongside her fisted hand. Her stomach felt jabbed by the sharp point of Mae's concern. *Who cares for any of us?*

"I've seen most ever'one hereabouts." Mae squinted at Bridget. "You don't look like no one."

"Her name is Kathleen." Bridget mimed Effie, swinging her hands behind her back. "Pappy's named Darcy?"

"There's a Davey. Even got us a Dewey. But they's Krauts. They ain't carrot tops."

Effie's breath caught.

"With that hair," Mae hurried on, "she ain't a Kraut. And yous," she looked directly at Effie, "best grow a thicker skin. We gets bullied down here. They call us river people."

"River people," Effie repeated. "That's ugly. Who says so?"

"Folks supposing they don't need no one but themselves. They's small inside. Small fills up with nothing."

Bridget went back up the stairs. "Mum is going to come."

Mae leaned closer to Effie. "You trade for her?"

"Of course not! She was a half orphan." Explaining any more would mean Mae staying to hear. It wasn't Mae's business.

"I was eight," Mae said, "when he traded me. I brung a gallon of whiskey. A gallon for the judge too, so he'd marrying us right there. Lifted his Bible and said it was done."

Just as Rev. Jackdaw had done. "Eight?"

"The law says a girl ought to be ten, but he promised me a store-bought dress if I lied." The chicken squirmed harder and Mae cupped a palm over its face, pushing down the head. "Lived with him thirteen years till he up and died. He never did buy me no dress."

We can't be friends, Effie wanted to say. *I'll never be as low as you.*

Mae's eyes crinkled and she smiled. "Talking to you is work. You don't help much."

"Rev. Jackdaw likes me quiet." During the long trip down from Minnesota, she'd hardly spoken. The first few days she'd tried, but he seldom answered. He bartered their meals and, when he could, a bed. "He speaks for us."

"Course he does." Mae's smile remained. "But what mens know about what womens got to say?"

"You don't know him. You shouldn't talk about a man you don't know. He's building a church and me a home in Omaha."

"That was a better string of words." She lifted a thin arm and pointed in the road's westerly direction. "I live up 'bout two miles. You'd be welcome to come by. I gets lonely."

Lonely. Effie's tongue felt dry. *I been lonely seven years.* But climbing into Rev. Jackdaw's buggy and leaving Homeplace had been about finding a better life. Not becoming friends with a woman worse off than her. Though Mae thought they were kindred enough to be friends.

Effie turned to Bridget. "Get back to your work. We got so much to do." Hopefully, the mention of work would send Mae on her way.

"I can help," Mae said.

"No. We can manage." Breadcrumbs sifted like ashes into her palm. Though decades younger than Granny, Mae carried a matching darkness. Something ghosted in her, just as something ghosted in Granny. Both were more eerie wind than solid.

Mae still didn't turn to leave. She could likely use a place to sit and rest, even a drink of water, but Effie couldn't force herself to extend the invitation. "Thank you for the bread." She forced herself to turn and face the steps.

"Why they let soldiers," Mae asked, "mens shot up and half starved to death, come home and name towns?"

Effie blinked and wished for her black cloth. "Bleaksville?"

"They come home looking like skeletons with 'ville' on their tongues. Mr. Thayer said half the mens in town come home from the war with pieces missing." Mae tapped one temple. "Sometimes the missing was gone from up here."

The leaves on the trees either side of the clearing breathed in raspy unison. "The lodge isn't fit for company," Effie said. "I can't invite you in. You want Bridget to fetch a cup of well water?"

Mae rubbed in wide, slow circles around the rim of her belly, her stained fingers disappearing and reappearing from beneath the chicken. "I can't bring 'em in alive," she said. "They wheeze. Can't breathe air." Her hand came around again. "Long as they are fish in me, they're alive. This here one, it's still using its gills. You know about gills?"

Effie's hand shook harder. More breadcrumbs sifted into her palm.

"I whelped one what lived." Mae nodded toward the boy waiting on the ridge. "That's Pete. He's got a white goodness."

A white goodness. Effie thought of Johnny, though the lad on the ridge looked older. Maybe fourteen or fifteen. "I have younger brothers . . ." Loss bubbled too close to the surface, and she couldn't go on.

"My boy," Mae was still admiring him, "helps me along in here with berries. Wood too. Sometimes he'll bring us crows to eat."

The hair on the nape of Effie's neck lifted. "Mr. Deet's wood?" She understood now why Mae hadn't left yet. Her shoulders drew back and the bristling on her neck settled. By the blessing of the saints, Mae Thayer hadn't come wanting friendship. She'd admitted to stealing wood, and now she wanted to trade her week-old bun for permission to continue. Effie brought the loaf from behind her back and held it out in the space between them. "I'm hired by Mr. Deet himself. You're not to come and steal from him."

The chicken, half perched on the top of Mae's belly, tried to flap and in the struggle caught a toe in the worn fabric of Mae's dress. The foot jerked, the wings flapped, but Mae held tight. "We only take wood that's down."

She did. The wall of newly chopped wood stacked against the lodge hadn't been touched. "Even wood on the ground is stealing."

"Wood goes to rot."

"That's no concern of yours." Did Mae even notice the struggling bird? The unsettling, half-clucking? "I'm to go to the sheriff."

"Berries'll go to rot too, call up blackbirds."

Effie couldn't look into the trees, couldn't bear to see their dark numbers swing out like an arm of the devil and back again. The scrapping and cawing of crows—a noise she'd been trying to deny since arriving at the lodge—rose higher. As if Mae commanded them. *Pick every berry,* she wished she could say. *Cut down every tree. Carry off every branch and stick.*

For the first time in her life, though, she had something of her own: authority. She turned on Bridget. "Go back to your work. Mae doesn't know your folks." What good did it do Bridget to keep hoping? "Your parents are dead."

Bridget stepped backwards, not stopping until she bumped into the door. She'd not noticed the horror at first, but now she couldn't take her eyes from Mae and the shadowy space ringing Mae's body.

"Go!" Effie shouted at her.

Bridget rushed inside, slammed the door, ran and sank onto the buffalo hide in the corner. Mae knew everyone, but she didn't know a Kathleen or a Darcy, and Mae had the death space.

From Bridget's place on the hide, the small brown box Effie had shoved far under the bed—where Rev Jackdaw couldn't see it—was in full view. Bridget fought the urge; she shouldn't steal. But her body felt loose inside her skin. She had to make it quiet.

She peeked out the bottom of the window. The older boy, Pete, still stood between the poles of his cart with its red peeling paint. She wanted to run up the slope and stand close to him. She'd tell him his mum had the space. But she wouldn't tell him Rowan had also had the space and he died.

"The wood belongs to Mr. Deet," Effie was saying. She'd yet to climb back up the steps.

Bridget ran across the floor, dropped to her stomach and shimmied beneath the bed. Only halfway under she was able to reach far enough to grab the box. It had no lock, only a tiny copper latch.

"You're a woman, same as me," Mae said, her voice rising and coming through the walls. "This one . . . if it lives, it'll need heat over the winter."

The pain in Mae's voice increased Bridget's tension. She opened the box, grabbed a spoon, and shimmied back out.

"Coal ain't free," Mae said. "He expects I can get my own wood."

Effie was on the stairs, each footfall a warning. "It's Mr. Deet, you understand."

Where to hide the spoon? Bridget hurried back to the wall where she'd been plastering and pushed the spoon onto a small shelf-like ledge between two logs. A handful of the mud erased the shine, but not the shape. The spoon *almost* belonged to her. Better and thicker mud and Effie would never find it.

Bridget also knew now where to hide Matron's silver pen.

Fourteen

Standing far enough back from the window to avoid being seen, Effie watched Mae and how the hem of the ruined dress drug in back as she worked herself up the incline. Why hadn't any respectable women come from town? Women wearing fine hats and riding in fine buggies and carrying fresh cakes and pies? She was a preacher's wife. People had watched them ride through Bleaksville the first day, and people talked. Smoke rose from the chimney. Rev. Jackdaw had promised to stop at the mercantile on his way back through to establish her with credit. People knew she was there. Mae Thayer knew.

She lifted her rag from the dirty water, balled it in her hands, and threw it at the glass. "My name is Effie."

Bridget, as frustrating a child as ever there was, stood at the same wall as before, smearing fistfuls of mud over the same area. Effie sighed. "What are you doing?"

She didn't immediately look up. When she did, her eyes looked weepy. "We are West, but Mae doesn't know Mum or Pappy."

There was no use letting the child's mind snag on the impossible. "Your parents are dead. Even if they were alive, the West is as big as a world. Nebraska is the West, but the next state is the West too, and the state after that. There's no way to be found here."

Bridget reached into her pail, drew up more mud, and squeezed. Brown squished through her fingers. She smashed the clay onto the wall.

"Telling you 'West' was lying to you. Same as Rev. Jackdaw lied to me, saying we'd live in Omaha." She shuddered. "They call us river people."

Two horses pulling a wagonload of new lumber came around the bend. The driver whoaed the team, and Mae waved her loaf. Had the man been sent to work on the lodge? Perhaps to add a room so that she and Rev. Jackdaw could do their business without Bridget listening ten feet away. Or was the lumber bound for Omaha and the new home Rev. Jackdaw was building for her there?

Wearing a battered leather hat with a large floppy brim, the teamster looped the reins once around the brake and stepped down. Effie took the combs from her hair, ran her hands back through the tangles, and secured the combs again. There wasn't time to change clothes.

"Go, go," she whispered at the dull yellow dress and hoped the man didn't think Mae was a friend.

He started down the slope, the sun striking his face. Broad with dark skin and a grayish braid reaching to the tasseled sash around his waist. An Injun?

"No. God, please, no." Effie gasped. Her knees went weak and her mind slapped back to Granny's stories. A house full of chatter and children's squeals. A door thrown open and the kitchen turned to carnage.

She grabbed the shotgun from its pegs, and swung it toward the door. She'd checked the shells in the chambers a dozen times since being left, but two blasts were little protection. How would they die? Stabbed? Raped? Scalped?

"Bridget, get away from that window. Get behind me!"

"He's helping Mae climb the hill."

Without realizing it, Effie had been backing up. Now logs knocked into her shoulder blades. She stretched just enough to see the Injun push one side of its lumber to the right and the other to the left, clearing a small cleft at the very back of the wagon. Mae wiggled into the space. The Injun drew out a bucket and started back down.

"He's got food," Bridget said. She had mud not just on her hands and arms, but on the ends of her hair and across a cheek. "There's potatoes and onions and carrots."

Effie's shaking hands were slick with sweat. Would she have the strength to pull the trigger when she needed to? Should she shoot now, try and scare it off? What if it didn't run and she was down one shell? Her tongue felt thick, her words half strangled. "Tell it to go away. Tell it I'm shooting."

Bridget waved through the glass.

"Don't do that! Get away."

"Maybe he wants to be nice. E-F-F-I-E."

"I'm going to shoot," she yelled. She kept the gun pointed and tried to think. The Injun hadn't touched the door latch. If it meant harm, wouldn't it already be inside?

"He's leaving," Bridget said. She shrugged and stepped wide of the gun barrel. "Can I get the pail?"

"We aren't eating that." Effie's knees still trembled. She needed to go for help, find the sheriff, and report the Injun. She'd be the first to sound the alarm: an Injun was off the reservation and had marched up to her door.

She waited until the wagon and Pete, trailing behind and dragging his cart, were out of sight before she crossed the room, and laid the gun on the bed. With trembling fingers, she worked at the old buttons on her dress. Mismatched every one of them. Buttons passed down from dress to dress from relatives long dead. She paused over her green; if she showed herself in the silk on the first day, what would she wear to picnics later? She chose a blue, faded but cleaner, and thought of Mae riding in the back of the Injun's wagon. At eight years old, Mae dreamed of a new dress. A little girl with no idea of the bargain she was making. Was getting in that wagon a choice just as bad?

"I'm going into town." If she hurried the two miles into Bleaksville, even with the days growing shorter—something like doors closing all around her—she could be back by dark.

"Should I come with you?"

Taking Bridget would mean company on the road and help describing the Injun, but she couldn't go in her mud-coated dress, and she didn't own a second. Effie had promised to make her a spare, and until that was done, she didn't want to give folks more reason to think them river people.

"You find the ox. No, wait a minute." Earlier, she'd had Bridget find the recipe in Dr. Chase's book for curing lice. Opening the book to the page, Effie tapped her finger on the recipe. "Read what we need."

"That's the wrong recipe. It's to 'Color a blonde'."

"There's a recipe to make your hair like mine? Right on the same page?" *Was it a sign?* "You want Rev. Jackdaw to stop calling you Rooster?"

Bridget answered slow, looking over at the hide and the red scarf with its braid. "Grandma Teegan's hair was my color, and my hair matches Mum's."

Effie swallowed a groan. Every time she thought to do something nice for Bridget there was resistance. "Read both recipes."

Bridget worked at the words. "Sulfide of pot-tat . . . potassium, distilled water, nitrate of bi-sm-uth . . ." She took a breath. "Rosewater, boric acid, cause-it"—a long pause—"caustic potash. What's that?"

"I think it makes lye. Ma uses it to make soap."

Bridget's voice caught. "Why do you want me to have hair like yours?"

Something in the tiny spray of freckles across Bridget's nose and the hope in her eyes, made Effie stiffen. *Baby Sally.*

"So we'll be like sisters?"

Effie looked to the tub hanging on the wall. She'd had a real sister, once. "Bridget, we just aren't."

A gust of wind made several walnuts drop from the tree shrouding the lodge. The strikes on the roof, then the skittering, rolling sounds, and more pings onto one of the narrow landings made Effie start. One more constant and sharp noise she'd never grow accustomed to. She hugged herself; she couldn't think about Baby Sally right now and the noise was only walnuts. Not Injuns throwing stones or knives or shooting arrows.

"Find the ox, throw that pail of vegetables into the river. That dead braid, too. I won't warn you again."

Bridget ran out the door and across the sand. Her thick and bright hair, even with the mud on its ends, bounced after her. She didn't hesitate or make the sign of the cross before entering the trees, only disappeared into the blood-colored foliage.

Effie closed the door. Bridget wanted to be thought of as a sister. *How could I ever do that to Baby Sally?*

Fifteen

Bridget hid behind a tree and watched Effie run down the road, grabbing up her skirt with both hands, her elbows swinging, making Bridget smile at the sight of her frightened ankles, her legs pumping, and her hair flying. Effie didn't want to be her sister, though she was no older than a big sister, and both of them were away from their families and alone together.

With Effie well down the road, Bridget backtracked and returned to the lodge. The single room with its small windows kept the corners hung with shadow. The mud-damp walls where she'd worked held patches of even deeper dark. She checked the wettest spot but saw no trace of her spoon. She needed to hide Grandma Teegan's braid the same way. Close but safe. The hair couldn't be buried beneath wall plaster, though. Not buried in mud.

Under the buffalo robe was too obvious and anywhere outside the lodge was too dangerous. Wind and rain would damage it or animals would carry it off. She paced. The floor planks were soft and rotting through in places. Even hiding the braid beneath a board risked it to spring floods and the prowling creatures she heard at night scurrying across silty leaves beneath her.

She needed to hurry. Effie wasn't brave and might stop and run back. With the next drop of a walnut, Bridget looked up. Rafters. She stacked the two straight-backed chairs onto the table and climbed both. On tiptoes and wobbly legs, she reached for the beam and stretched out the red bundle. It stared at her: bright and eye-catching.

She unwrapped the hair nearly as long as her arm, inhaled the scent of Ireland and Grandma Teegan, and stretched it out in the dust.

She had nothing else from her family. They'd never lined up like girls on steps and taken a photo. She didn't have graves to visit and not even one of the letters Mum sent from America. She laid her palm on the hair again. *My last thing.*

When she could, she brought the chairs down and spread the red scarf across the table. Effie would like having the color, and she'd believe the braid was gone. Taking up the pail from the Indian, she went out and stood by the river's edge. Her skirt made a sling to hold the vegetables—another thing she'd hide from Effie. She threw the pail as far as she could—it was rusty and old with splashes of white paint on one side, which would always mark it for Effie. The pail bobbed away in the current.

She hadn't yet reached the trees when she dropped to her knees, potatoes and onions rolling from her skirt. Without Grandma Teegan's braid, what was there to hold her up? Since saying good-bye to her, the snug scarf and braid had felt like a grandmother's hugging arms. Now she was unhugged.

She licked her lips and couldn't stop; Rev. Jackdaw would cut out her tongue.

The trees beckoned her. She stood. "Nera, Nera." She'd fight her sadness. She picked up the vegetables and stepped onto the narrow but worn path and into the light-splashed wood. *They often ran about the forest*, Grandma Teegan's story went, *and no wild creatures existed for them.*

The path tunneled beneath high branches and around bur oaks. The meandering route, first established by wandering animals moving amongst the trees, had grown to the width of a wagon. Or the width of an old cart with worn red paint.

At times, an oak was so massive she had to stop, put down her vegetables, and stretch her arms across the trunk. Early fall meant many of the leaves were gone, and those still hanging rustled. Jays chatted in high branches. Mourning doves lobbed their echoing sounds back and forth. Two squirrels scratched up a tree, rounded it like Maypole ribbons, and then peered from the backside to watch her. The woods felt as ancient and alive as the grove she'd often visited with Grandma Teegan. She pulled off her shoes, walked on leaves that crunched under her feet. Effie didn't want a sister, but Bridget had the river and trees. Being in trees, you climbed, even if your feet never left the ground.

"Trees are wise," Grandma Teegan had explained. "Their roots listen deep in the ground where the dead talk. Their trunks listen in the middle space where women pass on the stories. And the branches and leaves listen high where the spirits speak."

What did the trees know about Mum and Pappy? With what part did they know it?

She reached a small clearing where the biggest oak yet had fallen, making the path swing out and around like a cup handle. The tree's girth reached her chest high. Bleached and smooth, it had lain there for years, but unlike the trees felled at Effie's Homeplace, this tree was still alive.

She spread her hands slowly out over the trunk. "You are my new best thing." She considered. "Your name will be Old Mag." There was so much to tell her. "An Indian came. And a lady . . . but she wasn't Mum."

She climbed one end, where ragged roots made a ladder. Wobbly-walking, keeping her arms out for balance, she reached the opposite end where the trunk split into two arms. With the added height and the thinning leaves, she could see the river. Uncle Rowan, if he were still alive, could throw a stone that far and have it splash. She better understood the layout of the wood now. She already knew the trees followed the shape of the road on one side, and now she knew they followed the river's curves on the other.

Where the trunk split, one arm veered right and the other left. In the space between them, before more branches blocked the end, was a small V-shaped room. A perfect hideout and place to keep her food. She dropped in and lined potatoes, carrots, and onions along one side. All but one potato. As she ate, she raked up leaves with her fingers, threw them over Old Mag's side, and pulled the few brown weeds. Using a stick, she began a map, drawing a curved line for what she knew of the Missouri River and making X's to signify the two special trees she'd already discovered, Old Mag and Wilcox, the tree Effie thought of as the crow tree.

Sitting back between her heels, she drew the lodge next, a square with a single jot for a chimney and several lines underneath for its stilt legs. To the left of it, and nearly as close to the water as Wilcox-the-tree, she drew a smaller X for the smaller building Rev. Jackdaw called the skinning shed. And alongside that, just one tiny line for the winter sleigh kept there.

Maps were for safety, for today, for holding now together. Having the map would help keep her new home, the trees, and her safe place between the two arms of Old Mag. She could live at the lodge until Mum and Pappy found her.

Labyrinths were for tomorrow, and one day, she'd build one. They helped create the pictures you held in your mind. They went both clockwise and widdershin, and sometimes made you think you were going backwards or getting lost. Grandma Teegan had said getting the two of them to America was a labyrinth with so many widdershin turns she couldn't bear to look. But she knew to take a step. Then another. She knew if you stayed the course on a labyrinth, you were always going forward. Labyrinths were a way for the ancestors to help too. They walked with you, carried your wished for things in sacks over their shoulders.

Bridget knew she ought to start looking for the ox. The sun was going low in the west—the temperature was dropping, and Effie might already be back. She started to climb out. Two white hairs snagged along Old Mag's trunk made her stop and drop back in. Was the hair from white wolves? Or from Celtic hounds that carried lost souls into the Other World? Grandma Teegan, Mum? She had to be sure. Digging with her stick and scooping away loose soil, she carved out a fist-sized hole. She lay on her stomach, pressed her ear to the ground over the opening, and knocked beside it.

"Mum? Grandma Teegan?" She listened hard and after a minute smiled. Nothing. Rev. Jackdaw and Effie were wrong. Mum and Pappy weren't buried in the ground, and neither was Grandma Teegan. If they were, they would hear her and knock back.

Her breath caught. Sound! Knocking! Faint, but all the same, knocking. She pressed her cheek firmer against the rim of the hole, her ear deeper. She held her breath. Her heart kicked in her ears, but she was sure of the sound. A rhythmic knocking: *that* and *that* and *that*. Heavy hits even for their slowness, and the sound growing louder as she listened. Not her parents. She jumped up and looked over the wall of Old Mag's arm.

Grandma Teegan had kept sheep, and Bridget had seen plenty of cows across village pastures, but she'd never seen an animal as big as the white bulk swaying down the path, and never this close. With each step the beast took, her heart climbed higher in her throat.

"Shoo." The beast came on. "Shoo!" She waved her arms and swatted the air with her stick. She threw it. Missed. "Go away!"

The animal's large eyes fixed on her, one big hoof after the other just clearing the ground, curling up at the ankle and hammering back down. Was this the ox? Was the ox she needed to find white? She leaned out over her protective wall and tried to see down one long, furry side. There were markings on the animal's flank, but from where she stood, she couldn't be sure it was a Flying D brand.

The animal continued coming with its steady plodding. A part of her still wanted to scream, but a bigger part wanted to clap her hands. For sure, she planned to stay where she was.

The ox's head was the size of the washtub she'd stolen from Effie's mean brother. The head with sawed-off horns extended out from between the shoulders, not riding above them. It nodded with the motion of its massive shoulders. She stepped back and back until she bumped into the second arm. The ox reached Old Mag and stretched his head over the first arm as innocently as a lamb looking to lick salt from her palm. Even if her pockets were full of salt, she'd never stick the flat of her hand out to that mouth.

The brand was visible now: a D inside a pair of wings. This *was* Jake, Mr. Deet's ox, the animal Rev. Jackdaw expected her to tend. Had the ox been coming to Old Mag to scratch? Or was he so well trained that smelling chimney smoke or hearing voices told him he needed to return to the lodge? Grandma Teegan's sheep had known what it meant when Grandma Teegan came out of the croft with her staff. They'd known what it meant at night when she opened the barn door.

Jake wasn't pushing against the tree to try and get to her, and he couldn't jump over something so high. He wasn't even trying. She took two steps forward. "I'm not scared of you." She hoped he could see she was trying to smile. "You're way bigger than a ram, but you aren't mean. Are you?"

With her hands tucked safely behind her back, she advanced again until she could reach out and touch him. She wouldn't, though maybe if she just touched his leather collar, he wouldn't mind. He smelled of trees and musty fall leaves. She liked that. She also liked the depth of his large coal-black eyes and his long white lashes.

She'd found the ox, or maybe he'd found her. Either way, Effie wouldn't be so worried now, and she'd thank her. Maybe she'd even want them to be sisters.

Keeping her hand high and away from the ox's mouth, Bridget

reached and with one finger touched the curly hair across the bony ridge on the top of his head. He lifted his head and bumped her hand. "You like that, don't you." She flattened her fingers, petting now. "You're white and sacred bulls are white."

She rubbed the top of his head, and finally ran her hand down the long, loose skin of his neck and petted his cheek. *Nera, Nera.* She climbed out slowly, ready to jump back if necessary. A narrow band of just-visible flecks of red paint ran down his side. The same red as the handles of Pete's old cart. He and Mae not only took Mr. Deet's wood, they used Jake to haul it. Now she felt she knew why Jake had arrived just when he did; the Thayers were home and sent him back.

She wouldn't tell Effie. Pete had smiled at her, and Mae said he had a white goodness. Also, Mae had the space around her.

Jake was too strong, even if she had thought to bring the rope, to force back to the lodge. In Grandma Teegan's stories, wise women didn't try to boss mountains or trees. They moved boulders and oaks by making them want to obey.

With one outstretched hand on Jake's shoulder, she smiled at him. "Please come with me." They started for the lodge.

Sixteen

Effie reached the mercantile out of breath. A gray-haired man in an apron looked up from his scales. "Afternoon, Miss."

A bell clanged on the door she'd ran through. "I can't find the sheriff." She waved her hand in the direction of the lodge. "An Injun came out to where I'm staying."

The grocer had watched her; now he looked back to his weighing and the pile of beans in the teetering pan. "Hold on."

"It had a wagon full of lumber. I don't know where it came from." She'd survived a brush with death, and the man continued weighing his beans. "Bridget and I were alone." He brushed two beans off the scale with a hairy knuckle. "Rev. Jackdaw is gone."

"You're the one married to the old preacher?" He watched the scales.

"Welcome to Bleaksville." A woman's voice.

Effie turned to see her standing over a display of soaps and candles with a duster in her hand. She wore a white shirtwaist, so white it held a tincture of blue, and she seemed no more alarmed than the man. Did they think she'd made up the story? "It got off a wagon and ran down the hill . . . whooping."

The grocer tipped his scale. Beans rattled into a small sack. "That would be Chief. I ain't heard him ever doing any whooping." He rolled the top of the bag. "Chief didn't steal the lumber, and he ain't what you'd call a real Indian."

Effie felt herself shrinking. Something like Pa scolding her. "This was a real Injun. It had a braid and everything."

“His mother was a squaw all right,” the man said, “but his daddy was white.”

A half-breed was no less dangerous. In the back of her mind, Granny was weeping, tears running down her soft face and the jaw where half her teeth were missing from being clubbed. “I tried to find the sheriff. The office is empty.”

“I’m Cora, and you’re probably lucky the sheriff wasn’t there.” Her skirts made a soft rustle as she came forward. “This is Mr. Graf, my husband. I can assure you, Chief is a good man.” She touched Effie’s arm. “You have nothing to be concerned about.”

“He was raised out there on his land,” Mr. Graf cut in. “It’s his now.” The gray brows pinched as if the length of the conversation already tired him.

“He’s always there?”

“Shops here, buys lumber in town, sells corn and produce, builds coffins when there’s a need.”

Effie felt the blood drain from her face. “And people use them for their dear ones?” She’d never become like people in Nebraska.

“His boxes are beautiful,” Cora said. “He takes great care with them, and grieving families are happy to have him close by. I’m sorry, I didn’t catch your name.”

“Mrs. Jackdaw.” She hesitated and the catch in her throat surprised her. “Effie.” The name sounded so small.

“Chief’s always buying lumber,” Mr. Graf said. “With his wife high-tailed away, and his son dead, folks say he’s building himself a staircase to heaven. I reckon if he wants in, that’s his best bet.”

Jokes? Did no one in Nebraska know about Custer, Wounded Knee, the Sioux Massacre? “You’re all just letting it pass for white?”

“If he *wanted* to pass,” Mr. Graf said, “he’d cut off his braids. Maybe buy a decent hat.”

Cora made a *tsk, tsk* sound in her throat.

"He said you were young," Graf went on. More carefully weighed beans rattled into a sack. "I didn't expect a child. How old are you?"

Effie's palms tingled with heat. For the second time that day someone was asking her age. *How old are the two of you?* she wanted to ask. Cora was much younger than Mr. Graf, but not the four decades between herself and Rev. Jackdaw. She thought of Jury. She and Jury were nearly the same age. No differences between them.

She tried again. "The Injun came clear out to the lodge, all the way to my door."

"Now, settle down," Graf said. "Don't start making accusations. He didn't come all that far. He's your neighbor."

Sudden tears threatened. Mae and now an Injun? She'd tried to leave her nightmares at Homeplace, but this was worse. The growing horror threatened to send her running. She needed to leave, get back to the lodge, be alone, think.

"Effie," Cora said, "I'm sure you came to make a few purchases."

She wouldn't give them the satisfaction of seeing her run. She shuffled her feet, stuck them to the floor. "I would like to get a few things. Corn meal, fabric—"

"Your husband," Mr. Graf barked, "gave clear orders. I'm not to extend credit on any nonsense. Strictly essentials. And I need that man in here regular, paying his bill."

"Mr. Graf," Cora said. "You're putting Mrs. Jackdaw in an uncomfortable position. You must discuss your commerce with her husband." She touched Effie's arm again. "Let me show you the fabric we have left. We've stopped carrying it because it's just not a seller. Ladies order most of their dresses from catalogues or take the train to Omaha for the day and shop in bigger stores."

Effie had heard the train whistle blow in the morning and again in the evening, but she'd been too distracted to wonder where it went. "That train comes and goes into Omaha?"

"Twice a day. You can go in the morning and return at night, or stay the night and return the next morning. Your husband didn't tell you?"

"I'm sure he doesn't know."

"Mr. Graf explained the schedule," Cora said. "Perhaps your husband didn't think to mention it."

"Perhaps." A bright yellow gingham made Effie's heart ache, but it was too nice for Bridget's dress, given how they lived. And too lightweight for covering the windows and keeping an Injun from peeking through. The only other fabric was a bolt of black. So like Baby Sally's funeral cloth.

She fingered the mournful color. "I don't know, it's sad for a young girl. Rev. Jackdaw has taken in an orphan, and she needs a second dress."

"You want to get along in this community," Mr. Graf called from behind the counter. "Don't advertise you're harboring trouble."

"The orphan?" Effie asked. Was keeping Bridget considered harboring trouble, but the Injun running free was not? She wanted out of there. "I'll take two yards of the black." Surely, Rev. Jackdaw wouldn't think that nonsense. "I also need bismuth and potash."

"You make soap?" Cora's prim brows rose, and she pointed to a pink slab the size of a bread loaf. "Would you like a sample of mine?"

"No." Her answer too sharp, too quick. She ached to touch and smell the luxury, but she couldn't put that on her tab, and she didn't need charity.

"Of course not," Cora said. "You make your own." She started for a row of bottles behind the counter. "We have bismuth, but no potash. Do you want lye? It's what I use."

Effie tried to not show her confusion. Was there a difference between potash and lye? Both came from wood ash. Mr. Graf and Cora watched her and waited for her to answer. She couldn't admit she wasn't making soap. If people thought an orphan was trouble, mentioning lice would only make things worse. Lye sounded too caustic, but she knew it changed in the process of becoming soap. Ma stirred up a batch of soap every month, used lye, and in the end it was gentle enough for bathing a newborn.

"Yes," she said, "lye will be fine for my soap."

Seventeen

Four days later, the sound of the door opening made Effie pull off Sally's cloth. She squinted at bright light coming in a window and Bridget with a hand on the backdoor latch.

"You opened a curtain again. I made them for a reason." She sat up. "Where you going?"

"I told Jake I'd come back. I came in because I'm hungry, but the cornbread is all gone."

Effie didn't need reminding. They'd stretched the pound of mill flour and the pound of beans to last three days, fighting hunger each one of those days. After Graf tallied the price of the black fabric, thread, needles, and the ingredients for curing lice, she'd been too embarrassed to ask for eggs or butter or a second pound of beans. She dreaded going back—the long stretch of trees, passing what she now knew was the Injun's place, crossing the bridge into Bleaksville where they thought her river people, and facing Graf again.

"You've spent enough time today with that animal." She shook her head. "Don't say it. I don't care what Rev. Jackdaw wants. The days are so long. You gone off where I can't see you." She stood, letting Granny's Never Forget quilt slide off her shoulders. She'd been clutching Johnny's marbles, and she took them to a back window. She missed him. She missed them all. Even Skeet and his Pig Latin.

She set the marbles on the sill and dropped the curtain. In the end, she'd torn the skirt off one of her blue house dresses, cut it into four equal pieces and spent the better part of the day hemming and making curtains. For rods, she'd sent Bridget after long, thin limbs that she peeled with a knife. With the fabric from the mercantile, she made Bridget a shorter, black skirt and attached it to the dress top. The black and blue reminded her of bruising and the top was too big, but there wasn't fabric for a second attempt. Was it any wonder Bridget preferred the lighter blue dress given to her in New York? In the corner where she slept, the morbid dress hung on a peg as if waiting, knowing Bridget would gradually have to accept it.

A log in the fire shifted and Effie crossed the floor, used the rusty poker and jabbed at the split wood. She was keeping herself back from Bridget, keeping a wide, cold space between them, not asking where Bridget had come from or why her granny had sent her away. Getting close to the girl wouldn't be a justice to either of them. She couldn't say how accepting Bridget closed doors on her own family in Minnesota, but it did. She'd loved a little sister and that sister was dead. And Bridget? She was safer not trusting or relying on her. Who knew what Rev. Jackdaw intended once they settled in Omaha? Would he find Bridget another place? Or did he intend to keep his free girl?

"Jake and I will stay by the river," Bridget said. "You can see us out the window and won't be afraid."

It was more of Bridget's strangeness, standing by the river for long periods of time. Staring as if waiting for a boat to come around the corner of the bend. Or a sea creature to rise up out of the water.

Sparks popped and settled. The fall afternoons were chilly, but mostly, she just liked a fire burning. The flames gave her something to watch and made another presence in the room, distracting her from thinking about the future or the Injun. "They call him, Chief," she'd told Bridget. "Be careful out there. Don't walk that direction. His wife ran off and his boy is dead." Bridget didn't need to know the fright of the Injun building coffins.

Effie thought often, too, of Rev. Jackdaw, longing for the sound of Nell's clopping and the squeak of the buggy returning. It wasn't him she wanted, but to know he hadn't abandoned them. His demanding filled space. Like welcoming a storm because the distraction pulled your mind from yourself and made you think of the washing on the line or the tender plants in the garden. And there was something else. For all his big bossing and supervising and the awfulness of him crawling on her, he had dreams and they contained promises for her, too. He'd get her to Omaha where she'd be safe and find friends.

"Effie, can I go?"

She wasn't in the city yet; she was still traveling. The lodge was just a stopover. She wouldn't let herself forget that.

"Effie?"

Bridget had left the door and moved to the table. One hand toyed with the cover of Dr. Chase's book and the other rested on the red wool. Thankfully, she'd thrown away that dead woman's hair. At first, Effie had enjoyed seeing the scarf spread out, but it was beginning to look like a large pool of blood.

"Effie?"

More demanding this time. "What? I'm right here." How many times had Bridget called her name? Bridget didn't understand the distraction of loss, how it sucked at your attention. She'd lost only an old grandmother and had no idea how it felt to lose a whole family. Baby brothers who counted on you. And how to keep Bridget busy and not constantly wandering off with the ox? At Homeplace there were a hundred chores, but at the lodge, no eggs needed gathering, no laundry needed to be brought in, no vegetables peeled or babies held. There were not even more corn shucks to gather. The mattress, like the curtains, was done. Yesterday, Bridget made four trips, each time bringing back her burlap bag, lumpy with corn shucks given to her by the woman she called Old Mag. Questioned, Bridget explained that Old Mag threw her shucks in a wagon for her cows to eat but didn't mind sharing.

"Effie?" Bridget's voice a near shriek.

Effie started and refocused on the room. How long had she stared into space this time? "We'll color your hair. Find the page again." She had to keep busy, keep her mind from always skipping off. "What do we do first?"

"Do you want me to teach you to read so you can read the recipes?"

"Rev. Jackdaw said he didn't want me distracted from my work when I asked him to teach me to read the Bible. Said it was best if he read to me and explained what the words meant."

"Grandma Teegan taught me. Uncle Rowan helped, too."

"Men are scared of wives learning too much. They want wives to stay teeny-tiny so they can stay big." She shrugged. "At first, not reading seemed like trading something big for something small, being his wife. But Ma can't read. And I owe Rev. Jackdaw." Everything had a price. Mae sold herself for the promise of a dress, and Effie felt she'd sold herself too. Was it just to escape ever having to see Jury again? Away from New Ulm, he'd always remember her as she was now. But there was no going back, and dreaming about it hurt. Her life was this lodge and this child staring at her.

"Are you ready?" she asked Bridget. She wondered if she ought to part Bridget's hair and look for lice before the treatment, but Granny was smart. For all the times Granny didn't know thirty years ago from thirty minutes ago, for all the times she screamed "Thavages killing my babies!" she had other moments of clarity when she knew which jars of pickles hadn't sealed or how to smoke the henhouse free of mites. If she said "All orphans have lice," they probably did. Even without an infestation, there was still the issue of color. Though Bridget's red was less rooster's tail and more the rosy peach of a trumpet creeper, one of Ma's favorite flowers. Or it had been a favorite back when Ma cared about things like flowers.

She closed her eyes and took a deep breath. She'd done it again, let her mind float back to Homeplace and all the pain she'd caused there. "Maybe," she said, "if we change the color, Rev. Jackdaw will stop calling you Rooster. I'm not saying your hair is terrible, but if you look less Irish, good folks might start coming to visit. Even if you are an orphan."

"Maybe only river people visit river people," Bridget said.

Effie cringed. "We're not that." The hideous name lumped them together not only with Mae Thayer, but with snakes and mud. Even the Injun.

At the sound of a horse on the road, a single rider, not a buggy, Effie's eyes darted to the shotgun on the wall. She stood without moving, not breathing until the horse had gone by.

"It was probably Mr. Thayer," Bridget said. "I don't like him."

"Mae's husband?"

"Sometimes when I'm on the road with Jake, he spits tobacco juice at me."

"I'm sure he's just spitting."

"I followed the road to his house, but I didn't see Mae. I don't know if she had her baby."

"Stay away from there. I don't want them thinking we're friends and they can come running, asking for a woman's help with that birthing." She shuddered. "I don't know anything about that. We don't want anything to do with people so needy."

Loneliness settled over her shoulders again. Why had no suitable women come calling? She crossed the floor for a pan and the ingredients she'd purchased at the mercantile. Soft, loose boards moaned under her feet. On first arriving, the ghostly sounds rising whenever someone crossed the planks had stolen her breath. But now, at night when she couldn't sleep and the fire danced shadows on the walls, the undisturbed boards helped assure her no Injun was inside, sneaking to her bed with a raised tomahawk.

The pan was so dented it wobbled. Injun-touched the day of the massacre, possibly slammed against a wall. Maybe kicked or used to smash in a baby's skull. The Injuns made off with everything they thought worth carrying. They hadn't bothered with the pan.

Bridget ran a finger over the embossed letters on the red bottle.

"I'll mix both formulas together," Effie said, "and you can have blonde hair with no extra fuss. How much caustic potash do we need?"

"It says one dr."

Effie considered. "I know dr means dram. I mean I've heard the word before . . . but I don't know how much that is."

"It sounds like a little bit," Bridget said. "Like a drip."

"I think it's more like a cup. What use would a drip be?"

Bridget moved a finger back over the front of the bottle, touching each of the embossed stars and the letters L-Y-E. Concentrating, she read the recipe again. "It doesn't say l-y-e."

"Potash is lye."

"Grandma Teegan likes my hair this color."

"Hair isn't a serious thing," Effie said. "Would you rather I cut it off? One winter, because of lice, Ma shaved every one of the boys' heads." She drew back at Bridget's expression. "I won't shave your head. I'd go back to the mercantile for another round of ingredients before I did that."

"Are you sure potash and lye are the same?"

"Bridget. You're trying me. Even the grocer's wife said she uses lye. You aren't going to drink it; I'm just putting it on your hair."

"What if it's ugly?"

"Blonde hair isn't ugly." She estimated the amount in the bottle was just shy of a full cup. She poured what she hoped was half into her pan. She stepped away to the window, tucked up a curtain, and gave Bridget a knowing smile. She held the bottle up to the light. "I don't want to use too much, but if I use too little and the lice don't die, then I'm wasting." She poured in salts of tarter, substituted rosewater for a gush from the pump, added the other ingredients she'd bought and stirred. "Like I said, hair isn't a serious thing. That's what Ma told the boys."

"If I went to school," Bridget said, "I could learn how much is a dram."

Effie stopped stirring and looked into the mixture. There was no way to test its potency. If Ma or Granny were there, she'd ask their opinion. But she was alone, a married woman now, seventeen, and she had to learn to live without them.

"We could go to school together," Bridget said.

"No we can't." Effie rapped her spoon hard on the rim of the pan and laid it down on the red scarf. "You know how Rev. Jackdaw feels about you going to school." She held Bridget's gaze and swallowed against the lump gathering in her own throat. "If a girl has a smart mother, one who teaches her how to care for a man and children, she don't need schoolhouse schooling." Even to her own ears, her words lacked conviction. She'd longed to go at Bridget's age. Now she was married and too old.

Bridget's eyes pleaded. "I have to be a doctor."

Effie ached to say she would help with that dream, but what could she promise? "Lie out on the porch. Put your head over the side. That's how Ma washes Pa's hair."

Bridget rose slowly, moved to the door even slower.

"You lived back at Homeplace," Effie said, "Ma would drag you by the ears."

Eighteen

They stepped outside and Bridget saw Jake standing only a few yards away, swatting flies in Wilcox's shade and enjoying his cud. His chewing made Bridget think of food again and her hunger. The evening before, she'd eaten the last bit of potato. Some critter had stolen her stash, leaving her only a quarter of a potato full of teeth marks. Walking Jake along the road that morning, she'd found a mulberry tree, its branches nearly cleaned of fruit by the birds. She'd picked a half-rotten handful. Not enough, and too mushy and full of tiny fruit flies to bother taking back to share. She swallowed the whole sweet mess and licked her sticky hands. Even that was hours ago.

She lay down, the sharp edge of the porch cutting into the back of her neck.

Jake flicked his ears and moved from the shade to the edge of the clearing. Was it the smell coming from Effie's stinky pan?

While Effie fussed, brushing back Bridget's hair, making sure it all hung down over the side of the porch, Bridget watched the sky. The sun burned red in the west. Overhead, a string of clouds drifted, smallest first, followed by larger and larger ones. Woolly as Grandma Teegan's sheep. Fear scuttled through Bridget's stomach. Things were wrong. Big sheep didn't follow little sheep. Rams led the way in and out of pens. Lambs on their thin legs lagged behind.

But Effie was seventeen. She knew about lye and potash and mixing two recipes. She was already pouring a thin stream of cold over Bridget's crown and that proved she did want to look like sisters.

"Are you all right?" Effie asked. She poured more.

The tickly sensation might have been Grandma Teegan's comb making a part. "It tingles." Before Bridget could speak again, the touch changed to a narrow, icy finger. It scratched. Then clawed. "It's hot. It's really getting hot."

"Don't worry about that," Effie said. "Lice probably need a good scalding to die. Quit squirming. Hold still."

The finger widened. Became two. Three. Shatters of pain splintered over Bridget's scalp. Her arms flung out, one knocking Effie's pan away. It clattered off the porch. "It's burning!"

"All right," Effie said. "We'll rinse it out. What a waste. It's spilled clear across the sand."

Bridget couldn't lie still. She scrambled to her feet, stomped and danced. Her screaming ran through the trees, echoed back.

Effie was gone, the lodge door open, a bucket banging under the water pump.

Feeling picked up and shoved down the ramp, Bridget ran. Beneath her screaming, her scalp sizzled, still cooking like beans boiled dry over a fire. The pain flogged her, threatened to buckle her knees. She fought to stay on her feet, to keep moving, to obey the voices pushing her to the river.

Water reached her ankles, her knees. She splashed up to her waist and sank under. When she rose, she went back under. The third time she needed air, she rolled onto her back. Belly-up, she pushed her head deeper and let the river wash over her face. The cold helped cut through the worst heat. She forced her head completely under and her mouth filled with river. She had to stop screaming. Gagging and clearing her throat to keep from drowning, she lifted her head out of the water but that called back the torture.

Effie dropped her pail at Bridget's screaming. Pumping water was too slow. "Go to the river," she shouted, running back out. She'd hurt

Bridget bad. It seemed impossible; she'd not meant to do so. Water pulled at her dress, and she fought her old terror of drowning. She'd been overconfident with the recipes, so sure she knew what she was doing. How could this happen? She ought to have tested the liquid on her own skin. She'd been foolish and careless. She reached Bridget, wrapped her arms around her, "I'm sorry, I'm sorry."

"No!" Bridget screamed. She twisted and pushed. "Go away!" And again, choking on sobs, "Go away!"

Bridget didn't want her there. Trying to hug her only drew her out of the water, exposed her burns to the air, and made her howl louder. Effie let go. Bridget didn't deserve the additional upset of having her there.

Effie backed out of the water, her soaked dress dragging heavier with each step until it clung to her ankles. When she could, she turned and ran up the ramp, her stomach heaving. She'd never meant for this to happen. But it had all the same, and it proved something unspeakable about her.

In the lodge, she reached a chair breathless, the weight of what she'd done making her collapse into it. Seeing Dr. Chase's book with the hideous recipes, she swept it off the table. The pages fluttered in the air and the book landed on the floor. She grabbed up the spoon she'd used to stir the mixture and threw it against the wall. Still fraught with upset, she reached for the red scarf. Her breath caught. The lye on the spoon had eaten through the wool, leaving a hole the size of her palm and ringed by sickly yellow. If the lye had done this to fabric, how much more damage had it done to Bridget's tender scalp?

She tore the curtain from a window. Johnny's marbles rolled onto the floor and away. She couldn't see Bridget's head from where she stood, only the blue dress floating on the surface. Horror engulfed her. Her hands slapped against the glass. Bridget was drowning. "No. Please no." She pushed away, ready to run back into the water.

Bridget's knobby knees moved, then her arms, turning her body.

Her nose and mouth were above the water. She knew how to swim. "Not dead. Not drowned."

The best Effie could do for Bridget was stay away. She made it to the bed, dropped, and curled in her wet dress and shoes. The black cloth was there. She drew it over her head and in the darkness, bit into her fists.

Baby Sally's death had been an accident too, but what difference did that make? She saw the toddler lying on the kitchen table. A neighbor woman draped a black cloth over her to keep off flies. Overcome by the sight, Ma doubled over and the woman helped her away and into bed. Alone with Sally, Effie lifted a corner of the cloth, and ducked beneath. She was ten, so much older than Sally. She pressed a hand over Sally's tummy where her Sunday dress was wrinkled, fussed with her golden ringlets, counted her tiny perfect toes.

"I'm sorry," she wept. And then, "I want to go with you."

Nineteen

The cold water stabbed Bridget's ears, but she kept her head thrown back, letting only her nose and mouth rise out of the water. The river's current tugged her, carried her only a short distance before her arms knocked against one of Wilcox's roots. She grabbed it and wound her legs around roots as thick as her arms. Wilcox had reached out and grabbed her. Or Mum as a selkie had lifted her up and into the watery sling.

With her head thrown back and the last of Wilcox's leaves blowing in the October breeze, the pain gradually decreased. Minutes later, her head pounded, felt swollen with cold. Despite the fierce headache, she needed more minutes before she worked herself onto her knees. After so long in the water, her body jerked with cold and her ears pounded more than her scalp burned. Her bones felt locked in a frozen numbness. Brittle. If she didn't move now, didn't force herself out of the water, she'd never be able to do so. She couldn't give up; she'd promised Grandma Teegan she'd fight death.

Jake, his head high and the black pools of his eyes watching her, stood on the bank looking ready to charge.

"I'm all right," she said, but couldn't hear herself speak. She had to reach him. She'd ridden on his back and knew he was warm. They'd go to Old Mag and stay there forever.

Crawling from the water onto the silty land, she stood and pulled her hair over her shoulders to look for the blonde. Red hair. Rooster red. She didn't care what it was called. Her hair still matched Mum's.

Water streamed from the ends of her hair, growing it longer. Inch by inch, her hair lengthened while she marveled, unsure of what it meant. The long strands grew to her waist. Then dropped off, slid down the skirt of her dress, and onto the ground.

Jake stepped closer, sniffed.

Bridget stared at the clumps lying at her feet. Red nearly to the top, then three inches of ash-colored straw. She stood shivering, too frightened to move for fear the tug of the water dripping off her head would pull out more. She reached trembling fingers to explore how much was gone, but touching the scorched flesh made her wince in pain. She didn't need to touch her burns to know their size. The searing strip was three fingers wide and ran over her crown and down.

Jake kept pace at her side, and they hurried up the river's edge in the direction of Old Mag. Avoiding the easy path through the trees, they hugged the shore and when the pain rose again, Bridget knelt in the water and dunked her head.

When she thought they'd gone far enough to intersect with the tree, she geed Jake right, and they entered the woods. She'd not gauged right, and undergrowth and fallen trunks stopped them again and again. "It's only a labyrinth," she promised Jake as they worked forward and frequently had to backtrack because he couldn't slide through the narrow slits or crawl over downed trees like she could.

Once in the sanctuary of Old Mag's arms, she'd tell her she'd fought death. She wouldn't go back to the lodge. E-V-E-R. She was safe in the trees, and she'd sleep under the stars with Jake and the river nearby. She'd not think one time about Effie. Let Effie stand at the window, bawling and screaming all night.

Twice through the evening Bridget had to tell Jake "Stay" while she cut back through the trees and doused her head in the cold river. In the dark, she coaxed him to the southern side of Old Mag's trunk and out of the north breeze. "Down, down." She pushed on his left flank, not the right one where he'd been burned like her, only with a sizzling brand. His front legs bent at the knees, his rump sunk heavily on the ground, and then the front legs finished folding, and he settled with a grunt.

The temperature dropped lower through the next hours. She shook with cold in her wet dress and wished for the warmth of the buffalo hide and the fire in the lodge. But the cold also soothed her scalp. And she never wanted to return to the lodge and Effie.

She tried to curl close to Jake, holding her head up and sleeping against his warmth. But each time she dozed off, her head dropped against his side and she woke with a jolt of pain. And every time she woke, she heard, or imagined she heard, Effie's far away screaming: "Bridget!"

Finally, she draped herself like a saddle across Jake's warmth, her arms on one side, her legs on the other and her head propped up by her chin, a cheek resting against an outstretched arm.

She'd trusted that living along the river with trees meant she'd be safe. But an emptiness, painful as her burns, bore into her. She didn't want to think what it all meant—how maybe being West didn't mean a good thing at all.

Twenty

Jake's rising to his front knees made Bridget slide off, limp with chill and exhaustion. Night covered her. Even with Jake's warmth on her front, her back stung with cold. Her body shook and her chattering teeth rattled in her ears. She'd awakened off and on and told herself she needed to find the will to walk back to the lodge. But the cold made her so tired. If only she rested one more minute, she'd have the strength. The next time she woke, her legs and arms even more wooden, her shaking harder, she had even less will to move.

Beside her, Jake rocked forward to get his back legs under him. She'd slipped nearly beneath him, too close to his hoofs and massive weight as he gained the full extension of his front legs. She scooted out of his way, feeling Old Mag's trunk against her back.

Jake took a step away, and pulling herself forward on her knees, Bridget worked her body back into the leaves he'd left. She wanted to grab up the ground there, wrap the warmth all the way around her. She wanted to scold him too, make him lie back down, but in the next moment he vanished into the darkness. His disappearance startled her, made her groggy eyes open wider. She was alone. Even Old Mag seemed asleep and far off. The moon was a faint smear overhead and a thick fog had settled in the trees. Her heart raced with the realization. Fog! The stories all said fog was a doorway to other worlds.

A slight crackle on the path. She lay as still as her shaking allowed. Listened. Had she heard something large on the dead leaves?

The night was silent and heavy as the cold. Too quiet. Even trees that had swayed earlier, their ragged leaves swishing when she first sank across Jake, were still now. Then a hoot. The sound sharp. A hoot returned, distorted, both off and close at the same time.

Her heart beat faster. "Jake?" Her voice, a trembling thread in the night, waving shakily and exposing her fear. The sound of it sent shivers of a new kind up her back. *Nera. Nera.* She tried to be silent, to still even her breathing so she could hear better.

A minute passed, then two and three. She couldn't see through the fog, but now she didn't need eyes. The sound on leaves was soft, cautious. Not four feet, not Jake, but two halting feet. Advancing, stopping. Stalking. Whatever approached wasn't coming from the direction of the lodge, wasn't Effie, who would never come into the trees, and never, never at night. What approached came from the other direction, the direction she'd not yet explored. She scooted back again, pressing herself farther into the deep curve of Old Mag's trunk, making herself as small as she could. Her lips trembled, made sucking noises, and she pressed her cold hands over her mouth.

The sound came again, carefully placed weight on dry leaves. A twig snapped. A shape disturbed the edge of the fog. An almost form. A *something* that knew the night better than she did. That lived in the night.

Rounded and close to the ground, the dark shape stretched tall as a man. She tried to scoot deeper, but her back was already pressed hard against the trunk, and her movement in the leaves sounded near deafening in her ears. It watched her. A wolf on hind legs? A man? Yes, a man with his arm raised and holding the stub end of a branch like a club. He stepped through the fog at exactly the spot where Jake disappeared. For a fleeting moment, she wondered if Jake had shape-shifted.

Nera, Nera. But reciting the name didn't help. Her throat was trying to scream.

The man passed fully through the curtain. The man took the final few steps, dropped his stick, and lowered to one knee in front of her. The Indian! In his battered hat and his braids, and his face even craggier in the darkness. His name was Chief. He'd brought them food, and through the window he'd looked into her eyes. Her body went limp. She was crying.

He said nothing, but his face pinched as he looked her over, carefully moving each arm and then each leg. He took off his coat, spread it wide, and lifted her onto the warmth. She couldn't move, couldn't find the strength to mumble a thanks. He carried her, but not in the direction of the lodge. Her eyelids closed. The rhythmic walking was a gentle sea rocking her.

Bridget woke in a strange room, in a bed—a real bed. Something she'd not slept in since leaving Ireland. Her burns tingled and with a light touch she explored the wrapping around her head. She closed her eyes again and smiled. No pain, only the tingly sensation. She vaguely remembered Chief, his face in the night, but his carrying her seemed no more than a dream. Still, she was in a new room with cloth strips wound around her head. She wasn't dreaming. This had to be his house.

The smell of bacon rose from the floor below and made her stomach growl. She pushed back the blankets and realized she wore only her short bloomers. Her dress hung on the door, its blue color returned but more worn than she realized. She needed to save it.

At the bottom of the stairs, she stepped into a room with a fireplace, roll top desk, two wide leather chairs, and a leather sofa. On the long leather seat, blankets and a pillow told her someone had slept the night there.

Noise from the next room made her turn. Another door, this one ajar. She crossed the room and peeked through the opening. Chief sat at a table eating, a fork in his hand. She hadn't imagined how an Indian's kitchen might look, or that Indians used the same household items as other people: tables, chairs, knives, plates, and shiny pots.

"Come on," Chief said. "I haven't taken a bite out of you yet."

She stepped just inside the room. "Your house is big."

"Take this with you." A jar sat on the table, and he pushed it in her direction. The contents looked like sheep's fat with flecks of green herbs. "It'll help the pain. Keep the burns wrapped."

She thought to thank him for helping her, but if she did it now, she'd have no more reason to stay. Several other things lay on the table, and her eyes ran over them: a battered board only a foot long, a hammer, a small pile of bent nails, his floppy hat, a large toy ship. And his plate of food—eggs, thick slices of bacon, a hunk of bread as fat as a book and covered with butter. The sight and smell started a hundred tiny hands clawing in her belly.

He'd not asked her to stay, and the way he nudged the jar in her direction again seemed to say, "Take it and go." She couldn't. Her mouth watered and her hunger kept her feet rooted. She needed the bread worse than she needed the salve.

"Your name is Chief."

He studied her a moment and pushed his plate in her direction. "Eat. Then you best get on home. You already been here too long."

She hurried to the plate, using his fork, forcing herself to keep her eyes down so he wouldn't think she'd had enough and pull the food away. She finished the eggs and the bacon and held the bread tight. She'd give it to Effie. "Effie isn't my mum, and she's not my sister."

"Is that so?"

"Rev. Jackdaw signed a paper on me." Grandma Teegan, her hand shaking, had also signed a paper. Getting a kid was easy and so was getting rid of one. "The paper says I'm his now."

Shadow passed over Chief's eyes, and he answered slow. "The whole world's alone. Best get used to it."

"Are you used to it?"

He scowled.

"Why do you have braids?"

He rose with his coffee cup, walked to the stove, and refilled it. He lowered himself back to his chair. "My mother wore braids."

"I have Grandma Teegan's braid. Effie doesn't like braids. I hid it."

He sipped his coffee. "How did you find me?"

"Heard you crying."

Effie was right. Indians did prowl around at night. "I wasn't crying. I was sleeping."

"Then you snore like a girl crying."

She felt certain she'd been so cold and tired she hadn't been crying. Only inside. To hear that, a person needed a different kind of ears. "Were you on the path?"

Chief's black-gray brows pinched, and the furrows across his weathered forehead deepened. "Children oughten be crying in trees on cold nights."

She shifted her weight from foot to foot. By now, Effie would be screaming or sobbing under the black cloth. "Is that your hat?"

His hand, large and brown, lifted the hat to his head. Beneath the droopy brim, he nodded at the table. "Them are my nails. My hammer."

"Do you live here all by yourself?" Effie said he did.

"Ain't your business."

"The man from the mercantile told Effie your wife rode away."

"That ain't his business. Hers neither."

"He said your boy drowned in the river. Were you looking for him? Is that how you found me?"

He took the hat back off and laid it close to the toy ship. "I ain't got all day to sit and listen to your foolishness."

She shouldn't have mentioned his boy. He didn't think that was her business, but it was. Rowan was dead, and she didn't have a toy ship or anything once belonging to him. She wanted to talk about death and the dark emptiness she'd seen around Mae.

He pulled the board and hammer forward. Taking a bent nail from the pile, he held it against the short plank and with one blow straightened it. She'd seen the hammer rise and still the loud *whack* made her jump. He took up another nail. "I got work to do."

"Thank you for the vegetables."

He nodded at a pail in the corner. "Mae and Pete could have used them."

Bridget told her eyes not to look hard at the bucket, but they did. It was the same one Effie told her to throw in the river. A bit of white paint on one side proved it. She hadn't been strong enough to throw the pail far—even emptied.

"Effie wasn't hungry." That didn't explain why they'd thrown away a good bucket. With the bread still in one hand, she reached for the jar with the other and noticed a shelf on the wall holding a small painted box. "Effie has one that size, but it's not painted with marks. If I had one, I'd put in Grandma Teegan's braid."

She turned to leave, then stopped. "Do people homestead in Nebraska? Irish people?"

"Homestead?" He whacked another nail straight. "The government's still taking Indian land. Reservations and breaking legal agreements. That land is still being given to whites. You call that homesteading?"

Nera. Nera. She needed courage for the next question. "Do you think my face looks like someone?"

His thumb rubbed up and down the hammer. "What's your name?"

She swallowed. Changing the subject meant he didn't think she looked like anyone. He hadn't seen Mum with hair like hers. "My name is Bridget."

"Bridget. What happened to you?"

She licked her lips. Wider. "Effie can't read because she's Rev. Jackdaw's wife. She traded." She looked at the slice of bread she held and pinched at one corner of the crust. The whole outer brown edge peeled off like a ribbon. Her burned scalp wasn't all Effie's fault. Like Effie, she'd also traded: the message of the clouds for having Effie like her. "It was an accident."

"An accident happens once, you learn something." His eyes said she'd better listen. "Same accident happens again, you're a damn fool. You ain't a damn fool, are you?"

"No." The crust was in her mouth. With the remainder of her bread and the jar, she turned for the door. A basket sat in window light and inside it, something moved. She stretched and smiled to see the head of a sleeping dog. "You have a puppy." She stepped closer. The dog was wrapped in bandages around its middle and over one hip where a leg was missing. "What happened?"

"He ain't said."

She knelt. The dog, smaller than Ogan, had a black head with a white, straggly muzzle. His body, though the bandages prevented her from seeing much of his torso, was white with several black spots.

"Fished him out of the river," Chief said. "Looks like someone wrapped him in barbed wire and threw him in."

The food Bridget had eaten threatened to come back up.

"Did what I could. Leg so mangled, I needed to take it off to give him a fighting chance."

She couldn't see a shadow around the dog, but that didn't mean one wouldn't come. "Is he going to die?"

"I thought so. But he's a fighter."

"What's his name?"

"Going to call him Wire."

"He's like us." She turned and looked up at Chief. "He's left too."

He scowled for the second time. "Our business is finished. Go on before the sheriff comes looking for you."

The sheriff wouldn't come looking. Effie hadn't run into town during the night. Even in daylight, she'd spend hours before she worked up the courage to go for help and admit what happened. But it *was* time to go: Chief wanted her gone. She raised the jar. "Can I come back when it's gone?"

"You got plenty."

"Can I come back even if it isn't gone? I could help change Wire's bandages. I'm going to be a doctor. I have a doctor's book."

He stepped up to the door, opened it. "That dog ain't your business, and you don't belong over here. Not for any reason."

Bridget pressed her lips together to keep her tongue from licking. Chief wanted her away, and there was nothing to steal to fill the hole he was making. Not with him staring at her. *You don't belong in our trees, either,* she wanted to say. *Not for any reason.*

He pointed at her and swung the finger back to tap his own chest. "This ain't gonna be one of those fairy tales where the little girl makes friends with the wild and mean old bastard in the forest. I ain't and I can't ever be that man."

"You brought vegetables."

His eyes narrowed and he shook his head, but then the corner of one side of his mouth lifted. "You a piece of work. I got nothing against you, but you'll be moving on faster 'an rabbits breed rabbits. But the trouble you cause me is likely to stay."

She wasn't his trouble. She could take care of herself. "If the sheriff comes, you should tell him someone hurt Wire." She stepped out the door and stared at the wide yard and a road at the end of a long lane. Where were the trees, the river? "I don't know how to get back."

He walked with her around the corner of his house and pointed past two barns, one three-stories high, and across a pasture to a wall of trees. "That big oak. Tallest one. Path starts there. Taking the road's near a mile longer."

She saw the tree, but paid little attention. Five horses were in his corral. Four she'd seen hitched to his wagon, but the fifth was the most beautiful horse she'd ever seen. Sleek, taller and larger than Nell, it was also spotted like Wire and Ogan. Three matching animals meant magic. "I love your horse. What's his name?"

"He calls himself Smoke. Now scram." He turned back, then mumbled over his shoulder. "Likely it's the sheriff's dog."

She walked slowly from his yard, trying to memorize everything. A large fenced garden, the ground turned, which meant most of the root vegetables had already been dug. Two rows of fruit trees. One apple, one pear, only partially picked. A coop with red chickens, roosters, and laying hens. As she passed the door to his larger barn, shine on the ground caught her eye. She turned back to check that the grumpy man who didn't want to be "that man" wasn't watching. She grabbed up a nail.

Bridget tried the door to the lodge, but the bar was dropped across inside. She knocked. "Effie!" Knocked again.

The door finally opened and Effie stood huddled in her quilt, her eyes red and tired, her hair tangled around her face. "You aren't dead," she said. She opened the quilt into wings and wrapped it and her arms around Bridget. "You aren't dead," she said again. "I never meant to hurt you. You know that."

Feeling Effie's arms made up for all yesterday's pain.

"Who did that?" Effie held her back and looked at the tight bandaging, an edge rising in her voice. "Where did you go?" She touched the hair hanging down over Bridget's shoulders. "It isn't all ruined. Are you burned bad? Who helped you?"

Bridget lifted the jar. "I got medicine."

"Where'd you get that?"

"I ran to Old Mag and then . . ." She stopped. Hearing about Chief would shut Effie's love off. Effie'd be so angry she might insist the salve be thrown in the river. And when the awful pain returned, how could it be stopped?

Effie turned away, her feet dragging as she moved across the room. "A woman, Old Mag? She helped you?" She fell onto the bed, the corn shucks crackling as she curled, turning her face to the wall. "You were with someone while I was near dead of fright and thought you was dead too."

Bridget didn't know how to answer.

For minutes Effie didn't speak, her face still turned to the wall. Finally, "That woman, Old Mag, she'll tell the whole town."

"No, she won't. I told her it was an accident."

"She knows, doesn't she?"

Bridget stood rooted, staring at Effie's back. Every day it seemed there were more secrets to keep—spoons hidden in walls, Grandma Teegan's braid hidden overhead, the space she'd seen around Mae. And now Chief.

Taking up a log she'd carried in the day before, she placed it on the hot ashes and stirred the embers with the poker. Her heart skipped. Lying just out of the pile of ash, black and singed all around, was a scrap of red wool.

Twenty-One

Bridget woke, checked to see Effie still slept, and began unwinding the strips of cloth from around her head. The bands always loosened in the night and needed to be rewound in the morning. Something best done when Effie wasn't looking. So that her face didn't drop and her hands didn't start twisting.

With the soft pads of her fingertips, Bridget touched the burns. Most of the water had gone out of what she thought of as peeled eggs. Wren eggs, robin eggs, even hen eggs. She looked up into the rafters to Grandma Teegan's braid and whispered, "Can you see my eggs?" But braids couldn't see, and she promised herself Grandma Teegan was home in Ireland. Grandma Teegan hadn't stayed too long in America just for her. Wasn't buried this side of the water and hadn't died in the crossing. One day, they'd see each other again.

She wrapped Effie's cape over her shoulders and opened the door. The clearing lay under a shiny layer of frost, the air bunched and bullied with cold, the river steamed, and doves cooed in the trees.

"Wait." Effie crawled from bed. She reached for her bonnet. "That sound, I can't stand it. Close the door."

"It's just birds."

"It's not." She held out the bonnet. "Here, it will help keep your head warm."

"No," Bridget said. "I don't need it. My head is warm." The calico was worn and faded, and still too valuable to risk to low hanging limbs or anymore wear than necessary. Effie wore the bonnet every trip into Bleaksville and though nearly all women wore hats now, at least

Effie had head covering. When she tied the strings under her chin and tucked her hair up, she could force herself out the door. Bridget needed the cape for warmth and because it helped hide the ugly dress she had taken to wearing since seeing her blue hanging on a closet door at Chief's. That dress would be the one she changed into when Mum and Pappy came running down the slope for her.

She led Jake up to the road and across. A quarter mile of dry grass and weeds stretched between the road and the railroad tracks. "This way." He grazed, his square teeth chomping off bits of remaining greenery hidden in the taller, dryer grass. The shimmery frost burned off as they walked. A flock of turkeys with iridescent feathers pecked and gobbled in the distance. The squat birds pretended to be undisturbed by the slow approach of a girl and an ox, then one by one moved into the taller weeds.

The sun was high overhead by the time Bridget and Jake reached the end of Chief's lane—though Effie said not to walk in that direction. Chief, if he was working outside, might see her. If he was going into or returning from Bleaksville, he'd also see her. She'd stood in his kitchen, eaten all his eggs and bacon right off his plate using his fork, but they'd not talked since. She'd ask him about Wire. He'd ask her about her burns. Maybe she'd tell him Effie was scared of trees and birds that talked to her. And Mae had a gray shadow.

She saw no motion around Chief's house or barns. She stretched and stood on tiptoes, but there was no sign of him. Jake continued to stroll forward, but she held her ground, not moving until he'd grazed nearly around the next bend.

She followed, thinking of Mae and how Rowan had died when she should have found a way to stop it. Grandma Teegan hadn't blamed her, though. She rubbed Bridget's back, held her hand all night, and for the first time told the story of Salt Woman.

The sound of children laughing made Bridget look up. Watching only Jake and her black skirt kick out in front of her shoes, she hadn't realized how far they'd walked. Up ahead, Nettle Creek—she could see the sign—flowed under its wooden bridge, and just over that the school. As many as two dozen children played in the yard. Girls in clean coats, hats, and warm leggings rode in swings and jumped ropes. Boys whittled sticks and threw their jackknives at targets. None of them noticed her on the far side of the creek.

She left Jake and crept closer until she could hug a weathered bridge timber, half hiding behind the thick, rough support and half in the open. If a girl looked over and waved, she'd wave back.

The school doors opened wide and a man stepped out with a bell and a waxed mustache like a big, upturned grin. When he rang the bell, the students hurried toward him and for a moment they looked like ants, going in and out of each other until they settled into two lines. Younger students in one. Older students in the other. A two-room school, she decided. They followed him inside and the large doors shut.

Rev. Jackdaw had threatened a switching if she went into school, and she remembered the sting of a green switch to the back of her legs. That day, she hadn't been walking fast enough, hadn't kept up with Nell and the buggy. But the schoolyard was not school.

She glanced back at Jake. He would not put one foot on the narrow, hollow-sounding boards without getting spooked and backing off. Anyway, she'd be right back. She'd just walk around a bit, be in the yard where schoolchildren played. Then she could take that feeling back with her, build her labyrinth, and walk with it.

She crossed the bridge. The road continued on down Main Street where a few wagons were parked and horses swung tails and waited. None of the wagons looked like Chief's. She left the road and sat on a swing, then hopped in squares scratched in the dirt where she'd seen girls hop. It wasn't enough. She ran behind the school and dropped into a crouch beneath a window. Her knees felt doughy with fear and excitement. She was being Nera, and this was as scary as stealing apples from a vendor.

A woman talked, but her voice was too faint to understand. Bridget crawled on until she heard a man's voice. Likely the man who'd rang the bell. His voice was much louder and rose and fell, telling her he moved back and forth across the front of the room. His big mustache smiled, she was sure.

She sat in the sunshine, listening as he read about Abraham Lincoln and the Emancipation Proclamation of 1863. Out of the breeze and with the sun's heat radiating off the white building, she warmed. Her legs stretched out in front of her. She could see Jake, his bright white against the dying weeds, and she thought she'd never been so happy.

The window above her made a sudden, rough, dragging sound. She flinched and looked up. The man peered down at her. She thought to run, but he winked, smiled, and took a step back. His reading continued. The window remained open an inch despite the cold seeping into the classroom.

The next day she returned.

Twenty-Two

Bridget heard the knocking and opened the door. Pete stood on the landing, his shoulders slumped in his worn coat, his frosty breath heaving in and out. One eye was deep in a wide circle of black and blue. He turned his cap in his hands. "She died," he said. His bottom lip quivered, and he struggled to control it.

Bridget knew without asking, but her mouth made the words. "Your mum?"

Effie crossed the room, the Never Forget quilt around her shoulders. "What happened?"

Pete's hat moved faster, around and around through his fingers. "She's dead now."

They stood silent, though to Bridget they all screamed inside.

"The baby, too," Pete finally said. "I cleaned him. Got him buried." He swiped his wrist across his upper lip and nose. "I put him under the tree in the pasture. I thought Ma would live. She lived when the others died."

Bridget wanted to shriek, *I knew it, I knew it.* But what did that matter now? Her knowing hadn't stopped anything.

The cap in Pete's hands, the bill soiled and frayed, circled faster. "It's Ma. I thought, ma'am," he nodded at Effie, "you'd lend a hand. Mr. Thayer won't have a part to laying her out. She'd want cleaned up nice. A woman to do her hair."

Effie gasped. "I can't. I'm sorry." She hesitated, took another breath. "I know a son isn't the one to wash his mother, but I never washed a body." She stepped back from the door. "Can't your pa do that?"

"He ain't my pa."

To Bridget, Effie's face raced through a maze of thoughts. "Still," Effie said, question lifting her brows, "he was her husband."

"Ma wanted it. He ain't the kind what marries."

"We will help you," Bridget said.

"We can't!" The ends of the Never Forget quilt trembled. "I've never touched the dead. There must be other women. Church women?"

"I thought you, being a reverend's wife . . . Ma's never had a woman's help with her hair. I want her to be proud of how she's done up. One time 'fore the lid gets nailed."

"I can help," Bridget said. "I helped Grandma Teegan wash Rowan."

"No!" Effie grabbed her back from the door. "You aren't touching a dead person and then coming back in here." She faced Pete. "I'm sorry."

Effie stood at one of the front windows, peeking around the curtain, as the Injun's wagon rolled by with Mae's coffin in the back. Not even a cloth of respect over the box. The Injun walked in front holding the bridles of his team. The sheriff, a shiny star on his vest flashing in the cold sunlight, rode a horse alongside the wagon, as did Mr. Thayer. The two men talked loud, chuckling and randomly spitting tobacco juice out the sides of their mouths. Pete, his cap in his hands again, walked behind along with Cora.

"We should walk, too," Bridget said. She stood at the other front-facing window, her curtain nearly pulled off.

Effie's gut coiled. "No. This isn't ours." She'd tried to leave death back at Homeplace, and she'd only met Mae once. She lifted a corner of her curtain again. "I don't know why Cora is walking. I don't know what it means. Mae and Mr. Thayer weren't married. That's probably why Mae wasn't laid out at the funeral parlor. Maybe the place didn't want to serve her."

"Maybe it cost too much."

"Or Mr. Thayer didn't feel the need to spend it. Her not being his wife. Going out there, following them into town, would make things worse for us." They needed to gain footing in Bleaksville, and what would Rev. Jackdaw say of her partaking in such a procession? He worked to rid Omaha of prostitutes and Mae, it turned out, was no more than that. But Cora?

"When we took Rowan," Bridget said, "everyone in the village walked."

Mr. Thayer spat again.

"I said no. Mae isn't kin to us." They could perhaps stand on the porch as a sign of respect to Cora, but the Injun would see them. He might mistake that for an act of neighborliness. She dropped the curtain, went to Bridget's window, and slapped down that curtain. "It isn't safe."

Twenty-Three

Mr. Deet and five other men arrived in two wagons. The wagons stopped on the road and the men strolled past the cabin windows with their arms full and on to the skinning shed. Bridget ran out to tell Jake the news and be there for Deet to thank. She'd never met Deet, though she and Effie had been expecting him since the snow began piling up. She stood at Jake's side while the men made a trip back up to the wagons and came again with crates and guns, moving everything up the four steps to the skinning shed. Banging inside told her someone was starting the stove.

Bridget shivered, wished she'd grabbed the cape, and kept waiting. Deet would also want to speak to Effie and hear how no one had stolen wood—though Effie never left the lodge to know. Which Bridget wouldn't say.

The men wore beards and goatees, wooly hats and hats with earflaps that tied over their heads, coats that reached mid-thigh and heavy trousers. The largest man wore a long fur coat reaching to his knees. She didn't know if it was bearskin, maybe even bearskin over the bottom half of his face, but he looked like a bear standing there, towering over the others. *Bear-man,* she thought.

A man marched up to her. His beard was shorter than Rev. Jackdaw's and cut into to a point sharp as a pencil. His brows were heavy and the high bridge of his nose made his eyes looked punched in on either side. He had big ears. "Go on now. No need for you to be out here."

"Are you Mr. Deet?"

"Go on, get out of here."

He didn't want to talk to her. He wanted her rushed off, as if the sight of her offended him. Shamed him somehow.

"Go on." He waved a big hand in the direction of the lodge. One of the men made a snorting sound as he dropped rattling iron traps from the skinning shed onto the sled. Wind pushed at Bridget though all the trees were still. Having Deet there was a bad thing.

"Are they coming in?" Effie asked as soon as Bridget opened the door. She'd changed into her green dress and pulled the tiny copper combs from her hair and jabbed them back in.

"Maybe," Bridget said, trying to make the lie sound true. She wondered if Deet was ashamed of their living there, even if Rev. Jackdaw wasn't.

Deet and Bear-man carried out the yoke. With Jake harnessed to the sleigh, all but Deet climbed on. Men drug their large booted feet off the sides while Jake tugged over ruts and patches of winter-hard weeds. When they'd left the small clearing, and their backs were to the lodge, Bridget ran back outside.

Deet steered Jake along the river's edge on cutback, and Bridget was ready to turn back when men shouted. Arms flew up, and the back of the sled swung out at an angle. Jake let out a long and throated lowing sound, the men slid onto the frozen river, and the cut back finished collapsing. Jake's back legs sank even as his front legs on higher ground struggled for purchase.

Bridget screamed and ran for him. She felt the pain in his knee, sharp as a stick poke. More pokes. Jake not cursing the men but saying "ouch, ouch," and "yes, sir" as Deet cussed him.

While Deet, who'd not fallen, shouted "Heave" in Jake's ear, the men brushed snow off elbows and hips, no one bothering to grab hold of the sleigh runners and lifting so that Jake had a straight line pull.

She reached them winded and stopped, not knowing what to do. Men watched her like she'd come to deliver a message they must all hear. A man laughed. Then a second. Deet stared at her. The anger he'd shown in the yard was slight compared to the new rage in his eyes. He was a proud man, and now his sleigh, the laughter, Jake, and her.

She wanted to touch Jake, to feel his warm hide, and brush the muddy snow off his back knees. No one was doing that. Jake had regained his footing, and he was no longer saying "ouch." He was telling her, "Thank you very much for coming."

The men shouted even more when they returned the next day to drag in their traps. Their eyes were red, and despite the cold, they wore their coats open and their faces shown with sweat. At Jake's ear, Bear-man shot at a squirrel in Wilcox-the-tree. Missed. Jake's eyes were bigger than the first day, his shoulders tighter, his heart louder. He didn't like second days.

She followed because Jake had thanked her for doing so the day before. But she stayed far back so Deet didn't see her and tell Rev. Jackdaw.

Twenty-Four

"Start my coffee," Rev. Jackdaw barked.

The bed groaned beneath Effie as he sat up, his long feet hitting the floor. He'd pulled down her curtains and the sun was cresting in the east, but her body ached for more sleep. He had somewhere to go and so she must be up, too. After two months away, he was leaving again after only one night. His male Lord had important work for men.

He hadn't returned to spend time with her; he'd come to take his pleasure and see if she was pregnant. Had he also come to check she was still there, his property where he'd left it? Or did he have spies on her and already knew?

She forced herself out of bed and to the cold stove. He'd brought home six eggs, a bit of bacon, and a loaf of bread in a clean dish towel—the bread not from a bakery and wrapped in paper, but from a rich woman's kitchen where losing a towel didn't matter. He'd also carried in an armload of old newsprint. Sheets Bridget instantly started to read. Bridget reading at the table as he wrote in his journal at the other end. The two of them shutting her out.

Effie wanted to despise the papers—something Rev. Jackdaw had acquired for free, yet dropped in the corner like delivering a gift. Knowing she couldn't read. But she couldn't refuse them. Bridget would read to her on cold nights and the papers would go to their toilet or be shredded into the new mud they constantly needed for repatching the walls.

Bridget was awake now too, pushing back a flap of the buffalo hide. Effie held her breath. She dared not look at Rev. Jackdaw as Bridget unwound the long strips of soiled sheeting and exposed her scars like a skunk's thin stripe.

With the wrappings retied, Effie sighed. Rev. Jackdaw hadn't looked. He scarce noticed Bridget at all unless he needed something. But he hadn't been the one who hurt her. She'd done that.

Effie fed kindling into the stove. Already Rev. Jackdaw was readying his things. He had a new coat, something he'd shown her the night before. And a new inkbottle, a modern invention with a screw on lid rather than a cork and with a smaller well of glass just inside the rim. He could dip his pen into that and never go too deep, never get ink on the pen's shaft. Both the coat and the bottle were "gifts from Christ-ian women," he'd said, the word "Christian" drawn out—as though it indicated some long-standing goodness against which Effie couldn't compete. Both items befitted a preacher, and she scolded herself for being envious.

She cracked the last two eggs of the six he'd brought, the yolks bright in the blackened pan. To keep off the mice, she'd put a pail over the last of the loaf. He'd groaned at seeing her "unblessed and barren" and pinched her until she'd cried out. Then another pinch: "scrawny." Had he written those three words in his book? *Scrawny, unblessed, barren.*

She wouldn't beg him this time to stay. Doing so only fueled his anger and his need to escape her harping. Besides, her life in Omaha couldn't begin until he'd gathered enough flock there to support them. He had to go back. Still, his desire to be there was a rejection. Something she knew well.

She put his breakfast on the table. "My house . . ." She stopped as his cold eyes lifted and the scar, thick as a finger spooning his eye, threatened to throb and accuse her. She lived in squalor but asking even for plates without chips, and that hadn't been covered in the blood of Pa's family, angered him. How could she ask about the house he promised?

He finished eating and took up the union suit she'd washed for him and hung to dry on the back of his chair. "I suppose you been wanting to wash my drawers," he'd said the evening before. "You don't get much opportunity to be my wife."

He brushed at his new coat, flicking his fingers hard. He'd not take even dust from the lodge. Did they ask him to eat in their homes? She was afraid to ask.

Afraid to ask. Rev. Jackdaw was her husband, the man she'd trusted to bring her West, trusted with her life, yet she was afraid to ask. Because being accused of minding his business was worse than not knowing.

But letters? Had she the right to ask about letters? "You wrote Ma?" Her palms dampened. "No letters have come for me?"

"I'm your family now." He folded his old coat. "I get a minute, I'll write them again. Ask them, ain't you worth a penny post."

Standing beside the bed, Rev. Jackdaw pushed down on his aged coat and tried to force it into his valise. He'd worn the long, heavy duster on the buggy ride out and packed the new, thinner, shorter coat in his valise. He'd wear the new back to Omaha; Effie needed to see him riding off looking smart. The new wool marked his only gain thus far: one fastidious old woman's support. The squawk had acquaintances though, and with her coaxing some of them might yet convert to his cause. Not continue to clutch their purse strings in their withered fists.

Across the room, Effie stared at his breakfast plate as if not having the sense to know it needed washing. It was time she grew up. She likely coveted a new dress. Maybe even new shoes, but those wants were rooted in vanity. Lusting after material goods made women seek out whoredom—even if that meant the block-long alley of cubby holes, the fetid cribs.

He yanked at his coat sleeves. Her green frock served her well enough. She had no need to present herself in Bleaksville. She wasn't trying to get pulpit work, wasn't street preaching, or being scrutinized by the public. Wasting two dollars on a new dress made no more sense than investing in a litter of cats. Nor did it make any sense for her to have a fine rocker in such a damp place. He pushed down again, imagined he could hear the faint rustle of letters in the bottom of his valise.

He was doing nothing wrong. She was his wife, and he head of the house. Besides, she already spent too much money. He'd flinched at Graf's bill—putting down three dollars and swearing to pay the rest soon. *God willing.* He'd studied the list, counting week by week, and was surprised by how little she'd purchased to stay alive. No wonder she'd lost weight. Still, he'd pinched her. For her weight loss—there were other sources of food—but also for her failure in carrying a child. She couldn't shrink from his dreams. If she proved herself and conceived and bore him sons, then after he'd grown his church, he'd quiet her with a couple new dresses. Sensible clothing. Nothing like the gaudy, bright dresses whores wore.

He turned as Rooster ran in, nearly slamming the door behind herself. She shivered in Effie's cape and hurried to warm herself by the fire. "You watered my horse?"

She nodded. Pouty. Had been since his arrival. Was she up to something in his absence? Likely he needed to stay a few days, follow her some. But there was neither hay nor a barn here for Nell. If the nag dropped this winter, he needed it to happen when he was in Omaha.

He pushed down again on the valise lid, stopped, and pulled the coat out. He'd carry it. The hinges of his bag were weak with age and wear.

Rooster snuck up to his side, too close, and he scowled at her nearness. "We need the coat," she said. She took it from the bed, crossed the room, and hung his property on a nail by the back door.

Smart that one. Too smart. As though she weren't actually stealing from him, only moving his possession across the room. He thought to grab her by her rooster hair, but Effie's lethargy stopped him. Rooster at least had sense, wasn't folding up and quitting because her life carried a bit of hardship. "That one has a brain," he said to Effie. "You can thank me for getting you a sensible one."

Rooster faced him. She was at the fire again, slapping her arms. "Why does Mr. Deet have to use Jake for trapping? Their horses can pull the sled."

"That what's got into you? Come here." He'd forgotten he had a bit of business needing tended to. He waited until she'd sheepishly stepped close enough, then used the back of his hand to strike her across the cheek. She stumbled and hit the floor. "Deet paid me a little visit. Said last time they came trapping you got under foot. That animal ain't yours. Next time you bother Deet things will be a whole lot worse for you. Now git up."

She did, holding her cheek, her eyes brimming.

"Ox's got two toes for gripping," he said. "Better footing on icy river banks. You think an iron-shod horse can get traction on snowy slopes?" She wasn't looking at him. "A horse needs a bit of grain now and again, but brute that out there can stay alive on scrub." He paused. "You got something more to say?"

"They don't love him." She was close to weeping. "They don't care if he breaks a leg on the ice. They only care about their horses."

His eye twitched. Twitched again. Was she sassing him? Loving an animal was weakness. Pure weakness. "You act like a goddamned girl around here, and it's gonna turn out bad." His eye ticked, each pulse a tiny explosion of a nerve ending. "I've warned you now about causing Deet trouble. Your sniveling little-girl's ass . . ." He stopped. His father's voice boomed in his head.

Effie lifted the pump handle. Water gushed into her dishpan. "Bridget, come help me." When Rooster crossed the room, Effie put herself between Squawk and him. "An Injun lives down the road," Effie said.

He shook his head in frustration. She also had something in her craw. "The half-breed?" He nearly chuckled at the surprise on her face. His flapping eye slowed a notch. "You think I don't know what goes on around here? Don't know about his papoose drowning and his wife getting the hell away? You know what's good for you, you'll stay out of his business."

"He might be one of those who scalped and murdered Pa's family."

She and Rooster were a pair of squawks. One falling in love with an animal, the other scared of something ain't happened in more 'an a quarter century.

"You saying you ain't safe here? You saying the Lord's provision ain't up to your standards? That redskin didn't come all the way from Minnesota to Nebraska."

"We done it," she said. "We come that far."

She deserved what he'd given Rooster. He wrapped his pen in its square of soft felt, gave the cap on his inkbottle a second hard twist.

His eye was firing like a pistol. How could he impress followers with half his face jigging? He turned, his one steady eye facing Effie. "That Indian shows his face here, shoot him. No white preacher's wife's going to swing for shooting an Indian."

"Maybe Chief is nice."

Rooster had lifted her mug to speak, the grab of her words trying him. "He ain't nothing to either of you."

He put on his hat, turned, and saw motion out the window. He set his belongings back on the table and swung open the door. A man, one-third his age and riding a sleek chestnut mare, was coming down the frozen slope. The horse made Nell look like a graying dog.

"You got men coming down here?" He rounded on Effie. "I'll see about that." He stepped out, leaving the door open to the cold; Effie needed to hear loud and clear.

Rooster appeared behind him, sneaky as she'd been coming for his coat, her cheek red and swelling from the lesson he'd taught her. "It's the school teacher," she said.

"How you know that?" Was it guilt shining in her eyes? Or just fear of him? "I hear you been sniffing around that school, I'll lock you in the shed a week."

The rider finished the descent, his horse's ears high, its nostrils puffing steam. "Good morning, sir." He tipped his hat and began to draw a leg over his saddle. "You must be Rev. Jackdaw."

"What you want?"

The leg eased back over. "I'm headmaster of the school. I've come to talk about your daughter attending."

"Ain't no daughter here. You're looking at an orphan I'm housing."

He squinted at Rooster. "An orphan, you say?"

"That's right." He let the information sink in. "What use would this here orphan be to me, her head filled with book learning?"

The man leaned forward in the saddle. "Rooster?" White teeth showing. "She's likely to amount to more with a proper education."

"What sort of new-fangled nonsense is that?" He was glad for the new coat and tugged his hat down more to the right over his bad eye. "Just what is it she's supposed to amount to? I'm carrying the expense of feeding her. This one here," he thumped Rooster's head through her wrapping, "ain't in need of schooling."

"If she were to attend, she might become a school teacher herself one day."

"Hell, she's Irish. You think you're going to teach her to run a school?"

"Irish? Well." He looked back up the slope and to the road. "I wondered about that."

"I'm going to be a doctor," Bridget said.

Rev. Jackdaw snorted. She was talking nonsense in front of this man. Giving the im-pression she wasn't being raised proper. Wasn't being taught to respect her elders. "No man's ever going to let a woman doctor him. You know how to cook, clean out piss buckets, that'll be all the education you need."

The schoolteacher grinned. The conversation had turned comical to him. "An education might help her avoid the perils you fight against in the city. Aren't them 'ladies' mostly Irish?"

"Whoredom? You know about my work?" His reputation was spreading. "I'll kill her myself 'fore I let her ruin a man."

"Well, suit yourself, sir. I came out to be sure of your wishes."

Rooster spun around and vanished back in the lodge. Slammed the door again. *Fucking girl!* His father's voice once again thundering in his head. The flash of a boot toe aimed for his groin.

Bridget dropped back against the door and slapped her hands over her ears. She wouldn't listen to one more word. She'd hurried out to see the teacher who'd opened a school window for her to hear better, even winked at her. And did the same every afternoon she crept below his window for an hour or two. She'd trusted he came to tell Rev. Jackdaw she needed to be in school. She'd trusted he came on her behalf, and he could convince Rev. Jackdaw to let her attend school. He was a teacher, which made him the smartest man in Bleaksville. He knew all the right words to say. She'd believed he liked her. But she'd seen something in his eyes when Rev. Jackdaw said she was an orphan. Something again when Rev. Jackdaw said she was Irish.

She socked her stomach. She wanted to run back out, jump off the porch, pull off his stupid mustache and poke his horse with a sharp stick and scream it away. She looked to Effie. "They laughed at me."

Effie nodded, but so slight Bridget wasn't sure.

"They laughed at me." Her fists balled. "I'm eleven. They can't decide my whole life."

She couldn't go back to the school now. Not even to sit outside beneath a window. The schoolteacher had lied to her, pretending to care, pretending to believe having girls at school was as important as having boys. He was a L-I-A-R. He'd only ridden his horse down so he could pretend he cared. He didn't believe she fit in his school.

She'd bust open if she didn't make the crushing, crashing feelings go away. She looked at the inkbottle on the table. Stealing would help. She raced to grab it up.

Effie's breath sucked in. "Put that down. He'll whip you!"

Bridget agreed. Taking the bottle would be too obvious. She slapped open the journal. The pages, full of scrawling script, parted in the middle of the book with thick stitching running down the center. She tore out a page and saw the ragged edge left behind and had to take that half of the sheet too. Not enough. Another rip and its opposite half. Four ragged pages in her hand.

Effie's stifled moans sounded as if she'd slapped both hands over her mouth. "You'll get yourself killed." She hurried across the room and dropped to her knees in front of the bed. Pretending prayer. "Run." Her voice a sharp whisper. "Run out the back."

The latch lifted on the front door. The hinges squeaked. Rev. Jackdaw was inside, pausing, likely looking at Effie.

The pages in Bridget's hand shook. *Nera, Nera.*

"Green and gung-ho that one." Rev. Jackdaw strutted forward, his steps full of hard boot heels and purpose. "Made a damned fool of hisself. Coming here, acting like I don't know my own business."

Dr. Chase's book lay on the table, its black covers worn. Bridget stuffed the journal sheets between pages and slammed the book closed.

Rev. Jackdaw towered over her, his eyes going from her face to the book she'd slammed shut and pressed closed with both hands. "What's gotten into you?"

Effie let out a mumbling string of words that sounded like "Our dear Lord." Or "We're dead, Lord."

Rev. Jackdaw glanced at her on her knees again and frowned. He pulled Dr. Chase's book from beneath Bridget's hands and shook it in her face. "Anything you need to know about doctoring is right here."

"Yes, sir." She lifted her hands slowly, tugged gently on the book he held fast. The corner of a journal page peeked out the bottom, "Yes, sir," she repeated. She tugged again, her hands shaking, and when he let go, she hugged the book to her chest.

Twenty-Five

Bridget led Jake through the snow toward Old Mag. Rev. Jackdaw's coat hung to her ankles and rubbed the top of her too-tight shoes. Animal tracks ran in all directions through the trees and across the path. Deer, fox, squirrel. She looked for anything green poking up through the snow, both for Jake to eat and to take back to the lodge. If Effie had something happy inside, she might feel better. Grandma Teegan always brought ivy and holly in during winter to keep the croft cheery.

"Effie's never been in the trees," she told Jake. That wasn't the scariest thing she needed to tell him. Effie was quitting inside. Step one to something bad happening.

At Old Mag, she crawled over one arm and stared down at the snow-covered spot where she'd drawn her map. She had drawn it for safety and holding the day together, but it wasn't working.

"Hey."

She jumped at seeing Pete riding down the path on Mr. Thayer's wide plow horse. Since Mae's death, she'd seen him ride back and forth from Bleaksville on the nag. Going in mornings and coming home late in the afternoons. She imagined that without Mae to tend, Mr. Thayer had insisted he work. Atop the horse no sleeker or faster looking than Jake, Pete sat bundled in his coat and hat and looked plain handsome. His lips tipped up enough to say he liked riding, and he liked her seeing him do so.

He'd come from the direction of Chief's. She'd never seen him in

Deet's trees, but of course he knew about the path. He'd used the trail with his mother when they gathered wood.

"What are you doing here?"

"What *you* doing?"

She shrugged, then cringed as his gaze moved from the rags wrapped around her head to the man-coat with its sleeves hanging six inches too long. Was he thinking how poor she looked?

He nodded in the direction of the lodge. "Mrs. Jackdaw home? I have a message for her."

"I could tell her."

"It's business."

Effie was likely sleeping and wouldn't want to be woken up, but Pete needed her. "Follow me." She started back, leading the way with Jake beside her. She wouldn't hurry, her feet pinched in her shoes, and if Pete didn't believe her capable of relaying a simple message, she'd take her sweet time.

Opening the lodge door, she looked first to how the fire had burned down in her absence and then to Effie in bed, curled beneath the Never Forget quilt.

"Pete's here." She waited for Effie's eyes to open. "Pete needs to talk to you."

Effie sat up looking confused and still half-asleep. "Pete?"

"He's outside."

Bridget opened the door and listened as Effie in her wrinkled dress, hugged herself against the cold. "Pete, has something happened?"

"A rocker's come for you." He kept to his horse. "Two days ago. You don't fetch it, the chair becomes property of the railroad."

Bridget's chest warmed. She was Pete's friend; Effie wasn't. Pete wanted to deliver the message himself because it was bossy. Effie hadn't accepted Mae's loaf; she told them they couldn't collect wood; and when Pete stood with his black eye and his hat in his hand, Effie refused to help him dress his mother for burial.

"Granny's rocker?" Effie asked. "That means . . ." Her hair hung over her cheeks, but she made no effort to push it back. "Can't anyone bring it out? I don't have a wagon."

Pete straightened, making himself taller. "The railroad delivers as far as the depot. Going on a week now. Ain't your family sent word?" He lingered a few seconds more, turned his horse, and touched his heels to the animal's flanks.

"Pete," Effie called and waited as he pulled up and looked back. "I'm sorry about your ma."

He kicked the horse's flanks again. "Jackdaw wanted the chair sent to his room in Omaha. But no one's paid for that."

Bridget closed the door because Effie continued staring after Pete as if not making sense of what he told her. And not feeling winter blow inside.

"Granny's rocker," Effie finally whispered. "Granny's dead." She sank onto the bed, her face slowly falling and her eyes filling. "What could have happened? She was old, her mind, but she wasn't sick." She stared at the fire. "Her mind, but she wasn't sick."

Bridget watched Effie's tears but didn't know what to say.

"Not a line of post." Effie's face twisted. "Rev. Jackdaw knew. He wanted to take the chair, not even telling me it came."

"We should go right now," Bridget said. "You lost your granny; you can't lose your chair too."

"We can't carry it that far."

"Jake can."

Bridget shivered as Effie began to change dresses, letting the one she wore slide down over her hips and stepping free in her graying slip. Her collar and shoulder bones were beginning to look like ledges mice could run along. Grandma Teegan's body had looked the same way.

When Effie took the stained green silk from its peg, they both jumped to see a mouse drop and scurry away. Tiny new holes ran along the hem.

Bridget had never used the lasso Rev. Jackdaw tied in the rope, but this was different; she'd never taken Jake into town. She slipped it over his head knowing that even with the weight he'd lost, she wouldn't be strong enough to hold him back if something on Main Street spooked him. The length of the rope was too heavy to carry, and she let it drop and drag for fifteen paces behind. She stayed at Jake's head where she could talk to him. Hopefully, her voice along with the feel of the rope dragging behind would be enough to keep Jake from running off.

They walked first in a snowy runnel made by horses, then after passing Chief's—Effie's eyes down—they walked in wagon wheel tracks.

Effie didn't speak, but Bridget heard her sniffing and thought how much she missed Grandma Teegan. Someday, maybe she'd see her again, but Effie knew she'd never see her granny again.

Crossing Nettle Creek, Bridget tugged and coaxed Jake, and step by step he obeyed. The schoolyard was empty, and she hoped the headmaster looked out a window and saw her. She didn't know how, but she'd prove girls could be doctors.

Effie scrubbed her teary face with her hands. "I don't want people looking at me. Go down a side street."

Pete wasn't at the small stationhouse. A man Bridget had never seen, along with Mr. Thayer, carried out the rocker, one man on each arm. Effie didn't watch either. She stood silently while they hoisted the chair and used the long rope and strapped the rocker to Jake's side. She didn't notice how Mr. Thayer kept glancing at her—Bridget did. A tobacco-stained streak ran down from Mr. Thayer's bottom lip and deep into the wiry bush of his beard. He'd given Pete a black eye, and just like Effie, he hadn't helped Pete dress his mother for her funeral.

They finished looping and knotting. The rocker hung off Jake's side looking like a throne Effie could climb onto and ride all the way home.

The aproned man wished them a good day and went back inside.

Mr. Thayer lingered. He looked at Effie. "You don't come into town much."

She studied her shoes. "When I need things."

Tobacco juice squirted from Mr. Thayer's mouth. He'd turned his head, but the spittle made Bridget nearly gag. A bead of dark saliva curled over his lower lip and disappeared in the brown trail. "You staying for the eating and dancing?"

Effie grabbed one of the chair's rockers as though the ground beneath her feet had suddenly slipped. "Dancing?"

"Whole town's coming in. Christmas celebration at the church. They push back the pews and a young scrapper brings his accordion."

Bridget followed the line of Effie's gaze to the single white cross at the end of the block. Men carried in chairs and women baskets or small children. Red and green bunting hung in festive drapes. "We need to get home."

"That'd be a shame," Thayer said. "A pretty girl like you ought to be out more."

Effie looked again to the rocker. "I have to go home."

Bridget didn't want them talking, though she wasn't exactly sure why. "She has to go."

Mr. Thayer gave Effie a last long look.

As they walked away, Effie reaching out to keep a hand on one moon-shaped rocker, Bridget wondered about Mr. Thayer. Why had he looked at Effie like that? She wished he could have seen Effie when they first arrived. She'd been even prettier then. Bridget wondered too, about Pete. Were he and Mr. Thayer friends now?

"Jury," Effie watched the church. "Our first dance was at Christmas time. I wore this dress." They walked to the sound of Jake's hoofs. "Granny had just had it made over for me." She was quiet for a bit. "Turn Jake. Let's go right past the church and down Main Street. We'll stop at the post office and mercantile and everyone will see I have a fine rocker."

Bridget's heart sped. She was always hungry, but with Mr. Thayer ogling Effie, the Christmas celebration to which Effie hadn't been invited, and the sadness Effie felt over the death of her granny, Bridget didn't want Effie arguing with Mr. Graf too. "Let's go home." She smiled as big as she could. "I'll build a really warm fire, and I'll go and ask Old Mag for two eggs. You can rock in your new chair, and I'll tell you a story."

Effie didn't answer and headed toward the post office. Leaving empty-handed, her eyes were moist and her face red.

Waiting for her outside the mercantile, Bridget tried to push the rocker higher up Jake's side. Since leaving the depot, the cumbersome chair had slipped inch by inch, and now the heavy piece hung too low. By the time they crossed Nettle Creek, the rocker would drag under Jake's belly and be crushed with his hoofs.

"You! Irish!" She imagined she heard the sheriff, his badge bright on his chest, though he walked on the other side of the street and paid no attention to her. Wasn't even looking in her direction. Still, the man Chief thought mean enough to wrap a small dog in barbed wire yelled again in Bridget's head. "I been getting reports. A woman lost a sheet right off her clothesline. Missing turnips and cabbages." He yelled the same words in her sleep, using the voice of a mean New York policeman, reminding her the thin thread that had kept her from prison there was just as thin in Nebraska.

Chief's wagon sat empty across the street, only two of the four workhorses he owned harnessed to the front. She still hadn't spoken to him since the morning she stood in his kitchen, though she'd seen him at night through his windows, eating alone at the kitchen table. Or in the next room working at a desk and his ledgers. She never watched long, heading for his fruit trees or hen house before Wire sensed her outside and began barking. Or Chief rose and put on his coat for his nighttime walk.

In the mercantile, Graf frowned at seeing Effie. "If you haven't got money, turn right on out of here."

Effie clenched her jaws. *I'd like nothing more.* But they needed food, the community was gathering while she and Bridget were heading back to the cold lodge alone, and Granny was dead. "Rev. Jackdaw will pay you in full. Soon as he's able to make the trip. He's busy with his work in Omaha."

"It ain't mine to keep carrying you."

Had Rev. Jackdaw not paid the bill on his last visit? Had he spent all he had on his new coat, his fancy inkbottle? Not paid the bill for his wife and child's food?

Effie had been shaking since realizing Granny was dead. Shaking since seeing the chair and learning of the town's gathering, friends greeting friends. Shaking since hearing Pete say Rev. Jackdaw had wanted the chair sent to Omaha. How had he known about it? Had he heard from Mr. Thayer? Was there someone else in Bleaksville that spied on her, heard all the news, reported to Rev. Jackdaw?

"I'm not asking much," she said to Mr. Graf. "Just a bit to see us a few days. Maybe beans this time?" Could she pay off her debt with the rocker? But how could she part with it so soon? "I'm not asking for charity. Only a bit more time." She paused, motioned toward the door. "The orphan . . . Bridget, she's hungry."

Graf fisted the front of his apron, whipped it off, and slapped it down on the counter. Two small sacks hit the floor. Licorice drops spilled out and lay in week-old sawdust and mud carried in on boots and pram wheels and ground to dust.

"God dammit," he spat. He came around the counter, his cold eyes pinning Effie. "No reason I got to be the one to feed you." He grabbed the sacks in one hand and the soiled licorice in the other. He looked at the candy for a moment and then very slowly held out his open palm to her. Was it a test to see if she'd fallen low enough to accept it? His hand closed and he pulled the fist back.

Effie ached. She'd gladly take the sweets. She'd brush off the dirt and she and Bridget could have candy for Christmas.

Behind the counter again, Graf held the sweets over a trash barrel, paused, and moved his hand away. He laid the penny sweets on a shelf behind him. Was he keeping them? Did he intend to resack them?

"Tell your husband," his voice a low growl, "I have a business to run."

The Injun stepped out from behind a display. She knew not to scream, but she flinched and took a quick step back. Needles in her palms.

"You got what you need, Chief?" Mr. Graf asked.

The bronze face nodded at Effie. "Finish with her first."

Effie backed farther away, turned, and moved halfway down the aisle to Cora's display of unwrapped soaps. She wouldn't have the Injun hearing her beg.

The curtains parted behind the counter and Cora stepped through. She wore a crimson velvet gown. Effie once imagined that as a preacher's wife she'd have fine dresses, but she'd never imagined a dress so beautiful: boned through the bodice with wide, poufy shoulders and slender sleeves that ended with six-inch cuffs of lace.

Cora came forward. "Merry Christmas, Mrs. Jackdaw."

Shame over her poor bonnet, her dress with holes, her pauper's cape, washed over Effie. She didn't belong even standing beside Cora.

"Merry Christmas, Chief," Cora called.

As the Injun picked up his packages and nodded, his brown face as hard for Effie to read as Mr. Graf's. Had he smiled or sneered? With the door closed after him, Cora turned to her husband. "It's the holiday season. Surely we can offer Mrs. Jackdaw a little something." She winked at Effie, but the gesture was also for Mr. Graf's eyes. "My husband is a shrewd businessman, but he's kind."

The store buzzed around Effie. She was dissolving in the air, growing thin as fog, losing her substance, not like something drifting off that eyes could follow, but simply ceasing to exist.

"Effie?" Cora's voice was warm. "Are you all right? You've been crying. You're getting so thin." She turned and faced her husband squarely.

Graf's gaze lingered on his wife, then his hands rose in defeat. "One pound of beans."

"Of course," Cora said. "I'll wait on her. You're late dressing."

He hesitated before leaving. When he was gone, Cora snapped open a paper bag, added three large scoops of meal, and spoke louder than necessary. "That will be one pound of beans on your tab, Mrs. Jackdaw." She reached for a sack of beans, already round and weighed, from the counter behind her. She hesitated at seeing the candy, sighed and swept it into the dustbin. She brushed the area free of dust and pushed the beans across the counter to Effie.

Charity. Wasting candy.

"Merry Christmas," Cora said again. Then whispered, "Hurry."

Charity. The word still rattled in Effie's head. She hesitated, needing to say something about the wasted candy. Cora didn't understand hunger the way she and Mr. Graf did. But if the man came back and found them arguing, he'd take the meal away, and he'd likely be angry with Cora. That wasn't fair to her even though she'd been cold hearted in throwing away the licorice.

"He doesn't mean any harm," Cora said. "He has his demons. We all do."

Effie couldn't force herself out the door. "Why are you helping me?"

Cora checked the curtain—still closed. "Mae has died." Her eyes filled, and she touched the paper bag in Effie's hand. "Go. Hurry, now."

Effie stepped onto the wooden walk outside the mercantile and nearly dropped her things. The Injun stood beside Bridget and in broad daylight was stealing the rocker. "Get away from there." She rushed down the stairs. "Get your hands off my chair!"

"I asked him to help," Bridget said. "The chair's falling off. It's going to break."

"You what?"

The Injun with its foul hat and gray braids finished untying Thayer's knots and lowered the chair to the ground.

"Quit that," Effie cried. Two women with baskets and nearly to the mercantile door stopped to stare. Was it at the Injun? Or at her? She wanted to strike him, but she wasn't brave enough—even with two witnesses. Nor would she step so close she could use her fist on his back. "Thief! Someone call the sheriff."

The women smiled to each other. They didn't believe the Injun was stealing. They thought her as dim-witted as she'd thought Mae. The clenching in Effie's stomach changed from fear to anger. The pair would take their story into the church gathering. The story would walk around on its thin legs, collect strength, and split into new stories. By the end of the night, a hundred versions would come out. Each more embellished than the last.

The Injun lifted the rocker by the arms and swung it upside down above his head. "I'll sit it on your porch."

As he carried it across the street to his wagon, Effie silently cursed him, then sucked in a sudden, ragged breath. On the underside of the seat, in a finger-wide smear of paint, was a backwards J.

Bridget watched Chief carrying the chair. She didn't see a shadow around him. Not the way death announced itself, but his loneliness was there in the flop of his hat, the set of his shoulders, and in his worn coat—the one he'd wrapped her in. It was there, too, in the way he climbed into his wagon, flicked the reins, and the wagon rolled down the street, the chair rocking in back. The people of Bleaksville didn't cross the street to avoid him, but they hadn't invited him either to their Christmas party. *You can be with us,* she wished she could have said. Effie would have screamed, said no.

Walking at Jake's shoulder again, Bridget carried the sacks while Effie trailed behind, her head down. They passed the school, the windows dark now, and crossed the bridge. Dusk was settling, the wind blew colder, and the tips of tall grasses and weeds rustled either side of the road. The rope scraped over snowy ruts.

Effie let out a worn sob, and Bridget turned to see her cover her face with her hands and drop to her knees on the frozen road.

"Stay," Bridget told Jake. She ran back and knelt on the ground beside Effie, so close Rev. Jackdaw's coat touched the hem of Effie's cape. So close Effie could, if she wanted, reach out and hug, or just hold on. "I'm sorry your granny is dead."

"It isn't only that." Effie's nose dripped. "Johnny painted the rocker. He hasn't forgotten me."

The ground beneath Bridget rolled. Effie would leave her. Not that day, but one day. She'd go back to her family and Johnny. Like Grandma Teegan, she'd go.

"All this time," Effie said, "I thought they didn't know where I was. Thought that's why they haven't sent a single letter. But they know I'm here. These months . . . they've known."

Twenty-Six

Rev. Jackdaw shivered on the cold street corner, pacing back and forth for warmth. He held his slate high, the word "REPENT" fading in the wet, falling snow. No use pulling out his stub of chalk to write the word again. His overturned hat sat on the sidewalk close to his feet and served as a bucket for donations. His thin hair hung limp and dripped onto his brow. His eye slept quiet as a baby. This was the Lord's work; the cold was a privilege. God allowed those who would be great to be tested. Just as He'd allowed Job to be tested.

Half a block away, Storz Brewery stood six hundred feet tall. All fifteen buildings, the paper reported, had red tiled floors, stainless steel and copper fixtures. With that edifice to the devil in the background, the corner was normally profitable. A woman hurried down the street with her eyes lowered against the snow, and her hat tugged down on her forehead. He waited, watched her come, saw the moment she saw him: too late to step across the street.

"I see by the light in your eyes, sister." He'd seen only dread. "You are one of God's chosen."

Her stance softened realizing he was a man of God. "Good day, sir." A small tip in her lips as she tried to pass.

Some days his work reaped more profit than others. Today, the snow and cold kept most home, but on a good day, a bill or two was dropped into his hat, and women stopped to hear his preaching. He caught her elbow with his fingers, not pressing too tight. She didn't jerk away, though to keep hold he had to step forward with her backward step. A young man would shove him off, maybe raise a fist, but women were schooled to be inoffensive. They dropped coins in hopes of negotiating and considered themselves lucky to get away. "A bit to help our church," he said. He lifted a hand toward the brewery. "Together, we will rid the city of its evils."

She fumbled with her purse strings, and he let go of her arm. Though she refused to meet his gaze, she stepped the two feet ahead to his hat and dropped in a coin. He knew to keep his hat always three feet in front of him in the direction the pedestrian was moving. The placement allowed an easier escape; let a person drop in money and hurry on with no chance of being grabbed again. Trial and error had taught him relief made them more generous.

"The Lord's blessings," he said. Not all were as cold as this one. Some stepped up close as soon as he mentioned the light in their eyes or his desire to rid the city of its evils. Women mostly, prohibitionists who supposed they, too, had a calling. Those were the women who invited him to their houses and fed him hearty meals.

His stomach growled at the thought, and he wondered about Effie and Rooster. They were also hungry, though Effie didn't understand the benefit of suffering for a cause. He'd meant to return more often. Effie was young flesh going to waste, but there wasn't money to fritter away on train fare, and for weeks the roads had remained nearly impassable for a buggy. Even the man who pastured Nell expected payment every time he came for her. Nell wasn't but glue on hoofs now, and he couldn't afford to have her drop on the road between Omaha and Bleaksville.

The crack of a sharp laugh made him look up. A young man eyed him, aimed for him with a steady gait. A sneer on his face. Dangerous, looking full of spit and malice.

"Well, if it ain't my brother-in-law out begging on the street."

Skeet. At Homeplace, Rev. Jackdaw had paid little attention to the thug. No cause to with the Mad Matriarch and Effie's pa holding rein over him. But meeting him alone on the street, his size more than

Rev. Jackdaw remembered, his eyes beady with drink, there was cause to be uneasy. "Effie's not here."

"I heard."

"She's living the next town over. Bleaksville."

"While you live here."

"I keep a modest room. No space for a wife."

Skeet walked around him, peered into the hat, lifted it and pulled out a penny. Handed over the hat. "This it? A penny for your work?"

"You have no business with me." His eye was waking up. "What do you want?"

A slow smile spread across Skeet's wet lips. "I need to thank you. I didn't know about Omaha's treasures until you started bragging about them at Homeplace. Them ladies are mighty fine."

Rev. Jackdaw beat the snow from his hat. Put it back on his head. "You'll rot in hell."

"I will. I expect you'll already be there shoveling coal, keeping the place warm for me." He held the penny between two fingers, pulled open a pocket on his coat and dropped the coin in. His fingers remained still and wide for seconds after the coin disappeared. "So where is the church you're building?" He looked around, his palms lifting. "I don't hear any hammering, don't see any steeples being raised. I'll bet Effie's real proud of her preacher husband."

"Go home. She doesn't want you here. She's trying to put the sins of her past behind her."

Skeet smiled. "I'll tell her you said hello."

Twenty-Seven

The sound of horses neighing on the ridge made Effie quit rocking, work herself out of Jury's arms, and open her eyes. The lodge was empty. Bridget had been there only a minute earlier, Effie was sure, but now she was nowhere to be seen. *I only closed my eyes.* Finding Jury was as easy as shutting out the world and whispering his name. Only that to open the door on him.

Voices were coming down through the trees.

Effie spent so much time thinking of Jury that she considered it her living time, not the narrow slot of not-living time when she shivered with cold, hunger, and fear.

A moan on the front steps outside, sent a creak across the floor inside. The whole lodge being of one old piece. A hard knock.

She opened the door. "Skeet!" Was it possible? "What are you doing here? How did you get here?"

Cora, bundled in fur, smiled from behind him, lifted a basket as though that answered everything. "He came into the store looking for you." She spoke fast, keeping Effie quiet. "I told him I had your order ready, and I was heading out to make the delivery. So here we are."

Effie cringed as the pair, smelling of winter, stepped past her and inside. Cora went to the table with her things like she'd been there a thousand times, but Skeet stopped, his big shoes just inside. He gawked. Made a point of gawking. Savored every second of her poverty revealing itself to him. Thin skins of it peeling back like the layers of an onion, growing more pungent. Dark and cold, less habitable than the barn at Homeplace. Yet there was the barn's rubbish: the dented coffee pot on the stove, banged up pans, chipped plates. At six and eight-years-old, the two of them had taken the housewares from crates in the barn, set up a playhouse in the haymow.

"Olyhay hitsay," he said. *Holy shit.*

"How did you get here?" Had she already asked? Had he already answered?

"Train to Omaha, then here." He motioned to Cora, a shake of his head in her direction. He might have been trying to flick off a fly, a pesky mosquito, his concentration still on the lodge, taking it all in.

Effie scraped a chair back from the table. "Sit down."

Cora wasn't leaving, only taking her time unpacking. Effie tried to concentrate on Skeet, but she saw each item rise out of the basket: a pie, its top high and round, a square tin of tea, a bag of beans. *Charity.* But driven by something even more this time. Was she afraid Skeet wasn't really a brother, and she aimed to act as protector? Had something Skeet said in the mercantile frightened her? Or was it his drunkenness?

"How are the little boys?" She wanted to hear about everyone at once: Johnny, Curly, Henry, the twins, the baby. "How are Ma and Pa?"

Skeet sat. He ran a palm over a gouge in the wood. "Olyhay hitsay," he said again. Not surprised this time. Delighted.

Cora cleared her throat. "This is your brother then? No need to involve the sheriff?"

At the mention of the sheriff, Skeet looked ready to bolt. *Go on,* Effie thought. She wished them both gone and that Bridget was there in the lodge with her. They'd try to eat the pie quick, before they woke and it was gone.

Cora leaned in, closer to Skeet's drunken face, her eyes holding his. Maybe trying to gauge the amount he'd had to drink. "The livery needs that horse back by dark. The train leaves then too." She gave him a hard, hands-on-her-hips look. "But if you plan to sleep here tonight, I'll take the horse back with me."

Skeet looked around the room again, his gaze fixing on the sole bed with Granny's quilt on top. "I'll get the horse back."

A quick answer that struck Effie right then left. She was relieved to know he wasn't staying, wasn't expecting she'd give up her bed, but knowing he'd leave her as fast as he'd come, hurt.

Bridget came through the back door, smiling. Her fair cheeks were rosy, the tip of her nose red. She hadn't just stepped out. Had possibly been out hours. Effie reached for her hand, wanted to show her the pie, but Bridget glanced and frowned at Skeet and hurried past to Cora. "I saw your horse coming down the road."

Effie's stomach dropped. "You empty the pot today? You carried in enough wood for the night?'

The blush on Bridget's face deepened. "Yes." She hung Rev. Jackdaw's coat and dropped in front of the fire with her back to them, removing her shoes. Effie thought to scold again. *The floor is too cold; leave your shoes on.* But the rags covering Bridget's burns, the awful dress.

Cora left, and while Skeet paid no attention to Bridget, Effie cut the pie. Cherry. The filling spilling over plates that were once slick with blood.

"Didn't think I'd ever see a place hitched up in the air," Skeet said.

The pie was sweet and tart. Effie savored the taste before swallowing.

Skeet sneered. "Ain't really a house, is it?"

They'd grown apart since what she thought of as the pre-Granny years. Pre-Baby Sally's death. She didn't care. Years of his meanness had severed and burned away the ties. They were different people now, and she didn't care about the separation. She was no more interested in trying to foster a relationship with him than she was with the Injun up the road. "It's temporary," she said of the place. "Rev. Jackdaw is building us a house in Omaha."

"The man I saw begging on a street corner?"

Effie pumped water, set the pot on the stove for tea. Skeet thought her as gullible as Johnny.

"He ain't building you a house. He ain't building no church either."

He lied. He couldn't stand the idea of her having something nice. "Did Ma send a letter with you?"

"I didn't stick around." He grinned at Effie's surprise. "You think I was going to stay locked up in that room forever?"

"You weren't locked up. The bar across your door was your idea."

His eyes leveled on hers like two gun barrels fixing. He'd drawn a flask from his coat as soon as Cora left and taken a swig. She hadn't thought much then, but he'd taken more long draws since. Pa never kept a bottle, never drank a drop that she knew of. Maybe he had once and witnessed the whole bloody scene in his kitchen same as Granny had. Maybe he feared with whiskey in the house the ghosts would get likkered up and haunt even harder.

"You were always their favorite." He breathed heavily as if the alcohol clotted his lungs. "Even Granny's. You the one in her bed. Her giving you her good dress, the quilt. Why'd you do it?"

"I did the same as you. I needed to get away."

"She's here. You brought her here. The dress, the quilt, her dishes. I see you even got the rocker."

She looked away. Bridget sat on her hide, leaving them the two chairs. "You didn't know I was sent the rocker? You didn't help take it to the depot or see Johnny paint it?"

Bridget turned a page in Dr. Chase's book, pretended to read, but Effie knew she listened to every word, her ears big as plates.

Skeet took another swig.

"Did Granny suffer at the end?" Effie asked.

"The old windbag. Screaming all night for you."

"She had a hard life. Living through what she did."

"I couldn't take it anymore."

"Is that why you left?"

"Had to go this time."

Had to go this time?

A hand larger than Pa's, larger than Rev. Jackdaw's, lifted the flask, tipped it. Skeet hadn't known she was sent the rocker which meant he left before Pa shipped it. But seeing it, he wasn't surprised, which meant he somehow knew Granny was dead. How, if he left before she died to escape her screaming? The alcohol was mixing up his mind. She didn't want to think about how things could scramble in a person's head. She closed her eyes. *Be still.* She wouldn't question. She'd stay out of the darkness.

Skeet ate more pie. His flask was empty though he couldn't remember and tipped it up every few minutes, lips sucking. His eyes were red as Bridget's nose had been.

"Where will you go?" she asked.

He took his time as if looking for an answer. His drunken brain, she could see it in his eyes, chugged. "Denver," he said finally. "I planned on Denver all along."

Iarlay. Liar. He'd run off with no plan other than getting far away. She wanted him gone. "Livery is waiting." Because he was nothing to her. Because he was her.

When he finally started up the slope to the horse standing in the dark, Bridget stepped to the door to watch beside Effie. "He can't walk. Will he be okay?"

"If he can climb on that horse, the horse'll get him to Bleaksville. The livery'll be open waiting for him. He can sleep there. No colder than what we got here."

Bridget watched Effie, her eyes wide with questions. "He said a lot of things about your granny." A question even in that.

"Not you too. Come and eat your pie."

Twenty-Eight

Wind howled through the trees, rocked the lodge on its stilts, squealed and blew snow in under the door and around loose windows. Skittering sounds echoed from the walls. Not mice or even the big rat that too often at night showed his red eyes, but mud daubing crumbling with the blizzard and rattling down like loose gravel. The sharp slices of cold, knifing in between logs threatened to dig out Matron's pen, Effie's spoons, and throw down Grandma Teegan's braid.

In the glow of the nearly burned-out logs, Bridget peeked out from where she'd cocooned herself in the buffalo hide close to the fire. Effie, with her bed also pushed to the fire, finally lay still beneath her layers: two dresses, her shoes, her black cloth, the Never Forget quilt, and on top, Rev. Jackdaw's coat. For hours she'd cried over how the noise was Injuns whooping. At other times, when the wind lulled, "I'm left here." And later still, "I hate him. He don't care if we die. I can't give him sons. I'm so skinny now, I don't even bleed. I'm as dried up inside as Granny." Finally, exhausted and with paper packed in her ears, she slept.

Bridget pulled her knees up and hugged them. She didn't fear Indians circled the lodge; she wished Chief would come and carry them to his warm house. She did fear for Effie. Effie mumbled and cried too much. Jake, suffering out in the blizzard, was a worry too. After weeks of snow, with only half days of spattering sun, his haunches and ribs had floated up to where only his skin held them together. She needed to go and steal more hay from Chief's stacks. She'd done it before, walking over snow so frozen she didn't leave tracks, and the barbed wire fence separating the trees from his pasture was only a single strand rather than four. Using the gunnysack she found in the skinning shed and used to carry Effie's shucks, she crouched into the caves of hay the cows had made by all eating at the same spot. Out of the wind and out of sight of Chief's buildings, she filled her sack. Cows milled around her, their pools of frozen pee on the ground making shiny, emerald plates.

Each time Bridget carried a bulging gunnysack home, she rationed the hay, making it last a few days. But over the last two days, leaving the lodge to steal hay with the blizzard roaring outside had been too dangerous. Even going out for firewood stacked at the side of the lodge made Effie slip the lasso around Bridget's waist and tie the other end around the back of a chair. Then, at the door left open a crack to allow for the rope, Effie sat on the chair and gripped the rough braiding, letting it slide through her fingers, then tugging it back in when it grew slack with Bridget's return.

Taking wood from the snowy pile, Bridget called to Jake, but the wind sucked away her yelling before it reached her own ears. Snow blew sideways and whipped up and down in great sheets of white that blocked even a view of the skinning shed and Wilcox. Glimpses of what she at first thought was Jake's outline whirled, and disappeared.

Effie moaned in her sleep and turned over, the corn shucks in her mattress crackling.

Bridget sat up. She'd suggested to Effie that Jake could eat some of the corn shucks, but Effie shook her head and refused. Bridget even showed her the page in Dr. Chase's book where he prescribed boiled husks for sickly animals.

Effie's eyes had filled. "Give up even my bed?"

Another twelve hours had passed since Effie's refusal. In all that time, the storm had continued to pound against Jake's hungry body. Had he found bits of loose bark, tips of edible hanging limbs?

Bridget slowly folded back the heavy hide, felt the cold, and wished she could avoid doing what she knew she must. *Nera, Nera.* Effie didn't need all the shucks in her mattress, only the thought of them. If some were taken while she slept, she wouldn't know the difference. Just a small hole, a couple of inches along the bottom seam, would be enough. With that space, two fingers could be poked in and one by one, a dozen corn shucks slid out. Effie could mend the place easy enough if she ever discovered it.

Bridget worked herself to her feet, took a small step and winced. She slept in her shoes too, and over the last several days her feet had grown raw and painful. The shoes, like her dress, had been given to her before she boarded the train. Tight at the time, and now her feet had grown. And each time the leather got wet—almost daily—the shoes dried harder and smaller.

She tiptoed, clenching her teeth with each step, to the table and the knife she'd last seen lying there. With each board's creak and each gust of wind knocking against the walls, she stopped and watched for Effie's eyes to open. Would the paper in her ears be enough?

The large knife felt cumbersome and too big for the delicate job, but Bridget had no choice. At the foot of Effie's bed, she hesitated. Effie lay curled in the center of the mattress, leaving the thin ticking exposed at the bottom, but the room was too dark to see much. Bridget squinted and probed with her fingers to find the puckered seam. She fitted the blade tip between what she hoped was two stitches. She pushed. One nick. One popped thread. Then another. She pulled out a fistful of crisp husks.

A wind gust struck the back wall with such force Bridget jumped, felt the lodge sway and feared this time the box of it would topple off its sticks.

Effie's eyes opened. Wider. She screamed, the shiny blade in Bridget's hand catching firelight.

"It's me," Bridget screamed just as loud. "It's me. I'm not an Indian."

Effie scrambled out of her bed, yanking the paper wads from her ears. "You were going to kill me!"

"No." Bridget swung the knife behind her back and let the handle slide from her fingers. There was a soft thud as the knife tip stuck upright in the old floor, then a plink as it fell over.

Effie spotted the corn husks and descended on Bridget. "Oh, God!"

"Jake will die!" Bridget squatted and covered her head against the slaps raining down on her.

"It's *my* mattress. You have your hide."

"Rev. Jackdaw won't build you a house if Jake starves."

Effie slapped again, sank back onto her bed, and stared unblinking at her hands. After a long moment, she dropped her face into them. Sobs dragged and sucked behind her fingers. "I'm sorry, you scared me. I can't do this any longer."

Bridget sat beside her, a hand on Effie's back feeling the knuckles of bones that made Effie's spine.

They sat shivering to the sounds of the howling wind and rattling windows until cold forced them back beneath their covers. Bridget watched Effie stare out into the dark room, her fight for sleep with the wind and cold beginning all over again. Would this be the time her mind went too far and couldn't find its way back? Or didn't want to try?

"What if he never returns?" Effie asked. "What if we die here?"

"We aren't dying today," Bridget said. "And we aren't dying tomorrow. We are fighting death."

She wasn't so sure about Jake. She fought back a moan that sounded in her heart like one of Effie's.

Twenty-Nine

Carrying the smelly pail, Bridget entered the trees to the left of the lodge, opposite the path leading to Old Mag, and dumped her and Effie's waste from the last two days. She gagged and banged the tin against a tree to knock out the frozen layer in the bottom.

Jake was nowhere to be seen, but she prayed he'd spent the storm in the trees, seeking what shelter he could. She'd return the pail, rewrapped her stinging toes, and go look for him. Stepping from the trees, a wide whirl of snow like a summer dust devil lifted off the frozen river. The shape, thin and empty, looked like Effie's white underslip. The bit of ghost clothing danced onto the shore. Bridget stood fixed as it waltzed a few feet more before stopping and falling away. Was it an omen? If Grandma Teegan were there, she'd know. Would she say shadows around bodies aren't the only warnings?

The sound of wagons rumbling made her spin and look past the lodge to the road. The noise grew louder, squeezing her stomach: four large draft horses, four jingling traces, sixteen hoofs, four rolling iron wheels beneath a large, creaking wagon. Deet! That first wagon always carried the supplies she was now familiar with—bottles of beer and whiskey, piles of shiny rifles and shotguns with names engraved on the stocks, cages of pigeons under tarpaulins.

The sound swelled: four more draft horses, four more jingling traces, sixteen more hoofs, four more rolling iron wheels beneath the second wagon. That wagon held men.

The caravan stopped at the top of the ridge. Bridget looked again for Jake, this time willing him to stay out of sight. If Jake couldn't be found, he couldn't be yoked and mistreated.

Deet came around the corner of the lodge, a trail of men on his heels, and a long gun over each shoulder. He stopped at seeing Bridget. "Where's the ox?"

She wished she could lie and say Jake died in the blizzard, but Deet with his big ears and beady eyes would want to see the bones. Then to punish her for the lie, he'd send her and Effie away for sure.

"There's the beast," Bear-man said from the steps of the shed. He growled around a thick cigar.

Jake was coming from along the river, his eyes straight ahead, his ears up, his gait steady. Had he heard the wagons and knew to come? Too obedient, too trained and well behaved to save himself. He came to her and nudged against her chest, but she didn't wrap her arms around his thick neck.

"He ain't eating enough." Deet ran a gloved hand over Jake's ribs.

Bridget couldn't have another run-in with Deet. "There's been too much snow." She looked again at Jake, hoped he could hear her thoughts. *Do everything he says.*

She had a very bad feeling. She couldn't name all the signs. There weren't little sheep leading rams in the sky, but she'd seen a snow dress form and die. There was too much to try and make sense of. Last time, she'd followed the trappers and Jake only a short way, and she'd seen Jake fall and Mr. Deet yell and use his whip. She'd wondered why men thought they owned the world, thought everything in it had no more feeling than stone.

She took the ramp slowly and went inside. Effie sat close to one back window, the curtain lifted off. Huddled and silent, she stared through the frosty pane. At the second back window, Bridget lifted the curtain and saw Johnny's marbles. She touched them, longed to take them. If she stole them, her mind would be consumed with wondering how long before she was caught instead of worry for Jake. All Effie's spoons were buried in the walls now, and she didn't even know it. So were two of her copper combs, taken on days when Effie had stared straight ahead for hours and Bridget needed to keep the lodge from closing in on them.

She lifted her fingers from the marbles and scratched at the window. Ice crystals dusted like cold ashes onto her shoes.

"They don't even know I'm here," Effie said.

Effie's sadness added to Bridget's, and she felt torn between worry for Effie and worry for Jake. At the sound of shouting, she cracked the door open just wide enough to peer out. Deet and another man carried out the yoke. They settled the heavy top piece over Jake's shoulders, ignoring his collar, then the bow under his neck, and inserted the iron pins.

Knocking on Jake's knees with the toe of his boot and geeing and hawing, Deet backed him to the sled. He secured the chains in the rings, and three men dropped their steel traps on the bed then climbed on. Jake leaned into the weight and they headed upriver, leaving the remaining three men behind to drink and play cards.

Bridget closed the door and dropped her head against it.

The trappers always made the ache in Effie's stomach swell and spread. In Omaha, she was sure they ate big meals of roast beef, potatoes, warm bread, fruit stewed in juices. Even trying to imagine their parlors and the fine dresses their wives wore felt like trying to enter some impossible fantasy, a world apart from the nightmare that held her.

Her stomach growled, and she eyed the nearly empty pan on the table. They'd eaten the bread-like concoction warm the two previous mornings, then had slivers again last night. Cold, but dribbled with their last drops of molasses. There might be pigeons later, or the scrap in the pan might have to last until she found the energy and courage to face Graf. If ever she could. Was it three days already since she'd stumbled into the mercantile to the stony face of Graf? "Your bill's been paid," he said.

A wave of relief passed over her, but before she could enjoy the moment and wonder if Rev. Jackdaw had been in town, Graf stopped her. "I don't like it. A man ought to pay his own, but paid is paid."

His stance, like one of the long icicles hanging from the eaves in front of his shop, frightened her. "It wasn't paid by Rev. Jackdaw?" She could think of only one other person who even realized she lived there. "Was it Mr. Thayer?"

"Chief."

A wash of disgrace and shame burned her face and steamed down the length of her back. The Injun had heard her fighting with Graf. But to pay the bill! Did Graf now think they associated with one another? Did he think . . . ? She couldn't bear the thought. She began backing away. Everything she'd believed was good and right was spinning out of control.

Graf reached under the counter and lifted out a pound sack of corn meal. "Infested," he said. "No charge." He pushed it in her direction. "At Andersonville, men would have killed for much less."

Was it another test of her neediness or how like each other they were? What man saved such a thing? She picked up the sack she scarcely wanted to touch, let alone eat. She'd reached a new low. So had Graf.

Not yet out the mercantile door, she caught a glimpse of Cora stepping through the curtains, but she didn't stop. She heard them whisper behind her, then, "Oh, Mr. Graf, you didn't!"

What did Cora know of facing Rev. Jackdaw's jerking eye? What did she know of hunger? Or the shame of having to accept charity? From an Injun, no less. Could she ever understand how accepting infested meal carried less emotional debt and hurt than accepting good?

Back at the lodge, she spread the flour across the table with the flat of her hand. She picked out the black weevils and the squirming larva and tried to make bread.

Bridget was still at the other window, her head wrapped in rags like some sad cap. She'd gotten taller in the months since their arrival in Nebraska, but she was skinny and underfed.

There were times, frightful-awful times, needles in Effie's brain, when she lost her temper with Bridget for no reason. She knew what it was: pain swelling to her outer reaches, pain exploding through the ends of her nerves.

She longed to reach out, call Bridget over, hold her, and keep her safe. But affection might be as cruel as neglect. Bridget was better off not feeling any attachment to her. The child might still get away, and the less strings, the easier her escape.

Thirty

Bridget checked the door every hour for the sight of Jake returning safely. Late afternoon, with winter's early dusk settling, she saw him coming out of the trees. Lumpy shapes on the sled were two men with their long, wide boots dragging off the back, furrowing the snow and making extra work for Jake. But he looked unhurt. Nothing else mattered.

They wasted little time removing the yoke and climbing the slope. They fastened feedbags to the four horses they'd unhitched but kept tied to the sides of one wagon. Climbing into the second, they headed for the hotel in Bleaksville.

Bridget grimaced as she worked one painful foot into her too small shoe and then the other, carving the blisters deeper as the toes scraped against the rock-hard leather. The long arms of Rev. Jackdaw's tattered coat meant she could pull the sleeve ends inside and hold them closed. She thought to tell Effie she was going out, but Effie stared at the window, the glass sealed over with frost.

Bridget soothed the four draft horses, speaking to each one as she pulled the head straps of the feedbags first over one ear and then the other. She poured the oats from each paunchy bag into her pail. "Sorry, sorry," she said, re-attaching the empty bags. She remembered Rev. Jackdaw questioning her at the school in New Ulm. "No," she said aloud, "I'm not scared of animals."

She fed Jake only a small portion of the oats. She'd read in Dr. Chase's book about the ill effects on animals of a sudden, too-rich diet.

"You can have more tomorrow." She rubbed his shoulders where the yoke had rested. "Only one more day," she promised. Then in a whisper to herself, "One more long day."

Her feet hurt too much for the trek to Old Mag. She led Jake to Wilcox-the-tree and sat, looking out at the frozen river. Down nearly to Pete's back yard, steel traps lay waiting. They would snap through the night, and by morning the men would have pelts. She couldn't help the animals any more than she could spare Jake the morrow. The traps were invisible even in the daylight, covered with leaves and dustings of snow. If she tried to find them in the dark, she'd likely step in one, and the men would find her frozen there in the morning. And she'd leave footprints the men would know were hers. Deet would force her and Effie to leave, and she'd lose Jake forever.

She tucked Rev. Jackdaw's coat tight under her burning feet and huddled in the tent of wool. "Mum?" She looked out over the frozen water. "Are you there?"

No answer came and she dropped her face into her knees. In the distance, a fox yipped. Then a long rope of agony unwound in the night. She rocked as the eerie, agonizing howls rent the blue-black dark.

Thirty-One

In the morning, while Effie still slept, Bridget reached into the last bit of Chief's salve. Her fingers touched the bottom of the jar. She spread the ointment on her toes' weeping blisters and wrapped dry strips of newspaper around them. Only the thinnest layer; her stiff shoes were already too small. She tied the broken laces and hobbled back and forth in front of the fire, coaxing her feet into accepting the pain.

When Effie woke to the sound of the trappers returning, Bridget watched her leave the bed with the quilt around her shoulders, a red slash of fabric settled over her heart, and sit again at the window. Only blurred shapes of the men were visible through the thick ice covering the glass, dark and shadowy figures yoking Jake and climbing on the sled. Effie stared just as she had the day before, her bottom lip tucked beneath the top. "Rev. Jackdaw has abandoned us."

"No, he hasn't." Bridget said. "But Nell is old and the roads always have so much snow."

Effie's face struggled. She'd slept in her green dress and the front had places the size of Bridget's palm where the damaged fabric looked shattered. "He could ride with Deet. Take the train."

Bridget wanted away from Effie and how Effie's thin fingers clawed the quilt around her shoulders. Away from Effie's hollow cheeks and Effie's drifting eyes that saw invisible things. But Bridget had to give the men a head start.

Logs crackled in the fire. Flames reached up, but every corner of the lodge held winter and every wall breathed drafts. Effie continued to stare at frost white as a blindman's eyes. "I could hide under their tarps, but in Omaha I wouldn't have no money for a train ticket home." She looked down at herself. "I don't want Ma, or Johnny, seeing me like this." Her voice caught. "Pa wouldn't let me stay. He'd want quit of me again."

Bridget's stomach twisted. Effie had no way of leaving her, but she wanted to do so.

The hem of Rev. Jackdaw's coat was ragged from weeks of dragging on the ground and through scrub. Thorny thistle seeds had worked into the fabric pocket-high. Bridget pushed her arms into the sleeves and opened the door one cold inch.

The way the men cussed at one another on the second day no longer surprised her. Nor did the increased flash of whiskey bottles and flasks. On the second day, eyes were redder, the men moved slower, and they were angry. As if they'd not slept the night before, but gambled and lost their money and drank till dawn in the Bleaksville saloon. They were not only tired, the hardest work remained: recovering the traps, harvesting the pelts, reloading the wagons. And paying off debts. All of which made them meaner. On the second day, too, no longer concerned about their scents and noise, all the men went out.

"Step on," Deet yelled, and Jake leaned into his yoke.

She let them go into the trees in the direction of Pete's house and counted to ten before hurrying down the ramp on her sore feet. Following was dangerous. Effie thought it plain stupid. But Jake knew she was there. He knew she hid in the trees and watched him and that was everything. He knew he wasn't alone. Just as Grandma Teegan had held Bridget tight after Mum left, tight after Rowan died. Even when they needed to step a few feet apart, Grandma Teegan kept an invisible rope tied around Bridget. The other end tied around herself. When Bridget fell weeping, when she couldn't sleep or eat, Grandma Teegan felt a tug on the rope and held her again.

Snow began to fall. Bridget kept well back, avoiding the wider, easier path, crouching and working her way through the thick brush.

All that mattered was Jake knowing she was there, and he did. He was smarter than the men. The two of them were best friends, and friends stayed with friends even when staying right there was the only help they could give.

Men recovered traps and the iron hit the sled with loud clangs. The bodies of mink, beaver, and even a frozen wolverine landed with duller sounds. The smell of animals, blood, and death—kept low by the cold air—rose from the sled. Bridget looked away from the carcasses and promised herself Jake was doing fine. Today there wasn't going to be any trouble.

At the next stop, Bear-man climbed off and kicked at one of his traps. He bent and lifted the gruesome stump of a fox's foot. He hurled it into the river. "That goddamn varmint stole my pelt."

Bridget shivered. She thought of the pair of small foxes with their black-tipped ears and white muzzles that lived in the trees. She'd seen them darting, one on the red tail of the other. How many hours had it taken the snared fox to eat off its own foot? And how much pain?

"Next time," Bear-man growled, "I'll kill the sonabitch."

That day, Bridget knew, would never come. The fox was already dead. Or would be soon. A three-legged fox—even if it hadn't bled to death—wouldn't survive in the wild.

Jake was yelled onward. The men continued drinking and pulling traps from runnels where the river cut in under grass and scrub. Or snares set along paths where tracks had been seen. With each recovered trap, Bridget tried to reassure herself everything was fine. Her feet hurt so bad she struggled to keep up, but the day was nearly over. Soon she and Jake would be home. She could take off her shoes, sit by the fire, and warm her feet.

A quarter of a mile farther on, with Pete's house up ahead, Jake was stopped again. They'd nearly reached the end of the run, and the sled looked to hold as many traps as it had the day before when they left the clearing. Bridget crouched, waiting for the trap to be recovered.

Her feet felt swollen to three times their normal size. They throbbed and burned so bad tears ran down her cheeks, and she fought the urge to rip off her shoes. If she could just rub each foot for a minute or two. But she knew she might never be able to work her feet back into the awful leather. Panic washed over her. Could she make it back to the lodge?

"The son of a bitch stole my Newhouse."

Bridget's heart squeezed; they weren't done yet.

Bear-man cussed at a felled birch tree half on land and half submerged in the river under thick ice. Still-visible links of chain proved his trap had been pulled under the trunk.

"Walk that plank," a voice goaded. "Go get the sucker."

Bear-man paced, his face turning red. "Jesus Christ couldn't walk that log. Ain't no way of pulling that trap up in one piece."

More squabbling, though most of it was carried off in the wind and muffled by the bare branches sawing against one another over Bridget's head.

". . . not losing another pelt . . . my best Newhouse."

Then one remark, stark in its clarity: "That skinny, worn-out old ox."

The words hit Bridget with the force of a fist.

More arguing, then Deet. "I'll take that bet." He unharnessed Jake from the sled and took him to the water's edge. Again, the geeing and hawing and tapping on Jake's knees until Deet had him lined up. They fastened the chains hanging from the two sides of his yoke to the end of the tree.

"Step on," Deet yelled. And before Jake could move, "Heave!"

Link by link, the chain caught and snapped tight. Jake's hoofs dug into the snow as he leaned into the load, his head stretching out, his legs straining. The ice cracked behind him and small white splinters raced out from around the tree, but it didn't move.

"Christ, I'm cold," someone grumbled. "Leave the damn trap."

"Heave!" Deet bellowed again. "Heave!"

Again Jake leaned, his shoulders rolled, his front knees bent, his neck stretched long, and his whole body strained.

Bridget couldn't watch. She pulled her arms in tighter to her chest and slid down the backside of the tree she used for cover.

"I put a dollar on the blasted tree," Bear-man sneered. "Pay up."

Bridget peeked to see Deet searching for something to use as a club, then stepping up to the steel traps on the sled. Chains, closed jaws and pans.

Deet stood wide-legged, struggled a moment for balance as though an invisible hand pushed him into leaning forward, then into leaning backwards. He hoisted a trap.

Bear-man spat tobacco juice and put a bottle to his wet lips. His Adam's apple went up and down.

Deet blinked slowly, his ears bright red, and he stepped up to Jake. "I'll make the buzzard bait do it." He fisted the trap by its closed jaws; the chain and six-inch spike swung in the cold air. "He can't pull out that tree, I'll shoot him myself."

Bridget whimpered as the spike whipped at the end of its chain.

"Heave!"

Jake lurched sideways with the hit, his right rear leg jumping as the iron landed with a thud on his flank. He pulled again, the motion rolling up the length of his body, the chains straining. More ice cracked, shattering farther out from the tree in all directions. The tree trunk shivered.

Bridget's hands trembled deep in the sleeves of Rev. Jackdaw's coat. She slapped them over her ears. If she tried to stop Deet, she and Effie would be sent away. Jake needed her. No one else would move to the lodge and beat snow off scrub, steal hay, even corn shucks from Effie's bed.

With the next strike, Jake's lowing was a long moan. His back arched, his hind legs tried to step up under his body, his lungs sucked in blue air and heaved out white.

Deet dropped the trap and slumped forward, one hand gripping a knee, the other clutching his chest. He puffed clouds. "My heart can't take this."

"You goin' to shoot that ox, Deet? Or you a liar?"

"Not now," a man snorted. He shot snot from one nostril and pinched it off. "I ain't walking. Get us back first."

Bridget's stomach twisted hard. *Deet won't do it, he won't. He is a liar.*

Deet took his gun from the sled, opened his coat to the vest beneath and pulled a shell from a row of sewn notches. He cracked the gun, thumbed in a shell. "I said I'd shoot the thing. I'll shoot the damn thing!"

Bridget jumped from hiding and pain shot from her feet up to her knees. She tripped only a few feet from where she'd started.

Deet pointed his shotgun at Jake's head.

She screamed, the sound cutting through the underbrush, echoing off trees, and running out ahead of her. "Hit him harder; he can do it."

Through the brush, she saw heads turn in her direction. But they couldn't see her. They couldn't see her just as they couldn't see Effie sitting at the window wanting to go home. She was nothing to them, just as Jake was nothing, and *nothing* had no shape or size.

But Jake knew her voice and didn't understand why she'd turned on him.

Deet lowered his gun. With one hand on the gunstock and one hand on the barrel, he handed the weapon to Bear-man. He picked up the trap again—this time by the spike. The pan, with its clamped, half-moon of forged iron, swung in the air. He used the trap like a ball bat.

"Heave!"

Jake bellowed and jerked with the strike and a wide swath of skin on his flank opened like a small door on a flooding red room. His shoulder muscles shuddered and rolled.

The tree slid up onto the sand. The end of the broken chain glistened. No beaver. No trap.

Thirty-Two

The men finished retrieving their traps, but Bridget's feet hurt too bad to follow the sled the long trek back through the trees. She worked her way, climbing up toward the road through thick snowy brush. Several times a foot sank into a hole and needed pulling out. Reaching the road, her knees nearly buckled with defeat. She had well over a mile to home.

She fought against simply sitting down and giving up, but Jake was bleeding and he needed her. Limping and struggling to hold back tears, she started off. She took one step and then another, watching only the road crawling under her.

"Can't you hear?" Pete stopped in front of her, riding the horse he'd ridden when he came with news of the rocker. The snow was letting up, yet flakes settled over his cap and shoulders. "You okay? Why you walking like you can't?"

"My feet."

He glanced back over his shoulder at the distance to the lodge. "Come on, I got time." He leaned down, sliding off-center of the horse's broad back, and turned his foot out. "Step on my shoe."

She had no choice but to reach for the hand he extended—touching him for the first time—and then stepping onto his boot. He pulled her up behind him, surprising her with his strength. She grabbed around his waist, thankful he faced forward and couldn't see her relief and embarrassment. He'd changed in the few months since his mother's death when he'd stood with a black eye on the doorstep. He seemed a full year older. Was he as much as fifteen or sixteen?

“They must be trapping,” he said. “I saw the wagons in front of your place. Deet’s a mean old bastard. More ’an once he yelled at Ma to get off his property.”

Bridget held tight.

“Ain’t you got a decent hat?” Pete asked. “More’n just . . . ?” *Rags,* but he managed not to say it.

They finished rounding the bend with the lodge just ahead and Deet’s horses and wagons on the ridge. Did they remind Pete of his mother’s funeral procession?

“We watched you walk by,” she said. “Did Chief build your mum’s box?”

Pete ignored the mention of his mother but for a small suck of air. “I used to believe he was a vampire.” He spoke over his shoulder and the steady clopping, muffled by the snow, of the heavy horse. “He builds coffins all night long.”

“How do you know?”

“Hammers half the night. There aren’t *that* many folks dying around here. I thought he killed people just to fill up his handiwork.”

The inflections in Pete’s voice said he teased her, but still she wondered. “There’s bedrooms upstairs, but he sleeps on a sofa downstairs.”

“How you know that?”

She’d already said too much. “If he killed people, there’d be folks missing.”

“There’s talk he went loco during the Civil War.”

“How do people know that?” Chief had carried her out of the cold and given her salve for her burns. That wasn’t loco.

“The Union,” Pete went on, “put him working with the darkies, cleaning up the battlefields. He worked day and night burying the dead. Thayer said bodies had legs blown off, bellies ripped open, faces gone. The stink like nothing else in the world.”

Bridget clutched tighter.

"Chief was alright at first. Then he quit talking. Nothing but mumbling and swinging in his sleep. They didn't know if he was fighting Secesh or the clouds of flies and flocks of buzzards eating boys' bodies. He was older than most he buried and with a son back home. Heat cooked the dead, varmints came, and most soldiers got no more than a trough in the dirt. Just getting 'em outta the sun and under."

Bridget swallowed. She didn't want these things to be true, and she didn't like Thayer. "How does Mr. Thayer know?"

"He weren't but ten hisself. Went to school with Chief's boy. The town had a send-off at the depot when a carload from Bleaksville left to fight. Thayer's daddy was one of them, Chief, Mr. Graf, others. The army kept the Bleaksville lads in the same regiment, and those who lived come home with the same stories. They said Chief got to stinking like death, couldn't keep the smell off hisself. Got so he didn't even try. Or sleep. He hated shoveling dirt onto boys so much he started spending his nights looking for wood. Carrying back lumber from chicken coops, porches, privies—anything he could tear down to make a box. Couldn't stop himself. Still can't, though with a lumber yard in town our privies are safe."

How could anyone bury the bloody dead all day and not go crazy? Bury them young as Rowan. She'd gone some loco when she woke and found Rowan dead beside her. Loco when dirt hit his box. Effie had gone some loco when her baby sister was buried—though Bridget still didn't know that whole story.

"When he returned from the war," Pete shook his head, "and found his boy drowned in the river while playing on ice and the body never recovered, he started walking up and down the banks. And building coffins."

Bridget tightened her grip. She'd wanted to tell him about Jake's injury, but after the story of Chief, the whole world seemed too heavy for talk.

Walking the horse past one of Deet's wagons, Pete stopped on the ridge directly in front of the lodge. "Can you make it from here? It's too slick to ride her down."

Bridget could see in the closest wagon what she'd not thought to look for the night before: *Oats. Half a bag.* Taking them would help even the score for Deet's meanness, help Jake's hunger—he was one of Deet's animals too—and help quiet the fish jumping in her stomach.

"Bastard," Pete said, as if reading her mind. "I'd like to make him pay for hurting Ma."

"Let's do it," Bridget said. "He hurt Jake." Emotion caught in her throat. "He swung a trap and cut him bad."

Pete's breath eased out. "Ma never wanted me to make trouble where I couldn't win. Deet is something you ain't going to win."

"Why? Because I'm a girl, or a half orphan? Or Irish?" All day she'd been telling herself to stay hidden and not cause trouble. The worst still happened, and Jake heard her yell, "Hit him harder."

Deet's horses shimmied, shaking snow off their backs and making their long traces jingle. She thought of Rev. Jackdaw continually checking his lines. Cursing each new split in the aging rawhide.

"You got a knife?"

"Huh?"

She knew what she'd do and the decision made her brave enough to grab Pete's arm. Holding on to him, she eased off the horse rather than jumping and landing hard on her feet. Still, she winced as pain shot from her toes along the soles of her feet and up to her knees. "Give me your knife."

His eyes, just visible beneath his low hat brim, studied her.

"He was mean to your ma."

"You ain't going to fix that."

"Maybe he will stop coming back." She put her hands on her hips. "I'm not going to stick a person."

He worked a small knife from a pocket in his pants. "You ain't strong enough, anyway."

Her heels squished in her wet shoes and her toes felt hammered. She pushed back a coat sleeve and reached up, her hand blue with cold. "Give it. For your ma."

After craning his neck toward the trees for the sound of anyone coming, he handed over the knife.

She hurried. She wouldn't touch a neck or loin strap for fear of nicking a horse; she'd only weaken the traces and reins. And only on the rig Deet had taken to Bleaksville the night before. That way, no one could prove it hadn't happened there.

She pulled the blade across a leather strap and then again. Nothing. Not even a scratch.

Pete harrumphed. "I told you."

"You gave me a spoon." It wasn't fair, Chief was loco and Effie was becoming a ghost and Deet got to hurt Jake, and she couldn't do a thing to stop any of it. She turned, ready to give back the worthless knife when she caught her reflection in the eye of the horse less than an arm's length away. A tiny Bridget, wet and defeated. Left behind by everyone who was supposed to be her family.

The horse whinnied, stomped, but its large dark eyes never left her. Like the world in Jake's eyes. Pete didn't understand her need to fight death, but the horse did.

She bent again to the leather, stretched it over the blade and pulled up. The knife sliced and the leather opened. The two-inch thick strap now had only a half-inch still intact.

"Come on," Pete said. "Get away from there now."

Bridget picked another strap and watched as the leather breeched under the knife. "They'll make it back to Omaha," she said. "For sure most of the way."

"Gimme my knife."

Blood ran down Jake's leg and a flap of skin hung off his hip. She reached for another strap.

"Gimme my knife or I'll come take it."

She'd weakened the leather in only two places, but that helped.

"I'm not leaving," Pete said, "until you give it back."

She ignored him and went for the oats, the sack looking like a child hunched in old brown clothes. It weighed too much to lift up and over the sideboard from the ground. She climbed wheel spokes, the pressure like knives up her legs, stepped in, and dropped the sack over the side. Across the wagon lay a pile of saddlebags, male luggage that withstood the weather. And a second lumpy gunnysack—was it also oats? She widened the top. "It's a pair of boots." She looked at Pete's worn boots. "Do you want them?"

He stretched forward over his horse's shoulders and looked, squinting at the fancy red leaves twisting around the boot's ankle and the vine of red leaves winding up the sides. "I can't walk around in those." He settled back. "I want my knife. Or you planning to keep it?"

"Suit yourself." She threw the sack and its contents as far as she could. It landed only a few feet away with a dull sound and a small puff of snow. Still visible.

Pete nudged the horse even closer alongside the wagon and held out his hand. "Give it."

Keeping his knife was the only thing keeping him. "You didn't see Deet pick up a trap and cut Jake. I don't know what's going to happen."

He took his time answering, looking at her and then at the broken lodge with smoke rising from the chimney. "Lots can happen or not happen. You don't need trouble with the sheriff. He spits in the wind to see in what direction men like Deet want him to piss. You and yours ain't much liked around here. You don't want to cross either man."

She wanted to ask Pete if he was much liked, but she knew the answer: he was river people, and Effie said his mum had lived with Mr. Thayer as an unmarried woman.

Pete leaned over the side of the wagon, grabbed her arm, opened her hand, and took his knife. He folded down the blade.

"Get out of here. Let the snow work on our tracks." He also smiled and gave her a slow nod, saying he understood. Still, he would go.

His smile helped do what throwing the boots, stealing oats, and cutting lines hadn't. She let him reach over again, grab her around the waist, lift her from the wagon, and set her on the ground. "Go." He turned his horse, kicked the flanks, and started off. He liked her and wanted to keep her safe. He'd even lifted her out of the wagon. Maybe it was more that he'd pulled her out and kept her from falling, but all the same, he'd reached for her.

Expecting the men to come through the trees to the right of the lodge, she went down the slope to the left, carrying the oats. When she glanced back over her shoulder, Pete was already gone.

She sat the sack just inside the trees and thought about going back up for the boots. Would Deet find them and blame her? Even stuffed with paper or straw, walking in them would be impossible, and she couldn't wear them without Rev. Jackdaw and others knowing she'd stolen them. They were too big to hide in the walls. Rev. Jackdaw would like them, preach in them, but he'd knock her to the floor for taking them.

Effie still stared at the glass when Bridget entered. Her long yellow hair hung down the sides of her thin face, and she seemed especially small and pale. The room was cold.

Bridget dropped before the nearly burned-out logs. She gritted her teeth as she pulled off one soaked shoe and then the other. Finally, she unwound the bloody strips of newsprint from her toes, each with a weeping red eye.

She threw the paper scraps onto the glowing embers. Trying to keep her weight on her heels, she rose, added two logs, and set her shoes as close to the flames as she dared. She needed to go out again and tend Jake's wound, but she couldn't do that until the men left. While she waited, the wet leather would warm, and she'd use dry strips of newsprint around her toes. With the warmth and dryness, she'd somehow force her feet back into her shoes.

She limped back and forth to fight the itching and burning, then sat on the hide trying to massage away the pain. The boots she'd thrown worried her. If Deet saw the gunnysack, she couldn't blame anyone else. Pete was right: she was going to be caught.

She dragged one of the two straight-back chairs across the plank flooring and cracked the back door open only the slit she needed to see out. The men were back.

Over the next hour, some carried in traps, others carried out the pelts of small animals just skinned. Most of the pelts would go back with them to Omaha, but Deet nailed two muskrat hides to the side of the shed. Jake stood in front. Even after having his yoke removed, he stood obedient, his head down, his starving ribs visible, and his wounded leg bent at the knee. Deet hadn't yet commanded him to walk on. Twists of blood had dried down his leg from his flank. Maybe she'd saved his life earlier by shouting, and maybe she'd only postponed his death. Now that they were back, would they still want to shoot him?

"Walk on," she called as loud as she dared. "Walk on."

He didn't move.

"If that animal was dead," the floor groaned beneath Effie's rocking, "Deet wouldn't have a reason to keep us here. We could live in Omaha."

Bridget wanted to run to the rocker and tip Effie out. All Effie thought about was getting away. Leaving Jake behind and getting to Omaha. "It isn't just Jake. Deet would still want to trap, and he'd still need his pelts and trees watched." She flung open the door and screamed, "Walk on!"

Jake took a halting step, but stopped as the door to the shed opened. Deet wore his hat, but no coat. His sleeves were rolled to his elbows, and he carried a tub of skinned animals. Taking the rickety steps down, he bounced drunkenly against the rail, but regained his balance. He glanced at Jake's stance and the slice of flayed skin, but only walked around the backside of the shed to the river's edge and flung the waste. On his trip back, the empty tub hanging loose from his hand and dripping red into the white snow, he climbed the steps without looking.

"Walk on," Bridget said again.

Jake headed for the trees in the direction of Old Mag.

Bridget didn't allow herself a smile. Jake was only safe from Deet. Crows and turkey vultures dressed the ice with black wings, carrying off what Deet had thrown out. But once the cigar and pipe smoke had blown away and the trees were quiet again, the night hunters—wolves and coyotes—would come in search of fresh, warm meat. When they turned their noses up to the crisp winter air and followed the scent of blood, they'd find Jake.

The snow slowed, thinned, and stopped as the men finished inside and formed a loose circle outside. Deet pulled a small prayer book from his vest pocket—next to his rows of shells. It was Sunday. Those who held bottles or flasks in one hand took off their hats with the other and placed them over their liquor. Seconds later, they shouted "Amen." Hats rose, thick bottles glistened against wet lips.

Bear-man carried a crate from the shed. Opening a door on the top, he drew out a bird, one wing flapping loose in panic. Palming the pigeon's head, he used his thumb and with two quick jabs pushed in the bird's eyes. He threw it into the cold air. Wings flapping, the wounded creature flew, but crazed, right and left without direction. When it had gained a bit of height and a few yards of distance, guns exploded.

Eleven more targets, blinded and thrown, finished the cage. Bear-man carried out the second.

With the birds all blinded and dead, the men tossed two-days' worth of empty bottles. Tossed them drunkenly. Glass rained as the men shot bottles barely out of the thrower's hand. Beer, rum, wine. Bridget watched them flash in the sunlight, bottles of green, blue, and brown, some square, some round. Guns fired over the shouting and betting. Deet walked forward a bit, picked up a brown bottle with only the neck shot off, and tossed it again.

Guns fired.

As the explosions echoed into the woods, the clearing hushed. Deet dropped to his knees. Men lowered their guns. The side of Deet's face looked flayed opened, a swath of skin peeled back. Blood ran from the wound, off his chin, and down his front. One big ear was sliced half away.

"Bastards!" he howled. He managed to stand and take a wobbling step and dropped again. "I'm hit."

"They shot him," Bridget nearly screamed to Effie. "They shot his face. He's shot bad."

Men hurried in silence, grabbed up their possession—guns, dropped gloves, the empty pigeon cages—and helped drag Deet up the slope.

Once they'd left, Effie rose from her chair, paced back and forth in front of the table. "He won't likely die; he walked up on his own. Though he'll be uglier." She dropped back into her rocker, pushed her hands up and back along the arms. "Not even a scribbled note from Rev. Jackdaw, though he can write all day in his cursed book. Not even a 'how do' from the men." She rose again, swiped at the pan holding the two-inch square of infested bread, sending the metal spinning off and landing on the floor. "Stinking, rotten stuff." She picked up the knife still on the table and hurled it. The metal blade banged against the stovepipe and clattered to the floor. "I won't die here!"

Afraid of Effie's rage and the tears streaming down her face, Bridget worked her feet back into her shoes. The burning in her toes began with the first step, but she couldn't stop. If she hesitated, the pain might sit her down, and she'd not get to Jake until morning. She snatched up her coat, the bread from the floor, Chief's nearly empty jar of poultice, and the rope.

"You don't care about anything but that stupid animal," Effie cried.

He won't ever leave me. But the coil in Bridget's stomach kept her from saying it. She hobbled out and down the ramp. The air stunk of blood, tobacco smoke, and gunpowder. Dead birds and shattered glass covered the sand and the frozen river.

She found Jake several yards inside the trees, his head hanging. She feared the open skin on his flank wasn't his only injury. Had the strikes also broken a rib? Wincing, she touched salve to his wound, afraid it hurt as much as her toes. She rubbed more salve on the raw but still attached piece of hide showing half of the Flying D brand. The skin was already crusty with ice, and she rubbed it hard to try and warm it, then pressed the fur back in place. Winter meant two good things. No gnats or flies to lay their nasty maggot eggs on the injury. And the river was frozen, so Jake wouldn't be straying into dirty water to cool off. Running her fingers around the inside of the jar, she rubbed every bit of remaining poultice wide around the injury. Stopping his pain was more important than stopping hers. The salve might also help mask the smell of blood.

"I'm going to make you well," she said. And promised herself she would.

She pulled the bread from her pocket and rubbed his nose as his long, thick tongue reached and curled around the offering. "They shot his ear," she told him. She dropped her head against his cheek and though she couldn't wrap her arms all the way around his neck, she held on to him. "I'll never leave you. Effie can move to Omaha and leave us. We don't care."

Coming out of the trees with him, she widened the knot on the rope and slipped the lasso over his head. The free end she tied around the rail of the back ramp. He needed to stay close to the lodge where wolves were less likely to come. And he couldn't follow her while she picked up the worst shards of glass—the bottoms of the bottles that sat up straight as knives. If Jake stepped on one of those, stabbing it between his toes, Deet *would* shoot him.

With the worst glass cleared and thrown under the lodge between the stilts, she stepped again amongst the dropped feathers and picked up dead pigeons. Many had flown over the trees before being shot and dropped into the tangled undergrowth and others had flown over the frozen river. She wouldn't risk going for those. She picked up three, then four, then five birds along the shore. She and Effie would eat.

Thirty-Three

Using the iron grip, Effie lifted a lid on top of the four-hole stove and exposed the firebox. Cold and gray ashes, not the spark of a single live ember. She packed in kindling, a short log, and opened the small door on the front for draft. She'd spent the last weeks half starved. The last two days watching the shapes of men go about living. Two days of her mind wobbling like Granny's.

Cold hands fingered up Effie's spine. Daily she vowed to keep busier than the day before. To fight the fear of losing her mind, and daily she failed. Skeet's visit should have helped, but thinking of him and Homeplace only made her ache worse. Was he right? Had she brought Granny to the lodge?

She carried a trembling shovelful of hot coals from the fireplace, dumped them into the stove's firebox, poked and blew on the kindling.

The evening before, after the trappers left, Bridget lit the stove, plucked feathers from birds, used the tip of a knife blade and explored every tiny hole to pull out bits of feather and the lead pellet. Bridget who roasted two pigeons and pulled Effie to the table where they'd both eaten, letting juice roll down their chins, picking the last meat from the bones with their teeth.

Three dead birds remained in the pail at Effie's feet. Today, she'd cook for Bridget. She'd hold on. Was it February? In as early as a month, the weather would start warming. Afternoon temperatures would rise above freezing. Already she was noticing longer minutes of daylight and how the sun rose higher over the clearing. Winter's end meant workmen would finish her house in Omaha—Skeet had lied. She'd keep sane for the day she left this place. She wouldn't die in the miserable shack, and she wouldn't let Bridget die there either. She'd hold on for Omaha. Once there, she'd know what to do about her loveless marriage.

The back door swung open, and Bridget nearly fell through. Effie hurried to her. "What's wrong?"

Bridget shrugged off her coat, let it fall to the floor, hobbled across the room, and sank down in front of the fire.

"Are you hurt?"

The only answer was Bridget's whimpering. She cupped the heel of one shoe and slowly, no more than an inch at a time, eased it off her foot.

Effie cringed at the blood. "My God, what happened?"

Bridget sucked ragged breaths in between her teeth, slowly eased off her second shoe. She winced, bit her lips, and picked soaked and bloodied newsprint from around her toes.

The hope Effie felt moments before dropped away. She lifted each of Bridget's feet, turned them looking for gashes, but saw fresh blood only on the toes. "How long has this been going on? Why didn't you tell me?"

It's my fault, as much as the lye. Bridget hadn't come to her, hadn't trusted her enough. Effie's gut folded. Folded again. "It's you who's been carrying me. That's got to change."

She hurried for the pail, dumped the birds on the floor, and shoved the bucket under the water pump. Water rushed and stopped and she pumped again. From the nail above the sink, she grabbed the sugar sacking, stiff and gray with use. "It's that ox. You think you can't leave it alone a day. Like it's your only family." *Need it to be.*

She braced Bridget's right heel in her palm over the pail, dunked the rag and squeezed icy water onto the toes.

Bridget yelped and jerked, but Effie held tight. She dipped her rag and several times rinsed each small foot of blood and newsprint ink. Cleaned, Bridget's feet looked better. And worse. The blood came only from the tops of the toes, but the toes looked like half-chewed cranberries. Deep red gouges, bird pecked. Four toenails were pewter-colored and the toes themselves looked a sickly blue-gray. "Bridget," she choked, "how could your feet get this bad?" She followed Bridget's glance to what had become Bridget's corner and the empty jar of salve from Old Mag. "That stuff? It stopped the pain? A lot of good that did." She wanted to march up to Old Mag's door and give her a piece of her mind.

"Bridget," scolding now, "I know we have no money for shoes, but . . ." But what? What could she promise?

She threw the rag into the dirty water and sank back on her heels. Did a doctor need to be fetched? There was no way to pay the man anything. Would he even come to look at Bridget's feet, given they were river people? When Rev. Jackdaw found out she'd charge services for toes? "I can't stand it," she screamed, pushing herself up, pacing. "How does he expect us to live here? It's no wonder women sell themselves! Is that what I need to do?"

Bridget's face changed. She licked her lips. Again, wider, the way Effie had not seen her do in months. "Do you think my mum is a prostitute? Maybe she's in Omaha."

"Is that what you've been thinking? Hoping?" Effie sank back down beside her. "That your mother is living so close?"

"Rev. Jackdaw said they are Irish."

"I'm sure your ma is not a prostitute. But who could blame her?" She wouldn't tell Bridget yet again that the woman was dead. Had to be. She grabbed Bridget's shoes and threw them in the fire.

Bridget sprung to her knees and stretched for the flames. "My shoes!"

Effie grabbed her, held her struggling as flames curled up and around the shoes. Smoke rose from the tops, then licked through the small eyes. The cotton laces caught fire.

Bridget slumped, her body going limp.

Effie held her. "I miss my ma, too."

"We could have fixed them," Bridget said. "We could have cut out the toes."

"We'll share my shoes. Graf will never let us charge something so costly, but Rev. Jackdaw will be back soon." Dare she promise anything for that man?

Holding Bridget, rocking her, Effie remembered a night Ma held her. She sat in Ma's lap feeling too big and heavy to be held at ten-years-old. Yet Ma clutched her, not wanting to let her down. They were in a straight back chair near the kitchen stove, and Ma had only inches of a lap because of Johnny, who was days from being born. Her nearly non-existent lap was the reason Ma had to hold tight through the night to keep Effie from sliding off, so close they both felt Johnny's stirring in her belly. Then morning and a large pool of blood on the floor beneath them. As though both were giving birth.

"Nera, Nera," Bridget mumbled.

Effie dropped her arms. "What does that even mean? You say the strangest things."

"It means I won't be scared of the skeleton."

"When you talk like that," Effie closed her eyes, fought the picture of blood pooled beneath a chair, "are you doing it just to try and frighten me?"

The sound of a horse stopping made Effie stand. "Oh, not now." Was it Pete or Mr. Thayer and what did they want? She flipped a corner of a curtain. "It's Cora," Effie sighed. "I'm not letting her in. I don't want her seeing your feet."

On the porch, Effie thought to run up the ridge and stop Cora there, but the woman—who always rode like a man with one leg thrown over the saddle—was already starting down. Effie tried to relax her face, make it lie. Lifting her hands, she felt instinctively for her row of small combs. How could she have lost them all? She'd crawled around on the floor looking for them between planks.

Cora smiled, a basket swinging on her arm. She wore a hat, the likes of which Effie had never seen on a woman. Something of a man's bowler but with wide, scarf lengths of white silk or satin crossing over the top and coming down to cover her ears and cheeks and tie under her chin. A winter cape hung nearly to her knees and slim boots hugged her feet and reached up under pant legs so wide she might have been wearing a skirt. Cora wore pants.

How she must look to Cora, standing on a rotting porch, her hair hanging, and wearing a sorry dress that had grown two sizes too big.

"Good afternoon," Cora called. "How are you?" She giggled as she slipped in the snow and her arms, though she carried a basket, flew out and she caught and balanced herself. "My arse nearly became my sled," she said. Laughing now.

She's having fun. The thought struck Effie like a blow. There'd been a time when she and Skeet slid down snowy hills on shovels and pans until Pa built them a sled. Did the sled still exist? Had it been used once since Granny's arrival and Baby Sally's death?

"The sun's out," Cora said. "I'm so tired of winter. I knew if I didn't get out, I'd go crazy instead."

Effie gripped the porch rail and struggled to keep herself steady. *Crazy?* If crazy really threatened Cora, she wouldn't be joking about it. *Set the basket down*, she wanted to insist. *Don't come any closer.*

"We didn't talk the last time you were in the store," Cora said. She'd reached the bottom but hadn't yet handed up the basket. "I've missed you."

I took your bug-infested meal. Wasn't that enough? "Why?"

"Why have I missed you?" Cora's gaze stilled. "Effie, I'm sorry for Mr. Graf's actions. I'd like for us to be friends."

We can't be. Effie had thought the same of Mae—that they couldn't be friends. With Mae, she'd thought herself better, too good for such poverty and abject lack of hope. Or maybe she'd seen herself in Mae, knew what was coming, and been afraid. Now here was Cora, a woman so much better than her.

Womb, womb. Mourning doves harped from the trees. The wretched sound Effie hated; the mocking rising from the trees right and left of her. Worse than the endless hooting of owls and coyotes wailing through the night. The sound so haunting that on her worst days she was not sure if it came from outside or from inside her head.

"Effie," Cora said, "is everything all right? You look so . . . fragile."

The back and forth taunting went on. *Womb, womb.*

"Effie?"

She fought to bring back a scrambling attention. She would not die there. "I was thinking how much I miss Mae." If it was Mae standing there now, offering friendship, this time she'd invite her in. Cut a slice from her old loaf, sit and chat all afternoon.

"Such a strong woman," Cora said. "How she cried after each baby's death. Then in a few months, she'd be carrying again."

Womb, womb. Closer this time.

"She liked being pregnant," Cora went on. "Having a living baby inside her. She counted herself a mother for those nine months. Thought herself blessed even for that time."

Effie's hands lifted to her barren stomach, but she caught herself, kept her hands moving, smoothing her brown dress over her hips. "You were close to Mae?"

Cora frowned. "Not as close as I wish we'd been. Effie, are you sure you're all right? Is Bridget?"

"We're fine. Bridget is fine. She's reading." She tried to smile, but her lips tugged. "We stay busy. Old Mag visits often. She brings sweets, and we sit by the fire and talk."

One perfect brow lifted. "Old Mag?"

The muscles in Effie's throat tightened. "You must know her. Old Mag? She must shop at your store."

"Who could that be?" The ends of Cora's scarf fluttered in the breeze. "I can't think of anyone around here by that name. No Margaret or Madge. What does she look like? How old is she?"

Heat seared Effie's cheeks. So hot Cora had to notice. Bridget had lied; there was no Old Mag. Now Cora thought Effie a liar. She looked at the basket, wanting to trample it under her feet, but what of Bridget? Liar or no, she was only a child, half-starved and in pain without even a pair shoes to her name. The lying would have to be dealt with and all the things she claimed came from Old Mag, but not today. *I haven't the energy today.*

Cora set her basket on the edge of the porch landing and lifted out another large pie and a small object wrapped in cheesecloth. "I brought you a couple of things."

Effie's fingers trembled as she took the items—a tiny quaking she hoped Cora didn't notice. "Mr. Graf?"

Untying the scarf beneath her chin, Cora turned her face to the sun. "He's in Omaha on a buying trip. He doesn't like me too preoccupied in the kitchen." She smiled at that. "I have jars of last fall's fruit needing used, and I'll be spending the summer in New York. I need to start now, and I do love to bake."

"We don't need charity," Effie said. "Rev. Jackdaw will be back soon, and he'll pay off the Injun."

"I don't mean the pie as charity. Can it be friendship?"

"Rev. Jackdaw's moving us to Omaha."

"That's wonderful," Cora said, but her eyes held doubt. She motioned to the small object wrapped in cheesecloth. "It's a bar of my new soap. I added rose oil. I'm anxious to see what you think."

"Would it clean out sores?" Effie hadn't meant to ask.

Womb, womb. The haunting persisted. This time Effie didn't flinch. She deserved the mockery of birds.

"I don't know about the perfume in a sore," Cora said. "I don't think it would matter. Are you suffering?"

Shame. Standing there like Mae Thayer. Matching Mae but for the sticks in her hair. Shame for needing so much; shame for what happened to Bridget's feet—for falling asleep with Bridget's care, just as she'd done with Baby Sally's.

And now shame for being so rude to Cora, a woman she suddenly didn't want to leave. "I'm scared," she mumbled.

The pity and question in Cora's eyes made Effie look away. The black cloth was inside, but she pulled a mental one over her head. "Why are you doing this?" she asked. "Coming here with your gifts?"

Cora looked struck. "Our lives may seem wildly different, but all women share a world of sameness."

"I can't. Whatever you need, I can't hardly carry what I already got."

"All right." Cora nodded. She hesitated before turning and starting up the frozen slope. "If you need anything, you only have to ask."

Hurrying inside with the pie and soap, Effie shut the door with her foot. She stood well back of the window, thinking how often she stared out on others' lives. Cora mounted her horse and rode off. Not as a passenger in a buggy with a man holding the reins, but holding her own reins.

Effie forced herself to turn and face the cold room and Bridget's pain. "Look at this." The crust was golden, and its height promised a heaping amount of fruit beneath. It smelled of tart peaches and had a dusting of sugar. Buttery filling oozed around the edges. She brought two spoons, and they scooped and ate on the floor as Bridget's shoes burned.

Only then did Effie begin to slowly unwrap the wedge of soap. Lifting each of the four sides of the cheesecloth, her emotions went from despair to hope and back to despair. The soapcake looked smooth as farm cream and held flecks of pink rose petals. *Beautiful.* She closed her eyes and brought the soap to her nose. She struggled not to tear up as she rubbed the dry bar up and down her arm. Then Bridget's. How could she explain crying over a cake of soap? Who lived so poor?

She set the soap aside and tore the cheesecloth into two-inch strips and wound them back and forth, around and in between Bridget's toes.

"Don't cry," Bridget said when Effie finished.

Effie backed away, opened the rear door, and stepped out. Standing in the snow beneath the crow tree, she broke off twigs from low hanging branches. Later, after they'd eaten pigeon and more pie, she sat by the fire, whittled the sticks smooth as hairpins.

Thirty-Four

Bridget watched Effie and the funny way she stood and faced the door every time she needed to go out. Argued with her body like a bird cussing itself because it couldn't fly. Bridget had seen it once, a robin, big, with all its feathers, and the other birds from its nest catching air from limb to limb, but it was stuck on the ground, telling its dumb wings fly, fly.

Let Effie stand there all day trying to find the courage. Bridget didn't care. Effie was the one who threw away the shoes. Effie knew how to run up to the road and keep running until she reached Bleaksville, but she didn't know how to be in the trees and trust them. She shouldn't be the one who got to walk Jake in the sunshine.

Carrying the rope, Effie finally stepped out and faced Jake the hesitant way she'd faced the door. Bridget chuckled at the window to see her fumble with Rev. Jackdaw's knot in the rope until she'd widened it enough to put it over Jake's head. Though it was the second day, she was still scared to get close enough. Jake watched her and the loop hanging from her hands. Finally, he started forward, the lug, lug of his shoulders, and he walked into the loop himself. Nose first as Effie jumped back, then lifting and shaking the barrel of his head so that the rope wiggled down over his face and settled around his neck.

With Effie gone, the lucky one who got to be with Jake outside, Bridget knelt in front of the bed and pulled out the box holding the silver spoons. Only two left now. Four already hidden in the walls. She took the spoons, clicked down the lid on the empty box and admired it. Chief had a box like this, though his was prettier. She shoved it back under and fisted the spoons.

She and Grandma Teegan's braid had talked it over the night before, while Effie slept. Yesterday Effie, returned after hours outside, told how she'd found a pair of boots in a gunnysack. She knew they must be Mr. Thayer's because he traveled the road twice a day. "He was kind to me at the depot." So she walked to his house where he looked in the sack and smiled down at her. "You found my boots."

Pete sat at the table cleaning a gun, Effie went on. "Pieces laid out and him shining everything with an oily rag. He didn't say anything about Mr. Thayer's boots, but there was something in his eyes. I could feel him laughing at me, thinking how I hadn't helped with his mother. He isn't river people like us. I wanted to tell him, 'Just you wait. Your mama was, just you wait.'"

Using one of the spoons as a trowel, Bridget scooped out a patch of dry mud and weeds from the wall, letting it crumble into her pail. The spoons fit snug between the logs and with a bit of water into the dry, she had plaster to put over them. Seeing them disappear, it hurt less thinking about Effie being with Jake. And how Pete wasn't river people.

Thirty-Five

A knock on the door of Rev. Jackdaw's rented room made him lift his weary head from his prayers. After his days of repentance, had an angel finally arrived?

Taking advantage of the spring weather, he'd walked up and down the streets of the burnt district. "REPENT" written across his slate in large chalk letters. People snickered at him. Still, he'd marched in front of their pleasure dens, the cheap cribs and the houses with red lights in elaborate windows. Until a gang of young men in caps, with the same trouble in their eyes as he'd seen in Skeet's, approached him. Most of whom were already infected, he was sure, and didn't even know.

The jeering spiraled around him like the torment of his brothers in childhood. The months of failing to make any progress on a church, the hunger in his own loins for Effie, and then the heckling dropped him into despair, made him lock himself in his room, pull on the dress—degrading as a sackcloth—and drop to his knees. There, at the nadir of his soul, he'd been praying and waiting for God to send an angel of deliverance.

The knock came again. Harder, more insistent. He rose, stepped out of the dress, stood in his pants and shirt, and shoved the red into his valise. He opened the door of his room to a specter in black. A black-gloved hand lifted a black veil off a face and hooked the shroud over the wide brim of a black hat. "I'm the Widow Deet."

He wasn't certain he'd heard correctly. "The Widow Deet?" The mourning garb proved he had. "Your husband has died?" *What about the lodge?*

"A month ago at that horrid place . . ."

She rushed into a squawk's tirade about how she'd known for years the lodge was her husband's den of sin. A place where he drank and played cards. She dared not think what else went on when men left their wives and went off like a pack of prowling wolves. "We wives couldn't bear asking. Fitting, he died as a result of going there."

Rev. Jackdaw tugged his beard, tried to make the tug distract his suddenly ticking eye. "Died, you say?"

Her gray brows narrowed, but he saw no grief in her glum eyes. "You haven't heard? Shot. Infection it was that kilt him. God's will. I intend to have the place burnt to the ground."

He thought he ought to ask how Deet died, but he hardly cared. "My wife, a chaste," he nearly said girl, "woman, has need of the shelter."

"He never asked me to join him. Not even when the place was new. I won't concern myself with it now."

"I'm a man of the cloth." He looked around for his Bible, but it was in the valise. He couldn't lose the lodge, couldn't have Effie in her ragged dresses be seen on his arm, couldn't have her piling into his already cramped room. He needed privacy to work and think. And when necessary, the privacy to atone for his weaknesses.

"I want nothing more to do with it," Widow Deet said. "Hunting lodge? And I can fly! Did he really think me such a fool?"

Rev. Jackdaw scarcely listened. Effie's presence in Omaha might also stop the generosity of the few elder women in the community who pitied a man without a wife to look after his needs. Their foodstuffs and invitations to tea, even their bits of financial aid—a pittance though it was—might end, leaving him hungry. Suppose they frowned at Effie's age and mistook his reasons for acquiring such a young bride.

"I see by the light in your eyes, Sister." He laid a hand on the woman's fleshy shoulder. Her dress smelled of musk and long storage. "You are one of God's elect."

She flinched ever so slightly at his touch, but then nodded. The black veil slid slowly, falling back over her face.

"The Lord's work has need of the lodge," he said. Opening his wallet, he revealed its contents: twenty dollars—the whole of his money but for two coin dollars in his vest pocket. The week before . . . was it a week already? For how many days had he been on his knees? How long since he'd had real sleep, real food? He looked again at the money. The incredible sum had been passed to him by a grubby-handed old man with palsy. Near death no doubt, the bum hoped the sum could buy him a chariot ride to heaven.

Widow Deet lifted her morbid gauze veil a second time and peered at the money.

He fought the urge to slap his wallet closed, but he couldn't have Effie in Omaha. "Let me . . ." His Job's eye worked his whole cheek. Surely she wouldn't take the money. "Let me," he began again, "lift the burden of the lodge from your shoulders. I'm offering you the whole of my capital, so I may continue the work I've been commissioned to do."

The gloved hand plucked out his wealth. "I'll send a bill o' sale."

Alone again, the swish of the thick black skirts vanished, Rev. Jackdaw clicked the lock on his door. He stepped into his dress and pulled the vile thing up to his bearded chin. He'd lost to a woman. A loss as raw and ugly as any failing.

The next morning, his body was weak with hunger, but he'd slept better. He'd take a few days away from unredemptive Omaha, a city consumed only with building and profits. He'd escape to the lodge he now owned, tell Effie the news, bed her—a husband's duty—take an afternoon over his journal, and return to his commission reinvigorated.

First, he'd visit a few of the hens who cackled with their Christian piety.

The sun was low in the west when Nell finally reached the lodge.

Looking down on his purchase, Rev. Jackdaw felt sick. The place didn't look like it could survive the next good windstorm. He started down the miserable drop on foot. After the long, jolting ride from Omaha, each step of the short descent radiated new pain in his back.

The slope was worse than he remembered. The only way to fix it was to hire a man with a couple of mules and a heavy drag. No money for that. No money to fix the chimney or roof either. In his passion to keep Effie at a distance, he'd let Widow Deet swindle him.

He kicked at a runnel. He was too smart to be fooled again by squawks. Whether it was Widow Deet, Ma, or the wicked Miss Myra. The only schooling he had came from Miss Myra. Sitting at her kitchen table once or twice a month, always with a penny or a few eggs Ma had sent for her, it was Miss Myra who taught him his numbers and started him writing in journals. Sliding a ledger across her table, telling him to write out a Bible verse or what had happened to him so "the truth wasn't lost."

Sitting on her stool all those years ago, he'd trusted her and looked forward to that writing most. An hour longer in the kitchen where something good smelling always baked, free of Mister and his brothers. At home, he was a freak in his dress, his face twisted with scars not yet muffled by time and age, but at Miss Myra's his writing seemed atonement for his sins. First was the sin of showing a weakness for horses when the Bible stated man must have dominion over the animals. Second was causing his father to lose three fingers on his right hand.

Then he'd learned the truth about Miss Myra. He'd thought the pennies or bits of food he carried with him were to pay for those afternoons of Bible learning and forming a nice script. Until the afternoon Ma burst into Miss Myra's kitchen, and they shooed him out. He hadn't gone home like he was told, but hid under lilac bushes in the yard and saw Ma take off her dress and bloomers and climb into Miss Myra's bed.

By the time his ma quit groaning and breathing as if she climbed a mountain, night had come on. He stepped closer to the glass without fear of being seen. Miss Myra lifted a baby from between Ma's legs. A girl! He'd been so excited he'd wanted to run home and tell Mister the news. There was a baby girl. Somehow he'd believed that would make everything all right.

But Miss Myra took the baby, wrapped her up in a small white blanket—Ma not even watching—and half an hour later, he followed Miss Myra when she walked out carrying the infant. Walked for an hour until she stopped at a house and passed his sister through a door. He hadn't moved, though Miss Myra walked away. He watched until morning when a woman he'd never seen came out, carrying a small bundle against her shoulder. He followed her to the train station and watched her board.

Now he knew why there were no little girls in the house. Maybe even no brothers after him.

Nell's harness jingled. Happy for the distraction, he glanced at the horse, swaybacked and graying. He'd show no weakness with her. She didn't have many more miles in her, but those miles were his. He'd spend every one of them before nestling his shotgun into her ear.

For now, the horse needed to remain in harness for the trip back to Bleaksville. On his way through town, he'd considered stopping and putting a silver dollar against Effie's tally at the mercantile, but she needed to be there. He'd take her with him, have her stand facing him and Graf and, item-by-item, yea or nay every penny entry.

He opened the lodge door, spilling light across the floor. Rooster sat at the table and looked up from Effie's book.

"Cock-a-doodle-doo," he said. "Where is she?"

"Effie's with Jake."

His eyes narrowed. "Ain't that your job?"

"I hurt my feet. Effie's . . . helping."

There was more to the story. Something Rooster wasn't saying.

"Why you sitting there? Go git her." Rooster lifted her pitiful black skirt a few inches, showing bare feet with bandaged toes. "Well, put your blasted shoes on."

"Rev. Jackdaw!" Effie burst through the back door out of breath. "I heard the buggy, I was just coming in."

He studied her. While necessity kept him occupied in Omaha, she'd grown even skinnier. Lean faced, though her normally pale cheeks had a pinch of color from the brisk air. She took off his coat, ruined now, and hung it on a rusty nail. Her worn dress hung over her flat stomach. Near a year into marriage, she ought to have a son suckling by now. She looked no more ripe with child than Rooster.

She headed for the stove, keeping wide of his reach. She'd also betrayed him, letting him believe she was fertile as her mother. And he wouldn't let himself forget how on their wedding night she gagged.

He studied her hair, piled up like a nest on top of her head. Wildish, earthy. Something new in need of discipline and reining in. "Where're your combs?"

She didn't answer, only opened the stove's firebox. "Did you bring coffee? I'll start water." As though he might not notice how hardly moving, she slipped her feet out of her shoes. "Bridget," she nudged the shoes in Rooster's direction, "carry down Rev. Jackdaw's things."

"She lose her damned shoes?"

"Do you want Nell brought down?" Effie asked.

"What kind of answer is that?" She wasn't responding like normal. "Sticks in your hair? You lost your wits? That brother of yours, the stupid one, and your granny. Seems to me crazy runs in your blood."

He saw the sting of his comment. Her chin dropping an inch. Then her whole body pulling in as she moved to the fireplace for hot coals.

"What's that stink?" he asked.

She stopped, a respectful fear in her eyes. "What do you mean?"

He rose, grabbed her arm hard and pushed up her frayed sleeve. Sniffed. "A whore's stench."

"My soap? Mr. Graf's wife, Cora, she brought me some to try."

"On my bill?"

"No." She tried to pull away. "A gift."

He gripped tighter. "Why would she give you a gift? What you two up to?"

"Nothing."

"You think I want my wife accepting gifts from the likes of her?"

"I didn't think it—"

"That's what's wrong with you. You don't think." He squeezed her arm until she yelped. "We'll take it back."

"Mr. Graf may not know." She pried at his fingers. "Maybe Cora doesn't want him to know."

"What in your mind," his words slow, "tells you there's something right in that? A wife lies to her husband, and you being a party to it."

She jerked free.

He hadn't meant for his homecoming to sour. Was it seeing the place and being reminded of the poor deal he'd made? Was it the dread of telling Effie this was her home now? Or was it remembering Ma and Miss Myra? He carried too many weights. They hammered him down, and neither Effie nor Rooster with their easy lives cared about his load. They added to it. Effie couldn't even give him a blasted son. Not even a dunce like her brother.

Thirty-Six

In the buggy again, Rev. Jackdaw's back throbbed. At other times, the pain fired and he held his breath as the spasm passed through. He cursed the rutted road, Nell for every pothole she dropped a buggy wheel into, and Effie for making the trip necessary.

He slapped the reins without thinking and flinched as Nell jerked and the buggy wheel at his side lurched up a stone and bounced down. Why did he keep finding himself married to women who couldn't give him what he needed? Decades back, he'd broken his wrist and gone to a doctor to have the bone set. Hoping to find an elixir for his then wife, he'd asked the doctor. The quack suggested a man on his third wife and still with no children likely had "cartridges shy of a full load." The sawbones even asked if he'd suffered an injury to that area.

The question had filled his head with thunder, the sound of a wooden plank against horseflesh, and the pain of day after day pissing blood. The memories had threatened to unseat him, make him curl on the floor like a girl.

"Blasphemy," he barked at the non-believer. Why had he bothered to ask? A man's injury or no, if the Lord deemed a woman worthy, even if she were as dried up as Abraham's Sarah, He'd send an Isaac. The Bible was the word of God Himself, not to be abandoned by a quack's doubts, no matter how many pieces of paper he'd framed and nailed on his wall.

Sitting beside Effie, he stretched his back and shifted his weight. He didn't like the idea of putting her aside, young as she was. He had no other wifely prospects, and he didn't have long months, certainly not years, to court one. At his age, he was already having trouble sustaining the march. If it came to putting Effie aside, though, he needn't feel any guilt. If the Lord didn't think her worthy of children, the Lord wouldn't fuss over his leaving her.

He scowled at finding only Graf's wife behind the counter, her hair stacked, a full bosom. Tawdry.

"Rev. Jackdaw," she said, her voice pinched. Then in a kinder voice, "Effie."

"Where is he?"

The woman eyed him a moment as though answering a simple question took wits she struggled to muster. "Mr. Graf's gone on a delivery."

"Gone?" The Lord's hand. No need to even discuss the bill. "She's got something for you." He scowled and turned to Effie. "Give it."

The corners of the bar Effie put on the counter were so well rounded he knew he needed to come home more often, keep a better eye on his own wife.

Graf's wife let the soap lay. "Effie, how are you?"

"Skinny," Rev. Jackdaw said. He pulled his last coin from a pocket and dropped the dollar on the counter. The other had gone against Nell's fees. "You tell him I paid that." Then wished he'd hadn't laid down the money; Graf wasn't even there. Before he could reclaim the silver, the woman's arrogant hand snatched it.

"Don't put that in your own pocket." He tugged Effie's arm. "Come on. No use waiting for a man who's off and not minding his store."

"Effie," Graf's wife called to their backs, "take care of yourself."

He stopped and fired the woman a hard look. A rich squawk in her fancy clothes, acting as though she were a friend to Effie, acting as if he were some sort of demon.

"I hear you're barren, too," he said. "Not even a girl."

Enjoying the shock on her face might have held him up a moment longer, but there was no telling how soon Graf would be back. "Stay away from my wife."

He waited for Effie to climb back in the wagon. "Well, ain't that something," he said. "A man comes all this way into town to pay a bill and Graf ain't even there. Man's a crook. You don't see that? I don't want you buying in there. You hear me?"

Fear played across her face.

"You'll manage," he said. He'd planned on telling her he'd bought the lodge during the buggy ride back home. She didn't get buggy rides anymore, so riding with him was a treat, but now she stared straight ahead, her face as bereft of life as her womb. He'd tell her in the morning, just before he left. "Stay right there."

He crossed the street to the post office. The front-end of the establishment was no more than a counter for sorting and wrapping mail and a wall of numbered cubbyholes. He'd not reserved a slot like other folks in Bleaksville—better to have his mail held back during his time away.

The place was empty and he frowned. "Hey!" he yelled, hoping to bring someone from the back. "Hey!"

There was no point in waiting. Suppose Graf came back and saw Effie in the buggy? He walked behind the counter and pulled out a small box from beneath.

"Nothing there," he said, crawling up beside Effie. She still refused to look at him. Her face was more upset now than when they'd walked out of Graf's. "What now?" A few other horses and wagons waited on the street for drivers, but he saw no one who might have spoken to her. He glanced back at the mercantile. The "Open" sign swung ever so slightly on its chain.

"She give you back that soap?" He grabbed Effie's hands, pressed them open. Empty. "Wasn't no mail for you. Your family ain't missing you." He slapped the reins over Nell's back. "Leastwise, not enough to pen you a line."

Thirty-Seven

In the morning, Effie stood hugging herself. Out the window, Rev. Jackdaw slid Nell's tail through the crupper and began inspecting the leather lines. Once again the journal—his precious journal—lay open on the table. His pen propped across the inkbottle as if he still had some vital writing to do. She hated the book, all those words she couldn't read. His fancy script—loops and curly cues and scratches—not printed like the clear lettering she could read on a can or sack: Sugar, Flour. His thoughts kept secret, yet flaunted at the same time. The book was a mistress.

Bridget had stolen pages a couple of months back, but Effie hadn't asked to have them read. She didn't need, or want to hear, the crowing. She didn't need or want to hear what he wrote about her. She'd told Bridget to get rid of them.

Behind her, Bridget scraped Rev. Jackdaw's breakfast plate, collecting the crumbs and bits of bacon his horse teeth had snapped around and refused—morsels too brown or too white for his liking. "Keep them," she'd whispered to Bridget. Come evening, she'd heat his refused rinds for a bit of grease and fry some of the dandelion sprouts beginning to peek through the chilly ground. She and Bridget would eat at least that.

Tomorrow, she'd go and see Cora. Standing in the store, Effie had nearly fainted with the fear that Cora would reveal the bill had been paid. But Cora kept the confidence. If she'd told, Rev. Jackdaw would have assumed the worst: that Effie whored with the Injun.

Moments later, Cora had opened the door of the mercantile,

addressed Effie in the buggy. "Are you all right?" And frowning. "There's no Old Mag around here. No one by that name visits you. Why would you lie to me?"

Just after, Rev. Jackdaw told her that no one from Homeplace thought her worth a letter, and she felt wind blowing through her.

Out the window, Rev. Jackdaw turned from Nell and started back in. Effie hurried across the room to stand beside Bridget at the sink and pick up a pan to act busy.

He entered with his shoulders back as though some glad proclamation puffed him up. Did he have news about her house? She dared not hope, though he'd had the winter to see to the construction.

He sat down to his journal, picked up the pen as if to write, but stopped. "How is it you're getting along here?"

Effie's knees felt suddenly loose. They weren't getting along. Had he heard about the Injun? She took the few steps to the rocker and sat. His questions could snake around, bite from the front or the back. What was he really asking?

His gaze swung to Bridget. "I asked a question."

Bridget looked to Effie.

"Ain't there a goddamn one of yous can talk?"

"We were hungry all winter," Bridget said.

"Well now, you've got time to prepare for next winter."

Next winter? A rapping like knuckles from inside her chest. *Another winter?*

"Come here." He pointed to the second straight back chair at the table. "I've got something to tell you."

Effie found the strength to approach the table, but she couldn't make herself sit so close to him.

"Sit."

She sat.

"I bought this place for you." His hand lifted, cut the air. "No need for you to worry over a house in Omaha. I'll see if I can't find someone to fix the roof, chop you next winter's wood." The hand came down and he looked around, his gaze lingering on the mud-patched walls. "You've got a fine place here. You've fixed it up real nice."

Cold crawled up Effie's ankles. "My house?"

"You got a fine place here."

The freezing clawed at her knees, her arms, her lungs. "You bought this?" She was shivering. "This trashy hut!"

"You bought it?" Bridget asked, excitement tumbling in her voice.

The corner of Rev. Jackdaw's eye twitched. Jerked. "Not another word," he hissed at Effie. "I see your sins. Envy and pride. Coveting things of this world like Graf's whore." He rose, stood above her. "Thinking God ought to favor you more."

Effie's shoulders gave way, and she slumped against the table.

"You still expected a house in Omaha?" His voice boomed. "You ain't put that out of your head yet? I've the Lord's house to build."

"Did you buy Jake too?" Bridget's voice, sliced into Effie. "Is he ours now? You bought him too?"

"Look there." Rev. Jackdaw pointed a long finger at Bridget. "She ain't acting put upon. And she ain't even got a blasted pair of shoes. What's wrong with you?"

Rage lifted Effie from her chair. She faced him at her full height. "She doesn't know what she's saying. All she thinks about is that animal. Look at her." And Effie did: a child with fear in her eyes. "Wearing that raggedy dress. Both of us river people."

She'd never spoken back to him and now the force of her year-long silence rolled over her. She focused on his eye, jumping, blinking, watering. "We can't live any longer in rags. Eating off charity and your table scraps. We can't do it."

"God holds you over a pit of hell," he said. "He holds you as one holds a spider or some loathsome insect over the fire."

She'd heard the words before. The phrase came from Granny's Jonathan Edwards tract. The words no longer frightened her. On the lips of this broken preacher, they seemed as powerless as a little boy's ditty. Lines Skeet would bring home from school to torment Johnny. "You fool." She stared straight at him. "*This* is the pit of hell!"

She'd said it without thinking, without first rehearsing her words, weighing each one and its possible consequences before she let it out of her mouth. "What does that make you? A liar!"

"I wanted my sons to grow up in a fine house. I never promised for you."

"What about Jake?" Bridget asked again. Her voice softer, more afraid.

They both swung to face her. "That animal is mine," Rev. Jackdaw said. "Mine."

"You won't sell him because you're poor?" Bridget asked.

"What I do with my animal is none of your goddamn business. You understand me?"

Effie shoved the chair she stood behind into the table, knocking Rev. Jackdaw's pen off the inkbottle. A penny-sized spot of ink marred his page.

He bent to it. "Christ Almighty!"

"You brought us here." She could also be loud. "Took me away from my family. You ruined me, and you think this stinking roof is all you owe me?"

"I didn't ruin you. I tried to save you."

"You leave us here. With no food, in a shack, while you live in a warm place and eat fancy. What good are you to us? You're as worthless to me as—" Her gaze swung around the lodge and settled on Bridget, who cared only about a stupid animal. "You're as worthless as a girl."

He flinched as if she'd spat on him. She didn't see the fist though she heard Bridget scream. The strike knocked her to the floor. For a moment, her jaw hurt so bad she couldn't open her eyes. She cupped the side of her face with both hands and tasted blood.

He grabbed a fistful of her hair. "You've no authority to speak to me like that. 'Thy desire shall be to thy husband, and he shall rule over thee.'"

He dragged her. She twisted at the end of his long arm, her hands grabbing his, trying to free her hair and stop this new pain. She made it to her knees and then managed to get her feet half way under her. Unable to fully extend her legs and stand, she hunched along under his grip.

They wobbled and groped across the floor, nearly reaching the back wall before her foot caught on the hem of her dragging skirt. Then the other foot, tripping her as though her feet tried to run up the inside of her dress. She fell against his knees. As they both went down, he reached out and grabbed the end of the rope on the wall. It sliced and flicked and slithered down.

They landed with thudding sounds, him moaning as his back slammed against the wall's uneven logs. She lay caught in the vee of his splayed legs. Cursing, he drew the rope across her throat. Pulled tight.

She gasped at the sharp hitch to her windpipe. Gasped again for air that didn't come.

Using the rope, he pulled her back hard against his chest. The coarse woody fibers scraped off skin, and a bead of warmth crawled down beneath her collar. He leaned his head forward, pressing his cheek into hers. Words hissed through his gritted teeth.

"He looks upon you as worthy of nothing."

"Don't fight!" Bridget screamed.

Effie struggled to work her fingers under the rope, pushing her feet against the floor and bucking. She managed a single gulp of air, but he pinned her again, pulled the rope tighter. Panic surged through her. She couldn't breathe. Her heart and head pounded in unison. She clawed at the taut rope.

"Like fiends," his words floated through her mind, "whores move under men."

It took only moments before her chest felt near exploding. She tried to twist out under the rope, pry off his grip, even reach behind and hit him. Nothing.

Be still.

The words were a part of her nightmares. *Be still.* Her life depended on it. She couldn't go back into the darkness.

She was blacking out, curtains of shade rushing in from both sides, but she knew he wanted her to fight in order to justify his actions—as though killing her would then be self-defense.

Be still.

She had no fight left. No air. Her arms fell limp, her knees sank. Beams circled overhead, light corkscrewed down through a pinhole in the roof, pigeons flew leaving trails of sound.

A wisp, no more than a thread, of coolness flew in over her tongue, fluttered at the back of her throat, sank into her lungs. A single tiny stream of air resparking her terror, urging her body to fight again.

Be still.

Rev. Jackdaw's groaning increased. He drew in his own air with long whistling sounds. "I never *bought* a roof for the others."

Another thin string of air found her lungs. She feared moving even an inch. Feared he'd realize his back pain had made him ease his grip. *Be still.* She was breathing, though the painful rope rubbed and scraped, and the rattle of her panic remained.

"The world's headed toward damnation," he said. "Free lovers. Squawks calling themselves spiritualists, claiming to conjure up the dead, making their own prophets. Women supposing they know what's best for their souls, marching in the streets to vote." With a groan, he shifted his hips, then his back. His sweat dripped onto her cheek. "People wanting modern rules, ignoring ways set down for them in the Iron Age."

He rationed her air. Just as he rationed everything in her life.

She breathed shallow, her stomach nauseous. His teeth ground as he went on, and she hoped the grinding would make the teeth shatter like eggshells in his mouth. When he'd finished condemning her, would he kill her yet? Make one final quick hitch?

She couldn't risk moving. Not even turning her head away from the bearded cheek and the rancid breath, but her eyes searched the room for help. On the windowsill, the morning sun lit Johnny's marbles, and she thought of his struggles to protect them against Skeet.

"Iay atehay ouyay." A whisper. Slightly stronger. "Iay atehay ouyay." *I hate you.*

His body stiffened. His head tipped further forward, the rope looser.

Every muscle was limp with exhaustion, but her mind searched for more words to put into Pig Latin. "Odgay oldshay ouyay veroay hetay itpay of ellhay." *God holds you over the pit of hell.*

He ticked his elbows forward. His voice a whisper, dry and hoarse. "Tongues?"

She did her best to continue, trying to pick up speed and volume. "Odgay oldhay ouyay veroay hetay itpay of ellhay." He dropped the rope, letting it fall across her chest. His hands went to the floor at his sides and he groaned, pulling himself up into a better sitting position. He pushed slowly away and rolled to his knees, his face grimacing and his hands groping the wall for support as he stood. For a long minute, he looked down at her.

She didn't move as he limped across the room to the table, his backside floured with dust. He grabbed his journal and inkbottle. "I'll pray on this." He stepped around and opened the door. "I'll ask if the tongues mean you've been saved."

Her windpipe felt crushed, and her lungs still gasped. With the first creak of a buggy wheel, she rolled onto her side, drew her knees up, and hugged herself. She ached for the black cloth on the bed. The distance seemed miles.

She'd known she didn't love him, but now she knew she never could. She'd been lying to herself.

Bridget rushed over and knelt down, her red hair falling onto Effie's chest. "It's all right now," she said. "You can get up, he's gone."

Blood pulsed in Effie's ears. Hopelessness rent through her. This falling down hut was her home. Her husband had nearly killed her. The next time she angered him he would.

"Everything is all right now," Bridget said again.

Effie's whole body trembled. "Get away from me!"

Bridget returned to the sink. She watched Effie still curled and crying on the floor. Not wanting touched or spoken to. But it was more the fright in her eyes, ghosts looking out, that made Bridget back away.

She lifted a plate, dipped it in water, and wiped its surface with her hand. Rev. Jackdaw was gone now, the fight was over, and she needed to make things okay again. She'd wash the dishes, then tell Jake the news.

"Why didn't you help me?" Effie pulled the rope away and worked herself to her knees. "Why didn't you knock him off me?"

Bridget had no answer. She'd screamed several times for them to stop fighting, but that hadn't worked. Now Effie was crawling toward the bed, her eyes on the box where she kept her spoons.

"If you weren't here," Effie sobbed, "he wouldn't leave me alone. I'd live in Omaha." She reached the bed, dropped to her stomach, and grabbed the box from beneath. "He promised me a life. Not this!"

Bridget lifted another plate slower; her gaze going around the rim, searching the chips like scallops on a pie, struggling for distraction. She tried to lower the plate so carefully the surface of the water didn't move.

"Thief!" Effie threw the box, making it clatter across the floor. Gasping as though being choked again, she scuffled to her feet. "Where are my spoons?" She ran to the buffalo hide, dragged the fur from its place in the corner and screamed again at finding nothing beneath. "They're mine!"

Bridget wanted to tell where the spoons were hidden, even to dig them from their muddy graves. But so much red emotion, even with Rev. Jackdaw gone, still spun and howled off the walls. She needed the spoons too. "I'm not a thief!" Because stealing was a different thing than needing to quiet the fish in your stomach; needing to know you could take care of yourself though everyone you loved had left you. "I'm not a thief."

Effie rushed close, her hands twisting. "Stop washing those bloody dishes. Stealing my spoons. Lying about some Old Mag. You deserve this place. I don't!"

"Old Mag is real."

A bloody stripe two inches wide beaded around Effie's throat, but the wild in her eyes scared Bridget even more. This wasn't Effie.

"Don't lie to me." Effie's words burning.

A plate slammed into the side of Bridget's face, snapped her head back in an explosion of pain. She stumbled and fell.

The dish trembled in Effie's hands, slipped out, and shattered over the floor. "Oh God," she cried. She sank, swatted away pieces of plaster beside Bridget, and pulled her close. "I'm sorry, I'm sorry."

Moaning, Bridget pushed at Effie and scooted back against the wall.

Effie tried to reach for her again. "Bridget, are you all right? Talk to me. I'm sorry."

The wild had faded from Effie's eyes. Sorry and scared of herself. Bridget's pain still throbbed. "Get away from me."

Effie turned and groped, a hand finding the side of the sink. She pulled herself up. Clutching fistfuls of her skirt, she stepped back and muttered between sobs. "I'm no different than him. Worse. I'm losing my mind."

Bridget wasn't sure of all Effie's whispered and mumbled words. There was more about Granny and asylums and nightmares of black dungeons. She rose as Effie stumbled out the back door. She watched her stagger across the sandy clearing, and her body drift up the stairs of the skinning shed. She disappeared into the place where knives and saw-toothed traps hung on the walls and a scarred table smelled of animal blood.

Thirty-Eight

The river rushed high and fast. Debris floated, bobbed, and disappeared only to shoot back up to the surface farther down. The rolling water hadn't yet reached the lodge, but it rippled between the stilts of the skinning shed and wrapped around Wilcox-the-tree, tugging, and trying to bring him down. Bridget imagined the hungry Missouri eating trees all along its course and still it was hungry for Wilcox.

Crossing Chief's pasture, Bridget felt the cold in her bare toes. The ground had thawed and warmed in places, while other soggy and chilly patches made her run and hop off them. Three days had passed since Rev. Jackdaw left and Effie stumbled for the first time into the skinning shed, staying until dark.

Three evenings in which Effie stepped back into the lodge after her day in the shed and begged forgiveness. Not mentioning the burn around her neck or that the run-down lodge was now her home. Not cursing Rev. Jackdaw, only apologizing, her voice shaky, as if she didn't believe her words of contrition amounted to much.

Three nights of Effie rocking or pacing in front of the fire in her old slip, an orange glow reflecting off the once-white fabric. Hour after dark hour, as Bridget tried to sleep, worn and loose boards groaned under Effie's restlessness. Last night, when Effie thought Bridget asleep, she crawled onto the buffalo hide. She lay so close Bridget could feel her breath. Very slowly, she lifted one of Bridget's arms and laid it across her own shoulders—as if she were being hugged. Bridget left the arm there.

Climbing over Chief's gate, she paused to watch Smoke in the corral with his high-stepping gait and high-swinging tail. She passed Chief's two barns with their closed doors, before hearing the hammering and seeing him on the roof of his house. She wasn't going to bother him; she just wanted to spend a bit of time where he was. Wire caught her scent or saw her and came hopping and barking on his three legs, and Smoke whinnied and tossed his head. Now everyone knew she was there.

"Come on," she coaxed Wire and ran with him, not stopping until they reached the foot of Chief's ladder. "Hello."

From the edge of the roof, kneeling into the pitch of the slope, he looked down on her. Shaking his head, he sighed and turned back to his hammering. He didn't want her there, but she couldn't go home. She knelt and wrapped her arms around Wire. The dog had a hundred scars and only three legs. Someone hated him so bad they'd tried to drown him. He didn't think about any of that, though. He wasn't Salt Woman. He wagged his tail, jumped, and danced around on his three legs.

Several red chickens with feathers Rev. Jackdaw would say matched her hair gathered close—though not too close to Wire. The roosters pecked the ground and strutted with their long, high tail feathers trembling in the air.

"Rooster. Rooster." She pointed at them. "You're feathers are an ugly color."

Paying no attention to her, their long gold toes lifted and curled like fiddleheads before landing open again. Chickens the same breed as Mae's rooster.

She called up to Chief again. "Did you give Mae her pet?" He continued ignoring her. "Mr. Thayer killed it."

The hammering continued.

"He and Pete ate it."

Wire squirmed away. A box full of shiny carpenter nails, sitting nearly at her feet, caught her attention. Chief didn't want her there, and her hands itched to steal a couple of nails. She could bury them in the walls with the others. She thought then of Effie's box and the box she'd seen on Chief's table after he'd rescued her.

He started down. His worn soles scraped on and off the wooden rungs. She shifted, took a step back and adjusted the black skirt hem so it covered her bare and scabby toes. Her feet weren't his business.

Standing on the ground, Chief held his hammer, turning his wrist back and forth as sunlight panned across the iron head. "Belonged to my granddad. Father's side." He turned the tool again, watching her. "I've had to get a new head a few times and more'n once a new handle, but it's still Granddad's hammer." He let the handle slide down through his thick grip, caught the tool by the head, turned it over and repeated the action.

She hadn't talked to him since the December day he brought Effie's rocker home. And if he asked her why she'd come, she'd have to shrug and admit she didn't know. "My feet just came," she'd say.

"You all right?"

She spoke fast. "Rev. Jackdaw came home. They had a fight. A red one."

"She all right?"

"I wanted to stop them, but I was scared."

His face said he was angry. She thought he'd tell her again that he couldn't be "that man." His hat tipped in the direction of her eye. "Jackdaw give you that?"

She touched her cheekbone. The swelling was gone, and without a mirror, she hadn't wondered if the eye was black and blue like the one Mr. Thayer gave Pete. Was the sight of her face the reason Effie apologized every time she looked at her? Was that the reason Chief first turned away?

He tapped the box she'd admired with the toe of his boot. "Wouldn't be hard for you to make one. You own anything needs a box?"

"I'm a half orphan."

"No pencils, letters, anything like that?"

"Mum quit writing."

He took up a handful of the nails and started back up the ladder. "Being a girl and a half orphan to boot, I expect you're scared of hammers, nails. Brooms and mops, is it? You'll make a good maid, cleaning up after others."

"I'm going to be a doctor, and I don't know how to build boxes."

He looked down at her from the roof, his eyes deep in the shadow of his hat brim. "I imagine a girl's scared of learning."

"I'm not scared."

"Well then. Take some of that wood," he pointed at a scrap pile by a small shed, "and set about learning. You clean up around here, wood I can't use, you've earned."

She looked at the short lengths tossed into a heap. If she could build a box, she'd build it for Effie. But she didn't know how to even begin.

"Suit yourself. I got a roof to fix." He crouched, walking slantwise against the slope. "Change your mind, there's another hammer in the toolshed."

She had to say something. "Effie's happy you brought her chair home. She sits in it every day."

He didn't answer.

She huffed a minute as Wire bounced up onto the porch and curled in the sun. She started for the shed. Nearly at the door, she slowed. One end of Chief's clothesline was tied around a post, the other to a nail in the side of the shed. Clothes swayed in the breeze: two pair of short bib overalls. Too short for Chief. Too short even for Effie. Her size. The same with the two blue shirts and the pair of boy's high top shoes swinging by their laces. Shoes almost new.

She spun around, hollered, "You got another boy? One that's not dead?"

A long silence made her doubt Chief intended to answer. He stood, looking ready to step off the roof and fly. "I expect girls are too fancy for britches."

Maybe Chief was saying take the clothes, but could she? Accepting food from Cora—even if Effie didn't like it—was necessary. But clothes?

"Time I cleared out some things," Chief called, "but there's boys around if you're not interested."

She hurried into the shed where he couldn't see her pace and twist her fingers. She could take care of herself. That was the only reason Grandma Teegan signed Surrender Papers. Grandma Teegan didn't just give her away. Grandma Teegan loved her.

A hammer lay on a workbench along with other tools. The object with the most shine was a thin wrench. She slipped it in her pocket. Grandma Teegan didn't just give her away. Feeling better, she brought the hammer and nails outside to the sunlight. The clothes on the line waved at her.

Over and over she tried to pound in a nail, but it went no deeper than the tip before bouncing out. A nail stuck for three whacks, then leaned right and shot away from her with the fourth.

For an hour she pounded and had a row of nails in her board, though none of them had gone completely in before folding over.

"I got hogs to feed." Chief stood at her side. "Best you get home."

She didn't move. *What about the clothes?*

He nodded at her attempts to pound in nails. "You come back tomorrow and work on that."

"Really?" She glanced at the clothes.

He stepped ahead of her, gathered the clothing from the line, even untwisting the shoes. He pushed the wad at her. "They're ugly all right, but I can't do anything about that."

He was *making* her take the clothes because he didn't want them.

She didn't know how she'd explain them to Effie; she couldn't say they came from Old Mag. She started back across the yard, her arms full and the shiny wrench bumping happily against her leg.

She stopped at Old Mag and considered her wealth. She thought briefly of hiding them there, but what good would that do? They'd get soiled and the shoes ruined. Had Chief hung them out expecting her to come after dark and steal them? Did he know she'd lost her shoes? If he'd seen Effie with Jake, he'd probably figured it out.

With Jake at her side, she went on to face Effie. At the other end of the winding path, ready to step into the clearing, she hesitated. She was leaving the good world of the trees for the one where Effie suffered.

The clothes dropped from her arms. Effie stood in the cold river, the water quick and high with spring thaw. She wore only the old slip, the fabric floating and billowing around her waist. Her head was flung back, her arms stretched skyward, her fingers opening and closing, as though she meant to grab fistfuls of all she'd never have. Her hands dropped and scooped up water.

"I baptize me in this stinking river," she cried out. "I baptize me."

Bridget stared. This was the worst yet. She was going to lose the house, Jake, and Effie. Everything was ending now. Effie was scared of drowning, so scared she'd never learned to swim. One misstep, one too-strong surge, and she'd go under. Yet she was there, staggering as the water gurgled and released and made her find new footing.

Effie cupped more water, losing most of it by the time her hands reached over her head, but letting the drops she'd saved fall on her. "I baptize me with this stinking river."

Ten yards in front of her a large tree branch, carried by the stiff current, came into view. The sight slammed doors up and down Bridget's body. "Effie! Watch out!"

The branch sank in the churning water and reappeared half the distance to Effie.

"Effie," Bridget screamed, "watch out!"

The branch bobbed past, only brushing Effie's side, yet nearly toppling her. As Effie regained her balance, Bridget sank to her knees. "Please, come in. You're baptized. You're baptized good."

Effie faced her. Her eyes weren't wild like they'd been when she struck with the plate. They were horribly sad but focused, telling Bridget she knew exactly the risk she was taking.

"Please, Effie. I need you. We're going to take Jake and get away. I'm coming in to get you now."

Slowly, the slip lowering with each step closer to shore, Effie's body rose out of the water. Bridget ran to help her across the sand and up the ramp to the lodge.

Cora stood just inside the front door, and for a moment, all three stood locked in surprise. "I've only just arrived," Cora stammered. "The door was open and . . . what happened?"

"She was bathing in the river," Bridget said. She hoped she sounded casual, not as stricken as she felt.

"She's freezing," Cora snatched the quilt off Effie's bed and wrapped it around Effie's shoulders. But not before, Bridget knew, Cora had seen everything: Effie's skinny arms, the old slip—the straps mended again and again with black stitches—and Effie's throat, the rope burn still red as a velvet choker.

Thirty-Nine

Bridget sat on the back landing watching the door of the skinning shed with its smell of butchery and death clinging to the traps and knives and table. If Effie stepped out and started for the river, she'd stop her. A week now since the plate, and Effie still spent her days in there. Traveling all the distance she could from what happened.

The back door of the lodge jerked open. Bridget jumped at seeing Rev. Jackdaw again so soon. Defeat hung in his clothes, in his sagging face, in the eye that looked dying and paler than the other. "Where is she?"

Bridget froze. Effie hadn't asked about the clothes from Chief, either because she was too distracted to care or didn't expect the truth anyway. But Rev. Jackdaw? And would he be mad that Effie was in the shed? Bridget couldn't imagine why.

Anger muscled not just Rev. Jackdaw's eye but his whole face. "I asked you a question. She with that woman?"

Cora? "I don't know where she is." She prayed Effie would hear them talking and come out. Though she told her eyes *don't do it*, they glanced at the shed door and back.

Effie lay beside Jury. He was sorry for not choosing her. He'd made a terrible mistake in marrying someone else. The worst mistake of his life. He kissed her over and over, his hand sliding slowly up her leg, touching her, waking her body. Slow this time. Not taking her as he had in his parents' haymow, afraid of being found out before he satisfied himself. He was sorry for that, too. He'd keep her safe, build her a beautiful home, and they'd fill it with children.

The shed door burst open with an explosion of light that made Effie blink at the brightness. Rev. Jackdaw filled the frame, his eyes angry slits. Jury was gone. The soft bed they'd shared only a butcher's table. Loss sank over her.

"Sinner! Whoring with yourself."

She pushed her slip down and sat up. *Whoring with herself?* The idea confused her, but there was no confusing his anger. "No, I—"

He glowered, but stood looking as if weighing the severity of what he'd caught her doing. Weighing her worth and coming up with nothing. His face twisted, contorted, his eye, then his whole cheek took off, flapping like a bird trapped beneath his skin. A litany of evil names spewed from between his gritted teeth, and she imagined birds flying from his mouth the way they broke from trees: blackbirds, ravens, crows.

She scooted left, then right on the table, deciding where best to jump off and run past him. His body, rigid and feral, his arms wide, blocked her way.

"Leave me alone!" He'd been angry when he put the rope across her neck, but not this angry. This time he would kill her. "Please, please!" She'd learned not to call him a girl, not to fight, not do anything but plead.

He lunged and caught her by the ankles. Her heart pounded at the terrible, awful strength in his hands. He yanked.

Her hands flew up for balance then down as she tried to hold on to the table. She hit the floor on her back and cried out as her head struck, and the steel traps on the wall began to spin around her. He hoisted her up, pinned her against the table's hard edge. She struggled against her dizziness, tried to locate the door. If she could find her legs, manage to break away, she needed its location.

He cursed her for witching him into marrying her, his spittle flying in her face. She was damnation. Wicked as Eve. All women were. His work, his church, never had a chance because of his wives. Now this! "Making your soul unfit to carry my sons."

The nightmare was terrifyingly familiar. Righteous and loathing, he abandoned her for months, kept her trapped in a hovel, lifted her skirts and tried to farm her body for sons. He wrestled her toward the wall. She was reentering the nightmare. Next would be his threats of hellfire.

She was less dizzy, the pain in her head ebbing. Rev. Jackdaw was insane. His was a true madness. She'd brought fear and pain from Homeplace, but not insanity.

She fought, twisted, and kicked. "Let me go! Bridget, help!"

This time it wasn't the swish of a rope but the hard cold rattle of a trap and its chain. Her mind scrambled to find words in Pig Latin. How to say please or no? How to say I hate you?

He held her around the waist now, the pan of the trap clutched in his fist. The last metal links of the chain clattered to the floor. She drew her legs up, kicked the air, and put her full weight in his arms, hoping it broke his back. She landed on the floor a second time, and he pinned her there with a knee on her chest. Wheezing, he used his other knee to put pressure on the trap spring. The jaws opened.

She screamed as he pulled her hand to the teeth.

"If thy right hand offend thee," the words disgorging from his mouth, "cast it from thee: for it is profitable that one of thy members should perish, and not thy whole body be cast into hell."

His knee pulled away. The jaws sprung. The sound a soft, wet, sinking. Flesh splitting. Small bones crushing.

The unbelievable sight of the spikes through her palm and the blood pouring out shocked her into silence. Then pain seared up her arm. She cried out.

The agony brought dizziness. On its heels, darkness.

Rev. Jackdaw staggered back, out of breath and with his back nearly doubling him over with pain. Effie lay on her side, silent at last. Fainted dead away. On her side, her knees pulled up, she cradled her trapped hand. She looked thirteen, fourteen. Blood ran, soaking the undergarment she wore like a harlot.

He stepped over her and grabbed traps and knives off the walls. At the door, he turned back again. The sight of her reminded him of how he'd lain beaten and bloody. How pain could enter the body at any point and sear through the whole. The images in his head threatened to strike him down. He reeled toward the daylight and out. He would not compare what he'd done to Mister's actions. Effie's whoring with herself proved she was the culmination of every evil he'd spent his life fighting. Walking in on her, he'd seen the final, unutterable proof that he'd die having succeeded at nothing. Not even leaving an heir to carry his name.

He started for the slope and his buggy, seeing the row of sons she'd denied him. Remaining unworthy of receiving them, she'd struck them down as surely as if she'd drug a knife across their throats. She'd taken his children, and he'd issued justice. *If thy right hand offend thee.* When she woke, she'd know he was a man, not a girl. She'd know he was as strong as his earthly father and as just as his heavenly Father.

The traps were his possessions now, and he stowed them in the buggy's boot and marveled again at the Lord's divine orchestration. Even in the burly man who'd knocked on his door asking to have his traps and knives brought from the shed to Omaha. "They're my property," the bearish man had insisted. "Traps cost good money."

Good money? He'd tapped the deed in his pocket. "My property now."

The man's insistence that Widow Deet couldn't sell what she didn't own proved him a thief and made the trip to the lodge necessary. Before the thief came to take what no longer belonged to him.

With his second trip into the shed, grabbing the last knife and trap, Effie moaned, semi-awake, writhing even in her stupor. He didn't know where Rooster had gone, but she'd be back soon with a neighbor or the sheriff.

He took the back ramp in two long strides, pushed aside the bed, smashed the empty box, turned over the mattress, and searched the rags of Effie's dresses for the rest of his property: the silver spoons. Had she sold them, stealing from her own husband?

His back screeched with pain as he climbed into the buggy. Rooster was most likely to bring help from the direction of Bleaksville. Despite his suffering, he'd best take the road going the other direction, circle clear around. In his agony, he didn't deserve confrontation, too.

"Git up," he shouted at Nell and snapped the reins. "Git up, you damn mule!"

Forty

Seeing Rev. Jackdaw head for the shed, the tails of his black coat spreading and flapping behind him like a hawk with crippled wings, Bridget ran. Her arms and legs pumped and her lungs heaved with the effort. She raced through the trees, stopping at Old Mag to drop both palms on the trunk and suck in air. *I shouldn't run.* She wasn't big enough to pull off Rev. Jackdaw, and she wasn't brave as Nera. Ashamed, she ran on.

She reached Chief's fence, squeezed between two strings of barbed wire, and ran across his pasture with her side in painful stitches. She'd made another terrible mistake. She should have first grabbed up two pans—as Grandma Teegan told her to do with Rowan—and banged them the whole way.

Going over the gate into the barnyard, she screamed for Chief. He wasn't in his yard or on a roof and his house looked dark. She screamed again. Wire barked from inside the smaller barn and the doors flung open. The dog bounded out and Chief stepped into the doorway. His eyes full of question.

"Rev. Jackdaw's going to hurt Effie! Right now! It's a red fight."

Chief turned, disappeared back inside. Bridget feared he hadn't really heard, or had decided again that he couldn't be "that man." She ran in after him. He banged up the latch on a stall gate, made a loud clucking sound in his throat, and Smoke rushed out, his head high, his eyes wide, and his powerful legs trembling. Chief slid a bit into the horse's mouth, as easily as sliding in a sugar cube. "Jackdaw carrying a gun?"

She couldn't remember. "He has a shotgun."

From a box in the wall, Chief grabbed something with shine, tucked it into the back of his belt, and dropped his loose shirt over it. A gun or a knife, she wasn't absolutely sure. He swung onto Smoke in one motion, drew the horse up beside her, and before she could jump back, leaned down and grabbed her around the waist. Smoke was leaving the barn and her feet were off the ground. She screamed and found herself sitting in front of Chief.

"Heigh," he yelled at Smoke though the hoofs thundered and Bridget's hair flew back. "Jackdaw got the rope again?"

She'd thought only Cora knew about the rope burns. "Maybe," she shouted.

He drove Smoke on, the motion in his shoulders and the arms she gripped rhythmic, pumping, matching the horse's strides. Chief's breath quick against her cheek, mixed with her own panting. They breathed each other.

They skirted the pasture and came through trees and out onto the road through some narrow back way she'd not known existed. When they rounded the second bend, Mr. Thayer and Pete came into view riding ahead in the distance. Smoke didn't break stride as Chief let out a piercing whistle. Pete turned back. Chills ran down Bridget's spine. Mr. Thayer turned too. They drew up their horses, waited. She'd done the right thing. The three men would help Effie better than she could have done alone. But reaching the lodge and seeing Nell and Rev. Jackdaw's buggy gone, she nearly cried out.

Effie moaned on the shed floor, glassy eyed. At the sight of her, the blood and the trap, Bridget screamed. Pete and Chief cussed words of disbelief. Mr. Thayer barked loudest, "Jesus Christ!"

Pete held Bridget while she sobbed against his chest. Chief knelt behind Effie, wrapped his arms around her and held her still. Thayer slowly stepped on the trap's spring, and the teeth began pulling out of Effie's flesh.

Outside, birds exploded from the trees, their screams echoing the sound of Effie's.

Hours after the doctor, the sheriff, and Mr. Thayer had gone home, Chief and Pete remained. They sat in the two hard-backed chairs while Bridget rocked. They all turned to Effie each time she moaned through the heavy dose of laudanum the doctor administered.

"You think she'll want to live now?" Pete whispered. His gaze was distant, and Bridget wondered who he asked. Chief, her, the room? "I expect," Pete went on, "today will feel something like losing a baby. It's a death anyway . . . Jackdaw doing what he did to her."

Bridget watched the nearly imperceptible rising and falling of the quilt covering Effie. The slashes of red darker as evening turned to night. But she was still breathing.

"That where you sleep?" Chief asked Bridget. He nodded at her hide in the corner. "You ought to try. Come morning, she's going to need your help."

"I have to stay awake." She wouldn't tell him about Uncle Rowan. Her hands twisted in her lap. "I have to stay awake."

"She ain't likely to die from a broken hand," Chief said.

He'd done it before: Answered her thoughts as clearly as if she'd spoken them.

"Having the baby ain't what killed Ma." Pete's voice slurred with emotion. "He was born and looked whole enough. I thought they'd both live. Then his face turned blue and Ma was weeping, blowing into his mouth and rubbing his back hard." Pete's lips pressed tight. "After, she wouldn't give him up. Hours till I could coax him out of her arms. He didn't weigh nothing. I told Ma I'd lay him with the others. I could do that for her so she didn't have to make the walk. Thayer was at the bar in Bleaksville. She didn't answer me, just stared at the ceiling. Not dead, but a terrible *quit* look. Turned my blood cold." He cleared his throat. "I didn't know it then. She was done talking, done with this world."

Bridget wished Chief would read Pete's thoughts and know what to say, but his lips were still.

Pete's shoulders lifted with a deep breath and sank again. "I buried my brother under the same tree, shoveling in a different spot this time so I didn't hit tiny bones. Doc said there was nothing he could do for Ma. After a day, two, Thayer carried her out of his bed and to the floor by the fire."

Bridget shuddered to think of Pete seeing his mum laid out on the floor.

"He claimed she'd be warmer there." Pete leaned hard on his elbows. One hand was fisted and the other over the top like the fist needed held down. "All Thayer wanted was her out of his bed. He didn't want to wake and find her dead beside him. I didn't cuss him, figuring Ma would want away from a man more worried about his night's sleep than her dying. Or the baby they'd lost. And I wanted her where I could lie down close. I thought if I had her alone, I could talk her into living." He swallowed. "I thought I could talk her into living for me."

Chief rose, swung the back door wide open onto the night. Along the river, bullfrogs croaked and groaned, the sound rumbling in around him. "All this talk," he nodded in Effie's direction, "ain't of any use to her."

Bridget considered how Chief hadn't been able to stop his boy from dying either. Just as she'd not been able to stop Rowan. Maybe everybody carried a death on their backs. She glanced up to where she knew Grandma Teegan's braid watched them. Grandma Teegan carried several deaths.

"I tried to make her drink," Pete said. "Poured water on her lips, tried to close her eyes. Thayer said I was wasting my time. Said I needed to be a man about it and go do my chores."

What would Pete say, Bridget wondered, if she told him she'd seen the death space around his mum? She turned quick to look at Effie. With only a single lantern on the table, Effie lay in shadows, and even squinting Bridget wasn't certain what she saw or didn't see.

"The night Ma died," Pete went on, "even lying right there beside her, I didn't know when it happened. She left me that easy. Didn't wake me, never said good-bye. Thayer came out of his room in the morning and toed her. 'She's gone,' he said. 'She's cold as a log.'"

Pete leaned toward the open door, then picked up his cap and stood. He stepped closer to Effie, running the cap brim through his fingers as he'd done the day he came asking her help in dressing Mae. "I wasn't asking much."

"She didn't mean you harm," Bridget said. "She didn't know how."

"Ain't just that. Telling Ma she couldn't gather wood for the fire she needed. Not asking her in the day she came calling. Her just wanting to sit a spell in a woman's company."

Bridget was glad Effie, strands of her thin hair in tangled clumps and clotted with blood, had had enough medicine not to know of Pete's anger.

He stepped out and vanished in the dark. Bridget wanted to call out to him, ask him to stay longer. Someday, she'd marry him, and they'd live right there with Jake in the lodge Pete would fix up nice. She'd be a doctor then and never let anyone's mum die and leave them alone.

"Come on now," Chief said. "Time you got some sleep. I'll keep one eye open for Jackdaw."

Forty-One

Effie woke and tried to focus through the slits of her fevered eyes. Night, again. The pain in her hand burning as if she clutched red-hot coals.

"Bridget," she moaned, "my medicine."

Feeling the laudanum roll down her throat, she closed her eyes and struggled not to cry out again. She'd taken the drug enough times to know it would only take a minute. Less than two.

Caught in fevered loops of time, sleep, and wakefulness, the days and nights wheeled around her without divisions.

The pain in her hand—sharp as it remained—was grinding down. She sucked in air and tears stung her eyes when she rolled and bumped it, but she didn't cry out as often for laudanum. There were memories of Cora fussing and Chief—not even the Indian leaving her alone to die—and Bridget spooning in bitter broths. Along with the child's constant, "You have to fight death. You have to fight death."

Footsteps. Hard boots struck the floor. A man stood over Effie's bed, looked down at her, his badge leering. "I see she ain't going to die. Nothing else I can do."

The boom of his voice, like the boom of his boots, made her head pound. Using her good hand, she felt for Granny's quilt under her chin, wanting to drag it over her head. The pulling shifted the position of her wounded hand and throbs of pain made her stop, lay motionless.

"I got no jurisdiction," he said. "How a man treats his wife ain't my business." He faced others Effie only now realized were there. "This here's private. And there ain't no witness to say how she provoked him. Maybe got her hand caught."

"He did it," Bridget cried from somewhere in the room.

"How you know that? You said you ran. 'Less you lied to me earlier, you didn't see he did. Didn't see he didn't." He hawked phlegm from his throat. "Don't matter. A child's word don't hold in court any more than a wife's. Like I said, this here is husband business."

"God spare us!" This time it was Cora from somewhere near the stove.

"My job is upholding the law. Follow the letter."

"Don't you listen to him," Cora said. "His man-made laws, made by men for men. Same as your Rev. Jackdaw's. Church laws made to serve men. This madness has got to stop. And it will, just you wait. We'll get the vote." If the sheriff wanted to say something, Cora wasn't done yet. "Effie, a woman is half. Half of this world, and as long as men keep beating her down she's going to have to stand up again and say so."

Effie closed her eyes, ached for the strength to tell Cora and the sheriff both to leave. They didn't understand. Their arguing had nothing to do with her. She *was* caught and neither of them could help her.

"Effie? Tell me the story," Bridget's voice was hushed.

She opened sleepy eyes. Bridget was pestering again. Cora and Chief with his bitter broths were gone, but Bridget sat cross-legged on the floor beside the bed. Same as she'd been doing for days. At first, she'd told Effie to "fight death." Over and over. Now the harping had changed to "Tell me the story."

"Let me sleep. I told you before, I don't want to talk."

"Grandma Teegan said stories heal people. You need a lot."

"Go."

"You're the princess and you were taken away and trapped in a dark forest by a wicked man. I'm taking care of you like the dwarfs in the woods. I comb your hair and keep cool cloths on your head and make you swallow Chief's soup. Cora is my helper, too."

"Please."

"Rev. Jackdaw almost killed you with a rope, then with a trap. Two tries. The third time something happens in a story is the worst." Bridget's voice was still hushed, as if that were any less annoying. "In the stories, the maidens get away from wicked people and survive. Even the Goose Girl. Her pet horse had its head chopped off."

"Go away."

"Grandma Teegan said in the old stories, girls find their courage and take finger bones and save themselves."

She groaned as Bridget scooted closer, wearing boy's clothing. Likely things Pete had outgrown. A thank-you from Mr. Thayer for the return of his boots.

"This is a story-telling house now," Bridget said. "Pete told about his mum dying, and I've told you every story I know." She whispered again, "I even told you my hardest story. Remember? Rowan died when I fell asleep."

Effie moved her gaze down the length of the bed, searching for the black cloth. Easier to draw over her head than Granny's quilt. It lay at the foot, impossibly far away.

Bridget propped her elbows on the bedframe, as if she planned to sit there another week. Two if necessary. "If you tell the story of Baby Sally, I'll go away."

At Homeplace, Baby Sally's death had been a forbidden topic. Even conversations that *might* lead to the death were stopped well ahead. Now Bridget, bright-eyed—the skin under her eye healed, but her still wearing a rag over her burned head—insisted on the telling.

Burned and struck and starved, she'd still spent long days doctoring the one responsible. She deserved a bit of the story. "You promise to go?"

She nodded.

"Just after Granny came back," Effie began, "two, three weeks—"

"How old were you?"

"I don't know, Bridget. I can't think. Ten."

"I'm twelve now."

Effie closed her eyes, searched for the will to open them again. "I watched Baby Sally in the day and slept with Granny at night." Thinking about Homeplace was painful, but the story coming off her tongue, greased on lingering traces of laudanum and exhaustion, wanted out. "With me in bed with her, Granny had someone to clutch and shriek awake when her dreams started. I slept with Sally before that." She saw the toddler's perfect little sleeping face. The soft skin, the tiny eyelashes. "Ma had the cooking and washing. She was big with carrying Johnny. Tired. Now she had the extra work of Granny, a stranger to her, but needing everything. Granny's mind 'flipped back and forth like a dunce worrying a coin.' That's how the doctor described it. One minute eating her oatmeal and the next seeing her children crying out for her to help them."

Effie sighed; she was telling the story she hadn't told anyone since it happened. Somewhere, Pa was saying, "Be still." But the story wouldn't leave. "Ma was frayed to breaking. More than once, I heard her tell Pa that Granny had to go. The last time she insisted, Pa broke down. I'd never seen that. Her neither. Tears rolled down his beaten cheeks. He said he couldn't do it. Couldn't put her in an asylum. Said he'd prayed all those years for her to come back to him."

The touch of Bridget's hand made Effie open her eyes again. The dusty beams overhead were thick with shadows, but the afternoon of the drowning hung closer, as though she could lift her good hand and pluck the story from the air. Was it the days of being drugged sluicing open her mind?

"Pa and Skeet had another fight. Worse this time. That fighting started with Granny too. Pa was worn through, struggling to keep up with the farming and hewing down trees on winks of sleep so Granny would quit screaming at the sight of them, blaming him for their being there. He worried about Ma. Was scared and sorry for her, too. His ma hadn't returned. This crazy woman didn't love him like he'd dreamed she would. She wasn't proud of how he'd kept the farm going all the years she'd been away. She blamed him for living when his brothers and sisters hadn't. The harder things got, the heavier the work for Skeet, too. Only twelve, but Pa needing to work him like a mule. Worked himself the same way.

"That day, Pa came down on Skeet for being lazy and . . . I don't know. But the yelling went on quite a spell. It wasn't our Pa from before Granny's coming.

"Pa left for the field and Skeet started in on me, saying I had it easy with just Sally to watch. He didn't know how I wasn't sleeping with Granny bawling beside me, and how spooked I was getting listening to her bloody stories. My hands shaking all the time, my eyes staring at the trees yet to come down, believing they were full of Injuns."

Effie lifted her good hand and ran it under her dripping nose. "You promise you'll let me sleep?"

"I promise."

"I was tired and the sun hot. Baby Sally toddled around on the porch, then turned and slid down the stairs on her tummy. I thought she was safe on the ground. I saw the washtub on the new stump. Shiny in the sunlight. I saw her reach for it, but the stump was over her head. Being half-asleep, it looked too tall and like she didn't have the strength to pull herself up. Her being there didn't worry me. I must have shut my eyes.

"Ma's screaming woke me. Her hobbling down the steps past me, holding her big stomach to stop its bouncing. Skeet ran out of the house behind her but faster and reached the tub first. I couldn't see nothing wrong. Didn't understand Ma's screaming. Skeet's hands plunged into the tub and lifted out Sally. Her body was limp, her head flopped to the side." She choked and needed a new breath before she could go on. "So much water running off her and dragging out her curls. She was dead. Drowned as a puppy.

"This here place," Effie said, "maybe even what Rev. Jackdaw's done to me. It must be my just desserts. She was mine to watch."

Bridget stood and backed away from the bed.

"Don't look at me like that," Effie said. "Let me sleep. It's all I've ever wanted."

Her eyelids were heavy and her mind drifting. *They sat in the dark, she in Ma's lap, the two of them in a straight back chair. She was too big to be there. She'd let Baby Sally die and didn't deserve Ma's clutching, kissing, and weeping.*

Forty-Two

Effie curled in bed, faced the wall. Cora was gone. She'd come with two twisty loaves of bread, peaches even in that, and told them good-bye. Apologized for leaving at this horrible time. "I'll be back in August." And when Bridget asked why, Cora explained about a niece getting married and a trousseau needing purchased and packing and planning and arrangements to be made for guests and how the niece had lost her mother and counted on Cora. "I must go."

Effie hadn't really listened to all of that. Hadn't asked questions. She'd thought of her own wedding and the contrast between the two. And how Cora was going because she wished to. No mention of how Mr. Graf liked it, or didn't like it.

Now the Injun was in the lodge. Chief—he had a name. This time he hammered at the table with Bridget and made sleep impossible. The man angered her, but she no longer feared him. He wasn't going to kill her—though in the first days, dopey with laudanum and pain, she'd wished it. Instead, he'd saved her hand from gangrene, possibly saved her life. The doctor made a single visit. Chief visited every morning, unwrapping her hand and wielding a small knife. The first time, drugged and delirious, she'd struggled to lift her chin and bare her neck, giving him access to a clean swipe across her throat. Instead, he'd picked at pockets of pus or infected swelling, re-opening those wounds. Then starting on her forearm, he massaged downward until she bled cleanly and her arm throbbed from the work of his bruising hands. The wound was still a rope-thick line of soreness, a red braid across both the top and bottom, but Chief no longer fussed over it. The fear of infection was gone.

She flinched at the drop of his hammer on the table. With his coming and going, he didn't realize the hours she spent up, using the commode, rocking in her chair, her eyes on the road. But he wanted her on her feet now, her attention back on the world, supposing she slept too much. How could she face a life where her husband abused her so horribly?

"Get your nail through the first piece," Chief told Bridget, teaching her, as if building small boxes mattered a wit. "Then hold that side to the next."

Effie sat up slowly; what use in trying to sleep?

Chief put a piece of wood, half on the seat of a chair and half-extended out. "Downward strokes. The saw angled like this."

Effie stepped outside. It was quieter there, though the springtime air chilled her arms. She lowered herself gingerly to the porch floor, letting her legs dangle over the side. How often she'd sat on the porch at Homeplace, looking out at the openness, dreaming.

Chief's horse watched her from the top of the slope, its spotted head high. She wanted to run a hand along its side, absorb some of its surety. Now that she was better, she needed to face facts. Chief and Cora's visits and aid wouldn't last forever. Disasters called folks to attention, brought out good works, but that help faded quickly. Chief and Cora had other lives. Praise God! She wasn't a child, wasn't a beggar, and didn't want pity or charity.

But how would she and Bridget survive without help? All last winter, when she'd charged items at Graf's store—nearly dying of shame—she'd believed the bill would eventually be paid. Even Graf must have trusted Rev. Jackdaw somewhat, but that was over. No one trusted him now.

The door opened behind her. "You work on that," Chief was talking over his shoulder to Bridget. "I'll come by again tomorrow." He looked at Effie cradling her hand. "The pain all right?"

She ached for a sleeping tonic, but he wouldn't help her there. "It's better."

He gave a slow nod, delivering some wordless encouragement, and descended the steps. Reaching his horse, he grabbed the saddle horn and was up. Easy. Horse and man started off. Not a soul to say otherwise.

Watching the simple act was like watching a fog lift. A person could stand up and go. Cora, off to New York for the summer, going whenever she pleased. Effie took a deep breath, her mind racing, weighing. Since no lawman had knocked on Rev. Jackdaw's door to tell him of her death, he knew she was still alive. There was even the possibility of his having an informant in Bleaksville.

She had to go. The thought of a weeks-long trek on foot back to New Ulm, with no protection on the road, was terrifying. But even more terrifying was the thought of doing nothing, only waiting for Rev. Jackdaw's return. Suppose he came that night?

She stood and went back inside. "Bridget, it's time. We have to go. He's coming. Two weeks, two days, two hours. He'll come for the spoons or because God directed him to kill me. We've got to walk home."

Bridget's eyes widened. "He hasn't come back."

"Maybe he's been waiting to hear if I died. When he finds out I haven't, he'll be back."

"You aren't strong enough." Bridget's voice cracked. "You don't know the way."

"We'll find the way." How many weeks and what sorts of dangers would they face? Injuns, bad men, accidents? But they had no choice. Rev. Jackdaw's insanity was too deep; there was no hope for him, no possible way of living with him.

She crossed to the rocker, sank, and slid her good hand along one rough arm and its layer of new paint. She'd have to leave it. Plus Pa never wanted to see the chair again. He'd likely shipped it to her because he imagined Granny's ghost still rocked there.

"What about Jake?"

"We're not taking the ox." Effie ached for one last dose of laudanum. Just moving to the porch and back had awakened pain in her hand. She'd already taken all the painkiller the doctor left. She wouldn't go and beg for more.

"I promised Jake I'd never leave him."

Effie stood. "You're almost grown. Old enough to understand we can't take that animal. He'll slow us down. We might have to run, sneak into barns. How can we do that with a big ox?" A wave of doubt made her look away. How could she take care of herself and Bridget on the road? But staying and getting herself killed wouldn't help Bridget either. "Jake isn't ours. The law don't care if a wife runs off, but stealing a head of cattle is different. We don't want the sheriff after us."

"Jake'll be alone. He needs me."

"I need you. I can't do it alone." Bridget's eyes were filling. After all that happened, why would the child care about helping her? "I know I've hurt you and you don't trust me, but we can do this. But not with the sheriff riding down on us."

Bridget looked back at the box she was building. "I don't want to leave Jake."

"I'm not getting drug back here because of that animal."

"I don't need you." Bridget put down the hammer, crossed her arms. "I can take care of myself."

"If we stay and that man kills me, what do you think will happen to you? You think he's going to suddenly turn into the pappy you want? You think he's going to live here in this crumbling down place and let you keep the ox?"

"If you go, you'll get dead."

The thought of the trek seemed more daunting with each of Bridget's refusals. "You're coming. I need to get you somewhere safe, too. If he kills me, you'll be next."

She went for her dresses. The green, wilted and tired, hung from its peg like a long-dead weed. She spread the skirt out on the bed for a knapsack, pulled her shoes from beneath the bed and put them in the center. She'd save them, worn out as they were, for when the bottoms of her feet blistered. She put the black cloth with her shoes. "The spoons. It's time you gave them back. We can sell them along the way for food."

Bridget still refused to move.

Exhaustion threatened to sit Effie down again, and pleading with Bridget increased her weariness. "You can go to school in New Ulm." She stopped and swallowed back her emotion. "We got to go. You know that. If you were a baby, I'd pick you up and carry you."

She did her best to roll up the Never Forget quilt and add it to her bundle. Bridget was plain stubborn. She was also stronger and more cunning. Forced to come, she'd let a few days of travel pass and then she'd slip away, returning to Jake. What then? There'd be no use in doubling back for her. No use losing the miles already walked. Bridget would only run off again.

"Okay, I'll go alone."

Bridget's breath caught.

Maybe fear, Effie thought, *can do what pleading can't.* "Rev. Jackdaw touches you, he tries to take you to this bed, kill him first. You hear me? Killing him is your only chance. He does that to you, you'll die inside."

Bridget's eyes lifted. "Are you dead inside?"

Effie's hand throbbed as if it would speak for her. "I'm trying to live. I won't wait here and be murdered because you care more about that ox."

"It's not just Jake."

"What then?"

"Mum and Pappy are West. Mum might be in Omaha."

"A prostitute? That again?"

"There're no trees at your house. And Jake."

"But if you're dead!" Effie dropped a half-eaten loaf—another of Cora's loafs remained for Bridget—and the big knife on top of her things. *Poor protection, but something.* Folding in the skirt fabric to make a bundle, her own tears threatened. "You don't have a family . . . at least not one that stayed with you. Maybe you can't understand how I need to go home." She grabbed up the bundle. "Stay right here if you want."

"You're shaking. You're not strong, and you don't even know the way."

"I'll get stronger, and every day I'll be farther away from him and a day closer to home. That'll be my strength."

"Your pa said don't come home."

Effie lifted her hand with its rope of scars. "This will change his mind."

"Go!" Bridget cried. "Just leave me! I'll bet Rev. Jackdaw is coming right now! You better get out of here."

Bridget's hurting was all the more assurance that given a day or two—even an hour or two—she'd come running to catch up. When that happened, the decision would be hers, and she wouldn't run back.

Johnny's marbles lay on the windowsill. Picking them up, Effie felt their coolness. Johnny waited for her. With her cape and the bundle, she looked back at the lodge where she'd spent months and then to Bridget with her licking and eyes full of tears. Only a young girl wearing a turban of rags and in boy's clothes. How small she looked. Like some strange, lost doll.

"I won't go through town," Effie said. "Him likely to come from that direction, and Chief likely to see me walking past his house. I'll go toward Thayer's. Slow as I can walk, you can catch up. Bring the spoons."

She stepped out onto the porch, closed the door, but couldn't move. Where would she spend the night? She needed Bridget. She reminded herself she'd also been afraid the first day she stepped out alone to shepherd Jake. But she'd done it; she'd found the courage.

When she was sure Bridget wasn't going to come running, not yet at least, she made it down the steps, and started up the slope. She forced her face into a stiff smile. She wouldn't have to go far alone. Bridget would catch up.

Forty-Three

Bridget wouldn't watch Effie leaving; Effie walking away the same as had Pappy and Mum. E-F-F-I-E. Walking away the same as Grandma Teegan.

She waited a minute. Ten. An hour.

The sun set, and as shadows spread like a dark fog to cloak Effie's rocker and the bed where she slept, Bridget went out and sat on the back landing. This time, she wasn't the one stealing. Effie's leaving stole the colors from the sky. It stole the back and forth hoots of the owls. It stole crickets' songs and the throated honk of bullfrogs. It stole clear back a year and took Grandma Teegan again.

Where was Effie now that it was getting dark? Huddled in a ditch? Trembling beneath a bridge? She'd needed to go, but how could she? Wasn't she too sorry over her lye mixture? Too sorry over the blisters on Bridget's toes? Too sorry about hitting with a plate?

Jake left off grazing at the edge of the clearing and lumbered over. He licked Bridget's knees and bumped her hands with his head so she'd pet him. "I emptied the poop bucket," she told him. "I carried in wood and got food." She'd done everything to make herself too valuable to be left. But it hadn't been enough. There *was* time to catch up with Effie, but she wouldn't. Effie was going *east*. Her parents already had too many troubles and didn't want a half orphan. Not even Effie, with all those brothers would really want her once they arrived. "I'd only remind her of Rev. Jackdaw and the bad months at the lodge."

The second day was harder still. Bridget lifted the chairs onto the table and climbed. Dust sifted and made her cough as she brought down Grandma Teegan's hair. The pages of Rev. Jackdaw's journal dropped. The words hadn't interested her, hadn't interested Effie either. Effie had said to throw them away, but Bridget rolled the sheets tight as a pencil and tied them with strands of her hair.

With the braid fisted in her hand, she walked Jake along the road, keeping him close to the lodge. Up and down, so that from whichever direction Effie came, she'd see her. When Effie appeared, Bridget would run to her and carry the heavy green bundle. If Effie was tired and needed to lean on her . . . that would be all right.

The sun still slanted easterly when Chief came on Smoke and reined the horse.

"You can't stay," Bridget said before he could speak. "I'm too busy today."

He looked at her for a minute, then out into the quiet morning with Jake grazing just a few yards away. "I see that." But not leaving. Watching her. "You okay?"

How to answer?

"Effie all right?"

"She's sleeping." Had he seen Grandma Teegan's braid? She moved it casually behind her back. "I'm staying out here with Jake so she can sleep."

Smoke watched her and watched Jake. He shook his head and shimmied the shoulder closest to her. A large spot there shifted.

"You haven't seen Jackdaw?" Chief asked. "He isn't in there?"

"Maybe he's never coming back."

"Maybe I ought to go in and have a look."

If he did, he'd see Effie was gone, her dresses no longer hanging on pegs, the Never Forget quilt missing from the bed. He'd see what Bridget never wanted him to see: the shameful truth that she'd been left again.

"Effie's much better now." She squeezed the braid. *Nera, Nera.* "She doesn't want you to visit anymore."

Beneath the brim of his hat, she caught the squint of his eyes. He didn't believe her. Then he did. She wanted him to know Effie was gone, but that was only part of what she was feeling. She couldn't explain the round hole that formed when you were left. The hole was ten times your size and rolled alongside you. You had to be very careful and not fall into it. Anyway, Effie *was* coming back.

"You got something you want to tell me?"

She shook her head.

He rode off, Smoke's tail dancing, Chief lifting and settling with the horse's trot, his braids swaying. He hadn't gotten down, put a hand on her shoulder, told her everything would be all right. He didn't want to be "that man."

With each passing hour and no sign of Effie, Bridget's loneliness increased. That evening, she stood on the ridge and watched the train, its cars rumbling. Families coming and going. Inside the lodge again, she unrolled Rev. Jackdaw's journal pages, used her palm, and pressed them flat.

I'm leaving this record lest God forget

She'd glanced over Rev. Jackdaw's shoulders, or peeked at the journal left open and drying, enough times to know he began every entry this way.

I'm leaving this record lest God forget

Seven years old. Horses pounding into the yard. Four riders, each with a rope around the neck of the same wild stallion. Swearing, they struggled to keep the horse at a safe distance between them.

I'd seen plenty of wild horses caught and brought in for Mister to break. Never a stallion so magnificent. A wide, deep chest, powerful haunches. Black glass. His head in the clouds. Regal, at least twenty hands high.

Once in the corral, the stallion circled, pawed the earth, snorted, ran again. His mane streaming in the air. Never tiring, his eyes never leaving the row of us along the split rail fence.

When the men left, Mister and my two brothers, ten and fourteen, went in to sup. I sat in the dusk, seeing myself riding such a horse. And sick with what I knew was coming.

I spent most of the night at my bedroom window, looking down on the corral. The stallion still prancing, its head high.

The moon rose, the wind came up, and I got it in my head the stallion caused both. Mister broke horses across three counties, but none of them had ever ordered the moon and stirred the firmament. The drum of his hoofs circling, moonlight pouring over him like cream. Then he'd stop, turn, and start the stars swirling the other direction.

They dropped him at first light, his screams waking me. Snagged his front legs with a catch rope and brought him down. Tied his legs together. Mister barked the order and the stallion's hell began. My brothers, more bone in their backs than me, hitting him with flat boards. Not breaking the skin, breaking his will. Using constant irritation, wearing him down over the hours. Slapping him on the upturned flank and shoulder, keeping him scared all that day, his upward eye wide, rolling. Sweat sliding off him in sheets.

Mister broke them using his system: my brothers doing the meanness, while he stayed away, then him bringing trickles of water like some goddamned savior. Rationing. Fooling the stressed horse into trusting him.

By evening, the stallion foamed at the mouth. Mister came again with water. Poured a short, slow stream across the big, dry lips, the horse already knowing this was the man with the water, swallowing what he could catch as it ran through his teeth on one side and out the other. Just enough to wet his tongue and throat. Smelling how most of the water went onto the ground under his head, making a mud that, with his thrashing, closed his downward eye.

That night, the stallion still fought the ropes, struggling to stand and then going still with fatigue but for the panting. Dung and urine muddying his coat. His one open eye spied the stars. Then me at the window.

Bridget looked up from her reading. Out her window, fireflies blinked on and off in the darkness with the moon on the river just beyond. Jake lay in the starlight chewing his cud beneath Wilcox. With them in place she could continue reading the journal pages. She wrapped her feet around the legs of the chair, her whole body holding on.

The next day was never better. Sitting on the fence, watching the tormenting in the August heat, and Mister giving a little more water so the horse pulled up his lips, hungry at the smell, trusting more now in Mister's hand.

Mister grabbed me off the fence, called me a god-damned girl for my sniffling. My brothers and I were men to him or girls. Never got the chance to be boys. When he tried to make me be a man, insisting I take my turn on the stallion, I failed him. Too weak spirited to do it. He shoved me to the dirt, told me to get my "shriveling little girl's ass" out of his sight. He couldn't drag me to the horse, clutch my hand to the club, make me do it; he wanted the stallion to believe he was the nice one.

That evening, he knelt and tried the bit. Two days of suffering usually made a horse accept a mouthful of iron. But the stallion swung its powerful head into Mister's chest. Knocked him over. His face looking up and me right there in the window. Mister threw down the iron and poured the next ration of water a foot away from the horse's mouth. He'd already stressed the stallion about as far as a horse can go, and the tactics hadn't worked. A third day might kill the animal. Mister's reputation and good money were at stake.

Hours later, I heard the first howling. In the dark, the wolves took their time moving in until their baying told me there was no mistaking their target. On his feet, no wolf could take the horse, but on the ground, he didn't have a chance.

The stallion knew the wolves were there, too. I felt his heart booming inside my own. Did he want them to stay away? Or did he want them to come and end his misery?

When the whole world went quiet, nothing out of the wolves but their circling paws, I went out. I'd stand guard over the stallion, fight any yellow-eyed critter that came into the corral.

The stallion's eye widened and his nostrils flared when I climbed through the fence. I sat beside him hearing that same ragged breathing I'd been hearing since late afternoon. He knew me; he'd watched me all the hours I'd sat on the fence, then at my window, watching him. I stroked his head, feeling how it gentled down under my touch. Then it started. Him begging me to set him free. His one eye, blacker and deeper than the night, asking over and over. I believed I had to. If I didn't, everything that happened, the wolves or the next day's beating and thirst, would be my fault.

I brought water and ladled scoops from my bucket down his throat. I tried the knots on his front legs first. His struggling had pulled them so tight I couldn't do a thing. He lay still, believing in me, but I needed a knife and didn't know how I could go into the kitchen for one and come back out unnoticed. The wolves circled the corral, just yellow eyes moving in the night. I crawled in the dirt, tried the knots on the back legs. He'd pulled them just as tight.

The toe of a boot thwacked into my ribs, sent me flying over the stallion's rump. Mister came around the horse. The second kick caught my groin. Mister kept kicking while I twisted and howled. Him cursing how I'd undone two days of work and two days of the horse's stress. Giving the stallion hope, making him wild again.

More kicks rolled me in the dirt. One catching the side of my head, splitting open my eye. My body no more able to move now than a sack of feed. Ma's bare feet inches away. She didn't try to stop Mister. She stood there waiting for him to finish. Like waiting for him to finish gutting and quartering a deer so she could clean the bloody kitchen table and serve sup.

She'd pick me up if I lived, bury me if I didn't. Until she knew which it would be, she'd wait.

I remember shotguns and knew my brothers were shooting at the wolves.

When I woke, sun and heat poured in the open window. I was on the floor, my body too dirty and bloody for bedsheets Ma would have to wash. Mister's cussing in the corral made me pull myself up enough to peek over the windowsill with my one open eye.

On his knees, Mister was trying to force the bit again. His hands struggling against the powerful jaws. His arm suddenly flew up and he flung his hand. Blood sprayed in red strings. He fell to one side, howled, then staggered to his feet, the hand clutched to his chest. Blood poured onto his shirt, dripped down his pants. Stooped like he'd been shot, he started for the house.

He bellowed my name from the stairs. Throwing open my door, he came for me. A boot lifted off the floor, aimed, but his eyes rolled back and he missed and staggered. "Git up!"

I couldn't. He'd broken ribs, maybe my back, closed my eye, and put a gash alongside it. Fire seared in my groin. He reached down to grab me, his bloody hand splattering warm and thick on my face. Three fingers gone. Bitten clean off. "You fucking girl." The words slow. A struggle to pronounce. I'd seen him drunk a hundred times, but this slurring had a different tone.

"A girl's no use to you," Ma said. Her face pleasant as if she'd entered the room to see if Mister might need her to fetch something. "I could use a girl. I'm washing and cooking all day."

Mister stumbled wide-legged out of the room. He hadn't agreed with Ma. He was losing blood and in so much pain he didn't know where he was. A few seconds later, a boom and several thumps as he rolled down the stairs. Ma left the room to go help him.

The third day without Effie, Bridget led Jake into the trees to hunt for deeper scrub. They'd hide in case Chief rode by again. She'd lied to him the day before, but he wouldn't believe her two days straight.

She spent the day at Jake's shoulder or trailing at his heels. Staying that close to him, she wasn't lost. In her mind, she reread Rev. Jackdaw's pages, thinking of the little boy and the horse that stirred stars.

At the sound of the train across the river, Bridget led Jake to the road for the walk home. Dusk was lugging in shadows, a second world coming alive. Cora was gone and Chief had never visited at this hour, though she knew Mr. Thayer or Pete were likely to ride by. That was okay—they never asked to come in.

She and Jake had gone only a few yards on the easier surface when, just as she expected, Pete came around the bend. When he'd come abreast, he stopped his horse and touched his hat brim. "Hey."

Please, Bridget prayed, *don't ask any questions about Effie. I don't want to tell* you *a lie.*

He remained in the saddle while she did her best to smile up at him. He looked uneasy and full of something Bridget couldn't read. After a moment, he nodded at Jake. "Ma hooked him to our cart before I could even walk. He's older than me."

It was an odd thing to say, as though he struggled to find a way into a conversation. "He's not old." Pete didn't care about Jake, and he hadn't stopped to tell her what his ma did. Had he seen Effie walk by in front of his place?

She swung her hands behind her back, clasped them together. Suppose he hadn't, but her asking the question sent him off to the sheriff to report the news? Would the sheriff say she was a half orphan again and send her back to New York? Where police records said she was a thief and where Mum could never find her?

Pete touched his hat again, looked down the road he'd yet to cover. "You all right then?"

Chief had asked nearly the same thing. "Don't I look all right?"

She ached to keep him there. "Effie's strong now. She takes long walks. Probably even as far as your house."

Pete's face stilled, and he glanced up the road like something there needed inspection. She studied his profile. His jaw was leaner, harder even than the day she rode behind him. Her eyes widened. Shadow clung to his upper lip. He was shaving now!

Wait for me, her heart cried. *Wait for me to grow up, too.*

But she could N-E-V-E-R say that. "I better go. Effie will be waiting." She started forward and for a few paces Pete rode at her side. "You can take wood, if you want," she said. "It's not stealing. Rev. Jackdaw bought the lodge. It's our wood now."

"Collecting wood is women's work. Since Ma died, we buy coal." He clucked his horse into a trot.

She wanted to run after him. She'd tell him everything, and they'd talk until after dark. She'd ask how far he supposed Effie had gotten in three days. Did he think she was in Iowa by now? She'd ask him to stay and keep her company until she fell asleep.

Reaching the lodge, Bridget didn't want to go inside. No one waited there for her. Jake drank from the river, and she took off her shoes and climbed into the basket of Wilcox's exposed roots. "Mum?" Then louder, "Mum!" She screamed several more times before she had to quit and suck air into her heaving lungs. Jake came closer when she stopped. With his front feet in the water, he stretched his head to reach her. She stroked his cheek. How many times since arriving at the lodge had she screamed out over the river? Mum wasn't ever going to step out, but Jake was there and Wilcox held her.

A fish jumped, the large flash high and amber in the waning light, and then a splash with rings rippling out over the water.

"All water is connected," Rowan promised her the day Mum left.

The river, Wilcox and all trees, the sky with flying stars, Jake. It was all connected and all of it loved her. She was at home in the wide world, and she could unpack. Not unpack in a tiny room like she and

Grandma Teegan had in New York. Or even unpack all her shiny stolen things from the walls. She could lay *herself* out, unfolding all the things she believed, and be safe in her skin.

She leaned back against Wilcox's trunk and looked out at the quick-gathering stars. Mum and Pappy were walking under the same sky. Grandma Teegan in Ireland, getting her new sheep in for the night, Ogan at her heels.

"Grandma Teegan," she whispered, "we fit under the same heaven." And she realized that when a person fits under heaven, she fits everywhere.

Forty-Four

Before Chief walked up the back ramp, Bridget knew he and his horse had entered the clearing. Smoke's nearness always made her skin prickle with the sense of a larger world. Plus, they'd ridden through the trees, along the secret passageway, which made their arrival even more fairy.

She rushed to open the door. Effie had been gone five days, and by now Chief knew. His brown eyes said he knew, and when he took off his hat and stepped in, his open face said he knew. He'd spent so much time inside while Effie was healing he seemed fitted to the walls and the floor. Fitted to his spot at the table where for hours he'd taught her to hammer and saw.

He carried a small red, calico bundle and began unwrapping it. The fabric wasn't square like Effie's sugar sacking or one of Cora's dishtowels, but longer than his arm with green curly ques. When he'd exposed a sandwich of sliced beef piled high between thick slices of bread, he pushed it all at her. "I see you ain't been working."

She ate slow while Chief tapped nails into the box she'd not touched in five days. She thought to tell him building boxes was stupid. When he finished affixing the fourth side, he slid the box in her direction just as he had the sandwich. "What you planning? Just to make a nuisance of yourself in every garden within five miles?"

"Gardens aren't even growing yet." Grandma Teegan's braid lay on the table and she let her eyes rest there. Had Chief heard her crying out for Mum? Was that the reason he thought he'd better visit? "I'm all right now," she said. She wanted him to wrap her up, carry her again, or even to reach across the table and touch her hand. She couldn't ask. "Effie's coming back soon. She's visiting Old Mag."

His eyes said, *All right, whatever story you want to tell.*

She crossed her arms over the bib of the overalls he'd given her and looked directly at him. "Effie's probably coming home tomorrow. Anyway, I have Jake."

"That so?" His lips pursed. "She wouldn't want you helping me now and again."

Effie would call it charity, but Effie wasn't there. "Helping how?"

"Doing what's needing done. Helping me get in my garden, fighting hens for their eggs, washing up after we sup."

"You going to pay me?"

A corner of his lip turned up. He brought it back down. "Likely not."

Then it wasn't charity. His whole garden did need planting, he always missed one or two eggs she could find even in the dark, and she supposed old men didn't like washing dishes. Helping, she'd be doing him a charity, just like carrying off scrap wood and taking the boy's clothes he didn't want. "Only until Effie gets back."

"Only until then."

Grandma Teegan would like him. He was old, though not nearly as old as her, and he liked trees and animals and was quiet inside. The name Grandfather better suited him than Chief. She wanted to ask if he ever got lonely, but there was no gate into something so big. She reached up and began pulling the wrapping off her head, the long strips of fabric unwinding in her hands. She turned so he saw her scars.

He nodded. Then nodded again. "You finished wearing that silly stuff now?"

"I don't want anyone to see my burns."

"That the only reason?" He reached for his hat, tapped it against his thigh. "Tomorrow then," he said. He stopped at the door, his hat still thumping against his leg. "There's not a person in the world without scars. You might as well admit you're just like the rest of us."

Later, alone once again, she took the strips of soiled sheeting to the fireplace and tossed them onto months'-old ashes and stabbed at them with the iron poker. Starting at the crown of her head, she brought hair from the right up over the scar, then hair from the left, her fingers learning to braid.

Forty-Five

Bridget stretched Grandma Teegan's braid along the red cloth Chief had given her, twisted up the fabric, and tied it around her waist. The ends hung with a fringe at her side just like the sash Chief wore. If Effie ever came back and threatened the hair, Bridget would tell her no. She wasn't ever hiding it away again. Effie was small now, had grown small in her absence. She wasn't still the boss.

Bridget picked up the last pages of Rev. Jackdaw's journal.

I suffered days of fevers with the stallion running through my dreams. My back in spasms and making me cry out. The same with each bloody urination. My eye opened somewhere in the first week or two, though it jumped around my face, cried on its own.

I never learned whether the stallion lived or died. I saw how I'd wronged him with my girlish weakness. Maybe killed him. I'd cost Mister the use of his hand, too. Leaving him only one to grip a rope. Though two fingers could still grip a whiskey bottle.

Ma cut down one of her dresses and pulled it over my head. My begging didn't matter. I wanted to hide out behind the stove or behind anything, but she had no use for me if I weren't going to help her. I couldn't have survived another beating from Mister—even if my body did. I couldn't return to the corral where he'd be. So long as I was in a dress, wearing my humiliation, living behind Ma's skirts, and emptying his piss bucket, he could tolerate the sight of me.

He never stopped shaking his half hand in my face, reminding me I was responsible. Then a backhand would prove that even with two fingers, the hand and arm could send me to the floor. Maybe he wanted me kept alive so he could watch my shame in wearing a dress. They called me "girl." Mister had two sons now. If he'd ever had a third, that boy was dead.

My hair grew long, and people thought me a freak.

Spending my days in the house, I saw Ma's mind was a jar. She could dump out anything Mister did to her, rinse the glass with some lie she told herself, and despite her bruises, call him to eat an hour later. Not a trace of anger. Sometimes I wonder how Ma might have been before she married him. Did Mister break his wife the same way he broke horses?

The page ended there, and Bridget wished she had more. Slowly, she began tearing up the pages, then ripping the pieces into ever-smaller pieces. The words told a story, but they told a lie, too. Rev. Jackdaw hadn't written so God wouldn't forget. He wrote so he wouldn't forget, so he could live the past over and over. He was Salt Woman, but she was too, because in her mind, Grandma Teegan left her over and over again. Maybe everyone was Salt woman, all retelling their worst stories instead of their best.

Forty-Six

"Bridget," Cora hurried in. The lodge doors were open, and she came in without hesitating.

"Cora," Bridget, on her knees in front of the wash tub, scrambled to her feet. They fell into each other's arms.

"Is it true?" Cora asked. She smelled of flowers and a fast ride on her horse. "Effie has been gone all summer?"

"Did you have fun on your trip?"

"Yes, it was wonderful, but if I had known you were left in this dreadful place alone . . ." She looked around at the small copper combs and spoons hanging from the rafters by threads. "I would have returned immediately."

"Did Chief tell you? I've been working for him."

"He might have sent a letter." She took paper, ink, and a pen from a her satchel. "I came as soon as I heard. Is there someone you can write?"

"To come and get me?" Queasiness stirred in Bridget's stomach. "I'm not alone. I eat at Chief's, and when I'm in the trees with Jake I'm not alone, either."

Cora tapped the half-dozen sheets of paper she'd laid on the table as though she wouldn't accept excuses. "I hate to think of you moving away. I don't want you to leave Bleaksville, but that man," the word hissed, "Rev. Jackdaw is your father for now. And the law will honor that and let him take you. The only way to override that is to find some family. Aunts, uncles, lost third cousins, someone."

"He's not coming back. He's gone, and I'll be found."

"That's what I'm afraid of; him finding you. We don't know what he's thinking. We don't know he's never coming back. And Effie," she shook her head and pursed her lips, "that poor lost girl. I could take you home with me, but in this small town, word would pass in a day, and Rev. Jackdaw would know exactly where to find you."

"I don't have any aunts or uncles."

"Is there no one at all you can write? Where in Ireland does your grandmother live? I can't imagine," Cora went on fretting, "having to sign those papers. That must have been the hardest thing she was ever forced to do. How does a grandmother let a grandchild go? To strangers."

Bridget sank back to her knees. With both hands on the shirtfront she washed, she rubbed it up and down the bumpy washboard. She'd thought of writing Grandma Teegan before, but what if Grandma Teegan hadn't made it back? She wanted to believe Grandma Teegan had and never hear she hadn't. "I made her sign the Surrender Papers," Bridget said. And she had, though she'd been stabbed when Grandma Teegan actually picked up the pen, actually scratched out her signature with her shaking hand. "Then Rev. Jackdaw signed, too. I'm his free girl now."

"That scares me. But suppose you aren't legally his. If we could somehow find your parents—even a more distant relative, an aunt or uncle," she said again, "I have money for a lawyer. Bridget, maybe by now your grandmother has heard from your parents. You have to write her. When you're done, I'll post it. And your parents? What are their names? Where do you suppose they might be?"

Bridget stared down at her wet shirt in the cold water. The lodge had been too hot and stuffy to think about starting the stove. "They're West. Pappy's name is Darcy, Mum's name is Kathleen." She'd not spoken their names since Mae walked down the slope. "Mum's hair matches mine." Cora hadn't mentioned Bridget's braid, as if she'd forgotten Bridget had walked around for months with her head wrapped in rags.

"And the last name? Where are you from?" She asked questions fast. "Before New York?"

"Kathleen Wright and Darcy Wright. From Cork." She stopped. She wanted to add that Mum might be in Omaha, but she didn't want to say the word "prostitute." "Pappy worked in the mine."

That evening, Bridget stayed by Jake's side. When he walked, she walked. When he stopped and chewed his cud, she stood at his shoulder. Was Grandma Teegan still alive and wanting a letter? And what could a letter say? Bridget couldn't admit she was living alone and hadn't yet found Mum and Pappy. Grandma Teegan would worry. And she couldn't tell how Rev. Jackdaw put Effie's hand in a trap.

But Cora wanted her to write, and Grandma Teegan had loved the letters she received from Mum. Even when she worried over them.

Dear Grandma Teegan,

I am fine in America. I hope you are fine. I hope Ogan is fine, too.

She stopped, Matron's silver pen in the air and Cora's pen idle on the table. Grandma Teegan, if she received the letter, would read it sitting alone in the croft. A candle would be sputtering on her table. She'd want to read only nice things and hear she'd done right in signing papers. If Bridget asked if there was word of Mum and Pappy, Grandma Teegan would know they hadn't found each other. She'd worry more.

Jake, trees, a river—a happy list said more than all the things on it—roots of trees that hear the dead, trunks of trees that hear me, leaves that hear angels, your braid, curls on Jake's head, butterflies, selkies, hammers, boxes, Smoke, spots on Smoke, Wire, spots on Wire, Cora, Chief, Pete, Jake.

Love, Bridget

Forty-Seven

Bridget entered the mercantile carrying two boxes she'd finished. She'd spent the morning with Jake, then gathered eggs for Chief, washed and carried them to his cool cellar. They'd eaten strips of beef and fresh creamed cabbage outside under a tree. Sitting in the cooler shade with their plates in their laps, they watched monarchs and hummingbirds flutter over the last orange flowers on milkweeds.

Mr. Graf stood behind the counter wrapping a woman's purchases in paper and string. He glanced up when the bell over the door rang. His eyes landed on Bridget, a shadow passed over them, and they dropped. He returned to his wrapping. She'd not seen him all summer long, hadn't walked into the mercantile since Effie's leaving. But Cora was back now, almost three weeks, and on her last visit to the lodge she'd bought two of Bridget's boxes. Did she want to buy two more? But seeing only Mr. Graf and the shade that passed over his eyes, though it hadn't been anger, made Bridget turn to leave. She'd wait for Cora to visit again.

"Hang on," Graf called. He followed the patron with her purchases to the door, nodded good day, and turned the sign to "Closed." "Cora," he yelled in the direction of the curtain.

Bridget clutched her boxes, shifted her weight from foot to foot. She shouldn't have come. Graf was sweeping now, the broom's bristles swooshing on the floor. Cora scowled in his direction when she appeared, her brows pinched and her eyes heavy. Her expression fell further when she saw Bridget. "Oh honey, you're here."

The broom stopped. Dust motes swirled. "Tell her," Mr. Graf said.

Cora gave him a frustrated sigh and turned back to Bridget. "I was baking a pie. I planned to bring it out in the morning."

Cora's baking for her, despite the heat and even though Mr. Graf was home, meant something was wrong. Bridget felt as if she could only see the shape it, before Cora told her, then it wouldn't be news. When her heart crashed, when the fish in her stomach tried to make her throw up, she'd tell herself: *I already knew that.*

The boxes had grown heavy and misshapen. Earlier, they'd looked worthy of selling, but now, with something bad ready to step out, they looked wrong.

Cora took them, set them on the counter, and grabbed Bridget's empty hands. "I'm afraid I have bad news."

"I better go. He turned over the sign."

Cora held tighter. A moonstone hung from a dark ribbon at her throat.

Bridget tried to tug free. It was time to run.

"Will you bloody tell her?" Graf said.

"Bridget, the reason I asked so many questions," Cora's words sounded practiced, rehearsed through the afternoon. "I needed to know more about your parents so I could place ads in newspapers west of here, Denver—"

Bridget tried not to listen.

"—San Francisco, Seattle. A woman wrote who knew your parents." Her hands pumped Bridget's as if they worked together to hold on to something.

"Come," Cora said, "let's sit down." She steered Bridget through the dark curtain in the back of the mercantile. A few steps beyond, they passed through a second curtain the color of winter pines. They entered a fancy room and again Bridget thought to run. Chief's house was better. He had fewer things and his rooms felt more like her memories of the croft in Ireland.

Cora walked her to a sofa, sat her down, and then sat so close their hips touched. She squeezed Bridget's hands again. "There's just no easy way to say this. I'm afraid your parents have died."

Lying, lying! Bridget vowed never to bring another box, never to eat her cakes and pies again. She wouldn't listen either. She'd remember all the things in the room so she could tell Mum about them: sofas, plants, pictures, small tables with wood scrolling like tiny labyrinths, chairs with embroidered seats. All things Mum never had.

"The woman who wrote met your parents in Denver. A group of Irish, mostly from Cork, traveled together to Butte, Montana. They planned to work for The Company. Mining copper and silver."

Lying, lying.

"Many of them took ill the first winter. Your parents too. That spring, they died."

The last of the sun's crown was sinking and orange light streamed in through a window, warming a square on the carpet. Bridget pulled her hands from Cora's, slid off the sofa, and crawled to the brightness.

Cora joined her there on the floor. "Stay here tonight. In the morning we'll talk more."

Fish thrashed in Bridget's stomach, their wide mouths gaping and gasping. "Effie's probably home now."

Cora shook her head. "About Effie—"

Bridget couldn't bear hearing any more lies. She jumped up, ran through the first curtain and out the second. Mr. Graf stood at the mercantile door looking through its window. He'd already turned out the lanterns and hearing her, he jerked open the door as if afraid she planned to run straight through the glass.

She raced down the street, hardly aware of the other shops closing or the people who stared as she ran by sobbing. At the bridge she stopped, winded. Cora would be coming, not letting her be alone. But first, Cora would change and go to the stable and have her horse saddled.

Bridget swiped at her eyes, tried to clear them enough to see. She thought to hide behind the school and sit under a dark window, but she wasn't welcome there even when it was disserted. She ran on to Nettle Creek and, falling back on her rump, she slid down the embankment. Only catching herself when her feet hit the water. She hurried under the bridge, crouching, and keeping to the bit of dry bank along the side. She sat, dropping her face onto her drawn-up knees.

Dusk gathered. Mum and Pappy were never coming for her. She'd never see them again. She picked up a stone, hurled it into the water. Then hurled everything within reach: more stones, sticks, clods, a bottle, all splashing into the brown.

A horse started across overhead, sending down a thundering of dust. When the noise passed, she peeked around a wooden support beam: Cora's golden horse, Cora's skirt billowing over the horse's rump as she urged it on.

Bridget sank back into hiding. She'd been stupid to sit on the bank by the lodge and call for Mum. Mum wasn't a selkie. She was dead. Uncle Rowan had lied. He'd never seen Mum step from land into the sea dragging a sealskin.

Lightning bugs, first one, then two. Long minutes passed and the air filled with them. Barn swallows swooped and returned to nests along the beams and trusses over Bridget's head. Just outside the bridge's span, a raccoon with its mask and striped tail spotted her. It froze a moment and disappeared into the nettles lining the bank. She sobbed into her sleeve, licked her top lip and tasted the salt of her tears. Not Mum's.

She couldn't see overhead, but right and left of her tiny stars began to twinkle then grow fat and bright in the darkness. The slow gait of a horse's hooves made timbers creak and send down more dust. Cora was returning home.

Bridget longed for Jake. He'd never just leave her and then die somewhere far away. She'd go home, hug his big furry jowls, and tell him the awful news. He couldn't make the worst thing not be true, but he'd wish he could.

Grabbing weeds for handholds, even though they made her hands sting and itch, she crawled up the embankment. She walked without hurry. There were no horses out, only a million cricks and tweets and throaty-sounding night insects. If she did hear Cora coming, there'd be plenty of time to jump into a ditch and hide. She liked Cora, but Cora wasn't an orphan, or a half orphan, or river people, and she wasn't alone.

At the end of the long lane leading to Chief's, Bridget stopped. He understood people dying and having to live without them. Was he walking his pasture right now, talking to his dead boy? Looking for that dead boy's bones? She paced back and forth, searched the sky for a shooting star to tell her which way to go. If a star fell to the right, she'd stay on the road to Jake. If a star fell to the left, she'd go to Chief. He didn't like her there after supper. When the dishes were done, he always told her it was time to leave and he'd see her again the next day. He never said why he shooed her off, but she knew the nights were his to walk along the river and build coffins.

The stars weren't helping her decide. She didn't need stars, and anyway, she wouldn't bother Chief. Not even to talk a minute. She'd just go through his yard, hear his hammering, and know he was there. Then she'd cut through his pasture, maybe see Smoke, and go on to Jake.

Forty-Eight

The only light came from Chief's larger barn. Bridget had only been in the smaller of the two, and even that barn she thought large. Chief milked cows there and in the winter stabled his four-horse team and Smoke, each with a stall of their own.

Afraid of being seen by Wire—the dog couldn't keep a secret—she ran wide of the house and on to the lighted barn. There were no windows on the bottom floor and the wide double doors were closed, though light haloed around them.

From inside came Chief's hammering.

"He's loco," Pete had said the freezing afternoon when Bridget rode behind him, her feet bleeding and shrieking with pain. "He builds coffins." Building all night for dead bodies when coffins were already stacked to the ceiling—could mean loco. But other things were loco, too. Mum and Pappy left her behind in Ireland, ended up in a place called Butte, and now they were dead. That was loco, and so was Rowan's death and Grandma Teegan being back in Ireland without her. Chief hadn't been loco the hour they spent sitting under a tree, though that seemed days ago. Night changed everything.

Low on one side of the barn, a thin stream of light, narrow as the Matron's pen, caught her attention. The light reached out like a finger beckoning. She went to it, sank down in the dirt, and leaned against the barn.

A mosquito whined at her bare calf, and she rolled down her pant legs and then her sleeves. Chief had given her the clothes. He'd brought food, given a salve that stopped pain, taught her to build boxes, and saved Effie's hand. She didn't care if he was loco, and she wasn't afraid he would bite her on the neck and suck out her blood. But what if he was angry at her? He didn't want her sneaking around his place at night, spying on him. He'd think she came to steal vegetables and eggs. He might say he no longer wanted her help with chores, no longer wanted to be her friend. She thought of the wrench she'd put back on his worktable in the shed. He never knew she took it, so she couldn't tell him she'd put it back.

She couldn't go. Mum and Pappy were dead. She slapped a mosquito biting her cheek. Sniffed and slapped another mosquito on her leg.

Wire barked at her shoulder.

She nearly yelped with surprise. He was still inside, but he'd heard her or smelled her. "Shhh," she whispered through the crack. "Go away." He quit barking, and she pressed herself tighter against the building, trying to decide if she should run or if Wire was obeying and walking away.

A hand clutched her arm. "What you doing out here?"

Chief! She scrambled to her feet. "I'm sorry. I was just going by."

"This time of night?"

She couldn't move. She wanted to ask about the coffins he was building and tell him Mum and Pappy were dead, but she was anchored in silence.

"Well," he took his time, "you're practically living here." He slapped his neck with a wide, dark hand. "Come on in before the skeeters suck us dry."

Goosebumps winged down Bridget's arms. He wasn't sending her away. She was welcome to stay and be with him.

"Cora came looking for you."

She followed him around the corner of the barn. "A lady wrote her a letter."

"I heard."

"How far west is Butte?"

"I ain't been there," he said, "but it's a good piece."

"Maybe the letter was lying."

"That's possible. I expect you know it wasn't. Same names, same ages, from the same part of Ireland. I know it ain't easy." They stood in front of the wide barn doors. His hand on the heavy, metal latch. "It's time I showed you something."

He pulled open the doors and for an instant she blinked against the light. A row of lanterns burned paces apart down the length of the barn. More hung overhead from high in the third-story rafters. She thought of festivals and Beltane fires. When her eyes adjusted to the light, her mouth gaped with surprise. Her breath felt sucked from her throat. The structure filled the barn. Not coffins. "A ship!"

Its sides swooped up and out and ended in the rafters above her. Ropes strung from hooks in the ceiling supported large, curved arches that reminded her of a cathedral she'd once visited with Grandma Teegan. Reflections from the flickering lantern light all down its side rolled over the new wood like moving water.

The ship was magic. And on the very day she'd received word of Pappy and Mum's deaths.

She tried to steady her emotions enough to choke out words. "It's so big." She stepped around stacks of wood, carpenter horses, ladders, clamps, ropes, and tools she could not name. She walked the length of the ship, turned at the end, and walked halfway back up the other side. Chief couldn't see her now. She pressed both palms against the wood, dropped her head, and cried again.

She remembered looking out over the water with Mum and Rowan. They'd watched ships. It was Rowan who saved money in a jug for crossing, who most wanted to board a ship and sail across the sea. Not Mum. Pappy insisted he stay, "mind the lasses," Bridget and Grandma Teegan. "Soon," Pappy promised. But one day, after Pappy and Mum left, Bridget had stood in the sheep pen beside Grandma

Teegan. Wind gusted off the sea, blew Grandma Teegan's skirt and the ends of the red scarf tied under her chin while she offered ewes a dusting of salt from her palm. Giving one animal a couple of licks, then shaking out a bit more for the next, their wooly heads all crowding.

From outside the pen, Ogan began to whine. He sank slowly to the ground, but kept his head high and his ears up while his eyes fixed on the tall, rock-strewn hill. A knot of four men, their clothes and faces covered in black coal dust, wove slowly down, a litter stretched between them. They leaned in toward their load, their free arms reaching out for balance. Bridget knew the only person they could be bringing to the croft was Uncle Rowan.

Grandma Teegan—not seeing the advancing procession—continued shaking salt onto her palm until Bridget tugged her sleeve and pointed. The tin salt cup hesitated in the air, then fell to the ground, making the sheep flinch and scatter a couple of steps back. Grandma Teegan's old hands grabbed and lifted her skirts off her ankles. She ran toward the stretcher, leaving the pen gate wide, running crookedly, a half-hobble of old knees and hips.

Bridget bent between the sheep, pushed back heads and bodies as big as herself, and picked up the cup. The men scuttled their load through the narrow door of the croft and lifted Rowan onto his bed. They removed their soft leather derbies, held them to their chests. A small cave-in, they said, only Rowan was injured. "Not dead. Just a bad blow to the noggin. He'll have a right-good story to tell and a scar to prove it."

Neighbors came. A doctor by mule. He ran his hands up and down Rowan's bruised body. He washed and applied salve and bandaged the red slash that parted Rowan's hair and ran down the side of his forehead. He lifted Rowan's eyelids and for what seemed a long time, held a candle flame there.

Through all the commotion, Bridget huddled in a corner still clutching the shiny salt cup. His body was like a wet footprint drying on a warm rock, shrinking in from the outer edges. A dark rim growing around him. Fear kept her mute.

When the doctor left, Grandma Teegan peeled Bridget's fingers off the cup and drew her into her arms. "Rowan will be all right," she said. "He'll fight death. For us, he'll fight death."

For three days Grandma Teegan rolled drops of mutton broth off a spoon and through Rowan's dry and busted lips. She changed his head dressings morning and night and oiled the long gash with a poultice of mutton fat and herbs. Bridget stayed close, held the dressings as Grandma Teegan worked, but she kept her eyes from the shadow around him. At night, they slept with Rowan's curtain pulled open in case he woke and mumbled, and they needed to remind him to fight death.

On the fourth day, Grandma Teegan smiled, saying his eyelids had fluttered. "He's healing." She admired how the swelling was leaving his lip and even the gash was closing and turning pink. She told Bridget to nap in his bed, staying close while she drove her hungry sheep to a nearby pasture. "Only a few hours. If he wakes . . ." her voice hesitating, "bring two pans. Beat them as you run. I'll hear you."

Rowan hadn't needed anything. She lay beside him, crying to the ceiling. Maybe the space she saw wasn't real. She hadn't told Grandma Teegan for fear knowing about the space would crawl over Grandma Teegan and break all her bones.

"You're fighting death," Bridget whispered to him. She drifted off to sleep, and in the drifting she smiled at how he reached over and tucked the quilt they shared tighter under her chin.

When she woke, he lay just as he had. His body telling her he'd not moved. Not moved one inch to tuck the blanket tighter around her. He lay still as sheep after Grandma Teegan used her short knife on their throats.

Wind rose around her, filled her head with rushing and whirling. She needed Rowan to take her down to the sea and show her the flash of selkies she couldn't see alone. She needed him because when he held her, and she closed her eyes, he was Mum and Pappy both.

She couldn't move, only her eyes peeked sideways. His lips didn't look dead. She stared at them until finally one of her shaking fingers rose and touched them. Her fingertip went twice over the pink seam of healed flesh—a place where he'd gotten well.

Had he died through his lips? Everything that was Rowan folding up like a butterfly's wings and sliding out with his breath?

Only when she heard the small flock of hurried and disgruntled sheep bleating at being ushered back into the yard could she pull away and run through the door and out into Grandma Teegan's skirts.

Shaking, as if the still air was a gale, Grandma Teegan knelt down to her. With eyes red and brimming, Grandma Teegan kissed each of Bridget's cheeks. She untied the scarf from beneath her own chin and used it to wipe Bridget's face.

Seeing her grandmother's tears and how the old face looked terrible and collapsed, the lips and cheeks trembling, made Bridget's sobbing loud. Grandma Teegan already knew about Rowan. She'd come as soon as she felt his going. Or had Rowan gone out over the hills and banged pans and sent her home? Spirits always visited the living before they left for the next world.

At Rowan's bedside, Grandma Teegan folded down, sinking to her knees, her body dropping slack, her head landing on Rowan's chest. She looked crippled and broken. Her words were broken, too, and she sobbed in a combination of her old tongue and baby-shushing sounds.

Finally, her fingers moved, sliding up Rowan's chest to his cheek and the gash on his temple to touch his hair. Gently, as though he might only be sleeping. The way she often soothed Bridget back to sleep when the nightmares came. Brushing Rowan's hair back off the wound. Then harder, pushing back his hair with the flat of her palm, trying to make his hair obey, insisting at least on that.

With each stroke of his hair, the pitch in her cries increased until Bridget could no longer stifle her own. Just as she was about to cry, "Grandma Teegan, don't do that," it happened. Grandma Teegan's hand clenched, her head lifted, and her lips pressed into a line. She struck Rowan in the chest. "Ye didn't fight! Look at this." She stood, both hands trembling like her face. "The blankets still smooth. Ye didn't fight death."

Bridget stared at her uncle's lips. She wanted to turn small as a moth and bring her wings together like praying hands and slip through the slot of them.

Now she was in Chief's barn and he had a ship. She wiped her face on her sleeve again, wet to her elbow now, and walked back around.

Chief leaned over sheets of paper the size of newsprint. "Hey," he said as she came to his side. He lifted her chin, looked into her eyes, then nodded as though the two of them had an understanding.

She managed to nod back.

He let her chin go and rapped a finger on the paper he'd been studying. Lines went every direction—some curved, some straight—and they looked all drawn one on top of the other. He trailed a brown finger along a curved mark and she saw words she could read but didn't understand: side keelson, side sparing, stringer plate.

"What do we do next?" he asked.

We?

"Why don't you climb in," he said. He looked different without his floppy hat. Tonight, he wore a single braid like her. The end was black and white, but the rest, like the hair on top of his head, was white and shone in the lantern light. He pointed to a flight of stairs in the corner of the barn. "Go on."

The only way in the ship was up those stairs and across several narrow planks leading to a ladder going down into the ship. "I can't walk across those boards. I'll fall."

"I'll catch you."

She wanted to stay right there, standing beside him, where he kept her upright, as much as if his arms were wrapped around her.

"Go on."

She felt too shaky to resist. She climbed the stairs and looked out over the planks bridging the distance to the ladder. They looked as if they hung in space. She closed her eyes and took a deep breath. *Nera, Nera.* With outstretched arms, she started across, one slow step at a time. She couldn't look away from her wobbly walking to see if Chief followed along under her, but she knew he watched. Watched her walk overhead in the clothes of the son he'd lost.

When she'd gotten close enough, she reached out and gripped the top of the ladder. Relief flashed over her. She was Nera. "I'm going into the ship now."

The body of the boat smelled of new wood and hope. She trailed her fingers over ribs, believing Rowan stood with her now. Their sea was make-believe, but make-believe seas took you to more places. Like a labyrinth, they went nowhere and everywhere at once.

"I love your ship," she shouted.

"It's an ark."

She sat down on a long board running like a curved pew. She knew about arks. They saved things. They weren't built to sail and get from place to place. Arks were built for waiting out storms, for staying right there and keeping dry until the rain stopped and the sun shone again.

She remained sitting. She didn't move until her head dropped and the jarring woke her. The barn was quiet; Chief no longer hammering or sawing. Most of the lanterns were out, but the lights guiding her way back across the planks still burned.

Crossing the second time was easier. She reached Chief's side, not brushing against him, but standing close enough to feel his warmth.

"Why are you building an ark?"

His craggy face looked more weathered in the lantern light. "My boy learned about an ark in school. He came home wanting us to build one. Never quit asking." He sighed and looked at the massive shell. "I didn't take the time. Chores, crops, a war in the South I thought needed me."

"Pete said your wood was for coffins."

His dark eyes, the reflection of lantern light in each, held hers. "Everything's a coffin or an ark." He nodded at sections of new lumber waiting to be used. "Depends on what you do with the pieces. Grief's stoppered your ears at the moment. But a time will come when you'll look around and decide what you'll build: coffins or arks."

Forty-Nine

Effie opened her eyes. She'd not slept well even with Pete sleeping beside her. Morning streamed through the window and struck Mae's mustard-colored dress. The rag hung on a rusty nail, limp and faded with its tattered lace collar. Looking as ruined as had been Mae's life. Effie stared at the dress and thought of Mae as an eight-year-old, dreaming of a new one. A little girl with no idea of the bargain she was making. This dress had been Mae's 'visiting dress.' Effie's stomach fluttered at the thought. Mae had worn it to meet her new neighbor, hoping to find a friend. Someone who, like herself, was also river people. Someone she thought would accept her. Maybe a woman to sit with her while she delivered her baby.

Pete had saved the dress, hung it like a picture. Was harboring it like a companion. The rest of Thayer's house, three whole rooms—if Pete's alcove could be called a room—had no pictures or any other memento of his mother.

Effie looked over at him and slid slowly from the bed in her battered slip, trying not to wake him. She'd glanced at Mae's dress many mornings and not let her mind linger. Why this morning was she unable to look away? But it wasn't just today. All week she'd been staring at the dress. In the nearly four and a half months she'd lived there, she'd tried to keep her thoughts only on what needed to be done next. What to cook for Thayer and Pete? What clothes did they need washed? Which one would motion her to their bed for the night?

Pete stirred, though his eyes didn't open. A boy's smooth skin but for his hairy upper lip and chin. He looked part Skeet and part Jury.

Her gut moved again, a strangely physical—rather than emotional—stirring. More definite this time. She looked down at herself. Her pelvic bones no longer jutted against the slip's paper-thin fabric. She'd put on weight, three squares a day, eating as if she needed to make up for the winter's near starvation.

The small motion in her stomach came again. For a long minute, she wondered at the strange movement. Had she imagined it? One hand lifted, shaking its way to her belly's slight roundness and fanning across. Her breath caught. *Impossible.* She reached for a bedpost, steadied herself with one hand. Then needed to grasp with both. The slow slippage began, that sinking-away sensation of sliding down the dark and mossy walls of a well. Her mind clawing to grab onto anything that made sense and could stop her fall.

Was she pregnant? She couldn't be. She was barren. She had over a year's worth of proof. Lying with Jury, then Rev. Jackdaw. His constant cursing her for her barrenness. No, she couldn't be pregnant. Women knew, there were signs.

Signs. Her knees began to tremble. She'd been at Thayer's no more than a month when she woke mornings and had to run outside to puke. Dutchman's breeches had been in bloom. April finished in a haze, her hand still painful and demanding her attention—though Thayer was generous with his whiskey. Pouring for her throughout the day. She puked because of her ache for Homeplace and Johnny, and the sick of her loneliness. She puked with the shame of leaving Bridget alone at the lodge, and she'd puked with the humiliation of hiding at Thayer's. Consumed by how low she'd fallen and believing herself too undeserving of a child, she'd not even considered the possibility of being pregnant. She'd not bled the last several months at the lodge and had not bled once at Thayer's. Her body hadn't seemed to change in any way. If Ma or Granny had been there, women who knew . . . but how could she have known?

She let go of the bedpost and flattened both hands on her stomach, moved them across. She bit her lip and struggled not to scream. She'd wanted a child for so long. Now God would punish her with one. God mocked her, damnationed her while she still walked the earth.

Pete stirred, opened his eyes and glanced at her through half sleep. The horror on her face caught him and his eyes cleared and lowered to her trembling hands clutching at her stomach. "You sick again?"

Shock and disbelief and shame. She was to blame for not conceiving earlier and to blame for doing so now. She watched Pete rise, pull on his pants, and look out the window as if unable to face her and searching for direction.

"A baby," she breathed.

He turned, stared. His Adam's apple fell and slowly rose. "I have chores. You fixing eggs?"

Her mind, just as his had, caught on the handhold of a task. Her condition would settle over them bit by bit. "I'll make eggs." That was the thing needing done next. She would fix eggs.

Pete hurried out, and she faced Mae's dress again. She and Mae were the same now, women without souls. She slipped it over her head.

Fifty

Bridget looked out over the lodge. Whenever she stepped back inside after hours with Jake or Chief, it was as if the place had waited for her and let out a gentle sigh at her return. She'd taken down Effie's curtains, and the dangling spoons and combs reflected light as they moved back and forth. One wall held finds from along the river and road. Nothing stolen. Pink and white stones—smaller than wild plums—a ribbon, a small red tobacco tin, pieces of colored glass. When the sun hit the wall, the wall came alive. Larger river rocks, those too heavy for a mud glue, lined the windowsills and replaced Johnny's marbles.

She slept in Effie's bed now and in the corner she had used for sleeping, stones looped and wound around and made a labyrinth. It wasn't much larger than the tabletop, but she walked it, stepping ahead only a few inches at a time. The labyrinth grew as she moved, becoming as large as her imagination made it. The walk as deep.

The last week of working on the ark that went nowhere and everywhere had also made her better with tools. The nails in her boxes were flat to the surface without any hammerhead indentations in the wood, no splintered edges, and the sides were even. Building also helped her feel better about Mum and Pappy's deaths.

Cora didn't like her spending any time alone. Even if it was mostly just to sleep in the lodge. But Chief told Cora she "fussed." Though Bridget wasn't sure he liked it either. Both of them fussed. She liked sleeping there amongst the trees and with the river and Jake just outside the door. She liked being alone when the sadness came and she had to stretch out over Old Mag and cry.

Motion outside a front window caught her attention. Heat waving up off the sand made the air thick and smeary. She could squint a certain way and see rainbows. She stepped closer to the glass, her palms suddenly prickly. A ghost with slumped shoulders in a yellow, ill-fitting dress moved down the slope. The ghost of Mae Thayer? But with hair white as snow. A green bundle. A quilt with red, jagged slashes. Effie!

Bridget felt both pulled and pushed to the door. She wasn't sure she wanted to go and yet, this was Effie. Effie had come back to her. She ran out and up the slope until they met and fell into each other's arms. Bridget carried the bundle and they descended together, their arms around each other, their hips banging.

"Your hair is white."

"He lied," Effie said when they'd climbed the stairs and stepped into the lodge.

Except for Effie's white hair, she looked better. More like she'd looked the first time Bridget saw her at the clothesline at Homeplace. Her face was softer and bones weren't sticking out from beneath the dress's shoulders. She was pretty again. But she wore Mae's dress.

Effie watched her. "I'm not barren," she said. "Rev. Jackdaw is." She crossed the room and dropped into the rocker. Her pale eyes, flooded with tears, pleaded. "It's him barren."

Bridget wasn't sure where to stand. By a patched wall so Effie could see she'd kept up her chores? By the hanging combs or spoons so Effie could see she'd stolen them?

"Where'd you get that dress?"

Effie wiped a crippled-looking hand beneath her dripping nose. "I couldn't stay. I'm carrying a baby."

Bridget socked her stomach. Everything was wrong. Her hands clinched together, lifted, and set themselves on top of her head. "You got the dress from Thayer's? You been at Thayer's house? All summer?"

Her hands dropped. "Pete knew?" She rocked on her heels. "Mr. Thayer bounced the bed with you?"

"I walked till I couldn't walk no more. I got so scared—you know I can't stand being scared, especially alone in the dark. Mr. Thayer let me in."

"You slept in Mr. Thayer's bed? Why didn't Pete stop you?"

Effie's eyes filled. She used the thumb on her good hand and scrubbed hard over her scars. "The baby's just as likely Pete's."

Fifty-One

Bridget ran down the ramp, past Wilcox and Jake, over the hot sand, and through the gap into the trees, not stopping until she slumped against Old Mag. She hated Pete and she hated Effie. Marching back and forth alongside Old Mag, she considered running on to Chief, but she couldn't go to him. She couldn't show her face and admit where Effie had been or what Effie had done with Mr. Thayer and Pete.

She stood and paced. Could she trust anyone? Had Chief known where Effie was? If he had, and he'd not told her, then every time they'd been together he'd been lying to her. Pretending to be her friend. She slid down off the curve of Old Mag and sat on the ground. The world was spinning and everyone spinning away from her. Parents and grandmas and Effie and now even Pete and Chief.

What to do—how to punish Effie—came in a flash. She marched back down the path, and up the ramp, stomping, trying to scare Effie into thinking Rev. Jackdaw had returned. Effie was still in the rocker, fretting it back and forth like trying to ride it away.

Bridget took a deep breath. "Skeet killed your baby sister."

Effie looked up. The rocker stopped and for several long seconds she stared at Bridget. "What are you talking about?"

"He did it, and your parents blamed you. He drowned Baby Sally. You said she wasn't strong enough or tall enough to pull herself up onto the tree stump."

Effie made no sound, but Bridget imagined Effie's brain building a tower of the facts. When the last brick was laid, everything would come crashing down.

"He did it," Bridget said. "That's how he knew she was in the tub when you couldn't see her. That's why you didn't hear her cry or splash. He held her down just like he held all the puppies down. Then he went in and told your mum. He wanted you to be blamed." She stopped for breath. "He killed your granny, too."

Bridget watched it happen: Effie slowly crumbling inside, shattering down. Then the pieces falling again, splintering into even smaller bits. The clink and tingle of brokenness.

The ends of Effie's thin white hair stirred as she turned to the tub on the wall. She managed to stand, stumble to the bed and dig into her bundle for her black cloth before falling onto the mattress. She curled into a ball, tried to hide her whole self under the funeral cloth. Her bare feet poked out. The cloth shook.

Bridget felt better.

Then she felt worse.

In the morning, Bridget woke to find Effie in the rocker, staring straight ahead. Her eyes were heavy and red as if she hadn't slept.

"I wish I was dead," Effie mumbled. "All this time. Them letting me think it was my fault. Letting me believe I murdered my baby sister."

"Maybe they didn't know," Bridget said.

"I been thinking about it all night. You figured it out. They knew. I knew. That's why Pa put the bar across Skeet's door. To keep Johnny and the others safe while they slept." She took a shallow breath. "Even Ma let me carry the blame."

Bridget crossed the floor, yanking down combs and spoons and their strings. Why had she told?

"I dreamed it again," Effie said. "My nightmare, but now I know why."

"I shouldn't have told you, but you bounced the bed with Pete."

"It's always the same. It's what's made me afraid of sleep ever since."

"Your granny's story?"

"It's not a story. Not just a nightmare. It happened. Pa carried me to the barn. I was screaming, fighting him, and him yelling at me." Effie's hands grasped the rocker arms. "He shoved me into the pitch-blackness of the cement grain room. Once, for only a moment, I was accidently shut in. He knew the place terrified me. This time, I heard the door slamming, the latch dropping. I screamed, 'Papa.' Then my fear doubled over me. Just screaming. Terrible screams. A thousand monsters' hands touching my skin, pulling at me, clawing at me.

"Pa outside the door, called through every few minutes. 'It was an accident. Say it'." Effie choked with sobs. "I couldn't breathe. I threw up gagging, and sucking the bile back into my throat. I was ten years old. Locked in a black terror, dying, and Pa had put me there. I don't know how long before I fainted. An eternity.

"Pa was picking me up off the floor. I could see light coming in through the open door. He'd saved me. I clung to him. 'It was an accident,' I repeated his words. I said them over and over so he'd never push me back into the blackness. 'It was an accident!' I was begging *him* to believe me. 'It was an accident.' I couldn't ever go back into that darkness."

"Like nighttime?"

"He carried me back to the house and set me down in a kitchen chair. I must not have been able to quit sobbing. He kept scolding me. 'Be still. Be still.' I believed he'd put me back in the room if I moved." She scrubbed her eyes, the hand plaited with scars. "The story, Bridget. There's your story."

Bridget let the spoons and combs dangle from her hands. She'd done this, made Effie sick, just to get revenge. She couldn't take back her words, couldn't unsay the truth she'd already told.

Dropping her hand to her belly, Effie closed her eyes. "I haven't got a single thing to give a child. And Rev. Jackdaw won't let me keep it. He'll take my baby and lock me in an asylum. A place full of the same hell as the grain room. I can't go to such a place."

"He can't. You're not crazy."

"Those places are full of women men don't want. Murder a wife or lock her up, either works. If Rev. Jackdaw says so, after I ran away and come back like this, the sheriff'll take me in handcuffs. I won't ever see my baby. Rev. Jackdaw will raise her ruined."

Bridget dropped her things. She needed to think and figure out what to do.

"I'm not leaving you," she said. "I just need to go out and pee."

Bridget couldn't go as far as Old Mag this time. What if Effie needed her? She stood at the river's edge and stared out over the water. Some hurts were too big to heal. She'd given Effie one of those.

"Mum," she cried. "Grandma Teegan!"

Jake nudged her with his large head. "I can't fix it," she said. "I told Effie too much."

Several minutes passed as she and Jake walked around the edge of the clearing. Tufts of wild grass waved ripe seed heads. She snapped off a few, and Jake's big tongue, pink and long, wrapped around her offerings. She couldn't force herself back inside to face what she'd done to Effie.

"Bring him to the shed!"

Effie was staggering down the back ramp with the rope over her shoulder. She'd taken off Mae's dress and wore the old underslip she'd worn when baptizing herself. Her white hair blew back, and with her white shoulders and arms, she looked like an angel. "Bring him to the shed."

Jake? Bridget hesitated. She didn't want to obey Effie, but she was responsible for Effie's terrible sorrow. And Effie was only asking for Jake to be brought. That was easy enough; it didn't mean anything. "Step on."

At the bottom of the shed steps, Effie let the rope slide off her shoulder onto the ground. She picked up the unknotted end and tied it to Jake's leather collar. She picked up the other end, fisting the slipknot.

"Go," she said. "Go to Chief. Send him back. You stay there."

"No. What are you going to do?"

Effie wasn't crying now. She looked at the door of the shed. "Go."

"No. I'm sorry I told you."

"Go." Her eyes met Bridget's. "You don't deserve to be here."

Everything happening was a darkness Bridget didn't know how to stop, and Effie's yelling increased. "Go. Go. I don't want you here."

"No!"

Effie was screaming, pushing at her now. Stronger and bigger. "Do what I say."

Chief would know what to do. He'd ridden Smoke hard when Rev. Jackdaw put Effie's hand in the trap. And he'd fixed things. He'd fix this, too.

Bridget hesitated, but Effie yelled again, put her hands back on Bridget's chest, pushed harder. Bridget turned and ran into the trees, but went only a few yards before stopping and peering back through branches. Effie was mounting the rickety steps, the hem of the slip swaying against her calves as she climbed.

Bridget ran again, wishing she had two pans to bang together. Reaching Old Mag, she stopped, indecision and fear making her legs leaden. She couldn't see the shed or Jake, but she imagined hearing Effie yell, "Walk on!" Imagined she saw Jake stepping forward, his heavy footfalls striking the dry, silty ground and the rope crawling out of its coils.

Cupping her mouth with both hands, she screamed. "Chief!" Coughed and gasped and tried to catch her breath again.

There was no answer, just as Mum had never shown her selkie self, no matter how Bridget screamed. She was alone. She had to be as brave as Nera. And as smart. There wasn't time to fetch Chief. No matter how fast he caught Smoke and rode, it would be like the day Rev. Jackdaw put Effie's hand in the trap. Chief would enter the shed with the deed already done. If she hadn't run for him that day, if she'd stayed and fought like the maidens in Grandma Teegan's stories, used her fists or grabbed a knife, maybe it wouldn't have happened. And then, maybe Effie wouldn't have run and hid at Thayer's.

A hundred thoughts spun around Bridget, slammed into her. Effie would hang like Nera's skeleton: the body of bones Bridget needed to face. But before a person died, there was the death space. She'd not seen the death space around Effie's body. "No shadow!" She turned back, ran harder, her legs stronger, faster down the uneven path. "Effie, stop, there's no shadow!"

Leaving the trees, Bridget hit a wall of silence. The quiet, thick as stone, stopped her, threatened to push her to her knees.

Jake stood yards forward from where she'd left him. The rope, tight as wire, stretched over his back, hummed straight through the air, cut through the open door and into the dark skinning shed.

Bridget forced herself to Jake first, not hurrying now. She dropped her forehead onto his, and after a moment, tapped his knees and backed him until the rope grew slack and a large segment lay on the ground. She untied Effie's knot and let that end drop.

"Walk on," she said. "You don't deserve to be here."

The long climb up the four steps into the shed seemed like eight, then twelve. When she'd finally climbed them all, she stopped.

On the floor beside the table, Effie sat gripping the rope in her scarred hand. She stared at the old stain of her blood on the floor and the trap.

Fifty-Two

Effie found herself at the lodge table, working. She'd hated Chief's building and Bridget's constant pounding, and now it was her turn. Her combs held her hair off her sweaty neck. Even with the doors open, no breeze stirred the humid air. She'd rolled up her sleeves and left the top button on her dress open. The day before, she'd walked out of the skinning shed having only narrowly escaped herself. Still, she was terrified. Could she get away, survive on her own, raise a child?

She lifted the hammer again. The scars in her palm ached with the tool's weight, but they'd toughen. She'd get better too, at tapping in the small nails so that she didn't splinter the wood. Bridget had sold four boxes. *For money.* Effie didn't know the price of two train tickets home, but boxes might be an answer to her prayers. If four sold, why not ten? Twenty? Even more if the boxes were decorated. And there were silver spoons to sell.

Bridget wasn't helping. The saw lay idle again. Had been since Effie announced her plan that morning. Instead, Bridget stood at the sink washing wild plums she'd spent all morning picking.

"Bridget, please. They are clean. Help me."

"You didn't do it."

The words held such hope they made Effie's stomach grip. "That doesn't mean we can stay here." Rev. Jackdaw would be back. She'd keep a constant vigil. If he returned before they'd boarded the train, she and Bridget would still be gone. By the time he crawled out of the buggy with his rickety back and limped down the slope, they'd be out the back and deep in the trees headed for Chief's. There was the shotgun, too, if need be. She'd once kept it ready for Injuns, but now it was ready for Rev. Jackdaw. Maybe a white preacher's wife wouldn't swing for shooting a bastard.

"But you didn't do it," Bridget said.

A shiver ran across Effie's shoulders. She'd entered the shed with every intention of killing her life. "I had the rope around my neck." She touched the scarring on her throat, feeling the roughness again. "I started choking . . . like that day he used the rope on me."

Bridget tipped her pan, holding back the fruit and letting the water rush out between her fingers.

"My knees were rattling, but I yelled at Jake." The rope was lifting and her heart pounding when she saw the blood on the floor and remembered Ma's blood the night they spent in the chair. Ma telling her she was sorry. Not in words, but in the way she held her. "I almost didn't jerk out in time. I lost my balance and landed on the floor."

Out the lodge door, clouds moved, and shadow crept over the front landing. "Sitting beside my own blood stain, I knew my bad life wasn't just what others did to me. I'd always helped put the noose around my own neck."

"You bounced the bed with Pete."

Effie cringed. "I never meant that to happen." Emotion tightened her throat. "The first night, I was so thankful Mr. Thayer let me in, I cried." She took a breath and looked through the door and up at the empty ridge. If she'd somehow survived that night outside, her mind would have been scrambled as Granny's. She'd realized she couldn't walk to Homeplace, and she couldn't return to the lodge. "I was emptied out."

Bridget watched her, wasn't accepting only half a story.

Effie picked up a nail, rolled it between two fingers. She wouldn't tell Bridget how Mr. Thayer went to his room first, leaving open the door on his dark bedroom only to appear in it a moment later wearing nothing but his fancy boots with the red leaves. And his want. Standing there thinking the sight of him would call her like a hen to a tom's strutting.

"He'd taken my hand out of the trap," Effie said. "And he let me come in. I owed him." That wasn't the whole truth. Mr. Thayer's standing there had been an invitation. He'd seen her, wanted her. It didn't matter why or for how long; he wanted her.

"What'd Pete do?"

"He'd been sulking. He made a sad-sounding, uppity noise when I went into Mr. Thayer's room." She hadn't known if he was seeing her go or his ma. "One night, Mr. Thayer was drinking in town, and I got so scared I went into Pete's room and crawled into his bed." She'd known by his reaction that he'd never lain beside a woman. And he didn't at first move. "I'm sorry for what I did. Maybe I was trying to punish him for the guilt I felt over not helping Mae."

Bridget's face looked as much empty as angry.

"I never meant to hurt you. It was me being out of my head. And me who asked them not to tell a soul I was living there. Mr. Thayer kept quiet because he wanted to keep me coming to his bed. Maybe Pete was too ashamed to talk."

Bridget still wasn't speaking. She left the sink, walked to a corner, and pushed at stones she'd shaped into some sort of silly spiral. "Why'd you come back?"

"I realized I was having a baby. That morning, Thayer sat over his eggs and asked Pete was he fixing to call me his wife? Pete said, 'No.' The word quick, full of fright. 'You fixing to do it?' Both of them talking like I wasn't even there. Mr. Thayer put a fist on top of the table, looked hard at Pete. 'I ain't took a wife yet.'"

Effie turned from Bridget, walked to the back door, and looked out on the river. "Pete jumped up, his chair scraping back, like he meant to kill the man right there. I knew he was thinking of his mama. How she'd wanted Thayer—with every baby—to make her a wife and give their child a name." Effie felt the bump of her stomach. She'd yet to admit the hardest truth. "I'd done it. Pete's eyes filled up. I'd taken his white goodness. Breaking him was a way of breaking me. I wanted myself dead."

"It wasn't my fault?" Bridget asked from behind her. "You didn't go to the shed because I told you your parents made you take the blame for Baby Sally's death?"

"That's not why." She understood better now what she hadn't at ten: How badly a person can break. How Pa was trying to fix the broken pieces of himself when his ma returned. Then his son murdered a little sister. A baby Pa loved, too. How he must've blamed himself for not protecting his children. It was the thing Granny always blamed him for—not protecting the family. He couldn't see his twelve-year-old boy hang or be drug off in chains. Nor could Ma. She couldn't live knowing her boy was suffering in some horrid prison. They must both have blamed themselves, believed they could do better, find a way to save him. They couldn't risk Effie knowing the truth, talking about it to others, swearing it was Skeet.

"Maybe all families," she said, "hide horrible truths."

The sound of footsteps racing up the front stairs and across the landing made them both jump. Effie ran for the gun hanging on the wall, but she'd only gripped the stock when Cora rushed in breathless, a basket swinging on her arm.

"Effie, you *are* back!" She stopped, the smile leaving her face. "Oh, I didn't mean to scare you." She looked from Effie to Bridget and back. "I come at the worst times. I . . . I baked you a cake."

Effie eased her hands from the gun. It *was* a bad time; she didn't want to face anyone—the shame of lying with two men; hiding herself. But for Bridget, it was a good time; she needed Cora's brightness. "You can visit without bringing a cake or pie."

"Mother, God rest her soul, wouldn't agree."

"How did you know I was back?"

"Pete came to the store, and I asked about you."

Back at the sink, Bridget's pan slipped from her hands, clattered in the sink. "You didn't tell me."

"I'm sorry," Cora said. "I didn't know all summer of course. Then I didn't know what was right. Effie, I didn't know if you were staying in Bleaksville."

Doves cooed outside, the sound thick as their feathers. Then flew, the sharp clap of wings tearing the air. "Pete's talking?" Effie asked. All the more reason to leave. Even if Jackdaw never returned, she still wasn't raising a child amongst rumors. The town already considered her river people. Not a girl of eighteen, so scared of herself and full of guilt for a murder she didn't commit that she wasn't able to bear her own company.

Effie widened her hands across her stomach, smoothing her dress to draw attention to her swelling. She blessed Cora for not gasping in horror or pulling a look. "We're leaving. Bridget said you bought boxes." She didn't wait for a response. "If we build more and you sell them, we can buy train tickets."

Cora frowned at the tabletop of unfinished work. "I can't promise to sell that many."

"Maybe he won't ever come back," Bridget said. Her eyes were wide, pleading.

"If there's talk, he'll find out. And if he finds out I'm carrying another man's child, he'll kill me."

"You aren't safe here." Cora said. "But selling enough boxes? Let me buy the tickets."

Effie crossed her arms, held her opposite elbows. "I need to stand on my own feet. If I can't get myself home without charity, how can I survive there without it?"

"Stop being so proud! Take care of yourself."

"Mr. Graf won't let you buy the tickets for us."

"I've felt wretched since Mae's death, knowing I didn't do enough for her. She died without a woman present. I know my husband has been unkind," Cora went on. "He wrestles with himself for it. In his mind, he's still fighting in the war between the states. He spent months at Andersonville. Came out a skeleton. He has nightmares still, even if it's been over half his life ago. When he's weighing his beans and skimping on the scales, he's still living that starvation." She paused, her eyes asking Effie, then Bridget, to understand. "He enlisted, risked his life believing all men deserved their freedom. Negros, too. There are worse war injuries than losing a leg or arm."

Like Pa, Effie thought. *Or Granny.* Some things couldn't be put down.

"Chief was in the war too," Bridget said. "He buried dead boys."

The remark surprised Effie, but before she could ask, Cora spoke again.

"My friendship with you scares Mr. Graf. He's afraid I feel kindred to you and regret marrying an older man. I can see through his gruffness to his hurting, but looking into Rev. Jackdaw scares me. I can't see a heart there. Only a stone."

"Rev. Jackdaw," Bridget started, "is sad because—"

"You're coming with me," Effie snapped. "You're not staying here. I don't care what's happened to that man. He's ruined." A thought chilled her. "Suppose I'm not legally married. He did it himself in the kitchen. If I'm not . . ." She couldn't finish. *I have no legal claim on Bridget.* In which case, taking Bridget *was* kidnapping. She didn't care.

"Listen to me." Cora planted her hands on her hips. "A name on a paper or not, the Bible says, 'When need be, a lady must pick up her skirts and run.'"

Effie hated the look of confusion on Bridget's face, fear too. Bridget ought to be full of confidence, feel that going was the best thing for her.

"That's what it says," Cora continued, "lest some fool man over the last ten thousand years of male rewrites has struck it out with his goose pen." She looked back and forth between them. Her hands dropped from her hips, gripped the basket. "Did Bridget tell you about her parents? They're, unfortunately, gone."

Effie's breath caught, then eased out slowly. If Bridget no longer had any hope of finding her parents, she ought to feel better about leaving.

"Wait." Cora's hands lifted. "I almost forgot." She reached in her basket and drew out a pack of letters. "From your family."

Emotion flopped through Effie's stomach. She grabbed herself, wanting the letters so badly it was close to pain, but there were none for Bridget. Wouldn't ever be.

Cora set the letters on the table and pushed them slowly past the cake and into Effie's reach. "Normally Mr. Graf goes to the post office. The awful man behind the counter thinks mail is spelled m-a-l-e and women have no business in his establishment. When I went in, he took his time finishing up his sorting, letting me stand there waiting. I saw him reach a letter with your name printed on the front and flip it beneath the counter into a box. Easy, as though he'd done it many times. Had been told to do so."

"Rev. Jackdaw?" Effie's voice squeaked. "He told the man to keep my letters? Even though I came asking?"

"I was lucky enough to step in there when I did. Look at the dates." Cora rounded the corner of the table, tapped on the top letter. "They're all since he hurt you. He's not been back since then."

Effie's heart banged inside her ribs.

"You know what that means?" Cora asked. "There're likely a lot more earlier ones with him in Omaha."

Effie hugged the letters, carried them to the rocker. It didn't matter how many Rev. Jackdaw had kept from her. She had letters now.

Fifty-Three

"Slower," Effie said.

Bridget read slower. And when she'd finished with all seven letters, Effie insisted they be read again. Finally, as the sun set, Effie rose to stand staring out the door in the waning light and up to the ridge. Bridget went slowly back to the sink. Effie had letters, but Cora hadn't brought one from Grandma Teegan. Had Grandma Teegan even gotten her letter?

The train sounded on its way to Bleaksville, the noise distant but clear through the open doors. No more than a quart of plums were in Bridget's pan, but she picked at them. Was Grandma Teegan back in Ireland and safe?

"We'll go in the morning." Effie said. She turned quick to look around the lodge. The letters still fisted. "I need to bathe tonight, mend a dress. Cora's right, it's too dangerous to stay longer. Rev. Jackdaw's coming; I can feel it. He's been praying on it. He's coming."

The ripest plums ought to be separated from the green ones, but Bridget only stared at the fruit. In the three days since Effie's return, she'd thought many times of Chief and how he'd lied to her with his silence. He'd acted like her best friend, all the while knowing Effie was at Thayer's. It wasn't just anger over his knowing; she felt shame, too. Effie being right up the road but not caring enough to come home. Since Effie's return, which Chief knew about, he hadn't come. Hadn't come to say, "Bridget, how are you? Are you okay?" Now, they were leaving and she didn't want to go, but she needed to ask him to pasture Jake.

"I want my business finished here," Effie said. "Thanking Chief is part of that. Tie Jake up. I don't want him following, then running off and you leaving me in the dark to chase him."

What if Chief was working on the ark? "We should go see him tomorrow."

"We're taking the early train, and there won't be time."

"You don't like him."

"He helped save my life. And he's been looking after you."

"And you don't like your pa. So why are you going home?"

She took the rope from the wall and held it out. "Tie Jake to the rail. I'll carry the cake."

Bridget slipped the rope around Jake's neck and tied the other end to the railing. She couldn't tell him she was breaking her promise and leaving. And she couldn't promise him he'd like living at Chief's, even if Chief did say yes. Because maybe the bull in Chief's pasture would be mean to him. She led Effie onto the path.

"Pa was fourteen when his family was killed," Effie said. They'd walked nearly to Old Mag, darkness gathering and neither of them speaking until now.

Nera, Nera. I don't want to go. Bridget walked slow, letting her feet drag.

"Him hardly older than you," Effie said. "He isn't an awful man. All he's been through, other men would have saddled a horse and rode off. Or thrown a rope over a barn rafter."

Bridget paid little attention. Through the tree tops, a star close to the moon was already visible. In minutes the Big Dipper would be out. What if they were coming too late and Chief was already building on the ark? Effie couldn't see the ark, couldn't know the secret.

"He and Ma lost all three children in one day," Effie said. "Not just Baby Sally, but Skeet and me. Maybe Johnny too, him being born directly into all that mourning."

Passing Old Mag, Bridget ran her hand along the trunk. She'd never told Effie who Old Mag was, and she still couldn't. The secrets she took with her to New Ulm would be all she had of her time in the trees.

Crossing the pasture, Bridget was relieved to see Chief's barns were dark.

"I'm telling this baby," Effie said, "'Your papa is dead and your grandma's name was Mae. She loved a real pretty dress.' Rev. Jackdaw's always preaching about just desserts, and this baby—him having no claim to it—is his just desserts. Everyone back home knows I married, so carrying a child is just fine. That boy I liked, he doesn't matter. He feels like someone from another life."

They walked around the house to the kitchen. Light came from the window and through the screen. The wooden door behind it left open to the cooler night air. Bridget's breath came faster. Chief probably thought she'd quit visiting him because with Effie home he no longer mattered. And when he saw them walking into his yard after dark, he'd think she'd told Effie about the ark and brought her to see it. How could she promise him she hadn't said one word with Effie standing right there?

"Pa will have no cause to be ashamed of me," Effie said, "when I tell him Rev. Jackdaw's dead."

"Shh. His dog is going to hear us."

"Isn't that fine? My whole body's celebrating. Hearing you read those letters, I can't hardly stand waiting until I'm on that train. Rev. Jackdaw won't come after us. His crippled back can't take the ride, Nell can't make the walk, and he's too full of hate and poverty to take the train. Then there's the burn on my neck and my hand." She shifted the cake and placed her scarred hand over her belly. "Truth is, he wants scat of me. His heart'll quit soon enough. Couple years, maybe less, he'll be rotting in a box. I don't even need to hear he's passed."

Wire barked at the screen door.

"He heard us." Bridget's knees wanted to fold up and drop her. "Now Chief knows we're here."

Chief stepped into view behind Wire. Seeing them, he let Wire out and crossed the porch behind him. His face was hard to read in the growing darkness. Was he glad to see her, or angry that they'd come so late? Maybe angry that they'd come at all. He held a dishtowel, his braids hung over his chest, and after a summer working in the sun cutting hay, farming corn, and riding Smoke, his skin was dark as chestnuts.

He gave Effie a how-do nod, then his attention settled on Bridget. "You're all right then?"

She wasn't. She was sorry.

"We brought you a cake." Effie held it out. "That dog can jump."

"She wanted to come," Bridget said. She took a step, moving in front of Effie. *I didn't tell her,* she mouthed the words.

Chief held the cake, but his eyes hadn't left Bridget. "You lost interest in working here?"

That's not what she'd said.

Effie moved up beside her. "I didn't know you were *working* here. Thank you, Mr. Chief, but Bridget is white. She can't work for you." She hesitated. "Anyway, we come to tell you we are moving back east."

"East?"

Bridget watched his eyes change though his body remained still. She clamped her teeth hard. She'd miss building with him, eating supper together, and especially the long stories he told the way Grandma Teegan had told hers: *holy*.

"Cora made the cake," Effie said. "I don't have nice flour and sugar and such."

Chief wasn't saying he'd miss Bridget or that he didn't want her to go. His silence was saying, *I ain't and I can't ever be that man. You'll be moving on faster 'an rabbits breed rabbits.*

"We're moving on," Bridget said.

"Tomorrow." Effie wiped her hands down the sides of her skirt.

"East," Chief said again, nodding this time.

Bridget hoped he couldn't see the tears in her eyes or hear her sniffling to keep snot from appearing beneath her nose. If they were alone, she could explain everything: how Rev. Jackdaw would kill Effie next time. Effie had to go, and she too, or she'd be the one made to wash his drawers, and he'd put her in the buggy and take her to another place where he'd try to build another church. Traveling east with Effie or being taken off with Rev. Jackdaw—either way she'd have to leave Jake behind. And Chief. She'd already lost them both.

Chief still nodded over the word east. Bridget counted four, five, six nods before he spoke. "Good. Time you scrammed."

Bridget shoved her hands in her pockets. "You knew Effie was at Thayer's."

"I heard."

She felt slapped and tried to swallow back the sting. "You didn't tell me."

He took his time answering. "That wasn't my business."

I thought I was your business.

The sound of two horses charging down the lane made them turn. Cora leaned over her saddle, her horse's head stretched out. Pete rode just as hard beside her.

"Effie!" Cora cried when they reached the porch, their horses still edgy, like their muscles still ran inside their bodies. Many of Cora's pins had come out, and her knot of hair hung low and loose in the back. She panted trying to catch her breath. "You weren't home. We went there first." She looked at Pete. "He came and told me Jackdaw was wild acting. Thank God we found you."

Bridget's stomach, sinking since they'd left the lodge, dropped farther. She had to run with Effie now, without even giving Chief a proper good-bye or being able to swear to him that she hadn't told anyone about his ark. *It's a good ark,* she wanted to say.

"I didn't know if you were still around town," Pete said to Effie. "I figured if you were, you wouldn't listen to me, but I know you trust Cora." His gaze slid over Bridget, just as it did over Chief, and his attention swung back to Effie. "He's loco. Wearing a dress."

Effie slapped both hands over her stomach. "Where is he?"

"I was coming back from hunting." He patted a shotgun hanging off his saddle. "I heard a row of swearing. His buggy was hung up on the tracks and him whipping and yelling at his horse."

"Nell," Bridget managed.

"I helped lift the wheel out," Pete said. "Maybe I shouldn't have. He started swearing he's come to kill you."

"Someone told him I was back," Effie nearly screamed. She glared at Pete and then at Chief.

"Chief di-didn't!" Bridget objected so fast, she choked and the word came out broken.

"Likely our dear sheriff," Cora said. "Or that fool postman. He probably sent a telegram. We need to go. Hopefully you can still catch tonight's train. You'll never see Jackdaw again."

Effie hesitated. "Looking like this. Granny's quilt, Johnny's marbles. Tickets?"

Pete tapped his back pocket before Cora could speak. "I'll buy your tickets. I'm happy to get you back home."

"He's wearing his sister's dress?" Effie's voice trembled. "For everyone to see? He's lost his mind. We need the sheriff."

"You're not listening," Chief said. "He'll hand you over."

Bridget frowned as Pete reached down for Effie's hand. "You best ride with me."

"I can't leave Bridget. We must both go!"

Bridget felt close to sobbing. The whole world was shutting her out. "What about Jake?" She took a step back. "I'll bring him here. You'll hide him. You will, Chief, won't you?"

"I'll go find him come morning, pasture him." His eyes were coal dark in the scant light coming through the door. "But if Jackdaw comes with the sheriff, I got no claim."

"Bridget." Effie reached out. "I'm not leaving you again. We need to go. Forget about that ox."

"I'll run fast." She backed farther away, stepping out of the circle of light that held the rest of them close as a family. "I'll bring Jake here and meet you at the depot. I'll bring the quilt and Johnny's marbles."

Effie let her reaching arms drop. "Hurry."

"No," Cora said. "It's too dangerous."

"Effie!" Pete's voice was deep and louder than Cora's. A man's voice. "Climb up. Don't worry about her. If she misses the train, she can take tomorrow's. I'll shoot Jackdaw if need be to get you on the train, but I don't want to swing because you can't make up your mind."

Chief nearly dropped the cake, setting it down and paying no attention to Wire's sniffing it. He strode off the porch and grabbed Effie around her waist, hoisting her up behind Pete. "Go on," he growled. "You're asking for trouble you ain't up to."

Pete was already yanking the reins, turning his horse's head and kicking it in the sides. Effie's arms wrapped around him, hugging.

Bridget had once sat behind Pete, her arms around him, but her tears weren't over Pete. She was losing the trees and Jake. She was losing Chief too, without even the chance to say she loved him. But he didn't care about that.

Cora hesitated a moment longer. "I hate this. You run like hell."

Bridget ran for the trees and Jake.

“Hey!” Chief yelled. “Get the ox and come straight back! Don’t set foot in that place.”

Bridget ran past both of his barns and reached the gate. She didn’t need anyone.

Fifty-Four

In the pasture, Chief's cows were scattered dark huddles paying no attention to Bridget. Once across, she scraped between two strands of the barbed wire fence and ran on. At Old Mag, she stopped as she'd done many times before, struggling to catch her breath, pressing her sweating palms on the trunk, wanting the tree to give her hope and her legs the energy to run again.

She smelled smoke even before she left the trees and stepped into the clearing, winded again. Jake stood still hitched to the back porch. She saw no sign of Rev. Jackdaw, but the lodge windows were bright with flame behind them. Had Rev. Jackdaw built a fire even though the night was warm? Had a log rolled out onto the old floorboards?

She reached Jake, feeling the heat from the fire. "Come on, we've got to go." She fumbled for her knot at the rail, found it larger and tighter than she'd made it. She tried the rope around his neck. Coils and loops. Too tight.

Rev. Jackdaw stepped out of the darkness and glared down on her. His beard orange in the light, his cold eye white. "Where is she?"

Bridget's side stitched, her fingers stung with the effort of prying at knots, but the clench of fear in her stomach hurt more. Rev. Jackdaw wore his white shirt and black trousers, but over them was a red dress. Behind him, the orange in the window swelled.

"I asked you a question. Where is she?"

She worked at the knot. "Effie's gone. She got on the train . . . yesterday. She said she was going west. She's clear to Butte, Montana. It's very far away."

His bad eye bore into her, but the muscles around it were still. That stillness scared her; he'd made a decision. The fire was his, deliberate.

Inside, the lodge cracked and thudded with noises. She imagined the table collapsing, the bed with its dry shucks roaring. The Never Forget quilt turning black. She jumped back and Jake jerked his head at the next crash, his eyes wide, his body straining.

"You better come down," she said to Rev. Jackdaw. "It's burning fast." Her fingernails felt torn back, but she pried and pulled. She'd not tied the rope this tight. Rev. Jackdaw had. He'd planned on letting Jake burn alive.

"What devil got my wife?"

If she said the Thayers, Rev. Jackdaw would leave and go there. Mr. Thayer deserved having to face a shotgun, but she couldn't tell on Effie. She tried to sound convincing. "The Lord has blessed her, that's all. The baby is her just desserts."

He raised his gun slowly, stopped when the barrel pointed directly at her chest.

She couldn't move, felt that was exactly what he wanted.

Gray smoke, curling out from between the logs, circled Rev. Jackdaw, making him cough and his bad eye weep. "She'll never spend another night under a roof I paid for." He leaned forward, the gun barrel now little more than an arm's length away. "You either. You double-crossed me."

"I didn't." If she turned and ran, he'd shoot her in the back. He wanted someone dead and with Effie gone, a dead orphan would be good enough. "We can go to Butte," she begged. "We can find Effie. You can build a church there. A great big one."

A section of roof thundered down into the lodge, throwing light over many of Wilcox's upper branches. The swelling smoke stung Bridget's eyes and made her cough. The gun still pointed at her. The anger in Rev. Jackdaw's face said, "Run, Rooster, so I can shoot you."

Jake pulled on the rope, stood three yards back. The rail wobbled.

"Walk on!" she screamed.

Jake tugged again, and the short landing rail came off in one piece and hit the ground. He stopped.

"Walk on!" she tried again. Her throat was making silly, sucking noises. Rev. Jackdaw was going to shoot her. She could see it in both his eyes. He'd put Effie's hand in a trap, and now he'd shoot her. Even Jake knew and was staying right there. She clenched her eyes closed as tight as she could, her whole body trembling.

"Grandma Teegan!"

The shotgun blast knocked her backward. She hit the ground. Her ears roared. Her face stung in a hundred hurting places. She couldn't breathe, couldn't move.

With her ears still ringing, she felt the vibration of a lodge wall crashing down. Her stinging eyes slowly opened. She was dazed, confused to see the fire was still there, confused at still being in the same world as the fire.

The window shattered at Rev. Jackdaw's side, sending him cursing and crouching against the flying glass as he hurried down the ramp. His dress reflected red light on the side nearest the lodge.

Dizzy and unsure, she turned to see Jake drop to his front knees. She screamed. Blood covered his wide face, pulsed over his nose and rolled off his chin.

On all fours, she scrambled to reach him.

He struggled with the effort of staying on his front knees. She wrapped her arms around his neck. "Jake!" His face looked as though someone had taken a hoe and chopped at him. "I'm right here," she cried. "I'm staying with you."

His blood continued to pulse, running down over his wide dewlap and pooling on the ground. When he dropped over with a long lowing sound, she was holding so tight his weight pulled her over on top of him.

His back legs kicked, sawing through silt and sand.

She crawled higher, draping herself over his head, covering the raw flesh, burgundy, and white bits of exposed skull. The blood soaked into her clothes, and his breath grew louder, becoming half gasp, half moan.

She knew how it felt to be hit with a plate or fist, how it felt having lye poured on her scalp, but those pains didn't touch this pain. She lifted her head to scream at Rev. Jackdaw. "I hate you!" She should have run. He'd have shot her in the back, and Jake would be alive. "I hate you!"

Rev. Jackdaw had stepped wide of the fire. "She was yours to watch. Why do you think I bothered with you?" The hem of his dress brushed the back of his trouser legs as he rushed.

"Jake is dying. You killed him!" It seemed so impossible she had to repeat it again for herself. "Jake is dying."

She lay over the top of him, her hands on his cheeks either side of the large wound. Jake's blood soaked deeper into her clothes, filled up her sleeves, drenched her shirt and britches. But she didn't move. As long as the blood kept flowing, Jake's heart was alive, and he knew she was there.

"You and I are going away," she sobbed. "We'll live on an ark."

Fifty-Five

Crashing and splitting logs surrounded Bridget with deafening noise. Heat roared inside the lodge, rolled out and swelled in her direction. Though most of the smoke rose away from her and into the night sky, she coughed and choked. She ought to get farther away, but she couldn't move Jake, and she couldn't leave him. He was still alive. He needed to know she was staying with him.

His back legs kicked as if he struggled to run, and for long minutes a horrible lowing came from deep in his throat. With a hand covered in his blood, she stroked his long side, over his ribs and warm haunch. She sobbed too hard to say she loved him, but she could keep petting and petting and the feel of her hand would tell him.

In the distance a train whistle blew, the sound nearly lost in the boom of another crash from inside the lodge. Effie was gone.

Several logs thundered, a whole wall coming down in an endless crashing, log on log as though the fall of one brought down the next and the next after that. She yelped and covered Jake's bloody ears.

Somewhere beyond the din a horse screamed. Nell! But Rev. Jackdaw would get her to safety. She needed to stay with Jake.

From her position on the ground, she could see logs breaking through the floor and catching in the stilts. Other logs rolled through supports as if they were only upright twigs. A large red ember flew through the air and landed like a bird on her shoulder. She cried out at the pain burning through her shirt and slapped it off. Another wall collapsed, the logs stacking and rolling off those already on the ground, breaking out from beneath the lodge and stopping right and left of her. They brought more smoke that made breathing hard and stung her eyes.

She screamed as more timbers, rolling lines of flame, twisted and licked toward her. Stopping only feet away. She was caught. She could no longer hear Jake's moaning, and her eyes, weeping in the smoke, made her grab and try to rub out the pain. Blind, she couldn't see if Jake's back legs still kicked. She felt along his body again, smelling singed fur, and down a flank to his hard, two-toed hoof. It trembled under her hand and quit.

Jake, her best friend, who'd always done whatever he was told, was dead.

She sucked for air, but smoke burned the inside of her mouth, made her choke trying to swallow. She was dizzy and hot and even trying to force her eyes to slits, she couldn't see through the burning and watering. She pushed off Jake and stood wobbling, blind and uncertain of which way to run. The smoke was worse higher up, and after a moment she dropped back to her knees. Then dropped to her stomach, her face on the sand and in moisture she knew was Jake's blood. But there was less smoke with her nose just off the ground.

In the heat and smoke, she was too scared even to work her way back to her knees. The whole world burned and she didn't know in which direction to find the river. If she moved in any direction, she'd only catch on fire that much quicker. She'd stay there where she was almost asleep.

Like dancers around a Maypole, the world moved beneath her in a hot, wide, and sloppy circle.

"Ye didn't fight death," Grandma Teegan's voice screeched. "Ye didn't fight death."

"I can't," Bridget tried to say. She was huddled in the corner of the croft, crying behind Grandma Teegan's spinning wheel, clutching a tin salt cup. It was the place in the croft where Grandma Teegan spun wool and told stories of how all maidens survived—even the Goose Girl whose horse's head was cut off. The maidens survived when they stood up and fought death, facing their skeletons like Nera.

Grandma Teegan's voice screeched again. "Ye didn't fight death."

Bridget worked herself to her knees. She'd let Rowan die and Grandma Teegan hit him, and she had to fight death to make things right again. She swayed and fell back to the ground. On the second attempt, her knees held and she began to crawl, her foot knocking against Jake. She was leaving him. Her arms gave out in the effort and she dropped to her belly.

"Fight death." Grandma Teegan was angry.

Bridget inched forward on her elbows, pushing with her toes.

She crawled because Grandma Teegan watched and Grandma Teegan left her no choice.

Cooler air touched her face. Less smoke too, or she imagined it was less. She crawled on, her elbows digging in better now, helping her cover more ground. How much longer before Grandma Teegan would say that was enough and let her sleep?

Her palm splashed water. Then both hands. Her face. She dragged herself on. The cuffs of her britches sizzled and she realized they'd begun to burn. She tried to keep moving. She wanted the deepest water. She'd find a current and be carried away.

Something tugged at her, held her back. She kicked and slapped. She would be a selkie too.

"Hey, hey." A soft voice. Soothing.

Chief! He knelt in the water, hugged her close to his chest, and wiped her face with scoops of river and a big hand. He scrubbed her cheeks, her forehead, palms of water over and over as if trying to see if she was alive beneath the blood and ash.

Bridget could scarce think. The world was busted into pieces. Chief scouring her face, the lodge a huge Beltane fire, Jake's bloody face somewhere in the smoke, and the only visible thing she could make out through her burning eyes was Wilcox's limbs, flames dancing up like golden ivy.

There were other voices besides Chief's. Cora's as she came splashing out, gasping as if she'd been holding her breath since they parted in Chief's yard. "You're alive!"

Chief carried Bridget out of the water, kept his arms around her as he settled her on her feet, testing if she could stand before he let go. She clung to him. Her stomach suddenly rolled. She puked plums on their shoes, her throat burning. Chief held her forehead as she puked again.

"Effie?" she asked.

"We parted at the bridge," Cora said. "I'm sure Pete got her on the train in time."

The vomiting eased and Bridget wrapped her arms around Chief's waist again. His big hand on her back held her close.

"Effie left crying," Cora went on. With sad eyes, she reached out as if to take her from Chief. "She said you were never coming. If she waited a week or a year, it didn't matter. You weren't coming." She dropped her empty hands. "I hope I did the right thing. The train was leaving . . . it just seemed safest to have her gone."

Bridget looked up at Chief, his face still swimming behind her burning eyes. "Is Jake all the way dead?"

"He's left this world. He's not suffering."

Cora put a hand on each of Bridget's shoulders, tugged, but Bridget didn't let go of Chief. Cora was too small, couldn't hold her up against something as big as Rev. Jackdaw shooting Jake and the long lowing sounds he'd made dying.

Chief walked her wide of the flames around to the front of the fire. Men were gathered there, huddled in a circle halfway down the slope around an overturned buggy.

Bridget's knees began to shake. Chief's hand on her back pressed with a firmer touch. Flames from the lodge panned orange reflections over Nell lying on the ground. Bridget needed another minute for her eyes to clear enough to understand all she was seeing. Nell was dead, the hem of Rev. Jackdaw's red dress, a thin white ankle from beneath a wheel. His other leg at such an odd angle it looked to belong to a different body.

She screamed into Chief's wet shirt.

"I'm sorry, Bridget," Cora said. "I know you took pity on him."

Everything was gone: the lodge, Rev. Jackdaw, Nell. Even Effie and Jake.

"Where'd the other one go?"

Bridget hadn't seen the sheriff approach. He'd asked the question of Cora and Chief, but she spoke before they could. "Effie is in Butte." *The man didn't have the right to know.*

"The bastard's dead. Likely the horse spooked at the fire or stepped in a rut. Maybe just fell over dead. Its weight and the slope rolled the buggy. Jackdaw got hisself pinned."

"Nell did it on purpose," Bridget said.

Chief whistled and Smoke came from out of the darkness, his head bobbing and nostrils flaring. "There's enough help here."

Bridget clung to Chief as he grabbed the reins. "Whoa there, boy. Easy now." He pulled Bridget's hands from around his waist, held them both in one of his larger hands, and pushed her back the distance of his reach. He grabbed fistfuls of Smoke's mane and in one lunge, he threw his leg over the horse's back and was up.

I can't ever be that man, he'd said. Bridget knew what she'd do. She'd run to the bridge, sleep under there where no one would find her.

Chief leaned down off Smoke and before she could blink enough to clear her eyes, he'd pulled her off her feet as he'd done in his barn, caught her around the waist, and drew her up in front of him. He shook the reins. "The two of us," he said, loud enough for anyone listening, "are going home."

Fifty-Six

Bridget kept Smoke at a walk. The day was warm and the blue sky held skeins of honking geese flying north. She leaned forward in the saddle and patted the horse's muscular neck. Ahead were the barns and the house she loved. And Henry.

"Henry," he'd said a day or two after the fire.

She'd been surprised. "Then why does everyone call you Chief?"

"It keeps us separate. Lets them suppose they're different."

"Henry," she'd said, liking the feel of the name in her mouth.

Through the winter, they'd sat by a fire while Henry told his peoples' legends and she, Grandma Teegan's. She told him about hearing Grandma Teegan telling her to fight death the night the lodge burned. And how maybe that meant Grandma Teegan was a selkie in the river.

Henry hadn't told her she was being silly or that she must have heard the wind or the heat of the fire whistling. His face turned and he looked out across his wide yard, through his fruit trees and to the river beyond. "Selkie," he repeated the word.

She thought it pleased him to know Grandma Teegan was in the water with his son.

Smoke's gait quickened as they neared the end of the lane. Bridget reined in gently as she'd been taught. "Whoa." She wanted to ride for hours more, but Henry would be uneasy until they were safely back. He'd spent many afternoons teaching her to handle Smoke, but this was the first time he'd let her take the big horse alone, going the mile, then crossing the wooden bridge over Nettle Creek into Bleaksville.

Six months had passed since Jake's and Rev. Jackdaw's deaths. She liked remembering how she'd built Rev. Jackdaw's coffin. At least helped. Henry worked with her, helping saw and hold boards, giving step-by-step instructions, but she'd pounded in many of the nails. And she'd whitewashed the box inside and out on her own.

Rev. Jackdaw deserved the whiteness. She'd read his journal and been struck by the image of a little boy crying at a farmhouse window in the 1840s while his brothers beat a horse. That child got lost, and only the meanness he'd been taught stayed. She tried not to be Salt Woman and think about the man he became, who wore a red dress, mistreated Effie, and shot Jake. She tried to remember only the child and how he'd tried to do the right thing. By going out into the night against his father's will and trying to save a horse, he'd been Nera.

Six months had passed too, since Effie left, and now there was a letter. Bridget planned to save that for later. She'd read it to Henry after supper. Then he'd read it back to her.

The wide doors of the barn, where the unfinished ark had waited through the coldest months, were open. Winter's drafty corners warming. At the sound of Smoke's hoofs in the yard, Wire bounced out. Henry on the dog's heels. "You're back," he said, the muscles in his face relaxing. "I knew you could do it."

She nodded, hoping the silly grin in her belly wasn't showing on her face.

Grabbing the throatlatch on Smoke, Henry steadied the stallion. "You get what you needed?"

She put her left foot in the stirrup, grabbed the pommel, drew her right leg over the saddle, leaned on Smoke to free the left foot—just as Henry taught her—and landed solidly on both feet.

"Like you were born on a horse," Henry said.

She pulled off the saddlebags. "I got your coffee and my school paper." There were other items—butter, flour, salt—but they teased each other most about his need for good, strong coffee and her need for paper and pencils. Pencils he kept sharp for her with his penknife.

She held Smoke's noseband, running her hand down his long face as Henry unbuckled the tight billet strap. "How's Cora?" He stopped and squinted at Bridget before she could answer. "What you grinning about?"

"Cora said the whole town is still talking about the school recital. How good I did."

With pride in his eyes, he jerked the buckle loose. "That so?"

"She said you 'smiled the whole time.' And you 'truly seemed to enjoy joining the community.'"

"That so?"

"And she said I looked beautiful in my dress." She lifted a quick hand before Henry could answer. "I still like britches better."

He pulled off the saddle, held it against one hip and opened the pasture gate. Smoke tossed his head, his mane lifting left and right in the air, and he was off.

Henry swung the saddle over the gate and took up the saddlebags. "Supper's ready."

They sat over beef stew thick with meat, potatoes, and carrots. Wire lay on the floor between their chairs, his tail rapping. She told Henry about her afternoon, how she'd talked Smoke across the bridge, and how two mates from school had come running at the sight of her . . . perhaps at the sight of Smoke.

"And guess what? Mr. Graf is using one of the boxes Cora bought last year. Guess what for."

"Doubt I can."

"Seeds. He has a whole bunch of seeds in little packets. Watermelons, cabbage, tomatoes." She took another bite. "We could plant everything."

"That so?" He pushed back his empty bowl and refilled his coffee cup. "You been grinning for an hour. You about to that?"

"I was saving it for right now." She pulled out the letter. "Effie had a baby girl."

He leaned back in his chair. "She's fine then?"

"Yes. She has a wood building shop in town, and she lives in the back. Skeet never returned and her pa hired a farmhand." Bridget scanned the sheet again. "Effie's helping her ma plant fruit trees, and everyone's excited about her baby girl." She turned the sheet over. "She wrote the letter herself. Johnny's working in the shop with her. They've started making chairs." Bridget looked up. "That's because of you. You started us building."

Henry's eyes had narrowed and his lips set, but Bridget rushed on. "Guess what she named the baby?"

He looked at his cup, a calloused finger rubbing the rim. "You said she had a sister, Sally."

"Bridget. She named her baby after me. And Pete's mom. Bridget Mae."

Henry's thumb continued to circle. "Effie ain't asking you to come?"

Bridget's heart dropped. Henry's smile had faded and lines cut across his weathered forehead. She rose and wrapped her arms around his neck. "I'm never going to leave you."

He took her hands, held them, and searched her face. "How about we take the train to Omaha? Lawyers there helped Standing Bear. Said Indians have legal rights. Suppose we signed papers saying this is your home?"

"And you are my pappy?"

"I'd like you to sign too."

"I get to say?" She dropped her head back onto his shoulder so he couldn't see her tears.

He patted her back. "It's all right now."

About the Author

Margaret Lukas taught writing for over a decade at the University of Nebraska. Her award-winning short story "The Yellow Bird" was made into a short by Smiling Toad Productions in Canada and premiered at the Cannes Film Festival. She has writings in anthologies, magazines, and online. Her first novel, *Farthest House*, received a Nebraska Arts Council Fellowship Award. She lives in Omaha with her husband.